THE MISSING ONE

THE
MISSING
ONE

LUCY ATKINS

Quercus

New York • London

Quercus

New York • London

© 2014 by Lucy Atkins
First published in the United States by Quercus in 2015

Any member of educational institutions wishing to photocopy part or all of the work for classroom use or anthology should send inquiries to permissions@quercus.com.

ISBN 978-1-62365-989-9

Library of Congress Control Number: 2014957510

Distributed in the United States and Canada by
Hachette Book Group
1290 Avenue of the Americas
New York, NY 10104

Manufactured in the United States

10 9 8 7 6 5 4 3 2 1

www.quercus.com

California to London, January 1979

She knew she was walking because she was definitely upright, moving down a row of seated passengers, with the baby howling on her shoulder. She could hardly hear the cries, though she was aware on a primitive level that the sound was urgent. But everything was blurred and muted, as if she was deep under water and the world was shimmering somewhere on the surface. It didn't matter that people stared, or the baby yowled and writhed. Nothing really mattered.

He gave her instructions and she followed them. He issued his conditions, itineraries, and tickets and she accepted them all. He would be waiting at the other end for her. This was the start of a new year and a new life. He would put them into his car and take them to the house he had bought in some English village, with an apple tree in the garden. "You belong with me," he had told her, before he got on his plane. "You always did—I love you, I've always loved you. And—where else could you go?" He was right. So she did the only rational thing: she followed his instructions.

She couldn't feel the baby's mouth tugging at her breast, and when she looked down she was startled to find that it had come away and was open, red and wailing, the poor little face screwed up and purple with fury. And there was a smear of blood coming from her nipple, trickling over her white skin, and a rub of it on the baby's chin, too. The nipple was raw and glaring, as if articulating everything she couldn't feel. Gently, with the edge of her shirt, she wiped the blood off her baby's stretched out mouth. Two white teeth glimmered in the redness.

As the plane taxied along the runway and Elena latched the baby on again, she knew she would never go back. But this was not an escape. She could never escape because nothing would change what had happened—not Graham's kindness, not a new English life, not even this needy, upset baby, who should have been weaned months ago.

As the plane lurched into the sky she felt the physical fact of everything she was leaving behind, and the loss was as solid and loud and squalling as the ten-month-old on her lap.

Then, because she couldn't think about what was down there anymore, she closed her eyes, and as the plane nosed through the clouds she took herself back to their very first journey north. She traveled it again in her mind, because maybe once she got there she'd be able to rewrite the ending and something—anything—other than this could happen instead.

The plane banked, and the baby yowled and writhed and fought, but she was in the campervan with the windows wound down and the two of them singing James Taylor songs; warm California air on their skin. There was twelve hundred miles of highway ahead of them, and his hands were wide and strong on the wheel.

They crossed the Golden Gate Bridge in a fog, talking about whales, and then headed onward, skirting the wild beaches of Northern California, into Oregon. A night on Cannon Beach, with their sleeping bags laid on the sand under improbably bright stars: he twisted a strand of sea grass around her ring finger. The next day they drove on, farther north, into Washington State, and then sudden towers of downtown Seattle, the glittering arc of Puget Sound, Bainbridge Island, and Whidbey Island hunched to the west. Rain closing in now, they chugged on, with the Olympic Peninsula rising on one side, the Cascades crimped on the other.

Windows up, they found sweaters and blankets; coffee and cigarettes by the roadside waiting for the tow truck; a shared diner meal in the rain; a night in a garage forecourt, then—starter-motor fixed— they drove onward, crossing the Canadian border in a hailstorm. They arrived at the port just as the sky cleared. Lining up by the water with dive-bombing seagulls and freighters unloading, they clanked onto the ferry and away across the water, bouncing off islands like a pinball, passing between cedar-dense mountains that rose straight from the sea like fins; skirting the shorelines—a white flash of a deer's tail, a lumbering brown bear—rows of crowded pine, cedar, and hemlock—a slithering sea otter glimpsed; harbor seals basking on gray rocks.

Then there was Dean, Jonas suddenly more boyish, and Dean's big boat, sailing hours more through a hushed sea mist, talking about the research and the summer ahead of them. The big belching boat shuddering to a halt: the men rolling up sleeves, disappearing, coming back oil-smeared with puffed-up chests. As they muttered toward the island, the mist cleared to reveal a towering totem pole on the headland—the Kwakwaka'wakw tribe, the men explained—and there—on the very top, Max'inux, the sea wolf. It is fitting that a killer whale should mark the spot where her life began—and where it ended.

On that flight to England, with her breasts bleeding into her baby's mouth, she felt the totem of sorrow lodge itself inside her heart, stopping the blood flow and messing up the beat. She couldn't change what happened, but a part of her would always be there—out on the water, listening, watching, making notes, moving through storms and sunsets and defying the facts of her life.

Chapter One

It turns out that it's my job to locate the birth certificate.

"Dad doesn't know where it is," says Alice, "and I've looked everywhere else so it has to be in her studio."

She looks at me across the kitchen table and we understand each other: she can't go up there, and I can.

It is late, near midnight; Finn is sleeping in the travel crib upstairs, and I am heavy- limbed and numb. But she is exhausted too and we both know that going up there would be worse for her than for me.

Our mother's studio—a grand name for a storage room—is at the top and back of the house. I push back my chair and make my way up the two flights of stairs to the tiny landing. I peek into my old bedroom first. I can see him through the netting of the travel crib: his messy halo of hair and the lunar curve of his cheek above his sleeping bag. I tiptoe across and hover for a second, listening. At eighteen months, Finn is still my baby, still small enough that lurking somewhere in my maternal mechanism is the question of whether he will continue to breathe when I am not with him. I touch his forehead. I touch the back of his hand. He is warm despite the frigid air. I fold my cardigan tighter, hugging it around my body with both arms, and I gaze at him; he is perfect, curled on his side, breathing steadily, warm and safe. After a moment I go back out and cross the landing.

It is intensely cold up here. I hesitate, with one hand on the door. Then I take a breath and push it open.

There is an electric heater against one wall and a radiator, but clearly neither has been switched on for a long time. I pull the cardigan tighter, and go over to the window. The blind is rolled up and my face wavers back at me, eyeless and hollow-cheeked. My hair is witchy and mad-looking; I probably haven't brushed it for days.

I lean over the desk and press my face against the glass until it freezes the tip of my nose. In daylight there is a bird's-eye view over the houses, out beyond the village across the river and the water meadows. And under the stars I can just make out the road, whispering up the hill between the hedgerows like a secret.

I pull back. There's a bottle of jasmine essential oil on the fireplace, an oil burner, and two beach stones the size of babies' fists. There are fragments of beach everywhere—driftwood, pebbles, shells; a vase filled with sea glass, a knot of rope. Night creeps through the objects and the scent of my mother seems to bloom in it—jasmine and turpentine; salt winds and garden soil.

The housekeeper has spruced things up, but there are still sketches and paintings in piles all over the place. I have no idea what we are supposed to do with all this art.

Some canvases are stacked on the floor against the bookshelf. The one on the top is the ruined West Pier seen from Brighton Beach. The skeleton juts from the waves. There is no walkway to reach or escape it, just a rusting core on insect legs. There is decay and stolen gaiety in the structure; a feeling of lost lights and bandstands, ghosts of girls in swing skirts. Even in the murky light I can make out how angry the sea is. It occurs to me that my mother was a really good artist.

A memory surfaces even though I don't want it in my head. It was a very long time ago and we were standing on Brighton Beach, just the two of us, watching a swarm of starlings seethe through the sky, switching direction this way and that, before vanishing through the ribs of the ruined West Pier like a cloud of smoke sucked into a vortex.

"Why don't they crash?" I asked.

She looked down at me. "They do it by intuition," she said, "And trust." Then she knelt at my level and grabbed the tops of my arms. "Kali, I need . . ." she was breathing fast, as if she'd run somewhere. For a moment I felt as if she was really seeing me—just me—and I swelled into something important. But then the familiar cloud drew across her eyes and that good feeling crumbled as she dropped my arms. "No. It doesn't matter." She turned away and then she just walked off up the beach, calling sharply over her shoulder for me to hurry or we'd be late to pick up Alice from ballet. I ran after her, up the steep bank, but the stones slipped under my boots and it was like one of those dreams where you can't go any faster even though your life depends upon it.

I flick through her other paintings—almost abstract oils of the Seven Sisters, sailing boats at Seaford, pebbles at Beachy Head. All she ever painted was the sea—almost forty years of waves and boats and shingle and gulls, even though our village is fifteen miles from the coast, rooted in Wealden clay, with oak trees, bluebell woods, cow parsley, hawthorn hedges, and the line of the Downs changing with the light and the seasons. All perfect subjects for a landscape artist; all stubbornly ignored by my mother.

Her easel sits in one corner and there are boxes of charcoals and paintbrushes everywhere. Tubes of paint overflow from a wooden crate. Her worn black boots sit in one corner—but I can't look at those—and her green silk scarf is on the back of the door. It is the same shade as her eyes. I always wished I'd inherited her eyes, rather than my own, a sort of navy blue that Doug generously calls "violet."

But I can't think about Doug. Not now. I just can't. Not while I am doing this. Since I found his phone and everything torpedoed, I have been unable to think about Doug at all. Even if I try to think about what it means my mind shuts down, as if a blanket has been thrown over that part of my brain.

When I heard his voice earlier that day the fury was so intense that my words came out strangled, "I have to stay down here, and help with the funeral."

"But I'll drive down—I should be there . . . you shouldn't do this alone. You can't." I heard the guilt in his voice.

"No!" I barked. "I don't want you to come."

There was a second of silence. And then I hung up.

All I wanted was to run—to go far away where none of this could touch me. He would have put my inability to speak to him down to shock or grief, initially. Maybe he'd even have been relieved, on some level, that I was staying in Sussex with Finn. With us away he could work longer at whatever vital meeting, conference, or lecture he had scheduled and he wouldn't have to stress about being back for bath time or feel guilty that I was doing everything again. Or perhaps he would take off, to be with her.

But I can't think this sort of thought. Not now. The timing of all this is horrendous. I try to breathe. All I want to do is flee. Every single part of me is saying run. I want to be anywhere but here; I want to be gone, far away.

I have to focus and get this done. There is nowhere to run to. It's so late, my eyes hurt, as if they're shriveling inside my head. I just have to find her birth certificate and get out of this room.

Then, as if my thoughts have made it all the way to Oxford, the phone buzzes in my jeans pocket. I tug it out and hit "Ignore." He has been trying to call all night but I can't hear his voice, his excuses, or worse still, his confessions. I can't face either the truth or the lies. I drop the phone on the ground, kneel in front of the filing cabinet, and wrench it open. The phone rings again and I kick it under the desk. It bleeps and goes silent.

I am here to find my mother's birth certificate. When I've found it I will go and sleep next to Finn, and I will wake up in less than five hours with my baby laughing and singing and bashing his fists on the side of the crib calling "Mama! Mama? Mom-A!" And I will keep going; I'll keep moving through the next day and the next because whatever else I have lost, I still have Finn.

The hanging files are surprisingly organized. There are health folders containing her NHS medical card, some information about iron deficiency, and an ironic all clear from a mammogram three years ago. There must be a stack of hospital paperwork somewhere. I hope I don't find that.

I flick through the files—bank statements, random receipts. But no birth certificate. I pull out a file called *"personal"* and pour the contents onto the carpet. There is a Mother's Day card with a love heart that I made from stick-on sequins when I was little, and hopelessly trying to win her over—or make her feel better. There is a painting of the apple tree by Alice, aged ten, far more accomplished than any of my efforts, and some more Mother's Day cards—mostly from Alice. Then there is an old blue airmail envelope with my mother's name on it, and an address in California. I recognize my father's handwriting. It is careful and controlled, with each letter perfectly formed.

I look at it. I shouldn't. But I can't not. I unfold the blue paper into a single, crackling sheet.

It is dated around the time he brought us to England from California. I would have been about eight months old.

My darling Elena,

In just two weeks you will be here—I hope you still have the paper I wrote out for you, with the flight times. Kris will drive you to the airport—you have his number on the paper. But before you come, I wanted to clarify a few things since I'm not sure how much you could take in when we spoke before.

Please know that I will do my best to make you happy here in England. I will look after you, always, and do my best for Kali. The house is just about ready for you both, but I know you will want to make it your own so I kept it all very plain—white walls, neutral carpet throughout the house. I hope you won't find it too plain but you can do whatever you want to it once you're here—curtains and furnishings and such. There is a bedroom looking out at the apple tree that Kali might like. I like to picture her climbing that tree one day.

Please also know that we must stick to the agreement we made on the beach—we have to go forward from now on and not look back at all. This will be difficult for you, I know, it will take commitment from us both, but it is for the best because time will heal—we must have faith in that. Time will bring forgiveness and healing. We will have a good life together. I will make sure of that.

I want you to know that I do understand that it will take a long time for you to get over what has happened. But I do—fervently—believe that recovery is possible. And you must too. As agreed, we will not talk about this anymore—for all our sakes.

I think you'll like it here in Sussex. It is a lot as you have always imagined England to be—the village is pretty, and there's a small school for Kali when she gets to that age. The house stands right at the bottom of the main street where the roads fork. From our bedroom window you look down on the signpost and the roundabout, which is why I called it Signpost House. It is a proud Sussex Victorian, red brick and flint, original sash windows, good proportioned rooms though smaller and less airy, of course, than the Californian properties we are both used to. It has a pleasant (though rather small) garden, which I hope you will enjoy. It is a fine place to start a new life.

I shall be at the airport to meet your flight and will drive you both straight down. It takes about two hours to get to Sussex from the airport. I've been getting the London train every day from Cooksbridge—the station is a few miles from the village—and it is perfectly manageable, though it does make for a long day. I shall probably have to find a place to stay in London for some nights during the week eventually. Working at the firm is exciting, if exhausting and although Derwent treats me like a schoolboy, I think he is pleased with what I've contributed so far.

I do miss you and long to see you. You must know that I never stopped loving you—and I never will stop loving you.

Gray.

The paper crackles as I refold it and stuff it back in the file. I feel as if I have barged into a room that someone forgot to lock. My father would be appalled if he knew that I had read this. Whatever happened between them all those years ago, I have no right to know.

But it's obvious what happened—his guilt is palpable—and it makes total sense. They never talked about California or reminisced about how they met. There is no family story of a romantic proposal and I have never seen a wedding album. My mother always shut me down instantly if I asked about America. Now I know why.

It is hard to imagine my father doing anything so passionate, or so morally wrong as to have an affair. But it was California in the seventies, and maybe he was different then; priorities or morals were different then. I have never heard him call himself Gray. He has always been Graham.

I shouldn't have read the letter. The last thing I need is confirmation that all marriages are subject to betrayal, or that even my upright father could cheat.

I wonder if Alice knows about the affair. She might, since she and our mother talked about everything. I'd hear the chatting in the kitchen with Radio 4 in the background, spaghetti sauce bubbling on the stove, Alice's homework spread across the table and I'd walk through the door, and they'd stop talking and look at me. Then Alice would jump up, and make a space, or ask me for help with her math, trying, almost pathetically, to include me—as if it was her job to make me feel wanted. But at some point, inevitably, my mother and I would lock eyes over her head. It must have been exhausting for my sister to be stuck between us all the time.

But this is old news. I'm not going to do this, not now. It's much too late.

The birth certificate isn't in these files. It isn't here at all. I scoop everything back and scramble to my feet, resting my hands on the desktop. I feel the tightness around my heart, a physical reality, but a numbness, too. Somewhere in my gut the pain is organizing itself for another day.

The desk is rickety, with curlicues of woodworm running across the surface. There are two drawers. I slide one open and peer inside, as if, miraculously, the birth certificate will be lying there, waiting for me. But the drawer is packed with postcards. I prod at them.

There are pictures of pottery vases, a few Native American paintings, mostly cubic looking fish in bold blacks and reds, square faces,
square eyes, thick black outlines and curling designs on their bodies. I notice a painting of a man's face and turn it over. It comes from
a chapel in Ecuador. There is a single sentence written on the card:

> "*Thinking of you today,*
> *Susannah.*"

I turn the others over, one by one, and for a moment I think I
have lost my mind: my brain is short-circuiting. Every card says the
same thing, in the same cramped hand.

> "*Thinking of you today,*
> *Susannah.*"

Most of the postcards have Canadian stamps, though one is sent
from Taos, New Mexico, another from Seattle and a few from even
further afield—Quito, Moscow, Durban. Not all the postmarks
are visible, but every one I can read was mailed on the same date:
May 6th. The earliest I can make out was posted thirty-seven years
ago. My mother's birthday was in June, so these aren't birthday cards.

I notice that most of the later postcards, from the early nineties
onward, come from the *Susannah Gillespie Gallery*.

> "*Thinking of you today,*
> *Susannah.*"

I push them all back into the drawer and shut it, then open the
second drawer. It contains pencils and erasers, a paring knife, a
packet of Orbit chewing gum, a nail file, Post-its, a stapler, a box of
Swan matches, and an ancient silver lipstick.

The base of my skull throbs and I feel the fury massing in my
chest: who ignores a lump in the breast? Who sits and watches it
grow beneath the surface of their skin and does nothing? Tears are

coming down my cheeks, and I give in and lean on the desk, gasping for breath as they roll off my face and into her drawer.

Then I stop, almost as abruptly as I started. I slam the drawer shut, stand up, wipe my nose on my sleeve, swallow, breathe in and out. There is no reason to believe that my mother actually wanted to die. Maybe she just thought that she was invincible. I wipe at my damp face with both wrists. She didn't believe in illness. When we were young, if we ever complained of headaches, shivers, or fevers, she'd say, "If you think about being sick, you'll get sick."

I think of the time before this—the last time I saw her properly. It was August, just after the diagnosis. We were in the garden. Finn was on his haunches by my chair, putting dirt into his mouth then spitting it out. My mother was thinner and bone-pale, as if her skeleton was sucking away at her flesh. Her old jeans were rolled up, feet bare as usual, but her hair was lackluster, curls looser, scraped back, more silvery. She looked intensely small, with blue flowers towering behind her.

We sat with a pot of tea and a lemon cake that she had baked, but didn't eat. On my one day in the office that week I'd had to interview three women for the new "living with breast cancer" section. While they told me their intimate, awful stories, all I could think about was my mother and what she must be going through and how she would never—ever—talk to me like this. Afterward, one of the women, about my mother's age, clutched my hand and said the website was a "lifesaver." When she logged on and watched the videos of others talking about their similar situations she realized that she wasn't alone.

But my mother, sitting upright on her white wooden garden chair, was so alone that it hurt to look at her. She would never find comfort in videos of other people talking about this disease. The new section on the website wasn't even worth mentioning to her. I couldn't bear to look at her, so I looked at Finn instead, ruddy cheeked, squatting in his jeans with his fat fists buried in the dirt.

Doug obviously felt the tension rising because he pointed at the tall flowers, and said, in a slightly desperate voice, "They're such a nice color, what are they?"

"Wolfbane," she gave him a grateful smile. Even at the end, when she was so thin and her cheekbones so sharp and huge, her green eyes sunken, she still had dimples on each cheek when she smiled. Then she told him how the roots of the plant are used in Nepal to make a deadly poison, but in Chinese medicine, detoxified, they are a healing tonic. "Death and salvation," she said, "all in one lumpy root."

Finn set off in a crawl toward the blue flowers. I leaped up and lifted him back, but my mother didn't even move. She just turned her face to the blue sky.

"Granny's flowers are poisonous," I said, pointedly. "Don't touch them. Yuk." But I wanted to grab her by the shoulders and scream, "Oh my God! Your grandchild is right here! Don't you even care? Can't you see him? Don't you want to know him before you die?" But of course, I swallowed that back down, too, and turned away from her, setting Finn down on the grass, far away from her Wolfbane.

We stayed out in the garden for too long that day and in some ways it was as if nothing had changed at all. She was solicitous of Doug, as always, asking about university politics, his latest book, cutting him a second, thicker slice of cake. She didn't offer cake to Finn and I had to ask—is it ok?—and then she looked surprised, and a little embarrassed.

"Yes, sorry, of course."

She smiled at Finn in her distant way as he ate the little corner of cake I gave him, sitting on my lap and spraying crumbs over us both. He looked up at her, and grinned back and I saw her face melt. She leaned toward him, and touched her fingertips to his toes. "Do you like that cake?" she said, softly. "Do you?" Then a film came down over her eyes, and she blinked, and looked away, leaving him gazing up at her with his big brown eyes. I felt my throat tighten and put my hand on Finn's head. Doug stiffened next to me, perhaps antici-pating trouble. But I started to talk—something about Finn's eating, the first time I tried him on solids and how he didn't spit it out the way the baby books said he would, but wolfed it down madly. As I babbled she just stared at the sky, nodding vaguely, gathering what-ever it was back into that dark place.

I couldn't bring myself to ask her directly, that day, about the treatment she had refused. I couldn't find a way to lift my hand and touch hers; to say I was sorry, beyond sorry, and that I loved her despite all our difficulties and misunderstandings and furies; that this was unbearable—that she couldn't die. I couldn't tell her that I didn't just blame her for the way we were—I blamed myself too. This was both of us. I couldn't tell my mother that I loved her.

Only one thing was different between us that day. After I'd strapped Finn into his car seat, found his lost teddy bear, packed his rain boots and board books and bottles and clothes into the trunk, and snapped at Doug for not getting the travel crib down, we all stood for a moment by the car. Suddenly, she held out her arms and pulled me toward her, and kissed my face, "Take care, my lovely darling."

She hadn't called me that for years and years. Her words knotted themselves around my heart so tight it was all I could do to breathe and smile and get in the car with Finn and Doug, and roll down the window to say goodbye, see you soon.

But I didn't see her; I didn't visit again until the last day, just a week ago, when Alice called at five in the morning, and I had to get out of the leather armchair and come.

I straighten up. I really can't be in this room. This is hideous. I am so cold now, cartoonishly cold—my teeth are actually chattering. I wipe at my wet face with both hands. No wonder Alice couldn't face it up here.

As I come out of the studio I see a shape at the bottom of the stairs, standing in silence. The hall light isn't on and for a disorientating moment, I think it's a ghost, waiting to claim me. Then I realize it is my father.

"Oh!" I say. "Are you off to bed?" But his bedroom is at the other end of the corridor. He must have been on his way to the studio but heard me up here and stopped, not wanting to deal with my grief too. "Are you coming up?"

He says nothing, he doesn't move. For a second I wonder if he is about to collapse.

But as I come down the stairs, I smell the whisky on him. I realize that he is swaying, gently. I have never in my life seen my father drunk and I know without even hearing his voice that this is going to be appalling. The smell on him is all wrong. At seventy-two, he is still tall and upright. He doesn't move, but his faded gray eyes settle on my face.

"She loved you very much," he says, with no lead in, as if we're in the middle of a deep conversation, which has never, ever been the case. His accent, I notice, has become much more Edinburgh.

I lean away from the fumes. "Yes, well, I loved her too."

"Good God, Kali. You are so like her, that's the real problem: the two of you are just so stubborn—and so *entrenched*. But she loves—loved—you so very much. She loved Finn too—you need to know this . . ."

"No, it's okay. I do know it, Dad. It's okay."

"She just had . . . she had . . . she had awful . . . She had so many complicated memories—they got in the way of everything for the two of you—it was . . ."

"Dad, please—" I don't want to be reminded of how nightmarish I was and how perfect Alice has always been. But he holds up a hand so I close my mouth.

"She never," he enunciates carefully, ". . . there are so many things you don't know about your mother—oh Lord, so many things." He swallows, his upper body swaying slightly, forward and back. He rarely calls me Kali, almost always Kal. Hearing him call me by my full name has a strange effect on me: one part of me melts while another freezes.

He is, I assume, alluding to my mother's unhappy childhood—the death of her mother when she was just a child; the father she disliked so intensely that she could never even talk about him. Perhaps he's talking about his affair, in California. He probably wants to give me details, as if this will explain why she found it so hard to be my mother. Maybe I reminded her of her hated father.

"Okay," I say. "So, what things don't I know about her?"

He takes a long breath in.

"Dad?"

"I probably wasn't here enough," he clears his throat. "When you were growing up. I just left you all to it and I am sorry about that. Truly." He looks into my eyes, then. His are set deep, pink at the rims. I desperately want to look away, but I force myself not to.

"But Good Lord! I just couldn't stand all the drama. You and your mother were," his voice is loud, now, and suddenly outraged, "impossible!" We are back on slightly more familiar territory now.

I consider telling him that, yes, he probably should have been there more, but I'm not sure this is really true. What good would he have done if he had tried to be more involved? He kept his distance because all these messy female emotions were alien to him and no sane person could blame him for that. It must have been unbearable when I was a teenager, with my mother and me ranting around the house, me yelling and slamming doors, her shutting down and cutting me off, both of us crawling under each other's skin all the time, wriggling inside each other's heads.

Then there would be the remorse—I'd sob and she'd stroke my hair and tell me she loved me, would always love me, no matter what I did or said. I remember the softness of her body under my ear, the rumbles and sighs inside her belly, her steady heartbeat as we settled into a temporary truce. And then hours—minutes— moments—later we'd be at it again, something would change, some switch would flip in her or me, and we'd be at each other again. No wonder my father stayed up in London as much as he could.

I am suddenly extraordinarily tired. "Listen Dad, it really doesn't matter," I lean one shoulder against the stairwell. "You did your best. You really mustn't feel bad about anything."

"I always treated you and Alice exactly the same didn't I? Always. Exactly the same."

"Yes," I realize this is true, "Actually, you really did." It was only my mother who openly found my sister so much more delightful and easy.

He reaches out and grabs my hand, and pins it to his forearm. The tweed feels rough and his hand is chilly and leathery, but surprisingly strong. "I should have let her . . . We should have . . ." he says. "It might have made things better. She wanted to . . ."

"What, Dad? Wanted to *what*?"

"Oh God," he closes his eyes. "Oh dear God. This is not right."

"Dad. Please, it's okay." I pat his hand a few times with my free one. He is incoherent. He doesn't really know what he's saying. I realize that even if he does have something to tell me, I actually don't want to hear it. This is too much. I want to erase myself from this stairway. I just want to be somewhere else. "Look Dad, all this is just ancient history, all this, and anyway, we were fine, in the end, weren't we? Mom and I really got on fine."

He sways and his face is suddenly distressed. The muscles seem to collapse, presaging the elderly man that is just around the corner. It's as if a layer has been stripped off him by the grief and whisky and he's just pulsing there in front of me, exposed.

All my life, my father has been this beacon of self-control: a tall, dignified, priestly man with his unwavering routines, anchoring the family from afar. But now the structure of his face is unsteady, and I realize that he might actually cry.

But then he stiffens, raises himself upright again, and clamps his jaw tight. He would never let that happen, even in this terrible state. He lifts his chin and looks up the staircase behind me, and I turn, too, and I think we both half expect her to emerge from her studio, Medusa-haired, and order us to stop this nonsense and go to bed. The landing is dark and the door is shut.

"Well," he says, and clears his throat. "Bedtime I suppose."

His legs fold at the knee as he slowly walks away.

As I stand in the stairwell, listening to his footsteps recede, I feel an emptiness spread through my bones, as if I have failed him too. How can he bear to go and sleep in that room, in the bed where she just died? He must feel so alone. But maybe that is just it—maybe you cling to the space because the space is all you have left.

Chapter Two

It is only as I begin to read the Emily Dickinson poem out loud that I realize how totally inappropriate it is.

I chose it because I found the book under the coffee table, and my mother had marked this poem with a card. I wasn't thinking clearly. Finn was toddling around pulling books off the shelves with methodical focus. I didn't really read it properly, I just saw that the poem was about loss and thought she must have wanted it, or she wouldn't have left it out like this, as a sign—and that reading it would mean I didn't have to talk about her in front of all those people.

But now, too late, I realize that the poem is about the death of a lover. It is so completely wrong, and I feel my face getting hotter and hotter as I read on. My father will be mortified, Alice baffled. I can't look at either of them as I come back to the seats. I feel all the faces, some familiar, some not, turned on me as I walk.

I reach out and take Finn from Alice—he holds out his arms to me and I feel unspeakable relief as his solid little body anchors mine back onto the bench. I bury my face in his neck.

"Ba," he says, "Blah, ba, ba." He pats my head, reassuringly.

I kiss the side of his head, and smell the nape of his neck and close my eyes as if I might suck in some of his imperviousness to the awful event that is going on around us. There is an eerie silence in the crematorium, broken only by the sound of Finn's toy ambulance running up and down my arm. Finally, Alice gets up.

My sister is spookily beautiful in grief. Her eyes are red-rimmed, even more strikingly green today because her face is so pale. Her hair is pulled back in a ponytail. She's all bone structure, like our father. She's wearing layers of gray cashmere and her slim feet are slotted into ballet pumps. She's a couple of inches taller than me, and we're so clearly made from different materials that no one would ever guess we were sisters. It always seemed ironic that I was the one to take after our mother physically. But Alice got the beautiful green eyes.

She stands and talks movingly and simply about what an inspiration our mother was: friend and confidant, protector, and how she hopes one day to be half as good a mother herself. If I had stood up and spoken from the heart like this, rather than reading a bizarre poem, we would sound as if we had been raised by two completely different women: Alice's mother stable, loving, balanced; mine steeped in sadness, stormy, rising and falling like the tide, giving love only to withdraw it again the next instant.

But being so much younger, Alice has never seen the aspects of our mother that I remember all too clearly. Her first newborn summer, when I was six, our mother lay in bed on her side day after day, staring at the wall with one arm under her own head and Alice attached to her nipple like an afterthought. This seemed to go on for weeks, though I have no idea how long it was really. I just remember her dull eyes, and how she kept the curtains closed and spoke in a hoarse voice, saying, "Go play. The baby needs to sleep." I remember Alice's constant whimpering and the horrible sickly smell that my mother's body gave off, as if she was sweating out stale milk.

She didn't get up to cook or take me to the beach, so I spent a lot of time lodged in the apple tree, watching the cars as they came down the village toward the signpost outside our house. I invented a game of guessing which way they'd turn, and I'd keep score by slashing the bark with a penknife every time I got one wrong. Sometimes she sent me up to the shop on my own for bread or milk; I remember trying to make toast and not knowing how to work the toaster, and holding the bread in with a fork. That was the only time I remember her actually moving: her feet thundering toward me.

My father was presumably aware of the problem, because he'd take me for a drive or an ice cream on weekends. But he probably didn't have a clue what to do about any of it.

I should have taken against Alice. That would have been a healthy response to a new baby rival, but I didn't. I remember feeling protective of this strange little woodland creature, not quite in the world yet.

There were other episodes afterward, as we got bigger, when my mother would stay in bed all day with her face turned to the wall, her hair massed on the pillow like sticky tar and I would try to make things better. I'd take toddler Alice to the swings or tidy up the kitchen, or pick flowers and put them in a jam jar by her bed. Then, at some point, these episodes didn't happen anymore and I was older, almost a teenager. But my resentment had stacked up by then. I knew I couldn't trust her, and that's when the really big fights started. Alice and I really did have very different mothers.

Several people come up to me after the service to give condolences, and coo over Finn, who runs around grabbing handfuls of flowers, pinging off peoples' legs, dodging pats on the head, grabbing and tugging at things. No one mentions the poem but several people say, "You really do look like your Mom." A woman about my mother's age with hennaed hair and Peruvian earrings tells me that my mother's art should be exhibited. "She was a wonderful artist and a wonderful friend," she touches my arm and our eyes meet. Hers are kind, the color of soft leather. "I know you two had issues, but she always talked very proudly of you and her beautiful grandson."

I feel my throat constrict, and for a second it strikes me that this woman must be the magic link to my mother—she will find my mother for me, and bring her back. She hands me a tissue and says, "I'm so sorry, Kal."

The morning light is pale and the kitchen windows are fogged. I can see the outline of the apple tree; its bare claws sway in the wind. Alice is by the sink with her back to me. Her hair is swept up off her neck and she is on her cell phone. Finn has both arms wrapped around me and is still sleepy and snugly. The tiles are cold underfoot and I wish I had thick socks. The heating hasn't kicked in yet but I am in a warm old sweater of Doug's with the sleeves rolled up. I took it without thinking. It smells of Doug.

It is not even six thirty but Alice has obviously been going through our mother's papers: documents and files are strewn all over the kitchen table. I wonder if she slept at all. She is so diligent and so desperate to do the right thing all the time—she always has been.

I know she has to go back to the office today, but as far as I know no one will be there when she gets home tonight to make her dinner and hold onto her while she cries for our mother. She stands pluckily at the sink in leggings and an oversized sweater, nodding into her phone. Her neck looks fragile, somehow, beneath the weight of her head.

I will have to leave too. Only I can't go home. It's impossible to imagine even standing in the same room as Doug right now. I have to find somewhere else to go. Alice would have us stay. I try to imagine Finn and me in her clean white apartment.

"That's just not realistic," Alice snaps.

"Down," Finn squirms and I press my hand against his thigh, feeling its doughy give. "Down!"

"How about you sit in here, in your chair, and we'll have some breakfast first, eh?" I put him, swiftly, into his portable high chair.

"We can't do that," Alice says, curtly. She turns, looks at me over her shoulder, and raises her eyes to the ceiling. Who is she talking to at this time in the morning? Nobody seems to sleep anymore.

"Down!" Finn slaps both hands onto the high chair table then looks down at them—two chubby starfish. He slaps again, rather pleased by the noise.

"You just sit there for a minute, love, and I'll get you some milk." I hurry to the fridge, scraping my hair into a ponytail with the hair tie that was around my wrist. Finn watches me, edgily, as I fill his sippy cup, then he seizes it with two hands, and sucks on the spout, looking up at me from under his bangs. I kiss the top of his head and start to cut bread.

"Is Dad asleep?" I mouth when Alice turns around again.

She gestures toward the study.

Where else? Even at this time of the morning, the day after the funeral, he is up and working too.

I shouldn't be surprised, since this has been my father's response to almost any difficult situation for as long as I can remember: retreat and work. Go to London. Work a bit more.

But I am being unfair. He is reeling. Last night was awful. Why shouldn't he cling to anything that will keep him upright? The moment she died, a gray veil dropped over his face, and now he is halting and unsteady, as if the blood is no longer pumping quite so efficiently around his body. He did what he promised to do in his guilt letter: he loved and looked after her until the end.

Of course, nothing will be said about our encounter on the stairs. For as long as I can remember, my father and I have avoided discussing anything remotely personal. I imagine he will be mortified. I wonder how he is going to organize his life now. He can't come down here on weekends to a cold and empty house. I imagine him driving down the village street and letting himself into the echoing hallway every Friday night. He can't. Surely he'll sell. Without her our family home is just bricks and flint constructed around an unbearable, swollen absence.

I butter Finn's toast, spread it with marmalade, and slice it into soldiers. He takes one, and examines it as if it is a fascinating artifact. Then he crushes it in his fist. His hair is all over the place, tangled into fuzzy knots at the back, his bangs too long, and beneath it his eyes are wide and dark-lashed—Doug's chocolate brown. Finn shoves a bit of toast into his mouth. I lean over and smooth his hair out of his eyes.

And without warning I'm back there, by our bed, holding Doug's phone, reading the two texts that have changed everything. How could he do this?

There is a French coffee press on the table and I grab it and pour myself some of Alice's thick coffee and sit down next to Finn, sipping it. Alice drinks coffee all day. This is like molasses, growing cold. It can't be good for her. No wonder she doesn't sleep. I should eat something, but since I found Doug's phone, I have felt slightly sick most of the time. But I am so tired. I just want to go back to bed. I rub my face with both hands. I need a shower. Badly. Coffee.

Alice comes over, stands by the table, and holds up a finger at me. "I don't think that's realistic," she says into her phone. It's strange to see her dominant and brusque. My little sister, I realize, is probably quite intimidating in a work environment.

I have no idea how she could possibly focus on work right now. Still nodding into her phone, she points with one elbow at what looks like an old jewelry box on the table.

She will want to divide everything up. Alice is obsessed with fairness. Maybe it's a lawyer thing—or perhaps it is the old guilt at being the preferred daughter.

"Yes, quarterly." She gestures at the box again. Then she holds one hand over her phone. "I found that—" she hisses, "In the back of her closet. I think it's just a few bits and pieces from her university days in California—but do you want any of it?" She takes her hand off the mouthpiece again. "What's the price on that?"

It is about the size of a shoebox but less deep, and covered in blue velvet. The corners are worn and the material has faded unevenly, with an oblong mark pressed into the padded lid as if it has been wedged behind something for years.

Finn chews his toast. His cheeks bulge like a hamster—he looks at me, expectantly.

"Is that toast *really* good?" I say. He grins.

Then slowly, I open the lid.

An ivory carving about the size of a matchbox sits on top of a folded notebook. I lift it out and hold it up to the light. It is a fish-like creature with a hollowed belly and curling lines carved on its body. Something squats inside its belly. I peer at it from a different angle and realize that I'm staring into a leering human face, or almost human, an oversized block-shaped thing with two big eyes and a grimace that shows tiny, square teeth. For a moment I feel as if it's alive and might bite me. I put it down.

Then I pry out the notebook. The cover won't straighten. The paper is the color of weak tea but her neat high school cursive is unmistakable. It is the one thing from her American past that she never managed to shake off.

I am looking at a string of vowels—*"eeeeooooup."* I turn the page. There is a list of times in one column, starting at 6:00 and going to 18:18. Opposite the times are more vowel-heavy sounds, with notes—*"pectoral slap" "simultaneous dive" "B breach."* I flip forward a few pages—some scientific jargon, more odd observations: *"tail lob" "fluke lift" "still."*

I haven't thought about all this in years. It is easy to forget that my mother was once a scientist. I don't know if I ever even asked her what her abandoned doctorate was about—marine biology, I know; dolphins, I think. But I probably never asked her for specifics because she was always so prickly about her past. As I got older I realized that her abandoned research was a source of deep regret and possibly shame. This, presumably, caused the early bouts of depression. It is a common enough story: an intelligent, energetic woman forced to drop the career she is passionate about and live a life of domestic boredom. No wonder she was depressed. When I was a teenager I decided that since I was the reason she had to give up her PhD, I must be the root cause of her unhappiness. The last thing I wanted to do, after that, was to dredge it up for her.

Now, of course, I can see that it must have been more complicated than this. There was an undiagnosed postnatal depression for a start. But it's too late now. I'll never really know why she was so sad and I'll never know what interested her about dolphins, or why she gave up her PhD, and never worked again. They have marine biology departments on this side of the Atlantic too, but she'd never even take us to the aquarium. I will never know, now, about her childhood, or my grandparents, or why she disliked her father so much that she refused to even talk about him.

I can't imagine why she kept this ancient notebook. Why on earth would she want a reminder of a period of her life that she had tried so pathologically to forget? I flick forward and back a few times in case there are revelations or diary entries, but it really is just scientific notes.

Still, it is odd to hold this proof of her past in my hands. I have always felt as if this first part of her life, the bit before she married my father and brought me to England, when she was American and young and free and a scientist, never really happened. My father behaved as if she wasn't invented before he brought her to England. And she never seemed particularly American—though traces of an accent always haunted her speech—and there were the peanut butter and jelly sandwiches that she called PBJ and put in our lunchboxes every day.

She used to wrap them in acres of plastic wrap. It would take us half the lunch hour just to pry them open. She did this with other packages and envelopes too. She used feet of scotch tape wound round and round as if readying the envelope for a warzone rather than the post office. You'd actually need tools to get into them: Stanley knives, sharp scissors.

For a second I sit, reeling. It is as if someone has opened me up, scooped my insides out and, left a pulsing hole. I want my Mom. I want her back. She cannot have gone. This is just not possible.

I lay the notebook next to the carved fish thing. The walls swoop in and then out, and I feel quite sick. I try to focus on something outside my body. I'm looking at her painting. It has always been here so I hardly see it now. But it is actually a fantastic bright picture, in grays and blues, of Brighton Pier—the living one—with waves crashing toward the eye and white foam flying up, steeped in sunlight. I make myself breathe in and out.

"Are you okay?"

Alice is off the phone now.

"I was," I take another big breath, "just thinking about the PBJs—the plastic wrap. And the scotch tape—all the scotch tape she used when she mailed things . . ." Alice sits down, heavily, next to me. We look at each other and then we both start to cry. We grip each other's forearms and crumple.

"Mamamama!" Finn sings. He bashes his cup on the high chair. "Maaaaamaaa. Mammam!" I push back my hair, it is coming loose, and I wipe at my face with the backs of my hands. Alice does the same and we both turn blotchy smiles on him.

"Alish?" he flashes her his best grin. He has always, practically from the moment they first met, seen Alice as a personal challenge. He can feel both her unease and her adoration, and makes a point of offering her his most irresistible smiles.

Alice wipes her eyes, gets up, and runs a hand gently over his hair.

He stuffs some more toast into his mouth.

She bends down and smiles at his level. He offers her some chewed toast and marmite, crushed in his fist. "Oh yum," she says, pretending to take a bite. He thrusts it closer, leaving marmite on her reddened nose.

A white knitted square lies on the bottom of my mother's jewelry box. I pick it up and pricks of light shine through the fine stitches. I turn it over. Embroidered, in blue thread, is a curling *K*.

My heart turns over again: so she did keep a treasure from my babyhood. There is a box of Alice's baby things in the attic, but I didn't realize she had kept anything at all of mine when we left California. Gently, I lay the blanket fragment next to the box.

There is just one more thing now—a flat, gray stone, about the size of my thumb, and heart-shaped. It is smooth and almost weightless. I try to imagine my father giving it to her on a California beach at sunset, all those years ago when they met and fell in love, before he betrayed her.

But this scenario feels unlikely. I can't actually imagine my father picking out heart-shaped stones on beaches. He doesn't belong on

beaches at all, or in the California sun. He belongs in chilly northern cities, weaving through magisterial buildings in well-cut pants,
noting angles and lines with his architect's eye.

Alice leans over and pokes at the carving with an index finger.
"What *is* that thing?" She still has a smear of marmite on her nose
and for a second I want to reach out and hold onto my little sister. I want to stroke her hair and tell her that everything will be all
right and that this grief won't always be so intense. Maybe things
will be more straightforward between us now that we don't have
our mother to contend with. But this is not the way it works with
us. The way it works is that Alice is sensible and holds everything
together. She gets to worry about me, but I don't get to worry about
her. I can't comfort her, even though, when she was little and had
hurt herself, I'd be the one she'd run to first. But that all shifted as we
got older, and my relationship with our mother deteriorated, and
Alice became the peacekeeper, the smoother-over, the organizer.

She turns away, now, and pours herself another coffee.

"Alice?"

"What?"

"I'm sorry that I've been so crappy, and I didn't come, and you
had to take all the strain of her illness, and everything. I'm really
sorry I haven't been here."

"Oh, right. No. That's okay."

"The thing is, I just didn't know if she'd want me to be here," I say.
But I know this is not the whole story. The truth is I didn't know how
to be here: I was scared that she would push me away when she only
had weeks to live, and I knew there would be no deathbed recon-
ciliations. Or perhaps it's even more messed up than that. Perhaps I
couldn't face the thought that there would be a reconciliation—and
then she'd die anyway. I have been a terrible coward.

Alice drains her coffee then puts the mug carefully on the table.
It is an Emma Bridgewater mug, with a rooster on it. We both look
at the cockerel as if it might leap up and tell us what to do now.

"Doesn't it stop you sleeping?" I ask.

"What?"

"All this coffee."

"It doesn't affect me at all," she takes a sharp, efficient breath. "I sleep like a baby. You should try drinking more of it yourself Kal. You might be more helpful if you were less out of it."

I look at her. I want to tell her that babies do not, in fact, sleep—not mine, anyway. I have barely had an uninterrupted night in eighteen months. This might explain why my husband has . . . for a moment, the blood pounds in my ears.

"Sorry," she says. "No, sorry. God. I'm just . . . I'm tired too. I'm really, really tired." She rests her forehead on the heels of her hands. Her fingers are long and tapering, with soft cuticles and delicate pads and perfectly filed nails. "This is bloody awful."

"I know." We sit in silence for a moment. Finn chomps at his toast and kicks his heels against the high chair.

Our lives are so completely different. Alice spends her time in high-octane meetings and negotiations, flying business class to New York and Dubai and Singapore and Hong Kong, while I divide my time between Mommy and Me Music, Little Sunflowers Playgroup, Sainsbury's, the swings, and the office—where I am becoming increasingly superfluous.

"So when are you going back to Oxford?"

"I don't know. What about you?"

"Well, I have to head back to London today. I have this thing going on at work . . . you know what it's like."

I really don't, at least not anymore, but I nod. "It's okay, you should go. You've done so much here already." Finn has his sippy cup upside down now, and is pouring it onto the plastic table, then smashing his hand flat into the milk and sodden toast, splattering it across the floor.

"Should he be doing that?" Alice says, anxiously.

I get up and take the cup away. He wails and holds out both hands for it. I give him back the cup and he spurts it into my face. As I wipe milk out of my eye, I remember I have three recorded interviews in the car. I should have left them in the office for someone else to work on. But it all fell apart so fast.

I used to care about qualitative research into patient experiences. I used to put huge effort into getting the most truthful, enlightening story from each person I interviewed. But my work has been squeezed into one-and-a-half days a week and has, therefore, rendered itself almost pointless. The pay barely covers the babysitter. I leave things undone, half done, badly done—to be tidied up by others. But if I let my work go—the job I once loved, and worked so hard for—then what? I cannot see myself at home full time—I saw what that did to my mother. So the only answer is to work more, not less. But I can't do that because then I'd have to hand Finn over to the babysitter for even longer, and that feels wrong too. He is so small and he needs me. He needs to know that his mother is always there for him; always puts him first.

It would be easier if Doug's work were more flexible. But as my job has been crushed into fewer and fewer hours, Doug's has expanded, with the promotion to senior lecturer, the book, the global speaking invitations. Each month his schedule gets a little more demanding, with more travel, more meetings, more talks, readings, conferences, while my life is shrink-wrapped around Finn and our home. It is not clear how my years of education and ambition have funneled me into Mommy and Me Music but I do know one thing: there is a sharp red line leading from that to this to what is happening with Doug right now.

I can't believe that it's only a week since I tore through our closet at five in the morning with him behind me saying, "Stop, stop, please—wait—I should come with you."

I couldn't even look at him.

I had been up all night in the leather armchair downstairs while he slept. I had just about decided to go and wake him up and confront him with what I'd found when my cell phone rang. I wasn't really surprised to hear Alice's panicky voice telling me to come down to Sussex. I'd been waiting for her call all week.

I shoved some of Finn's clothes and diapers, his bunny, his sippy cup, and his bag of toy cars into a bag. Then I went into our bedroom to grab some of my own things before I woke Finn, wrapped him in blankets, and coaxed him, gently, out into the January pre-dawn fog, and into his car seat.

Doug would have put my behavior down to shock, initially, but at some point, after I'd gone, he would have noticed that his phone was downstairs on the leather chair. Then he would have known that I'd seen her other text, too. Maybe he thought I'd forget about it all, with my mother's death.

But of course I have heard his guilt behind every interaction we've had since that morning. I have felt it licking at my heart the whole time. His guilt is how I know that this is real and not just a made up paranoia, a silly misunderstanding.

Alice is tapping at her iPad and Finn is battering his cup on the side of the table, singing a nonsense song to himself while drumming his heels.

"That's a lovely song." I sit back down.

"Are you all right?" Alice says. "Are you actually okay?"

I look at her. "I'm not sure. Are you?"

"Not really."

We both stare at each other. Finn goes quiet and watches us, perhaps concerned that we may be about to bawl again.

Then Alice takes a breath. "Kal—you don't have to answer this, but why didn't you want Doug here? I know you said there was a good reason, but obviously . . . he wouldn't . . . I mean. This must be serious. What's going on with you two?"

I glance at Finn. I can't possibly explain all this to her with him sitting there, covered in milk and marmite, his brown eyes fixed on our faces.

"It's okay," she says. "If you don't want to talk about it, that's okay too."

I take a gulp of coffee, then I lean over and with one hand I stroke the hair off Finn's face. "I can't really, at the moment." His bangs really need cutting. "I just can't really even think about it to be honest." I try to slide the bits of soggy toast into a heap on his tray.

"No. That's okay. Don't worry," Alice pushes her chair back, gets up, and starts scraping her papers together. I heave Finn out of his chair and put him on the floor. Drunk with freedom, he toddles off in his spaceman pajamas toward the open dishwasher. "It's all right," she says. "I can see why you wouldn't feel able to face anything right now. So. Look. You know what? I still can't find the bloody birth certificate."

"But we don't need it now do we?"

"I know, but I want to find it. It feels odd not to. It feels incomplete."

This is why Alice is the high-earning city lawyer, and not me. "But maybe she never brought it with her from America in the first place?" I suggest. Finn is taking dirty cutlery out of the dishwasher and laying it out, quite neatly and slowly, on the tiled floor.

"You can't become a British citizen without a birth certificate."

"Was she ever a British citizen? Do we even know that she was?"

Alice frowns. "I suppose not. I found their marriage certificate though. Did you know they didn't get married till you were ten months old?"

I nod, surprised that I know something about my mother that Alice doesn't. "They got married just before Dad brought us to England."

"That's quite cool of them, when you think about it," she says. "There must have been a lot of pressure to get married."

"Well, it was California in the seventies, maybe not?"

"But from Dad's parents?"

"Actually, that's true . . ."

The phone buzzes in my jeans pocket.

"Kal!" Alice cries.

I follow her eyes to Finn. He is brandishing a Sabatier kitchen knife, feet apart like a warrior. The blade glints. I hurl myself across the kitchen and wrench it out of his hands. He looks up at me with startled eyes.

"Dangerous!" I say, in a horrified voice, holding the knife high above us. "Dangerous! Knives are very, very dangerous!" I put it in the sink. My hand is shaking.

"Mine!" He holds out both hands, outraged. "Minamineamine!"

"No. Dangerous. It will cut you. Knives cut you. Ow!"

"No. Mine. Mine!"

We wrangle for a bit, but eventually he settles for the soapy washing up brush. I gather up the cutlery from the floor and close the dishwasher, aware of Alice behind me.

"They're quite a handful aren't they?" she says. "Toddlers."

I sit down, again, and watch Finn scrub the kitchen cupboard.

"You're not tempted then?"

"He's gorgeous," she smiles. "But I'm quite glad he's yours."

I don't know why Alice is single. She is so kind and clever, and immensely beautiful. Maybe she is just too busy for boyfriends. Or maybe she has someone, but hasn't told me. There is something so self-sufficient about Alice though. I can't imagine her as part of a couple, even though she has had boyfriends in the past. Now does not seem to be the right time to ask her about her love life. I look at my phone. There are voice mails and texts, probably all from Doug.

Suddenly, I just want to be left alone.

"Listen," Alice glances at my phone, then at me. "If you'd like to pick out some of her jewelry, before you go . . ."

"No, it's okay. I don't want anything, I really don't. You can have it."

"What? Why? You should take something. I'm not keeping it all."

"No, really, Alice. You deserve it. I don't want her jewelry."

"Well, you can choose things when you're ready," she says.

"Look—how about you have the jewelry, and I'll keep this box," I pull the blue box toward me. "It's got her American things in it. I'm the American-born one, so I get this, okay? You have the jewelry."

She raises her eyes to the ceiling and sighs. Then she gathers the rest of the paperwork.

"So I have to go back to London around lunchtime . . . I'm going to finish up here and . . ." She walks to the door, pauses, and then turns back to me. "Kal, whatever has happened with Doug, you two will work it out, won't you? You have to."

I nod but I can't speak. I finish the last of the coffee with my eyes shut, and then I get a cloth and kneel down and wipe the marmite off Finn's face. He squawks. I kiss him, push back my mess of hair, and survey the carnage—milk, toast, and smears on the floor by the dishwasher and all over the white kitchen cabinets. I hear the door close behind me and Alice's light feet on the stairs. Then I reach out and gather Finn's solid body tight in my arms. He smells of marmite and milk, and somewhere beneath it, sleep. I squeeze my eyes shut so that stars appear. This is the only thing that really matters. How could Doug throw this away? Finn wraps his arms around my neck and presses his sticky face into my hair. "Mama," he coos. "Mamamamamamamama."

At some point I am going to have to confront Doug. I can't just run away from this. And then suddenly, with Alice's strong coffee buzzing through my head, I think I'll just do it. Now. Tell him that I saw the texts and that I know he's having an affair. I put Finn down, kiss him, and get several pans and a wooden spoon from the cupboard. He seizes the spoon and begins to bash.

And before I can change my mind, I press "Doug." The room spins as it rings, twice, and he picks up.

"Thank God, Kal. I've been calling and calling you! Why didn't you answer? Oh my love, are you okay? What's happening down there? I've been going out of my mind—I can't believe you wouldn't let me come down, why . . ." But I hold the phone away from my ear. I breathe in and out.

I can feel his guilt bouncing off the base stations toward me, and my body vibrates with it. I can't hear what he is actually saying because everything else is too loud. He has taken our small family and smashed it to pieces. The past eight years suddenly feel like a story that I made up because I needed to believe that love could be simple and constant and he has ripped it up now. This cannot be happening.

"Stop," I say.

"What?"

"I saw your phone. I saw it Doug. Stop lying to me."

A pause. "What did you see?"

"You know."

"You mean . . . ? Okay. Okay. Now, okay—look . . . this isn't . . ."

"I can't talk to you about this now!" I yell. "Jesus!"

"No—listen to me Kal . . . I . . ."

But I can't hear it. I hang up.

A moment later, it rings again. I throw it across the room and it bounces off the plasterwork, making a dent.

Finn looks up—his eyebrows are knitted, his eyes wide.

"It's okay, sweetie, it's okay."

For a while, I don't know how long, I sit and stare at the pier painting above the table, unable to move, or think, while Finn crashes the spoon onto my mother's redundant Le Creusets.

Then my father comes in. His face is still ashen against his white shirt and navy blue sweater, his cords hanging loosely off his long legs. He asks, slightly formally, whether Finn might like to come into the garden for a stroll. I bustle around finding Finn's coat, hat, and his red rain boots. I wonder what my father overheard, and I am embarrassed, but also rather touched that he is stepping in like this. Then again, I suppose he knows all about infidelity.

The two of them go out the front door together, my father bending sideways like a tree in a gale, to reach Finn's small hand.

I sit at the kitchen table. I can't go home today, that's clear. The thought of confronting Doug makes waves of fury and fear rise inside me one after the other so I have to steady myself with both hands on the table edge. I just have to find a way to think clearly. All I want is to get as far away as possible from this mess. I can't think—or talk to Doug. I can't go home. But I can't stay here, surrounded by my mother's belongings, and all the memories of my complicated childhood and the ghosts of so many lost opportunities. I have to get away so I won't have to face this anymore. I basically want to vanish.

I always thought there would be time. I never thought she'd die like this, before she even turned sixty. She always seemed younger and more intrepid than other peoples' mothers. She was fit and strong. She had odd, adventurous skills, an odd fit to a life of supermarket shops, dog walking, and painting. She could not only make a fish spear, but actually skewer a carp with it in the shallows of the River Ouse. She once taught me to start a fire like a boy scout, using only twigs and a mirror. She had a witchy attitude to the countryside, gathering fungi and picking herbs for medicinal teas; she could name constellations and understood things about the moon and tides. She could tie nautical knots too. I'd forgotten that. A buried memory surfaces: summertime on the beach at Birling Gap, a brusque wind, me sitting in a terry cloth robe as she showed me different knots. As she manipulated the rope, she gave their names: the cleat hitch, the clove hitch, the bowline, the sheet bend, the square knot. The skin on her hands was weathered and hard—more farmer than artist. There was always a line of soil or oil paint under her nails.

She was just so physically robust. She never got sick, never made a fuss over cuts or bruises—ours, or hers. I remember one night she slashed into her palm trying to cut wax out of a candleholder and I came into the kitchen to find her twisting a pair of underpants into a tourniquet with one hand. There was blood everywhere, like a slasher movie. She hadn't thought to call for help even though I was next door watching TV, and Alice was upstairs doing homework. I called 911 and an ambulance came. She needed ten stitches.

She was supposed to be invincible but it all happened so fast—for us at least: diagnosis, decline, death. I never thought I'd have such a short while to make things right.

This is exactly what Doug warned me about on our Boxing Day visit, a year ago, before her diagnosis. As we drove out of the village, I remember him saying that he thought that she was scared of me.

"You're kidding." I gave a dry laugh.

"No," he said. "Honestly. She sometimes watches you when you aren't looking, and she has this sort of anguished look, like she's desperate to get through to you, but too scared that you'll brush her off or something."

"She's the one keeping her distance, not me." I felt the resentment rising again and I was surprised by how near the surface it still was. I had successfully protected myself against my mother for years but now, with Finn, I was wide open again. I hadn't considered this when I was pregnant. I didn't realize that a baby shoots up the generations and stitches them together, like a strong thread. Having Finn had crushed me up against my mother again, and I couldn't do anything about it.

"She isn't scared of me, Doug." I tried to sound reasonable. "It's not fear that keeps her distant, it's a total lack of interest. Haven't you noticed what she's like with Finn? She hardly even looks at him. It's like he isn't there."

"Come on, that's just not true."

"Why are you defending her? I don't think she held him once today, not one single time. Even my dad held him for a bit and he has never liked babies. And they've never even been up to Oxford to see him, have they? I tell you what, Doug, she can come to us next time. I'm not going to keep driving down here like this."

"Kal . . ."

"I expect she was like this with me as a baby too—uninterested. It explains a lot."

"I actually don't believe that, Kal. I mean, look how you are with Finn—she must have done something right with you because all that love and patience you have with him—and your goodness and kindness—*you*—all that doesn't just come out of nowhere."

"Do we have to do this?"

"Why not? We haven't talked about you and your mother for years," he said. "And there's Finn now and that's changed things. She bought that high chair, for God's sake. She's really not uninterested."

His hands on the wheel were broad, strong and clean—hands to hold, hands to be held by—hands to keep things safe. I swallowed hard. I was not going to open all this up again. I turned and looked back at Finn in his car seat, gnawing on a teething ring. Seeing me, he let it drop and his face cracked into a great big grin. For a few seconds, my beautiful baby and I just smiled at each other, and the world was simple.

"All I'm saying is I think she's sad that you two aren't closer." He really wouldn't let it go. "I actually think she wants things to be better between you, but she doesn't know how. She might not want to hold Finn and coo at him, but she's totally aware of him. I saw her today, watching you while you were feeding him and talking to your father, and I think she was almost in tears. She really isn't uninterested, Kal. Whatever this is for her, it's definitely not lack of interest. Can't you just try talking to her?"

"Doug. Stop. Just leave it. My mother and I are totally fine."

"But this is surely a chance to put things behind you and . . ."

I looked out the window, silently daring him to say "make a fresh start." But he knew me better than that. "The two of you are complicated," he said. "I get that."

I stared at the expanses of plowed clay, the bare oaks flicking by, then the chalk quarry looming above us like a giant's tooth. We turned onto the London road.

"But don't leave it too late," he said. "Or you might regret it one day."

I should clean up breakfast—the French coffee press, the mangle of marmite and milk. I can't sit here thinking about my mother and Doug. I can't. While we had that Boxing Day lunch, her tumor was there already, growing in her breast, a deadly secret that she was hiding from us all.

It is also possible that Doug was keeping his horrible secret too, even then. Maybe he was already lying to me as he ate honey-glazed ham at my parents' table. A vivid image rises in my brain of a curtain of strawberry blonde hair and Doug's broad hands pressing on pale flanks. All I want is to erase myself from this nightmare, completely.

A surge of nausea brings saliva into my mouth. I have to decide what to do next. But I can't think. These images are too much to hold in my head. I just want to get away.

I wonder what my father is doing outside with Finn. I imagine him leaning down and trying to explain the Victorian architectural features of the house to his small grandson. I pick up my mother's notebook. Holding it in my hands brings a sudden and unexpected comfort. Her handwriting, though younger, rounder, more girlish, is definitively hers. And it's still here—still physically present. This small part of her is here and that must mean that she hasn't really gone.

*

Alice leaves, but I don't. After I have given Finn his bath, and read him three storybooks, and tucked him up in his sleeping bag in the travel crib, then sung "Baa Baa Black Sheep" until, finally, he really is asleep, I creep back downstairs.

My father is in his study. I can see the crease of light under his door. I walk through to the kitchen and put the kettle on. Her old notebook is lying on the kitchen table, where I left it, next to the jewelry box. I take the notebook, make myself a cup of peppermint tea, then go through to the living room. I curl up on the old Habitat sofa.

It is chilly in this room, and the floor lamp gives off a yellowish light, casting long shadows up the bookcases. I pull a scratchy tartan blanket around my shoulders. The house is eerily quiet, except for the far-off moan of the wind and the occasional creak and tick of the radiator. I feel as if she might pop her head in at any moment, and ask why I'm sitting here, all alone. Is something wrong? Has something happened?

I open the notebook. Maybe there is something in here that will give me a clue about who she really was. Maybe this book will help me understand why the two of us were so twisted and knotty.

But it is just lists and scientific jargon. I flip through pages of incomprehensible notes, tables of numbers, and columns consisting mainly of vowels. Then I realize that there are little scribbled comments, dotted here and there. They are often written vertically in the margins, or scrawled along the bottom of the page: little hints of a life outside the research. I flip from one to the next.

4pm tomorrow—S

—Find out about OMP—

S bday

<u>Where</u> *is B's family? Puget Sound/Salish Sea?*

I notice that the initial "S" crops up frequently but I can only find one reference to what could be my father: "*G to NY Friday?*"

The last fifth of the book is blank—old, empty lined pages, waiting for something that never came. I wonder if it stops because she got pregnant. Maybe this notebook represents her last days as a scientist. Is that why she kept it?

Then something connects in my head. This *S* could be Susannah, the postcard sender. There were thirty-seven annual postcards, which means Susannah started to send them the very first year my mother got to England.

If there are old friends out there, like this Susannah person, then maybe there is family somewhere too. My mother was an only child, her parents are long dead, but maybe there are cousins, or at least, old family friends. There must be people out there who knew her as a young woman, as a child. Perhaps one day I could take a trip out to the Pacific Northwest and find the people who knew her. Maybe it's not too late to understand my mother—and if I can understand her, then perhaps I will be able to let her go. Then something occurs to me. I could go—now. I could take Finn and get on a plane and go.

The metal band that has been clamped around my heart for days immediately feels less tight. Just the thought of getting away is a huge release.

And I could do this. I really could. Why not?

If I leave then I won't have to sit in our home and listen to the man I love explain how he fell for his ex-girlfriend all over again—or worse, how he has longed for her since college. I won't have to hear him tell me how motherhood has changed me, or how having Finn has exposed the cracks that were always there in our relationship, I just didn't see them. And I won't have to hear him tell me that he understands, now, that he never should have left her in the first place and that marrying me was a mistake. He doesn't love me in the right way. He loves her. He's so sorry.

I put my mother's notebook on the coffee table. My hands are shaking. An escape plan has dropped from the sky, and I must pick it up and use it before it shimmies away again.

I get up and go through to the kitchen and get my laptop. I take it back to the sofa, pulling the blanket back up as it falls to the floor.

My mother kept her maiden name, Halmstrom, listed before my father's: *Elena Halmstrom MacKenzie.* I have no idea how people go about searching for family members—there are probably millions of websites dedicated to this. But, not knowing where to start, I just google *Halmstrom, Seattle.*

Some long ago Ellis Island slip must have turned a vowel because there are ninety-five Holmstroms in Seattle, but not a single Halmstrom. I feel the disappointment settle solidly in my belly. Maybe there really are no surviving members of my mother's family.

I skim down the Google links for Halmstrom, and then something catches my eye: *Harry Halmstrom, The Ida May Assisted Living Facility, Vancouver, British Columbia.*

Seattle and Vancouver aren't that far from each other. I click on the link. The Ida May Assisted Living Facility lists the names of its residents and there is a Harry Halmstrom, along with the phone number of Jenny Zimmerman, his caregiver.

My mother's father is dead and I'm pretty sure that his name was Theodore. She never talked about him and yet I grew up knowing that she hated him and he died. I have no memory of any conversation at all, in fact, about my grandparents. Presumably she shut me down if I ever asked. This, I realize, is just not normal. It's not just my genetic inheritance, it's Finn's now. Doug can trace his family back to the 1700s. My father's MacKenzie clan goes back through generations of priests and bagpipe players. But the other half of our lineage apparently vanished the day my mother died.

I think about getting up and going through the house to the study to ask my father about all this, but then I'd have to explain to him what I am doing and I couldn't even begin to do that because obviously it's not normal to be doing this. So I pick up my phone and call Alice's cell.

She doesn't answer. I leave her a slightly strangulated message saying that I was just checking to see that she got back to London safely.

It is nine o'clock in Sussex, but only 1 p.m. in Vancouver. I finish my peppermint tea, get up, go to the kitchen, and pour myself a large glass of red wine.

I drink half of it, then I dial the number of Harry Halmstrom's caregiver at The Ida May Assisted Living Facility.

I don't really expect anyone to pick up, but someone does, after just a couple of rings.

"Oh. Hello," for a moment, I can't think what on earth to say. Then I take a breath. "I'm calling about one of your residents, Harry Halmstrom. I'm calling from England because I wonder—I think—though I'm not sure—that there's a possibility he's a relative of mine."

"Really?" she says. There is a pause. But she doesn't say anything else.

"Well, I don't know. We have the same family name—well, my mother's name actually, and, well, I might be coming to Vancouver so I thought perhaps I could find out if we are related." As I talk, I am realizing how tenuous all this is—how completely deranged. It occurs to me that I could just hang up.

"Well you sure have to come see him then don't you?" she says brightly. "If he might be your relative!"

"Yes. Well, that's right." I'm bolstered by her enthusiasm. "That's what I was thinking."

"I just love your accent," she says. "What did you say your name was again?"

I'm not sure why, but I give my mother's maiden name. "Kali Halmstrom."

"Well, Halmstrom's not exactly a common name," she admits.

"Do you know if he was from the Seattle area, originally, by any chance? Or had family there?"

Her voice lightens. "Oh, you know what, honey, Mr. Halmstrom lived all over the place, he may have lived in Seattle. Yes. I think so. I do know he was born in Sweden—is your family Swedish? Mr. Halmstrom came out West on a boat when he was just a teenager."

My head buzzes. I remember my mother telling me just once, a very long time ago, that I have Swedish blood and that's why my eyes are blue, though my hair is dark.

"I think so," I say. "Yes. I do think there is Swedish blood somewhere."

"Well Mr. Halmstrom has no family that I know of and he never gets a single visitor, so if you'd like to come visit him, honey, you'd be more than welcome."

"Do you think perhaps I could talk to him? On the phone?"

"Oh well no," she says. "He really isn't so good on the phone. He's very elderly. He gets awfully confused. And he doesn't hear too well. But you drop by if you're visiting the area. I'd love for him to have a visitor! When are you visiting?"

I take a sip of wine. "I'm coming this week," I say. A wave of nausea runs through my belly.

"Well how wonderful!" she says. "So, what day would you like to come by? I'll put it on the calendar."

I put down the phone. It's like the blood is pumping faster through my brain, bringing blooms of color instead of this heavy gray. It's mad, but I could do it. I could go. It doesn't matter if he's a relative. I could just go—to Canada. Vancouver is as good as anywhere. And I have to get away. That's clear. I have to go somewhere.

Suddenly, I think about the postcards. Many of them came from a gallery in Canada. I try to remember the name of it—the Susannah something gallery.

I google "*Susannah, Art Gallery, Canada.*"

The Susannah Gillespie Gallery.

I recognize the name instantly. It's in a place called Spring Tide Island, off the coast of British Columbia—reachable, surely, from Vancouver.

I skim the gallery home page. There is some blurb about the artists and various buttons to other pages. I click on *"Interviews with Susannah Gillespie."* There is a magazine article from a year ago. I tuck the tartan blanket tighter around my shoulders and, with the wine glass in one hand, I read.

Our Island Treasure,
By Zadie Hagan, arts reporter.

When I visit Susannah Gillespie's Spring Tide home, I'm struck first by the eclecticism of the art—there are paintings, ceramics, carvings, objects in vastly different styles—a mix that is testimony to a lifetime of travel, curiosity, and creativity. This should come as no surprise, since Gillespie travels widely through Europe, South America, and North America looking for new talent and giving lectures. She is truly a cosmopolitan Spring Tider!

A native of Nanaimo, Gillespie, 62, first came across Spring Tide Island in the late 1970s, she tells me, after a stint teaching in California. "I was escaping," she admits, "My heart was broken. I was looking for a retreat."

"The moment I stepped off the boat I knew I'd found home," she continues. Her Isabella Rock home, perched precariously, overlooking the sea, was built in the late 1960s by Ian Lao, now one of Vancouver's best-known architects. Set on the westerly-most tip of Spring Tide, the home is fully exposed to the elements. It is also an integral part of the landscape. And nestled behind the house is a custom-built pottery studio, which Gillespie added in the late eighties. Here, she also has a special room dedicated to yoga. But she will not show me around. "My studio is out of bounds," she tells me. "Nobody goes in there but me." She also keeps a small cabin, hidden away in the archipelago, though she will not discuss the location. "Everyone," she says, "needs a bolt-hole."

The Susannah Gillespie Gallery, established twelve years ago, has become a mecca for art lovers who flood over from Vancouver in the summertime. Her exhibitions are characterized by a devotion to the art of British Columbia, but she also selects works from around the globe. She is friends with famous artists such as Dale Chihuly in Seattle. And she has the Midas touch! Those lucky artists who exhibit at the gallery are almost always snapped up by big time collectors.

Gillespie, whose husband died two years ago, is the picture of serenity, sitting cross-legged on her couch with her two golden retrievers. How does a busy woman achieve this Buddha-like calm? Her answer is surprising. "Yoga helps," she says, "but we all have our demons. Most of us spend our lives trying to distract ourselves from them. We build businesses, houses, marriages to keep them inside, but these are external distractions. Look beneath the surface of anyone you know and you'll find chaos."

Well, this writer has to disagree! Gillespie is anything but chaotic: with her beautiful home, her thriving business, her artistic talent, and her professional standing. She is fully in control—our very own Spring Tide treasure.

I peer at the grainy picture. A handsome woman sits on a sofa with two golden retrievers at her feet. Her wavy hair is pinned up, her back is straight, gaze direct. There is no ingratiating smile for the photographer. She certainly does not look like a person carrying demons. She looks like a woman who knows how to control the world and everything in it. She looks like someone who is completely in charge.

I go back to the main page and click on "artists"—a list of potters, painters, and jewelry designers pops up. Then I click "*About Susannah Gillespie.*" There she is again, in color this time. Her hair is graying, and dangling turquoise earrings bring out extraordinarily pale blue eyes in a sun-lined face. She has high cheekbones, deep eye sockets, a serious mouth, and is looking sideways at the camera. Her body is muscular and she holds herself like a tall person who has worked hard not to stoop. You would not, I think, want to mess with Susannah Gillespie.

I go to Google Maps. Spring Tide Island is not far from Vancouver. A drive south and a ferry ride.

The plan seems to be taking shape, as if it has a life of its own. I imagine getting on a plane with Finn. We could go and meet this old Harry Halmstrom, stay a couple of nights in Vancouver. Then we could go and find Susannah, the postcard sender. I could ask her about my mother. I would be away from here: this, Doug, death. I realize that I don't really care whether this plan holds water. I just need to not be here. Canada sounds perfect. I finish the wine and pour myself another glass.

A buzzy feeling spreads inside me as I compose a brief e-mail to Susannah, introducing myself, telling her I'm going to be in the area, and asking if I could possibly come visit—this week. Then I dial the gallery number. I suddenly feel nervous and I almost hang up—but I just get her answering machine message, a deep-voiced Canadian woman instructing me to leave a message. She does sound in control. I give my name and cell number. "I hoped I might drop by and say hello," I say. "I think you might be a friend of my mother."

She must be. She sent my mother a postcard every year. They must have been good friends once. She will know things about my mother's past. Maybe she knows who taught my mother to spear fish or build a tepee, tie nautical knots or construct a really good snow shelter. Were these skills handed down from my grandparents? Susannah may know about my family too—what happened to make my mother so bitter about her childhood. It is too late to make things right but it's not too late to find out more about who my mother was, where she came from—where *I* came from. Where Finn comes from.

Suddenly, nothing seems more important than going to Canada. It feels like survival.

I google the Spring Tide Island ferries. They are few and far between in January, but they leave from Tsawwassen, a port outside Vancouver.

I search for B&Bs on Spring Tide Island. The first two I click on are closed in wintertime. But there is one, right in the port, and it looks lovely—window boxes, gingham duvets, homemade organic breakfast pancakes, cribs available. I dial the number. Nobody answers but I leave a message, with my cell number, saying that I am just going to fill out the online reservation form, and giving my dates.

I formulate rapid plans. I will drive back to Oxford first thing in the morning to get our passports. I'll pack warm things for

Finn—presumably it's bitterly cold in Canada in January—and then we'll just leave—on the overnight flight to Vancouver, before Doug gets home from work. My plan feels both deranged and perfectly reasonable.

I gulp the last of my wine and before I can think too much, I get out my credit card and click on Expedia. When I see the price of the British Airways flight I stop. My fingers hover over the keyboard. I can't possibly do this. The number represents a third of our entire joint savings. I stare at the screen. Blood pulses behind my eyes. It is an astronomical amount. But if I don't go—then what? Then there is a gaping hole.

And, as if I am in a dream, and not really participating in this lunacy, I type in my credit card details. I blink several times, and, with a fizzing sensation in my limbs, I click "purchase tickets."

Finn and I are booked on the last BA flight of the day to Vancouver.

A clammy sickness rolls right though my body. What the hell have I done? I stare at the flight details. A prompt asks if I want to print out my boarding pass.

And my phone rings. It's Alice.

"Were you trying to call me?" Her voice is muffled and anxious. "Sorry it's so late—client dinner." I can hear voices and bustle, faint music, in the background. Hearing Alice, sensible, rational Alice, reinforces the insanity of what I have just done. The tickets are nonrefundable.

"Are you okay Alice?" My voice sounds disembodied, as if it has very little to do with me.

"I had this dinner, I couldn't get out of it," she says. She sounds tired. "What is it? You sound . . . Is everything all right? I have to get back in a minute."

"No. It's fine. I just wanted to let you know that I'm going away for a bit with Finn. Just to . . . clear my head. I need a bit of a break."

"Oh Kal," she says. "Is this thing with Doug really bad?"

"It's okay. It's not that. I just need some space. I need to get away so I can think."

"You could come stay with me. I'd have to be at work, but . . ."

"No, it's okay I've booked something already."

"What?" The background noise is louder now. I realize she must be walking back into the restaurant.

"I'm just going away."

"Did you say you're going?"

"Yes!"

"Where are you going?"

"Vancouver."

"What?" she shouts. "I can't hear you at all! This place is—"

"Never mind," I bellow. "Don't worry. I'll call you tomorrow, okay?"

"They're waving at me. Speak to you tomorrow."

"Okay." I say, "And take care of yourself, okay? Get some rest." I hang up, but I know I won't call her tomorrow because if I do she will feel duty bound to stop me, and I will realize that I can't possibly do this. But it's too late. The tickets are nonrefundable. And I can't go home. Not yet.

Southern California, 1975

The Sea Park whales performed their show twice a day in an above ground tank with steep glass walls and bleachers stretching up on all sides. The male, Orpheus, had been captured in the North Atlantic by Icelandic fishermen when he was five or six years old—now he had a chest the size of a tanker and his dorsal fin was taller than a man. The female, Bella, was three years older. She'd been taken from the Pacific Northwest in the sixties, when orcas became big business. The two whales had been trained together and the Sea Park guys said they were docile: there was no threatening behavior and they did their job placidly. The public loved them. Since the orcas arrived, park revenues had gone up by a third—all across America the crowds were going wild for killer whales.

Elena had only watched one show, early on when she first got access to the dolphins. She stood in the wings with her backpack on one day and a hat pulled down to block the glare. In one routine, Bella had to open her jaws to allow the trainer to brush her teeth with a giant toothbrush. The crowd whooped and yelled. Some school kids threw popcorn. The male had been trained to drink what seemed to be the contents of a giant can of gasoline, then swim the perimeter making the sound of an outboard motor. After that Elena stayed away when the whales were performing.

Between shows, the two whales would move in slow circles around their cramped tank. Sometimes when she passed she'd find them just floating there, completely motionless, staring at the glass sides. The head trainer, Dan, said they were sleeping but maybe he was just *trying to make himself feel better because they both knew that orcas in the wild swim for miles while they sleep. They shut down half their brain at a time. They don't hang in the water.*

She'd seen sleeping killer whales in the wild once—a few summers ago, up in Puget Sound, she was on a field trip with some other students, monitoring Chinook levels, when they spotted a pod out to sea. Twenty or more whales were lined up in sleeping formation, moving eerily across the horizon, surfacing to breathe—a tiny pause—then submerging for a long time.

In the wild, an orca will swim up to a hundred miles a day; here at Sea Park they could only move in tight circles. Out in the ocean, they'd dive hundreds of feet to the sea bed; here, they'd hit the bottom at thirty feet. They lived, essentially, in a bathtub.

She noticed one day that the male's dorsal fin was beginning to collapse. Dan said it was nothing to worry about—it happened to captive males, he said, it definitely wasn't a sign of ill-health.

She had somehow managed to get past all this when it came to the Bottlenose family. They seemed active and healthy and she couldn't spend her time feeling bad for them. She'd had to shove these thoughts out of her head because she had work to do, and she knew she was lucky to have unfettered access. As she monitored their play patterns, and language of their play, she'd grown used to their environment— mostly she managed not to think about the life they could have had outside it. The dolphins seemed to have adapted to captivity. It was possible that they didn't remember the wild or what it felt like to skim through the waves like the pods she sometimes saw down on the beach. She felt attached to the Bottlenose family, but distanced from them at the same time. They were what they should be: research subjects of whom she'd grown fond.

But the killer whales were different. They sat like capital letters in black and white, quietly making their point.

Perhaps because she wasn't studying them, she didn't manage the same scientific detachment. She couldn't avoid them either—she had to pass their tank every night to get out of the park. Sometimes, she would catch the eye of the big female and she had an uncomfortable feeling that the whale knew all about her. She dismissed this as tiredness—the hollow feeling you get at the end of a long day, when you are alone in a public place that has emptied out for the night.

One day she noticed that the male had scabs across his back, and the skin, which should be glossy black, was peeling and mottled. His dorsal had collapsed fully now, and hung limp, like the tail of a dejected dog.

Each night, as she passed their tank to let herself out of the lush tropical park, she would feel their silent longing settle on her like a cloak. She felt like they were asking her for something, quietly and insistently. She could not shake off the guilt.

CHAPTER THREE

I can't sleep. Every part of my body is jangling and my head pulses with the effort of containing all the thoughts that I can't allow myself to think. The flight is almost empty so we have a whole row of seats just for the two of us. Finn has finally fallen asleep after rampaging up and down the cabin for the first four hours with me behind him, trying to stop him from grabbing things and bothering people. He is sprawled across my lap now, fingers uncurled, mouth open, but his hair is static and wild, as if it, alone, refuses to admit defeat.

I sip some water and shift gently to get my back in a better position, fearful of waking him because I know that he is perfectly capable of staying awake for the whole nine hours, slowly spiraling through excitement and hyperactivity into full-blown hysteria.

I see my face reflected in the window and for a second I don't know who it is that I am looking at. I thought I loved my hair but its absence is intensely liberating. I touch my head and it feels smooth. My fingers expect length and weight, even though I know it's gone. I can feel my curls in my hands as I twist my hair up off my neck, the same way I can feel Finn's newborn mouth suctioning onto my nipple, or Doug's hands cupping my chin. Body memories; lost things; life moves on.

The cut was an impulse. As we waited in the drizzle outside the bus station for the Heathrow Express, I found myself staring at a hairdresser's sign across the road: "Walk-Ins Welcome." We were far too early anyway. There was time to kill.

While bored hairdressers fussed around Finn, giving him a lollipop, and letting him play with the brushes, I shed my hair. The girl kept asking if I was sure, but I could tell she was thrilled to slice off great, satisfying chunks. She held them up like curling brown bouquets as she snipped. Afterward Finn looked at me with a sort of respect and tentatively patted my head with both hands. "All gone!"

I could watch a movie. Or read. I pick up the *High Flyers* magazine and flick through it. There is an article about Totem Poles of the Pacific Northwest. I skim paragraphs about totem meanings—pride, remembrance, bereavement. How the poles, made of rain forest wood, will disintegrate over the years and how they are built in the understanding that they will be reabsorbed into the earth one day. Nothing lasts forever. We are all part of a bigger cycle, birth and decay. A subheading catches my eye—*Shame Poles*—totems erected by tribes to shame people for their unpaid debts or crimes. But I can't concentrate properly on the text. My eyes are so tired. The words won't quite line up. I stare at the pictures—faces, symbols, black beaks. I close the magazine, shut my eyes.

I mustn't think about what I'm doing. I am in flight.

Another memory surfaces—I must have been nine or ten. I told the teacher to shut up and then ran for my life—out the staff door, down the steps. As I pounded across the playground I glanced back and saw the faces of my classmates pressed against the picture window, thirty mouths hanging open. This is the feeling that I have right now: I am galloping away, but beneath the adrenaline-fueled outrage is a strong sense that this can't end well.

When I got back to Oxford this morning—only this morning—I called Doug.

"You're home."

"No—I'm going away for a bit. I need to think."

"What? What—where are you going? Back to Sussex?"

"I'm going to take Finn to visit relatives—in Vancouver."

"You're what? You're going to Vancouver? Canada? What relatives? You haven't got any relatives in Vancouver. Kal . . . Jesus . . . This is—"

"I need to get away, Doug."

"Is this about the texts you saw on my phone? Look—listen—I know you're in shock right now. You just lost your mother. It's not—"

"Oh my God!" I cut him off. "Are you honestly about to say 'it's not what you think?'"

"Okay. We have to talk about this. Wait there. I'm coming home. Just wait there. I'm coming now."

But I didn't wait for him to come home and explain to me that he'd fucked her because I was preoccupied with our baby. Or that he loved her—and had never really loved me. That he was leaving.

I hung up, then strapped Finn into the baby carrier, and hauled him up onto my back. I hooked my bag across my body, and then I left, bumping the case behind me down our front steps.

Doug, presumably, got home soon afterward. I wonder how he felt when he saw that I had gone—furious? Upset? Confused? Guilty? And that's without knowing how much of our savings I had just spent.

I kept my phone switched off after that. The only way is not to think about this, and not, under any circumstances, to read his texts or listen to his voice mails.

I reach over Finn's sleeping body and delve gently into my bag for a book. I wish I'd worn yoga pants rather than jeans. I feel as if my whole body is swelling. My hand closes around my mother's notebook and as I pull it out, the wedding photo flutters onto my lap. I forgot that I slipped it in there as I packed our things in Sussex. I catch it before it slides off my lap. Then I hold it up to the yellowy cabin light.

My mother is wearing a long seventies-style dress with flowing sleeves, and she is laughing up at my father. Her hair is loose and

hangs in thick dark waves around her shoulders, in a middle part-
ing, like Yoko Ono, and she's holding a bunch of wildflowers.

You can't see my father's expression because he's cut in half by
the crease and obscured by the shadow of a building. All you can
see is flared pants and a narrow, floral shirt. He looks sportier; surprisingly cool. They are standing outside a red brick building. It is
frustrating not to be able to see his face with the crease and the
shadows, but from his thrown back shoulders I feel sure he is grinning back at her.

I am not in the picture but I must have been there somewhere,
in someone's arms. I wonder who held me during the ceremony.
It is odd that in all these years my mother never mentioned any
friends from school or college. She didn't even mention the woman
who sent her a postcard every year for thirty-seven years. She was
a student in California for—what—six years? It is astonishing how
easily she cut off from her American life. But then, she always was
excellent at cutting off.

The pilot dims the lights. All around me people shift and murmur. Another baby lets out a high-pitched wail and Finn's arms
twitch, but he doesn't wake up. His eyelids flutter. I wonder what
he is dreaming about—I imagine him in there, right now, perched
on the backs of dragons, or diving headlong into a giant chocolate cake. He is so beautiful, with his tawny bangs and his perfect
Sistine-baby mouth, the dimple on his chin. I stroke the hair gently
away from his eyes and remember how, when he was born, and I
breastfed him day after day I watched his eyelashes grow.

I look at my watch, still on British time. It is 9:45 p.m. I should be
on the sofa with Doug, all the toys cleared away, the washing up done,
the dishwasher trundling through its cycle, and Finn asleep upstairs
in his crib under his car cell. Doug and I should be drinking a glass of
wine and watching TV. I didn't buy dishwashing detergent. Or butter.
I forgot to tell Doug to turn off the electric heater in the basement. I
forgot to tell work that I won't be back this week, after all.

I should tell my father what I am doing too. When I woke up
this morning he'd set off for London, leaving a note in his elegant

handwriting: *"I have gone to the office. Please stay as long as you wish (though lock up if you leave). I will be back on Friday."* I left him a note. *"Thanks Dad, I had to go but I'll see you soon. Take care."*

He will be alone in his London apartment now, shattered—but working. I wonder if he even has friends. I might have known nothing about my mother's past, but I always understood her present. But with my father I really know nothing. Beyond the layout of his office and apartment, I am completely unfamiliar with his life in London. I don't even have his cell phone number. All I have is his e-mail, and a work number. Usually we communicate by e-mail. Every few weeks I send him a message—these days usually about Finn—and he replies, often instantly, in one or two sentences. He signs his e-mails *G.* Not "Dad," not even "your father," but *G.* It is a way of communicating that avoids any real connection. But still, he is my father and he should know what I am doing. And he may be able to tell me something about Susannah or Harry Halmstrom. Asking him about them in an e-mail seems more doable than asking face-to-face.

I get out my phone and, without looking at the inbox, I compose an e-mail. I'll send it when we touch down.

To: Dad <G. K.MacKenzie>
From: Kali
Subject: Getting Away

Dear Dad,

I hope this won't worry you too much, but I have decided to get away for a bit—I'm actually on a plane right now, in fact, typing on my iPhone—will send this when we land. I'm going to Canada of all places. I decided—rather spur of the moment—to go and find an old friend of Mom's, Susannah Gillespie. She owns a gallery on an island near Vancouver. You probably know her? Don't worry if you can't think about much right now. I just felt you should probably know what I'm up to. I needed to get away, and Canada seemed as good a place as any.

I was just looking at your wedding photo. Mom is so beautiful. It struck me that I know nothing about your wedding. Maybe it's the shock, but I can't stop thinking about how little I know about Mom's past.

Anyway, I hope you're managing—are you back in the office? Will you be staying in London now or haven't you made any plans? I will e-mail again soon.

Love

Kali

Ps. Was going to call but then I realized I don't actually have your cell number. Only your office.

I stare at it for a few moments. Mentioning Harry Halmstrom seems like a step too far. Seeing a description of my plans in black and white gives me a fleeting, almost drunken perspective on myself: this is unstable behavior.

The e-mail sits in the outbox. I snap my phone off and then a poisonous thought lands in my heart: right now, Doug might be on his phone to her, telling her that I know—that I've just left, taking Finn. They might be discussing what on earth they are going to do about me. Maybe she is saying "well, she had to know sooner or later."

As I shove the wedding photo back into my mother's notebook, and the notebook and phone into my bag the urge to scream is overwhelming. Then suddenly, irrationally, I am furious. Livid. Enraged—with my mother. How could she just die like this, without the two of us saying all the things that needed to be said? I feel as if she's reneged on a deal or broken a promise. It seems grimly fitting that she should die exactly when everything else is falling apart.

But these are ludicrous thoughts. I have to get a grip. I never would have turned to my mother for support over Doug anyway. I absolutely would not be sobbing on her breast right now. But still, this loss is awful. It is a disorienting, panicky feeling. I feel as if I'm a small child and she has vanished. I suddenly remember being lost on a rock face—one of my earliest memories—I was about four, I think, at a French picnic spot. I clung to the boulders and the sunlight bounced off the granite around me, and I couldn't see my mother. I howled for her under the hot white sun. I was alone in the world. Then she was calling my name and as she came around the corner I felt a tsunami of relief.

I close my eyes. The plane shudders through turbulence, seatbelt signs ping on. I lay my arm over Finn's heavy body.

I have been incredibly blind. That's really what I'm angry about. I have deluded myself. I am not angry with my mother for dying—of course I'm not. I am angry with Doug. And I am angry with myself for being so clueless and trusting. And so distracted.

I should have known better. I learned all too well from my mother that love is not to be relied on. It is a state of uncertainty. But over the last eight years Doug persuaded me—or perhaps I persuaded myself—that our love was different—it was safe. It was solid and equal and—above all—permanent. I am built on this belief now. What I didn't realize was that Doug lay beneath this conviction of mine, propping it up. And now, apparently, he isn't doing that anymore. Apparently Doug's love was never permanent or safe, it was just another thing to be given and taken away.

I have messed up. Doug has messed up. We have both messed up and the one person this is going to ricochet into is the child that we, above all, are supposed to protect and love, constantly, safely, permanently. I look down at Finn, spread across my lap.

What have we done?

*

Driving out of Vancouver International Airport in the rental car, with Finn dazed in his car seat behind me, what I need most is caffeine. The flight has left me parched and blurry and everything feels very far off. The shock of how much the rental car cost didn't help. With insurance, and a ludicrous surcharge for the child car seat it came to a jaw-dropping sum. But I can't think about money. The expenditure is reckless, but not half as reckless as being here.

As I pull onto the busy southbound freeway, it begins to rain hard—I fumble about trying to find the windshield wipers and for a few shocking moments, I am spinning down a five lane freeway completely blind.

I twist the right lever and the windshield clears for a moment. It is morning rush hour, and all I can see are blurry red taillights and driving rain. It is hard to focus on the lines dividing the freeway lanes. The wipers shove at the rain but everything still looks watery and far off.

I should never have made the appointment to see Harry Halmstrom the day after a transatlantic flight. What was I thinking? In fact, I should never have made the appointment at all. But I have to show up now. I can't possibly leave a lonely old man waiting for his only visitor in years. Besides, I probably need a destination and purpose more than I need sleep.

I try to remind myself that this trip is a positive choice. I have always wanted to travel. This is me, traveling. I hear myself think this and I actually laugh out loud. The weird, barking sound of my own voice shocks me back to silence. I think of our vanishing savings, and Doug, at home, outraged, talking about me with—her. I fold a hand over my mouth.

A car undertakes and sweeps in front of my hood. I grip the steering wheel with both hands again and resist the temptation to slam on the brakes and skid across the lanes. My heart is beating far too fast now. I have to stay alert. There is a metallic taste against my back teeth. I glance in the rearview mirror. Finn is still and peaceful, eyelids drooping. He trusts me to get him wherever we are going. He doesn't need to know why we are here. He doesn't care about rain or traffic or where we are, or what we are doing. He trusts me to keep him safe.

Wheels swoosh over wet tarmac and rain drums on the car; the wipers thud rhythmically. The road signs are too small and the fonts are all wrong. The road markings are the wrong color. There are too many expansive lanes, too much traffic, no identifiable fast or slow lanes—the cars all seem inflated and high up; their license plates are diminutive, letters and numbers lost in too many red taillights; vast gleaming trucks coming out of the gloom. I tell myself that all

I have to do is drive straight and then the exit will be marked. This isn't hard. It is just driving in a straight line. I have a B&B booked, not too far from the Assisted Living Center.

But I need coffee. My brain and eyes are not working well together.

Through the rain I see a sign for a shopping mall. I somehow manage to pull across three lanes to get off the freeway. Blaring horns—the flash of taillights too close—but I am on the off ramp. I glance at Finn again—still relaxed, half asleep—I am in a fast-moving dream over which I have no control. I whisk the car onto the exit ramp to the mall. The wipers thump like angry fists.

In Starbucks, after a triple espresso for me, and a cup of warm milk for Finn, it occurs to me that I really am not prepared for this climate. The walk through the indoor parking garage left me shivering inside my thin coat. I have Doug's thick sweater but that's about all. I packed Finn's warmest clothes, his fleeces and layers; I remembered his bunny, his sleeping bag, Tylenol just in case, his red rain boots and Huggies and wipes and his sippy cup, but I packed randomly for myself. Apart from Doug's old sweater, my clothes are far too thin. I didn't even bring the fleece I use on walks, or waterproof boots of any kind. My old coat, and Finn's little puffy jacket from Marks & Spencer are clearly unsuitable for January in British Columbia.

Finn is whacking a paper cup with a straw so that it flies off the table. The mall sound system plays a chirpy version of "Don't You Want Me" and the lighting turns everything a sickly yellow. I glance at my phone. I need to call Alice, but I can't face her incredulity, or trying to explain what I am doing. I send her a quick text.

Hi—arrived safe in Vancouver. Finn happy. All fine. Needed to get away. Don't worry. Can't talk now but will call later. K xxx

I go into my e-mails.

The message I wrote to my father on the plane was sent when I switched on roaming in immigration. It's not beyond him to have replied.

There are three e-mails from Doug, titled, "Why are you doing this?" "Call me the minute you touch down!" and "We have to talk." I ignore them. I'll deal with him later. There is my father's prompt reply: two lines, typed at ten past midnight his time.

To: Kali
From: G. K.MacKenzie
Subject: re: Getting Away

Kali
    Susannah Gillespie was <u>not</u> a friend of your mother's—suggest you alter plans <u>immediately</u>.
    G

Finn whacks the cup off the table, laughs, then kneels down, picks it up and puts it back. Bash. Whack. Laugh. Kneel. He glances up at me. "Dat?" he points at the cup.

"That's a cup." I try to smile. "Cup. Can you say *cup*? Are you bashing it?"

Two lines. Even for my father, that's impressive.

"Bash!" Finn thwacks at the cup again. "Bash" was his first word. I should write that down because one day when he's grown up I might forget it. He comes closer and holds out his hands to my face, then pulls me toward him and kisses me on the lips. Bash: Kiss. The male template.

"You." I hug him. "Are you completely daft?" He wriggles off and grabs the cup again.

A text beeps in.

Vancouver??????? CANADA? In mtg till this eve. Call u when out. Bloody hell Kal! What in god's name ru doing in Vancouver????

I text back.

Bit of an impulse. But all good—don't worry! Call u later. x

Despite the temperature outside, it is airless and sweltering in the mall. Finn is bouncing around between the tables now but since we are the only ones here, I let him—he needs to stretch his legs and shriek and let it all out. I realize that I can't remember what return flight I booked. The neon lights hum overhead, and the only person other than the Starbucks barista is a cleaner trudging along with a wide fluffy sweeper. It feels as if this journey is happening to me, not the other way around. It occurs to me that running away is not necessarily a purposeful act of control.

My father's high-handed tone rankles. It is so distant and peremptory, right down to the lack of personal pronouns. With one eye on Finn, I type a reply with my thumbs:

To: G.K.MacKenzie
From: Kali
Subject: re: Getting Away

OK, thanks Dad—but I'm not sure if you mean Mom didn't know Susannah Gillespie, or that they were enemies? I'm not sure why you're telling me to alter my plans? It would be good if you could expand, just slightly, on this? I know this is awful timing. I didn't say in my last e-mail that I'm also going to see an old man called Harry Halmstrom today, who might be a relative of ours. He's in his nineties and in an old people's home in Vancouver. Could he be a relative?
    love
    K

I click send, feeling as if I've thrown down a gauntlet. Then I get out of my e-mails.

My father actually has a point. The sensible thing to do is to stop this nonsense right now. I should take Finn to the rental car and head straight back to the airport. But even as I think this a small voice of defiance tells me to press on. Keep running across the playground and don't look back. The alternative—going home to Doug—is far worse.

And besides, this is not random running. I do have a purpose. I am here to find out about my mother. I am here to work out what went before, so that I can free myself and stop running. It's a brilliant justification. But even I don't believe it.

The Starbucks woman is staring at me, so I gather up my bag, and steer Finn off down the echoing, shiny mall. Half the shops aren't open yet but we pass the doors to a department store. I hesitate, then guide Finn inside. I let him toddle up and down the clothing racks while I find hiking boots and socks, underwear, and, at the last moment, a huge gray North Face parka that is on sale, though still horrifically expensive. It goes down to my shins. I find a bright red, all-in-one weatherproof suit for Finn, also on sale, and a pair of waterproof mittens and a woolly bobble hat with earflaps.

I do not look at the total on the credit card receipt, I just sign. Given the huge chunk of our savings that I have already blown on flights and rental cars, another couple of hundred dollars is neither here nor there. And these clothes will make the difference between feeling vulnerable and feeling prepared. Suddenly, the clothing seems vital.

Before we go back to the rental car, I take Finn into the mall toilets to change his diaper. Then I peel off my coat and boots and dump them in the bin. I pull Doug's thick sweater over my head. As I glance in the mirror, I run a hand through my shorn hair, and feel the shock of it again. The silver hoops in my ears look brighter and bigger without hair to hide them and my face has changed shape. It looks more angular. I hardly recognize myself in this angular stranger with large eyes. But I'm glad. It feels cleaner and simpler like this. I should have cut my hair off years ago.

Finn has stopped, and is looking up at me.

I smile at him. "I know," I say. "My hair is really very short, isn't it?" I kneel to his level and he puts both hands on the crown of my head. Then he lifts them, and bashes them back down again. "Ow!" I laugh through the pain. He pats my head, more gently, and presses his nose up against mine.

"You are my lovely boy."

He thinks about this, then toddles off to pull paper towels out of the dispenser.

I stand up and slide on the North Face parka. The fake fur hood feels as if it would keep out even the worst of storms. I zip it right up and tie it tight with toggles, Inuit-style. The label says it will keep me warm in temperatures of minus 30 degrees. I pull the hood off again. As I put my phone in the pocket of the coat, I glance at my e-mails. Nothing from my father.

I look over for Finn. But he isn't at the paper towels. I spin around. He is there, in the stall, pulling toilet paper out of the holder and flinging it skywards, in grand, extravagant ribbons.

"Hey," I cry. "No. Stop! That's a big old mess." I shove the phone in my pocket and scrape up the reams of paper, wondering if I should try to flush it, or just ball it all up and put it in the garbage can. He thinks this is a game, and runs to the next stall. I nip in after him, sweep him up, and he giggles, deranged, disoriented. "Okay you," I look at him, firmly. "Enough."

I decide not to even try and get him into his suit—he'll boil in the car anyway. He wriggles and kicks as I wash his hands, roaring "No!" So I put him down and he's off again, in a flash, back into the stall, pulling toilet paper out again, gleefully.

"No. You stop that." I go back in and sweep him up, prying his hand off the toilet roll. "Let's go love. No more toilet roll. Let's go now, okay?"

He considers a tantrum; I see the thought march across his brow as I sweep out of the stall with him. "Look!" I point, pathetically, at the lights. "Lights! All those lights!" I will just have to leave the mess behind us. Before I had Finn I thought people like me were antisocial monsters, letting their children destroy public property. But now I know that motherhood is largely about damage limitation and survival tactics. I wonder if we are being watched on a security camera. Vandals.

"Let's go now, love." I hang onto him as he wriggles and squawks. "Come on." I blow his neck and it makes a farting noise. He shrieks with joy.

"Again! Again!"

Tantrum averted. I blow and slobber on his neck again. His laughter is slightly deranged—a whisker away from screaming—and I can't blame him because, essentially, I feel the same way.

With my free hand I shove the other things I've bought into our suitcase, gripping his heavy body against my hip with the other arm. He clings to me like a baby chimpanzee. "Again! Again!" I blow his neck again. He roars.

And then we go. I don't look at my phone. I try to make this a positive decision, too. I will text Doug from the B&B, and call Alice, and e-mail my father again later. Geographical distance is nothing. With modern technology there is no escape anymore. It is basically impossible to flee.

As Finn and I step hand in hand from the elevator into the massive multi-story parking garage, it occurs to me that I have absolutely no idea what the rental car looks like, or even which floor I parked it on.

*

I pull onto the I-90, remembering to drive on the right. The automatic gears are surprisingly easy to use and there is less traffic now, since we took so long to find the car, walking around the parking garage, pressing the key, listening for a beep. The rain has eased to a drizzle. Finn loved the "find the car" game, but I became slightly panicky. What if I never found it?

There is no view of the mountains above Vancouver, or of the skyscrapers that are presumably behind us somewhere, or of the sea stretching out to the right: all I can see is tail-lights and a rodent-gray sky. Mercifully, Finn looks dozy again. His cheeks are flushed and his blue bunny is pressed under his chin like a travel pillow.

I switch to a local radio station and try to relax. It isn't far to the turn off. I have Google Maps on my phone. This is fine. I keep to the 60 mph speed limit and stay firmly in the middle lane. It occurs to me that right now, no one knows that I am driving down a freeway in Canada.

I should call Doug. At the very least he should know we landed safely. But Doug is the last person I can face calling. My hands tighten on the wheel. It's like walking in a circular maze where every thought leads, eventually, to the same dead end: Doug, and what he has been doing.

I have worked so hard to keep her words out of my head, but suddenly, they are blaring through my brain.

I miss you, spiritually, emotionally, and physically.

It is the intimacy of the phrase that undoes me. These are not the words of an ex-girlfriend with regrets. This is a present tense missing; a lover's longing—ludicrous and overblown and intrusive.

I don't know what made me pick his phone up. Usually when Doug's phone beeps I ignore it. Doug's phone beeps all the time—texts or e-mails from paranoid students, lazy students, confused students; texts about staff meetings, faculty meetings, University sub-group meetings, college administrative meetings; alerts about conferences, papers, supervisions, committees; editor queries, publisher queries. His phone beeps endlessly.

But maybe I sensed her the way you sense the burglar in the house without hearing a footstep. He must have felt the energy in the house shift, too, when I picked it up, because he called through from the bath: "Hey, Kal? Was that my phone?" Or was he expecting her message?

I stood there by the bed and her words marched in hobnail boots across my heart.

"Kal?" Did he, in the bath, sound anxious? Guilty? Fearful?

I held onto his phone and struggled to work out what I was reading. For a moment I thought maybe I sent this text. I could say the same thing. But then I understood. And it made an awful kind of sense.

That is the worst thing. It makes sense.

Her words form a tiny door that leads onto precipitous, awful roads inside me. There are all sorts of details that I don't want to know, but probably will have to hear at some point. Did she wear him down, or was it easy? Did he leap at the chance to get away from the exhausting reality of me and Finn: the sleeplessness and resentment and diapers and feedings and teething and preoccupations? The first time it happened were they in some foreign city where it almost didn't count? On how many occasions has Doug, specifically, lied to me?

I heard the squeak of his feet on the enamel of the bath and the slosh of water as he stood up and I put the phone on the bedside table. I went downstairs and stood in our kitchen, hemmed in by the Ikea cabinets that we chose together. And as they swayed in and out overhead, I made myself a mug of peppermint tea. When I got back up, more than an hour later, Doug was already asleep—or pretending to be. I picked up his phone again.

He had deleted her message.

He must have deleted others from her, too, because I took the phone down to the living room and searched through all his texts and there was only one more from her but it confirmed everything.

She had sent it the previous Tuesday. He'd been to a meeting in London that day. She sent it at 8 a.m., when, presumably, she knew that he would be stepping onto the Paddington train.

Have a great day, gorgeous.

Words that small can only come from something huge.

I sat on our leather armchair in the front room that we painted together—*Sail White*—when we bought the house. There is a tide mark now on the walls, marking Finn's progress from pulling up to walking: a band of mucky fingerprints, crayon trails, the round imprints of bouncy balls and above this, pure Sail White. I sat on

our chair all night, surrounded by the sea of our little family life—
toys and board books and socks and biscuit crumbs, a pile of bills
waiting to be dealt with, the rug we chose last year, way too expensive, already stained by fruit juice. And I plucked facts from my
memory like poisonous berries.

I found that I could remember all sorts of surprising things about
her. She directs documentaries, mainly on classical or archaeologi-
cal subjects. Her apartment is somewhere off the Goldhawk Road.
She reached Grade 8 in piano. She knows how to walk glamorously
in stiletto heels. She earned first-class honors in Politics, Philoso-
phy, and Economics. She wears Issey Miyake perfume. She went to
a girls' school in Berkshire. She was devastated when Doug finished
their relationship. She told him her life was over, and she was only
twenty-one. She threatened to take an overdose. Then she took a
whole year out, in Florence, or Paris, to get over him. Well, it clearly
didn't work because sixteen years later, she still wants him back.

They met for a drink in London, sometime around Christmas—a
year ago, almost exactly. I remember it. Finn was almost six months
old. Just learning to sit up, wobbling and grabbing at things, starting
to eat solids, beaming and pointing and giggling, teething. Is that
how long this has been going on? A year ago, I was still breastfeeding our child. It is all such a tired old cliché.

I remember Doug telling me that she'd been in touch after Sean's
wedding. He looked uncomfortable when he told me this. I remember that now. He wouldn't meet my eye. He said she wanted to talk
to him about Cantor or Pythagoras or something for a documentary she was making about mathematicians. He ran a hand through
his hair, saying he'd have to get the late train home. I remember that
I was furious with him: yet again I'd be doing the bedtime routine
alone. Then I felt guilty because he had dark circles under his eyes,
too. And his job paid the mortgage now.

I didn't even ask how their meeting went. She was ancient history and I had too many other things to think about: Should Finn
be allowed peanuts? Was baby-led weaning really safe? Should I
try Gina Ford because this lack of sleep was killing me? Was he

teething? Or was this a genuine fever? If so, could it be the first signs of meningitis?

I just never tuned in to Doug because all my wavelengths were bursting with Finn. Perhaps that's why he was sucked in by her. I was too busy with the epic task of keeping our baby healthy and fed and clean and safe to notice him. She, in contrast, noticed every detail; validated him from the inside out—or the outside in.

I remember once, last autumn, we got a babysitter for the first time and drove out to the White Hart for lunch. Doug was stressed about some panel, or committee, some new piece of university bureaucracy and I just wasn't listening—I was somewhere else entirely, circling high above the pub, floating over the russet countryside with the glint of the Thames in my eye as Doug's voice mingled with the wind. The sheer relief of being out of the house was overwhelming and yet, simultaneously, anxious thoughts bubbled up, one after another. Would the babysitter remember to give him his bunny? Was he crying right now? Would she microwave the milk causing hot pockets to burn his mouth? No wonder Doug fell for her: a glamorous redhead, who had adored him for more than sixteen years, and was hell-bent on getting him back.

But even so. How could he?

I realize that if I do this—if I let myself think all this—I'm going to have to go back over a whole year of academic conferences, meetings, trips, and work out exactly how many times he might have been with her, and lying to me. And I can't do that.

But how many times did he lie to me? Casual mentions of her name seem electric now. Sometime around Easter, someone's fortieth in Shepherd's Bush; her name among a list of five or six of his old college friends. I didn't go. Finn still wasn't sleeping through the night. He'd wake four, five times and need to be coaxed, sungto, held, then eased back into his crib, inch by inch. I was sleepdeprived to the point of lunacy, forgetting to wash the shampoo out of my hair, driving out of Sainsbury's with the week's groceries still in the cart in the parking lot; losing keys. I didn't care where Doug was or who he was with.

But the thing that I really can't get my head around is that this is Doug. This is not some other man. It's as if I'm dealing with two entirely separate people here. There is the Doug, my Doug, the solid husband, the good father, who would never, ever do this because he loves me, and always will. And then there is this other Doug, this out-of-reach stranger who has betrayed me, lied, and broken us apart.

Presumably it started at Sean's wedding. I remember her in a very short dress; long, strawberry blonde hair, a Pilates core, and those legs. Doug even introduced us. I remember feeling shabby with my belly stuffed into Spanx, my leaking breasts tamped down in a big maternity bra, and baby vomit on the shoulder of my black dress. I remember growing dumpier and scruffier every second that she looked at me. And she did look at me—I remember her eyes. How intensely she looked at me.

Then I forgot all about her. I was mildly curious, but nothing more. After the wedding I put her into a list of his posh Oxbridge friends, people I never really felt comfortable with, even now. I forgot about her when I should have seen her coming at us like a juggernaut.

I could check his Facebook. I know his password. In situations like this that's what spurned wives do; they dig for proof. But I can't do that. Really, what is there to find out? It's obvious—surely. Isn't it?

I wonder if I'd handle this differently if it had happened at another time. The timing is certainly unbelievable. I would have just confronted him. I was going to do that. I was waiting for dawn in our leather armchair, because I was going to go and wake him up, and show him what I'd seen on his phone and demand to know what the hell was going on.

The blare of a car horn jolts me back—an elbow-straight, furious bellowing. Yellow headlights loom. I jerk the wheel, swerving out of the oncoming lane with just inches between my hood and the bumper of a towering silver truck. The horn continues to sound as it vanishes behind me. Finn lets out a high-pitched, baby animal noise—part terror, part question.

"It's okay love, it's okay." My arms quake at the elbows, and there is that metallic taste in the back of my mouth again. The rental car wipers swish and thud and I try to hold the wheel straight but my arms are wobbling. "It's okay, everything's okay. You're just in the car. I'm right here." His wailing escalates. I have to get off the freeway before I kill us both.

I veer off at the next exit and pull into a gas station. My heart is battering in my throat. I get out and walk around to open Finn's door. He is, rightly, hysterical. I undo the restraints and haul him out. He howls, red-faced; snot and confusion and protest surge out of his whole body. I hug him tight and shush him; I try to kiss his wet face, but he struggles and wails even more loudly so I pin him to me and run through the rain to the kiosk.

The woman behind the counter looks at me as if I'm a child murderer. So I take him straight to the toilets and lock the door. I lay him on the diaper changing table, but he screams and kicks—his foot catches me on the cheekbone and anger suddenly surges up, "NO!" I bark. "Stop!" He pauses mid-yell, his eyes round and startled. Then he takes a huge breath and begins again, louder, from the gut. Proper tears roll down his cheeks like shining gel balls.

"Oh no. I'm sorry. I'm sorry, it's okay. Mommy's tired too, that's all. Poor baby, my poor little boy." I wipe at his tears, close the snaps on his jeans and scoop him up, holding him close against me again. His cries are more pitiful, now, less rage, more genuine distress. He clings.

"What about a treat?" I suggest. I know it's desperate. He pauses mid-sob, and looks at me with big, tear-filled eyes. "A lovely treat! What about chocolate?" He hiccups. I wipe the snot from his face with my sleeve. "Chocolate would be nice, wouldn't it, love?" He gives a weak nod. "That's right. Chocolate will cheer us up." This, I realize, is exactly what the baby books tell you not to do.

I take him to the counter, and buy the smallest chocolate bar I can find, which, this being North America, is not very small at all. I rip off the wrapper and hand a chunk to him. He hiccups again, then stuffs it into his mouth with both hands, palms flat against his face. I glance at the woman behind the counter.

She is still staring, judgmentally. She probably heard me shout at him in the bathroom. I want to explain to her that I am not quite as bad as I look; that I make him eat fruit and vegetables; that I breastfed him for eight months, through three excruciating bouts of mastitis—that he is the love of my life, this little boy. But instead I buy a horrible hazelnut flavored coffee and stand by the newspapers while Finn covers me, and himself, with melting Hersheys.

I want to go back out with him into the freezing rain and gun the engine and get away from this place, too, but I know I can't. I have to wait until my limbs stop shaking before I get back into the car and drive my child along a fast-moving freeway in this weather.

Rain dribbles down the windows. The woman's peroxide hair glows in the fluorescent light. I can feel her hostility swelling across the counter packed with sweets and gum, filling the air between us.

I clear my throat, and ask her how far it is to the turn off I need.

"'Bout twenty miles north."

"North?"

I have overshot The Ida May Assisted Living Facility by twenty miles.

Then, abruptly, I feel tears welling. I turn away and take Finn back into the bathroom. I am going to have to claw back some sense of control. I can't fall apart like this. Finn stands by my leg, slightly wobbly on his feet, mouthing the last of the chocolate, while I lean both hands on the basin. For a moment I feel as if I've unplugged myself from life and I am swinging at its borders, completely lost. This would be okay if I didn't have Finn. I have to get control. I can't lose it.

I stare down at my hands on the filthy basin. I splash water on my face. The enamel is stained and the drain is clogged with a bird's nest of dark hair. I look up at myself. The silver hoops glint in the harsh light. On the wall above the mirror someone has scratched: "*Smile! Today could be your last day!*"

Southern California, 1975

She let herself into the condo and put her bags down. There was a smell of sizzling butter; someone was moving around in the kitchen. She should go say hello. She could see the archway to the kitchen, just across the living room. She'd met the guys, but not the third roommate, Susannah. Maybe she could just slip into her room, without being noticed.

"Hello?" A summons.

She forced herself to walk across the living room.

The kitchen was a mass of greenery, with plants cascading from tall shelves. The woman standing at the stove was barefoot in faded jeans. She was tall, but not willowy. Blonde hair rippled down her back. She turned her head, and the first impression was of extraordinary pale blue eyes with pinpoint pupils.

"Hey." There was a studied lack of interest in the flat tone, but it didn't quite go with the intensity of the eyes.

"Hi—I'm Elena. I'm your new roommate—I'm just moving the last of my things in."

"Uh-huh?" The woman looked at her for a moment, then turned back to her eggs.

It didn't matter. Elena had no desire to be part of some pseudo family—she didn't want new friends or roommates. All she wanted to do was finish her research. Having to move off campus was bad enough at this point—she'd been fine there, with her routines all worked out and the recordings and notes piled high around the tiny space, a complex system that worked. Now she'd been forced to unpick all that, and everything was in boxes. It would take forever to sort it back into a system. That alone had set her back weeks. Being here was bad enough without some prickly blonde roommate to contend with.

The move had made her realize just how set in her routines she had become over the past few years—since meeting Graham, really. The time they spent together had settled into an orderly and manageable pattern and she really didn't need anyone else. Graham planned breaks in their work schedules where they'd eat together, or see a movie. They sometimes crammed into a single bed for a night—his or hers—but not always. They didn't crowd each other. Theirs was a gently sustaining relationship: they were rooted and shaped differently, but had become quietly linked and harmonious, two plants sharing an ecosystem. The dolphin research took up the rest of her time and energy.

"So, I probably won't be here much," she said, quite loudly, to the back of Susannah's head. "I'm mainly just going to sleep here, my research is—I'm trying to finish—"

"You're a marine biologist, right?"

"Yeah, that's right." She was surprised that Susannah should know this. "What about you?"

"Oh," Susannah turned, and this time she smiled. She was striking, with high cheekbones, long hair middle-parted, and those unnatural eyes. Under her white gauze tunic she was braless. Elena could see the shadows of her nipples. She shifted her gaze to the plants behind Susannah. "Well I guess I'm at the other end of the spectrum," Susannah was saying. "I'm on a teaching sabbatical in the art department. Ceramics." She turned away and reached behind a ficus plant to get two plates. She divided scrambled eggs onto both, then put a hunk of sourdough on each. Elena glanced around, in case there was someone else in the kitchen that she hadn't noticed.

"Here." Susannah held a plate out, across the breakfast bar. "You look half-starved."

Elena hesitated and then perched on a stool. Susannah poured two coffees from the espresso pot on the stove, sat down opposite and, without speaking, began to eat. She ate with her head down, putting food rapidly into her mouth, chewing fast, and washing mouthfuls down with coffee. She ate like someone from a big family, Elena thought, someone near the bottom of the food chain. Every time she leaned forward for another mouthful, the Indian necklaces around her neck clanked between her loose breasts. Elena bit into the sourdough. Susannah was right; she was starving.

Susannah swallowed her last mouthful, wiped around the edge of the plate with one thumb, and sucked the eggy mixture off it. There was a thick silver ring on the thumb, and a line of clay under the nail.

"So," she said. "I'm kinda with Greg—the good looking one—you met him I think when you came around before? But he was quite taken with you, so he's all yours if . . ."

"No, God. No," Elena swallowed. "Seriously? No. I mean. I'm really not . . . I'm with someone already, and the last thing I want right now is—"

"Huh?" Susannah pushed her hair back off her shoulders and then leaned forward again. "He wears odd socks on purpose. He thinks people notice other people's socks. He told me odd socks make a guy seem intriguing. Odd socks and Birkenstocks."

Their eyes met and she caught something in Susannah's—a hint of wildness, or not-caring. This weird, disjointed talk, felt like a challenge.

"I had a boyfriend once," Elena said, chewing her mouthful of sourdough, "who folded up wedges of paper and wore them in the heels of his shoes to make him look taller."

There was silence for a second then Susannah lifted her chin. Her laugh was loud, quite startling—almost a howl—and it filled the small kitchen, bouncing off the wood-paneled walls, the plants, and out into the small patio, making birds flutter out of the tree, and sweep up into the sky.

By the time she carried her bags to her room, Elena had agreed to go swimming with Susannah, who knew the very best place, just down from the condo and around into a deserted cove where you weren't supposed to swim. The tides were dangerous but it was fine if you knew what you were doing.

The friendship, from the start, seemed to be out of Elena's hands.

CHAPTER FOUR

Harry Halmstrom has obviously done well in life. The Ida May Assisted Living Facility is shiny, newly built, with limestone steps. The sign outside says: *"Bringing Joy and Purpose to the Lives of Seniors."*

The interior is done out in shades of yellow, even down to the bouquet of roses and baby's breath on the circular table beneath the hall window. There is an artificial lemony smell. I have no idea what I am doing here.

I have Finn in the backpack and I'm glad, because I can't imagine chasing him down these corridors, crashing into walkers and trays of cranberry juice. But I wonder what I'm going to do with him in the old man's room. I feel like a fraud. Worse than a fraud. Like an unstable loon.

The receptionist calls Harry Halmstrom's caregiver, Jenny. As I stand waiting for her in the overheated vestibule, my phone rings. I pull it out. Doug. I can't just ignore him. It's unfair. He'll be worried. So I pick up.

"Jesus Christ, Kal! What the fuck are you playing at? Where are you?"

"I'm in Vancouver."

"I know you're in bloody Vancouver, but why? What are you doing there? Is Finn with you? Is Finn okay?"

"Of course he is Doug."

"Okay, but for fuck's sake love—look, I'm sorry, but—what are you thinking? You can't just leave like this. I came home yesterday so we could talk and you weren't here. This is completely bizarre behavior. I know you're in shock but . . . didn't you get my texts and e-mails? I've been calling and calling you."

"I couldn't think straight."

"Okay. You're having a crisis. I don't blame you, I really don't," I can hear him trying to get his tone under control, trying to be sympathetic, "Your mother just died. This is horrible for you. You saw the message on my phone. It's—she's—"

"Doug!" I bark. "Just stop!"

"Can't you JUST—"

The receptionist is staring at me with a mixture of disapproval, and fear.

"Doug," I hiss. "I can't do this right now. I'm standing in the lobby of an old people's home."

"You're WHAT?"

"I am visiting a relative of my mother's."

"What? What relative?"

"Listen. Finn is fine. He is fine. He is perfectly safe and happy. You don't need to worry about him. And I haven't gone mad. I feel perfectly sane and perfectly fine but I just need to be left alone. I can't talk to you about this right now. I just want to be left alone—please—please—can you just do that?"

"Kal—okay—look. I'm going to come. Okay?"

"Oh my God. Didn't you hear what I just said?"

"But—"

"Doug!" I snap. "The woman I'm meeting is here now—I have to go. I will call you later." I hang up. Then I turn my phone off.

A woman in late middle age, short and plump, with a gray bob, wide pants, sensible shoes, and a floral blouse is clip-clopping toward me,

beaming as if I am her long-lost daughter. I hang up. The receptionist starts typing again.

"You must be Kali?" She fusses over Finn "Oh—what a cutie!"
She leads us down the main corridor, asking questions about my
journey, where I'm staying. We pass signs to a gym and a pool and
a "physical therapy" center. There is no soft broccoli smell, just the
pervasive scent of artificial lemons. There are no communal TVs
and no old people. In fact, it all feels more like a pleasant four-star
hotel than an assisted living home.

Finn kicks his legs against the backpack. Jenny beams up at him.

"He's just such a cutie," she says, again. "How old is he?"

"Nineteen months."

She lifts a hand to him and I hear him giggle flirtatiously. "Hey
cutie," she says. She glances at me. "You must be excited to meet
Mr. Halmstrom."

"Well," I say. "Kind of." I can't begin to explain to her that this
was an impulse, born of distress, and that this man almost certainly
has nothing to do with me; that if it wasn't so socially unacceptable,
I'd be turning and running right now.

"So, Mr. Halmstrom can be a little . . ." she hesitates. "He may not
fully understand who you are. Just keep an eye on the baby, okay?"

I slow down. "What do you mean?"

"Mr. Halmstrom gets confused," she says, brightly. "He's very
elderly."

"I hope this isn't a bad idea," I say. "I probably should have established whether we really are related or not . . ."

"Oh no, honey!" she says. "It's wonderful that you came. I've
been here three years and he hasn't had a single visitor. Isn't that
sad? You can live your whole life and end up with nobody?"

I nod.

"But you know what?" she says. "Halmstrom's not a common
name and you do have family out here don't you. So I'm sure you
are related."

I run a hand through my cropped hair. Finn is heavy and with
the parka on too, I am becoming horribly hot. A drop of sweat

trickles between my breasts. Finn pats the back of my head with flat hands. A nurse passes us, pushing an empty steel cart. She smiles and says hello, and beams up at Finn. Her shoes squeak on the polished floors.

I feel as if the lining of my nose has been sprayed with ersatz fruit and flowers. A pocket of nausea gathers in my belly. Finn will be boiling in his new red suit, too, and when he's hot, he gets grumpy. But I can't stop and take him down and start undressing him in the corridor.

Jenny stops at a door. "So, this unit has a lovely view of the park—there's a little patio, though of course, at this time of year you can't sit outside . . ."

I feel sweat prickle my scalp. Finn kicks his legs, urging me forward, like a cavalryman.

Jenny puts a hand on my arm. "He may not understand why you've come." She smiles. "But try not to let that spoil the visit."

The room has peach walls, a thick pile carpet, and there is a walnut dresser by the door. By French windows there's a rug and two wingchairs, one turned with its back to us, looking out at a balcony. The air is moist with smells of medicine, disinfectant, butterscotch, urine, and that other familiar yet disturbing smell that I know too well from my mother's deathbed. Harry Halmstrom isn't here.

"Mr. Halmstrom? I have a very special visitor for you today. This is Carly, she's come to see you all the way from Great Britain with her little boy." Jenny comes around behind me and walks toward one of the chairs. I realize that some hair, like a little puff of white smoke, is just visible above the chair back.

"Mr. Halmstrom? Helloooo?" Jenny calls out. Presumably she is used to walking into rooms to find the occupant dead.

I unhook the belt of the baby backpack and lower it to the ground. Finn looks up at me and holds up his hands to be carried. I glance at Jenny and the chair. Jenny is looking at me, expectantly. I pull Finn out and kiss him quickly on the cheek as I put him on my hip.

"Okay, so Carly, I'll leave you and Mr. Halmstrom to catch up. Let me know if you need anything. There's a phone right there, on the bureau; just press zero for reception. There's coffee and tea in the kitchenette." She points behind me then exits, swiftly, like someone who has just pulled the pin out of a hand grenade. Finn is lodged on my hip. Unusually, he doesn't kick and wriggle to get down.

The head doesn't move so I step closer. The knee poking out of the chair is covered in a blanket; a slipper protrudes. A veiny hand rests on the knee, plant-like and still. My heart is bouncing off my rib cage.

"Hello?"

Sensing my nervousness, Finn clings tighter.

The sunken figurine is purple-nosed, his spine a question mark, chin almost to navel. Brows hang over his eye sockets like dripping wax. He doesn't move, but the hairs on his eyebrows twitch. Perhaps he is trying to look up.

"Hello?" I bend so I'm more on his level. Finn grips my ribs with his knees. "Up," he says. "Up, up."

The brows suddenly shoot up and a pair of surprisingly dark blue eyes, set in curdled egg whites, fix on me. White hearing aids comma his skull. He stares and then, slowly, his lips droop and the tip of his tongue protrudes. It is gray.

"I hope you don't mind me coming," I say, perkily, "but I think there's a possibility that we might just be related. At least, you have the same surname as my grandfather and my mother—Halmstrom. I think we have some Swedish blood too, so . . . I really hope you don't mind me coming like this? Jenny said not to call. But I just . . . I wondered did you know my mother, Elena Halmstrom?" I realize, as I talk, that this is preposterous. What am I doing? "I'm sorry," I mutter. "We're probably not related at all, but I—"

"You! YOU?" His voice is reedy, and spiteful. He is staring at me. "YOU? Here?"

"Me? Yes. I'm Kal. And this is Finn, my son. My mother's name was—"

"What in God's name are *you* doing here?" he interrupts.

"Well. Okay. I came to meet you because of your name. I found you on . . ." he has to be too old for Google. "My mother's name was Halmstrom so . . . I wondered . . . are we maybe related . . . ?"

"You think I don't know who you *are*?" he spits. "I haven't lost my mind you know, just because I'm old. I know you *Goddamit*! I know you all right. Changed your hair though huh? What is that—some kind of disguise? I always said you'd show up again one day, but you took your time about it, didn't you? Took your damned time to come face me."

I move backward, gripping Finn. I realize what's happening here. Time is bent out of shape for him. But surely this is recognition.

"Mr. Halmstrom. I think you might be confusing me with my mother—Elena?"

"What?" he trembles. "Speak up dammit."

I search his face for any familiar feature but he is so folded and warped by time that it is impossible to glimpse the young man he once was.

"I came from England to see you."

"England? Why? What?" He looks lost. "*That's* where you went?"

"I live in England . . ."

"England, huh?" he nods to himself, as if confirming a long-held debate. "So, that's where you ran to? *Fugitive*." Then he mutters something I don't catch, something about a baby.

"Mr. Halmstrom, I'm Kal—Kali. My mother was called Elena Halmstrom," I say. "This is Finn, my son."

There are spider veins across his cheeks and his hair is so thin that I can pick out the splotches on his head. My arms are aching from holding Finn so tightly. I look around and grab the other arm-chair, pulling it toward us.

"Make yourself at home," he hisses. "Then you can . . ." again. I don't catch what he mumbles.

"Then I can what?" I have Finn on my lap now. He buries his head in my neck, peering at the old man with one eye. I shift Finn around to the side of my body furthest away from Harry

Halmstrom, and lean forward. "Sorry, I didn't quite hear what you said."

"Tell me!" This explodes from his mouth with balls of spittle. "Then you can tell me! That's why you came, isn't it?"

Finn yelps. I wrap both arms across his back. "Shhh, it's okay, love. It's okay." I have to remind myself that this old man can't hurt us. The poor man can't actually do a thing. For a moment, he just pants. His brows fall. His hand twitches. I notice a panic button near his arm. I consider pressing it.

But he is staring at his knees now as if it is too much effort to raise his eyes. He seems to have retreated somewhere inside himself. I wonder if he is actually going to die. The room is so airless. With the heat and the stink of medicine and decay I am beginning to feel queasy. The idea that this ancient man and I are going to sit and chat about my mother is nonsensical. This is a colossal mistake.

"I'm Elena Halmstrom's daughter," I say, again, pointlessly.

"Stop that," he snaps back to life. "Stop talking nonsense."

"Okay. Sorry."

I can see his sunken chest moving up and down too fast. Then he lifts his head, just a little and stares out the window, chomping on an invisible object. There's a paved area with two chairs, outside, and a dead fern. Shrubs squat on a lawn behind this. A sparrow lands on the table, looks sharply at us, then flies away.

"Mr. Halmstrom?" I say. "Do you remember an Elena?"

"Elena—that's right. Forgot the bitch's name!"

I recoil again, covering Finn's head with my hand.

His hand reminds me of a bird's foot, gripping the arm of the chair—just skin and gristle. I should leave.

But it is as if he has submerged again. His body is roped here by the stubborn beat of his ancient heart, but his mind is clearly moving between two worlds.

I wonder if he even knows who he is. I try a different tack. "Mr. Halmstrom, did you have children?"

"Me? All gone. All gone. Worked my whole life, real hard work for my boys . . ."

"You had boys?"

"Oh they just . . ." He lifts the hand then drops it back down. "They go . . . all of them . . . they leave you in the end . . ." He frowns and his jaw hangs. "Yes."

"So you had boys, sons?"

"First one, just a pup—you don't get over that, you think nothing worse can happen but it does, dear God it does, and their mother too, eggs in a skillet one minute then the next—gone. But him. Him! My poor boy. Lost. Oh dear God. Everything in life. Everything. Here one minute then taken away from you. They don't tell you that, do they? No one tells you how to be alone."

I nod at this. "No. No, they really don't."

For a moment, we sit in silence, listening to his harsh breathing. Even Finn is still and silent.

"It's all smoke and mirrors," he snaps, and I jump. "Including you. You! Back here! Smoke and mirrors . . ." His fingers spasm on the arm of the chair.

"But I'm not smoke and mirrors," I say. "I'm real. Finn and I are really here right now."

"You got that wrong, missy."

"Up," says Finn. "Up." He tugs my T-shirt.

"It's okay, sweetheart. We'll go in a minute. Just a minute."

"Why are you even here?" It is almost a whimper, and I see that he's in pain. His mouth is contorted. I am confusing and upsetting him. This feels very wrong indeed.

"I'm so sorry," I say, gently. "I don't want to upset you. I'm sorry. It's okay."

But it seems brutal to just leave. I pat Finn's back with one hand, and jiggle him on my knee. "So, what was your work, Mr. Halmstrom? What line of business were you in?"

"What?" he says, "didn't even tell you that did he?"

"I'm sorry—*who* didn't tell me what?"

Nothing.

I keep patting Finn's back, like I did when he was a newborn, and he gradually settles down. His fist is clamped around my T-shirt and he is sucking at the fabric.

"Construction," Harry Halmstrom says suddenly. "Sold for big money in . . . oh . . . He wanted me to give him it for . . . I forget what. I forget! Saving the world, saving the . . . you know . . . money to save his . . . those . . . black and white . . ."

"Whales?" I say. "Killer whales?"

"A dreamer!" he yells. "Gave it to him too. Maybe that went down with him. Or you took it. Huh? Did ya take it?"

"Take what?"

Nothing.

"Mr. Halmstrom, are you talking about your son?"

His head swivels. "Yes! My *son!*" ball bearings of spittle pellet my face. "My SON . . . whatchamacallit . . . my SON goddammit!"

Finn yelps. I get up, whisking him onto my hip. I smell the sweet medication on the old man's breath and have to wipe his spit off my mouth with a sleeve.

The queasiness is swelling in my stomach and throat. "I'm really sorry." I look down at Harry Halmstrom. "I'm upsetting you so I should go now. I should let you rest."

A hand shoots out and grabs at my leg. His bony fingers pinch me just above the knee. "Stop messing with my mind, girl, and tell me what you did to him. What did you do to him?" I push his hand away—it feels like paper—and I step backward. "He could swim like a fish!" he shrieks. "What did you do to him? Did you want the money? Was that it? What did you do to my boy?"

Finn lets out a high-pitched shriek, and clutches around my neck, trying to climb up my body to get away from the old man.

"Okay," I shout above Finn. "I have to go now . . . the baby . . . I'm sorry!"

I lurch toward the door and grab the backpack with one hand, and then wrestle with it, the door handle and Finn's weight. Above Finn's yelps I can hear Harry Halmstrom's high, wavering voice.

"What did you do to him you *bitch*? He could swim like a FISH. You murderer! Murdering bitch. I KNOW IT WAS YOU!"

*

Finn and I drive around for a while, past suburban houses with shrubby gardens, and basketball hoops and double garages. Slowly, I begin to calm down. I cannot believe I put myself—not to mention the old man—through that. It serves me right for concocting absurd plans.

There are no pavements, no shops, no humans here. I am not far from the B&B but I can't take Finn there, not now: it is far too early. What would we do? I have to keep him awake for much longer than this. We both need fresh air. The lemony scent of the old people's home is somehow still in my nose. Finn has been cooped up. He needs to run and play and yell. We both need to fill our lungs with fresh air and forget what just happened. I need to call Alice. She'll be worrying. And I have to do something about Doug though God knows what. For a moment, it occurs to me that I have been completely mad. Of course Doug has not been sleeping with his ex-girlfriend. That's just insane. Then the clarity is gone and a sort of fog closes in on my brain, washing over everything, and I can't think straight. I am suddenly profoundly tired. It is an effort just to keep my hands on the steering wheel.

I spot a swing and a blue plastic slide—a playground—and pull over. I get out—the freezing air slaps my face—and go to the back. I unclip Finn's seatbelt. "Look!" I point at the playground. "Swings!"

Delighted, he wriggles to get out then toddles across the grass with his arms sticking out slightly in his red padded suit. I run after him, across the sand pit, zipping up the parka as I go, beeping the car locks. The air is freezing and damp and I can smell the sea. He holds up his arms to the swing, looking back at me with pained tolerance, as if I'm an old lady moving interminably slowly.

"Up! Up!" he shouts. "Up!"

I lift him up and put his chubby legs into the seat, then give him a gentle push. "Wee"

"Higher!" he bellows, the upset of Harry Halmstrom forgotten already. There is salt on my lips. I'm suddenly ravenous. "Higher!" Finn cries. "Higher!"

I push him harder and he shrieks and sticks out his feet, pigeon-toed.

"Wee! Look at you!" After a few minutes of pushing, I feel more awake. I get out my phone. There are three missed calls from Alice.

"UP!"

"Fly you to the moon." It's bedtime in England. She picks up after a few rings.

"It's me. Sorry it's so late."

"Where are you? Are you okay? I've been worrying all day about you."

"We're fine!"

"Okay. Listen. You have to call Doug. He called me earlier, and he's really worried about you. What are you *doing*? Why on earth are you in Vancouver?"

"I'm fine. Honestly. I had this crazy idea that I'd track down a relative of Mom's. There's this old man out here called Harry Halmstrom and, actually, I just went to see him. He's in an old peoples' home here. I thought he might be related to us."

There is a pause as my sister absorbs all this. "You're investigating our family tree? *Now*?"

"No, I'm just . . . I'm having a break. I stumbled across his name. I . . ."

"Do you have any idea how bonkers this sounds Kal? Do you know how weird you're being?"

"Why can't anyone allow me to get away?"

"Is this about Doug?" I imagine her sitting up in her white bed with her laptop open, surrounded by legal papers. "It's about Doug isn't it? Can't you tell me what's happened?"

"Okay. Things are . . . difficult. I found texts on his phone . . . but I can't really talk about all that right now—Finn's here. We're in a park. I'm pushing his swing. It's freezing."

"No? You found texts? What texts? You mean—texts from a woman?"

"Yes, from a woman. His ex-girlfriend. But I can't talk about it now."

"Shit," she sounds taken aback, but also satisfied. Now, at least, I have given her a logical reason for my behavior. "Oh Kal. Oh dear."

"Yes," I say. "Oh dear."

"Okay. All right. You poor thing. Okay. So, what happened with the old man then?"

"Ah, that. It was actually a bit awful. He's senile and confused and he started yelling at me and eventually I kind of ran away."

She laughs, despite herself. "Look, I think you really do need to come home. You need to sort out whatever this is with Doug—you need to talk to him about it. You shouldn't be out there on your own in an old peoples' home. Come home, Kal. I'll pick you up at the airport, and you and Finn can come stay in my apartment if you can't face Doug yet, but being there . . ."

I think about her cream, thick pile carpet, her glass coffee table, and the immaculate kitchen. She doesn't even have a spare room. It is sweet that even now, she feels she has to look after me. "No, really—it's okay. Thanks, but I want to be here; I'll be home in a few days and honestly, I really am fine. I really am. I just wanted to see if Harry Halmstrom might be a relative of Mom's. He's the only Halmstrom in the Pacific Northwest as far as I can tell."

"Okay. So look—our grandfather is definitely long dead, if that's what you're thinking. He died before Mom even went to college. And his name wasn't Harry, it was Theodore. The old man you just met definitely isn't our grandfather, Kal."

"Did Mom talk to you about our grandparents then?"

"Barely!" I can hear the concern for my feelings already. She has never lost the habit of trying not to let me feel excluded. "She really didn't talk to me half as much as you think, not at all. She'd just say that the past made her sad and she'd rather not think about it."

"Me too."

"Well, there you go."

"But you know the weird thing about today—that old man—he actually seemed to *recognize* me. At one point he called me Elena." I don't tell her what else he said, about whales, and theft and murder. Or the names he yelled as I fled.

There is a pause. "You know what I think?" she says. "I think you're overwrought, grieving, and very upset. We all are. I'm sure there's an explanation for whatever you saw on Doug's phone—there must be—and I think you really need to talk to him about that. As for this random old man—he has dementia. He picked up on the name Elena—no doubt you used it before he did. I think this is not a productive situation for you right now, Kal."

"I know. You're right." The wind batters my head and I feel my lack of hair—I really need a hat. "Hey, I had my haircut off before I left—it's very short."

"Are you leaving Doug?" she says this gently. "Is that what this is?"

"No." I push Finn higher, his hair flies up. "I don't know." His hat is in the car. His ears are red. "Higher!" he kicks his feet. His hands are bright red on the metal bar too. His gloves are in the car.

"Come home and show me your haircut," she says. "Please?"

"I will, in a few days."

"Should I be coming out there to get you? Because I am having a bit of a nightmare at work and it's going to be hard to do that, but if you really are cracking up, I will come, you know that, don't you?"

"Oh my God! I don't need to be taken home. Why does everyone think I'm cracking up? All I wanted was to get away for a bit. I'm totally sane. Finn and I are going to go on a ferry tomorrow and spend a couple of days in a nice B&B on an island and then we're flying home. I've bloody pre-booked, Alice."

"This is grief," she sighs. "You know that, don't you? You're grieving. You're in shock, in denial of what's happened. So am I. So is Dad. This is the first stage of grief: denial. We're all in the first stage."

"Yes I'm sure we are but . . ." It is typical of my sister to have categorized our emotions into stages already. It would be endearing if it wasn't so infuriating.

I push Finn and he laughs, riotously. "Weeeee!" he shouts. "Weeeee!" I push again. He flaps his legs and arms, shaking the swing, his entire body filled with joy and freedom and I realize that Alice is right. "Up to the moon!"

"What did you say?"

"I'm just pushing Finn. Look, you're right. I am grieving. But I'm grieving in a perfectly pleasant, if freezing, Vancouver suburb. We're booked into a lovely B&B tonight and we're about to go and get pizza. Then tomorrow we are going on a sweet ferry to a little island. I'm going to pop in on an old friend of Mom's who owns an art gallery. And then we're coming home."

"Okay, fine," she actually sounds reassured. "But you'll talk to Doug?"

"I did talk to him earlier. Listen, though, do you think you could call Dad and tell him I'm fine? We've exchanged a couple of e-mails so he knows I'm here too. He may be worrying."

"Okay," she sighs again. "But could you stop visiting old men now? Take Finn to the aquarium instead. There's a great aquarium in Vancouver, I've been there. And call me tomorrow when you wake up. I'm eight hours ahead of you."

"I know you are."

"I have to give a breakfast presentation to thirty pissed off executives at 7:30 a.m."

"Sorry. Okay—go to sleep now. You have to stop worrying about me, Alice. You need to look after yourself too, you know—don't work too hard. Be kind to yourself, too."

After I've hung up, I grab the swing and sway with it, as my weight slows it down. "Are you cold?" I hold out my arms to Finn. He raises his to be lifted and he hugs me tight for a moment, and then he spots the sandbox. "Down!" he shouts. His nose is red but his eyes are bright. He kicks to be put down and hurtles toward the sand. I watch him go, feeling like an impersonator: a woman with cropped hair and a North Face parka who says she's me, and is fine.

*

It's three in the morning, and Finn is finally asleep, sprawled across the double bed, diagonally. The B&B's travel crib is all set up, but I daren't move him in case he wakes again and we have another five hours of bashing and board books and escalating hysteria. I hadn't thought about how jet lag would affect a toddler, but it is not good. I never would have thought that even Finn would be physically capable of staying awake for twenty-two hours straight but, apparently, he is.

I am wired, overwrought and buzzing. I lie for a bit, on the very edge of the bed, but there's no way I can sleep. I get out my phone. Two missed calls from Doug and one text: Call me.

I open my e-mails. Two from Doug titled, "Where are you staying?" and "This is mad." He is everywhere, exploding at me through every point of contact. I feel the anger bubble up and I press his number.

"You have to leave me alone," I say when he picks up. "Finn is fine. I am fine. I don't know why you can't understand that I just need to be left alone."

"Okay," he says it slowly, as if pacifying a mad person. I can hear the hurt in his voice, and the confusion.

"Please."

"Okay. But we do need to talk. So, before I leave you alone, can I just tell you what's been going on—what that text . . ."

"Oh my God! NO. I can't do this. Not now. You have to stop!"

"No! Kal, I don't. I really don't—you have to bloody listen to me! You taking Finn out there like this—it's just not reasonable."

"Not REASONABLE?"

"No! Look. I don't care if you want to hear this or not. I am to blame. I haven't been honest with you, I've been hiding this from you and I feel horrible about it—she . . . she—she got in touch for that thing she was doing for Discovery on mathematicians. Remember? When I met her in London, that time. We were e-mailing a bit after that—just stuff for the documentary—and then she started sending—"

I hang up. My whole body starts to shake. I go to the bathroom and throw up pepperoni pizza into the pine-scented toilet.

Back on the bed, I stare at the ceiling for a long time. Eventually, I sit up. Finn is out cold. He hasn't even twitched. I go and get a glass of water. Then I sit on the bed. My phone pings: another text from Doug.

> I'm sorry. I'm sorry. I love you. I will leave you alone for now. Just call me when you are ready as we have to talk. Obviously.

I delete the text. Then I open my inbox.

There is no reply from Susannah Gillespie, but there is an e-mail from my father. After Doug, I feel completely numb. Nothing my father can say would really bother me right now.

To: Kali
From: G. K. MacKenzie
Subject: re: Getting Away

You are utterly mistaken about this Gillespie woman. Your mother cut off all contact with her decades ago. Do not even think about going to see her. Also, I cannot believe you are finding people called Halmstrom and visiting them at random. Have you lost your mind? Your maternal grandfather's name was Theodore and he is deceased. He died before you were even born. I cannot imagine what you are playing at. Are you actively trying to make this terrible time worse for all of us? I urge you to stop this wild goose chase and come home. If you come home, I will answer any questions you have about your mother's family—any that I *can* answer. I understand that you are having a difficult time, as are we all. Have you spoken to your sister? I suggest you call her immediately. Perhaps she can persuade you to stop this if I can't.

   G.

His tone makes me feel like a teenager. At least he is writing more than two lines now. The main effect his words have is to make me want to meet Susannah, really badly. What on earth does this woman know about my mother that he doesn't want me to find out?

How does anyone ever flee these days? I feel a sense of defeat. It is apparently impossible to run away with e-mails and texts and phones constantly connecting me to the people I am running from. I could throw away my iPhone but I have a small child and need to be able to make emergency calls. I could switch it off. Maybe I'll just switch it off. But then Alice will worry if I fail to respond. And I'm not running away from Alice—at least I don't think I am.

   I look at the—G—at the end of my father's message. It is like a little shove to the chest.

   I click "reply."

To: G.K.MacKenzie
From: Kali
Subject: re: Getting Away

Dad I'm really sorry to upset you, I know you don't need that. But I am perfectly fine, and so is Finn. I've already seen Harry Halmstrom and you're right—it was a wild goose chase. He was senile and shouted at me about fish and murder. He did call me Elena which was weird. Alice (yes, I called her) says he probably just picked the name up because I used it first—and I think I did. Anyway, I'm trying to forget about that now—silly of me, you're right. It's good to know we can talk more about Mom when I get back as I actually have tons of questions. I realize I don't know anything about her childhood or my grandparents, or her studies—or why she quit? Was it because of me? I think losing Mom has driven all

of this home. But you're right, we can talk about this face to face
Sometime.

Tomorrow, I'm going on a boat to the island where Susannah
Gillespie's gallery is. I'm here now, so I might as well go. If I do meet
her, and she has nothing to say it won't matter, will it? I'm staying in
a B&B and I'm just going to pop by the gallery and say hello—she
may not even be there anyway. You say she and Mom had no contact but look in Mom's desk drawer.

You never answered any of my questions about your wedding btw.

Love

K

ps. Your cell number at some point would be good.

I click send and go to the bathroom. I take a shower, towel dry
my hair—the advantages of the crop—and brush my teeth. I didn't
bring any pajamas, so I just put my dirty T-shirt back on. When I
get back to bed his reply has already pinged in.

To: Kali
From: G. K. MacKenzie
Subject: re: Getting Away

I do not know anything about any postcards. You must stop this:
Susannah Gillespie was not a friend to your mother, and she is <u>not</u>
a reliable source of information. I am not sure why you are doing
this, unless it is to distress me, but I feel certain it cannot be helpful
for you. It is certainly not helpful for me to think of you getting on a
ferry in British Columbia in January with a very small child to visit
that woman. When you come home, we will talk about all of this,
calmly.

In the meantime, to answer some of your previous questions:
your mother's childhood was unhappy. Her father was something
to do with the logging trade, she was not fond of him and he traveled a lot. He died before she went to college. Her mother died,
very unfortunately, when she was just a child. She had no brothers

and sisters. She moved to California on a scholarship when she finished high school—your mother was very bright. She started a PhD (we met at graduate school) but stopped all that, to have you, marry me, and come to England. She did not want to go back and nor did I—there were some very, very difficult times. We both found it easier not to dwell on the past. Our wedding took place in the registry office closest to the university campus. It rained, which was unusual for southern California. Your mother did, indeed, look beautiful. You were held by my friend, Dan Josipovici who now runs Josipovici & Associates, an architectural firm in Manhattan. You cried all the way through but thankfully the ceremony was brief.

It seems extraordinary to me that you should choose to do this now, Kali, after all this time, when everything is so raw for all of us.

—G

I stare at the e-mail. It contains more information than I've had from my father over my entire lifetime.

I type right back:

Dad, see—that's what I mean! I didn't know when my grandparents died. I didn't know my grandfather was something to do with logging. I didn't know it rained at your wedding. I didn't even know you got married in a registry office. Why don't I know these things? Maybe that's why I'm here. I am truly sorry that this is painful for you and I am not trying to hurt you. I suppose this is grief, and shock—denial even—but it matters to me, it matters a lot. It's not normal to know so little about your own mother. I understand that you don't want to remember painful things—I do know that you had an affair. I'm sure there are all sorts of other things that made Mom the way she was. I just want to know who she was.

Please try not to worry. I'm only going to pop into the gallery and say hi. Susannah probably won't be there anyway, in the dead of winter. And if she is, I'll be sure to take what she says with a grain of salt. Finn is loving the adventure, and we will both be home in a few days. Love Kal x

The minute I press "send" I regret it. I should never have mentioned the affair. He is vulnerable and grief-stricken and we don't talk like this—ever. I can't know what I've just brought up for him, or how that feels. He may have done thing he regrets, but he must be in pain right now, and I have just made it worse.

I start another e-mail.

To: G.K.MacKenzie
From: Kali
Subject: Sorry
    Dad, sorry, I should never have mentioned the affair—it's none of my business. Finn and I will stay tomorrow night in a B&B, have some fun walks, then come back to Vancouver, then home. We will see you soon, Kal x.

I shut down my e-mails and chuck the phone into my bag aware that every time I open my e-mails this situation gets worse.

I look at Finn, fast asleep on his back, hands thrown up. As long as he has me, he really doesn't care where he is. I certainly won't be taking him to any more old peoples' homes. All that does feel deranged now. I'm sure there was something I didn't tell Alice about Harry Halmstrom, but I can't remember what it was now.

If I do meet Susannah Gillespie, and find out things about my mother as a young woman then maybe this jet lag will be worth it. I begin to feel sleepy. I feel as if I might wake up in the morning in my bed in Oxford, with Doug, and all this will have been a deranged dream.

As I begin to slip in and out of sleep, I suddenly remember what it was that I didn't tell Alice. My eyes snap open. It was something else that Harry Halmstrom said as I stood in his overheated room.

"Changed your hair though . . ." he said. "Changed your hair . . ."

Southern California, 1976

Lately, Elena had taken to pausing at the tank on her way home to spend a few minutes with the whales. It didn't feel right to just walk by every night. No one was ever around at that time, so she'd sit with them for a bit. The male always kept his distance, but the female, Bella, recognized her and would swim slowly over. Once, while sitting on the edge of the tank, Elena leaned her head right down so that her hair trailed into the water. The whale came up and nosed the strands, curiously, and very gently. She knew that each tooth in the whale's mouth was the size of a man's thumb, but there was no sense of threat; Elena could feel the whale's curiosity. There was something tender about it.

But today Bella wasn't paying any attention to humans. Elena could picture the massive heart pumping inside Bella's chest as she circled the tank. She felt as if the sound of that heart should be audible through the headphones but all she could hear was the rushing noise of the colossal body pushing through the water as Bella circled. Then the contraction passed, and she sank again, obviously exhausted.

Elena yanked off one side of the headphones and addressed the backs of the men's heads. "Do you think it's getting close?"

None of them turned around, or answered.

She leaned through them, and poked Dan's arm. "Dan? It feels close. Doesn't it?"

The head trainer turned to her. His face was pallid. Like her, he'd been up most of the night before, and this had been a long day. Still no sign of a baby. He shrugged and turned back, hands in the pockets of his shorts.

The truth was none of them had a clue how this would pan out, not even the vet with his Yankees cap drawn down and a beaten-up jacket always on, despite the warmth of the evening, and a toothpick perpetually twirling at the corner of his mouth. None of them knew if this was how a killer whale birth was supposed to go. They were all impotent, standing there like distressed spectators at a show that is somehow going wrong.

She flipped the headphones back on and glanced at the sound dials on the tape recorder. She peered, again, through the glass tank wall at the hydrophone, down behind the ladder. The whales had ignored the black wire at first, when she dropped it into the tank. Finally Orpheus had come over to inspect it: he stared at it, carefully, for twenty minutes. Then he swam away. Neither orca had looked at it since.

The whale was silent during her contractions, but between them she spoke to Orpheus in low chirrups. He didn't make any sound during the contractions either, but he replied as she spoke to him, and moved across the tank to her. Elena wondered what the exchange meant. Their sounds were so much deeper, and slower than the dolphins. They had an almost spiritual effect on her as if they were tapping into a hidden rhythm in her subconscious. Every time they stopped, she felt a wrench.

Orpheus seemed calm, coming close but not too close, and even when he was out of her way, he kept his eye on her all the time. Elena wondered if both of them understood, instinctively, what was happening. Perhaps he knew, through echolocation, that there was a baby inside her. Then again, how could they know the true implications of this? Neither of them would surely remember the births they might have witnessed in the wild. She wondered if they were afraid. Were these sounds reassurance? She had to be careful. It was far too easy to anthropomorphize. But they did seem to be talking to one another.

There were more contractions, each one coming a few minutes after the last. She had to remind herself that the baby was likely to come out just fine. She knew from anatomy that orcas are better adapted to birth than humans: their babies don't have to navigate a narrow pelvis and they emerge through soft tissue, not bone. But still, this seemed like an awfully long and hard process. The baby could be stuck, or in the wrong position—or dead—but none of them would know, or be able to help even if they did know. There was something brutal and experimental about just standing there, watching. She looked at the men's backs, and wanted, suddenly, to shove them between their broad shoulder blades and shout, "Do something!"

Another hour passed.

And then, suddenly, the whale pulled away from her partner. She began to swim fast and then to corkscrew just below the surface, moving around the rim, as if she was rehearsing a new trick, swirling in tight spirals, astonishingly quick.

The guys pressed closer to the glass.

Elena slid off one headphone again and heard their voices— "What?" "This is it!" "What's this?" "Come on!" They were a crowd, heckling at a sports game. She pressed the headphones to her ears to block out their voices and she heard the rush of water as the whale spiraled—no vocalizations—she glanced at the sound levels again and made a couple of small adjustments.

Suddenly, there was a collective gasp. A pair of folded flukes appeared from Bella's underbelly.

A little tail flipped like a torn flap of skin. The mother whisked onward, round and round, twisting even faster now, her body arched in pain or effort, or both. She was silent—no cries or whistles—and then, in a bloom of blood and fluids, her baby was born—her perfect, miniature replica, flukes still folded, dorsal flattened.

It floated, motionless. And then it sank.

"Oh fuck!" shouted Dan. "Jesus shit!"

The baby didn't move. It was dead.

The men stood, aghast, faces pressed against the glass. In the headphones a terrible watery silence filled Elena's ears. The only sound was the thud of her own heart.

And then Bella turned and prodded her limp baby with her nose. And at her touch, life flooded through its body; it flipped a couple of times as if orientating itself and then floated toward her. She eased it to the surface, tenderly, with her flippers, four hundred pounds of slippery perfection.

The men cheered as if the victory was theirs. Dan even punched the air.

The baby took its first breath, blowing out at exactly the same time as Bella. And after that, mother and baby moved together, breathing in synchrony, swimming slowly around the tank side by side. Bella's breaths were far more frequent than usual: she knew, instinctively, that she had to breathe with her baby.

Dan was running alongside the pool, now, following them with a big grin on his face, the blond hairs on his thighs glistening in the late evening sun. One of the new guys had a movie camera and was loping alongside too, slightly slower, trying to keep the camera steady. The vet's assistant, a skinny guy with acne, snapped pictures with a zoom camera. The vet chewed his toothpick and watched.

The blush pink baby orca—it was too early to tell the sex—was a tiny match for its mother's belly and dorsal patches. It nosed steadily alongside her. Then Orpheus, who had been floating to one side, slowly swam over and joined his family. There were no vocalizations, but the three whales lapped the tank together—the baby slid in between its parents.

The guys were slapping each other on the back, like they had pushed the baby whale out themselves. Even the vet grinned, abruptly, showing crumbling teeth, his face splitting oddly, lopsidedly, beneath the rim of his Yankees cap.

Elena took off one headphone and their voices boomed. She looked back at the whale family.

It was the perfect birth.

She bent and switched off the tape recorder, flipping the switches one by one. She knew this was insane: she should keep it running and continue to collect the data; these were groundbreaking, unique, once-in-a-lifetime sounds. But she couldn't listen as the family circled its cramped glass prison.

There was a deep thudding in her ears. She felt sick. She couldn't look at the men anymore, or the new family. Without a word she let herself out of the park, and walked away through palm tree-lined streets toward the ocean.

It wasn't long after the birth and its aftermath that Elena saw the documentary about the whale captures.

There was a screening on campus in the central auditorium, and she would have missed it entirely, because she never bothered to read campus newsletters, but today there was another anti-war demonstration outside the dining hall, so she took a detour on the way to Graham's room. She almost bumped into the billboard.

It was just about to start—there was no time to run all the way across campus to Gray's room, tell him, and get back for the start of the film. So she went inside.

It was about orca captures, from the first in 1961, a female called Wanda, who threw herself against the tank walls all night and then died in the morning. Then there was Moby Doll, who survived being harpooned for an art project in 1964, and was kept, wounded, in the Vancouver Aquarium, refusing food for fifty-five days. The capture stories went on like this, grim and depressing tales of human greed and ignorance. But the climax of the film was the Penn Cove roundups.

Elena knew about these. She remembered the public outcry when the three drowned orca carcasses washed up near Seattle. Their bellies had been cut open and stones put inside—because the hunters thought they'd sink to the bottom and then no one would ever know. At least six live whales were taken to theme parks across North America that day.

One scene, in particular, was almost unwatchable. After chasing down the pod with planes and speedboats and seal bombs, the hunters dropped nets, and herded the frightened animals against the Puget Sound shoreline. The whales were panicking. You could clearly hear parents calling out to their children; babies screeching back. The hunters singled out a baby orca, and a scuba diver attempted to net him. The diver, along with ten or so other men, drove the baby away from his mother. She thrashed around in the water, distraught, making haunting, high-pitched cries. The whole family stuck their noses up out of the water, perhaps to try and hear what was happening above the surface, or to search for a way out. Meanwhile, the hunters tethered the baby tightly, nose and tail. He lay trapped and completely immobile but his family didn't stop calling out to him. The men hauled him into a cradle and lifted him with a cherry picker up into the air.

The baby's terrified cries, as he dangled above his family, were human. And from the water beneath him, his mother's screams echoed out, louder than the others'.

The camera panned back to the original scuba diver as he clambered out. He pulled off his mask and bent over, hands on knees, and as he raised his head for one last look at the captured infant his mouth distorted. Tears streamed down his face.

When the film came to an end, Elena sat in the muggy darkness with her hands on her knees, churning with rage and guilt and shame. There weren't many people in the audience but no one spoke or moved. The film whirred and flickered to a halt. Someone, somewhere near the front was crying. The lights came on.

Afterward, there was a talk. She wanted to get out. She badly needed air. But she didn't trust her legs to stand.

A bearded researcher—he'd been involved in the documentary in some way, though she wasn't sure how—stood on the stage in front of the dark screen. He said that legislation had just been passed to outlaw orca captures in Washington State. It was a direct result of this footage. Finally people were noticing what was happening just off their beaches, and they were objecting to it. After ten years of this, people were beginning to understand that ripping young animals from their mothers, and taking them to die in stone fish bowls, was not such a great idea.

And that was it. Her instinct had been telling her that this was wrong—every time she passed the orca tank. The birth had confirmed it. But she still hadn't worked out what to do—how she fitted into this. Now she did and there was no going back. Everything she had worked for had just disintegrated. Her time at Sea Park was over.

She completely forgot that she was meant to meet Graham that night. Instead of going across campus to his room, she turned and walked back to the condo. As she walked down the long path off campus, crickets rasped and the antiseptic smell of the eucalyptus trees coated the insides of her nostrils, but she could still hear the sound that the mother orca made as her baby was hoisted out of the water above her. This must have happened to Bella—whether at Penn Cove or somewhere else in Puget Sound. She would have been through a similar blood bath—ripped from her distraught mother and her screaming family. Her family must still be up there—however many of them had survived the captures. Somewhere out there, in the Pacific Ocean, was Bella's mother.

Back at the condo, Elena found a scrawled message on the kitchen countertop. Graham had called four times. She picked up the scrap of paper and went to her room, but she didn't call him back. He wouldn't understand. To him they were just animals; it didn't matter if they were in a sea or a tank.

She was going to have to find the orca guy and get more information—he had talked about a project going on up in the Pacific Northwest to photo-identify all the region's remaining killer whales. They were assessing how much damage the captures had done to the orca population. They needed to find ways to protect these animals and to rebuild the decimated pods. He said estimates, so far, put the damage from sea park whale hunters at up to 30 percent of the region's killer whale population. She shouldn't have left so fast: she should have waited and found him, because she had so many questions.

That night, the researcher's voice ran through her mind long after she was asleep—not his words, but the tone of his voice—the deep echo and rumble. The sounds wove their way through her head all night so that when she woke up with the sun streaming through the open blinds onto her bed, she was startled to find herself alone.

CHAPTER FIVE

I drive off the ferry at Spring Tide Island in a fog so thick that I can't see three feet in front of my face, let alone read any signposts. The gangplank clanks and a ferryman's face looms, yellowed by the headlights, then vanishes, swallowed by fog.

Finn and I woke up after lunch so we missed the morning ferry. The lunchtime one left forty-five minutes early: we watched it go from the port café, unaware that it was the Spring Tide boat until I'd lugged Finn and all our baggage downstairs at the right time, only to see that the sign on the departures board had changed to: "Departed."

Nobody could explain what was going on. The final ferry of the day left at five, but I didn't dare leave the port in case that one left early too. So Finn spent the afternoon running around an empty café, climbing up and down the stairs, counting seagulls through the windows, running outside into the freezing air to watch the cargo boats come in and out, and burly men load and unload crates from the mouths of enormous ships. He was thrilled. With the chips and ketchup in the café, this was, for him, the perfect day. I tried to call the B&B to tell them I'd be late, but they weren't picking up so I left an apologetic message. I only let myself check e-mails once—one from Doug: *"ready?"* One from my father. None from Susannah. I couldn't face Doug's, so I opened my father's.

To: Kali
From: G.K.MacKenzie
Subject: re: Sorry

If you do not want to distress me further, then stop what you are doing. You are wrong about the affair. Your mother was the love of my life. Do not go looking for this woman—you have Finn's well-being to think about. I will tell you more about our wedding and any-thing else you need to know but you will not find reliable answers by chasing unreliable strangers.
    —G

I replied right away.

To: G.K.MacKenzie
From: Kali
Subject: re: Sorry

Dad, I'm glad we can talk—I'll look forward to that. I really am sorry to have said that thing about the affair but I do wish you could be just a bit more forthcoming about Susannah Gillespie. I'm not chasing her, and while she is a stranger in one way, she must have known Mom well at one point. Why is she so unreliable? I am about to get on a ferry, so if there is anything specific I should know then I would really appreciate it if you'd fill me in. Try not to worry. I'm not being irresponsible. The B&B looked lovely on its website: it's run by a retired British couple from Barnstaple—what could be safer than that? They make their own bread. It's been a long day (we've somehow missed 2 ferries!) and Finn is hyper. But rest assured that my son's safety is my top priority at all times. I hope you're ok.
    Kal

I realized as I clicked "send" that my relationship with my father was not really much better than my relationship with my mother. It was just a different brand of noncommunication: more civilized, but no less dysfunctional. It seemed extraordinary, really, that we were having this sort of interaction over e-mail. But even if I had his cell number I could not imagine picking up the phone and actually speaking to him, openly, about his relationship with my mother. It would be like asking to see him naked. I should never have told him where I was—it was only ever going to upset him.

In the end the last ferry to Spring Tide Island pulled out of the harbor an hour later than scheduled. It was already dark.

And now it is a bitter, foggy night—a ridiculous time to be arriving somewhere remote and unfamiliar. Fortunately the B&B is only a few streets away from the ferry port. Everything will be fine. This is far away, but it's still civilization.

I imagine warm flannel sheets, a friendly welcome—a cup of tea for me, a snack and warm milk for Finn, a hot bath for both of us, a story, sleep. He is clearly tired now from all the fresh air and running around. Surely this time he will sleep. I imagine a flowery bedroom looking out at the port where the sun will rise in the morning.

Slowly, I drive away from the ferry and up a murky main street. The fog is so thick that it feels like I am driving underwater.

Finn is yelling to get out.

I can see him through the car window, furiously kicking his legs on the car seat, his mouth wide open, eyes screwed up, his howls muffled.

There is an empty feeling in the pit of my stomach. I knock on the front door again. There is not a single light on in the house. The Magnolia B&B—a low, pretty, clapboard house—is quite obviously closed.

I can see the blurry halo of a porch light on the house opposite, but it is impossible to see up the road to other houses. Fog swirls around the car headlights. It freezes onto my face and my breath puffs out in front of me. I have to stay calm. There will be other places to stay.

I knock on the door again. "Helloooo?" Then I get out my phone—maybe they're somewhere out the back and can't hear me. Maybe because I'm arriving so late, they thought I wasn't coming and they went to bed. But it's only 7:30 p.m. Finn is yelling at full throttle now; his face is contorted and purple.

The last ferry back to Tsawwassen was the one we came on.

I go over to the car with the phone at my ear, and open the door. A blast of wailing. "It's okay, love. Just a minute. I'm just . . . just a minute sweetheart." His face is blotchy and big tears roll down his cheeks.

"Up! Up!" he howls, holding out his arms.

"Just one minute, lovie. Hang on just one minute. Mommy's right here, okay? I'm not leaving you." The B&B phone rings on. I can hear it through the windows. I go and I knock at the door again. Then I hear something over the road. A man's gruff voice, "Hey?"

I hesitate. Do I leave Finn yelling in the car, or go and haul him out, and take him to a stranger's doorstep in the fog?

I call out across the street, "Hello?"

"You need something?"

"I'm booked into the B&B but no one seems to be in." I squint, but all I can see is a shadow in the fog.

"They're on vacation."

"No. They can't be. I have a reservation!"

"For two weeks."

"Are you sure?"

I hear his front door slam.

I swallow. I let the phone drop down to my side. Finn carries on wailing.

It is bitterly cold in the street, even with the parka. I get back into the car. Finn sobs and hiccups behind me. "Up," he sobs. "Up, up, up, up, up." I could go and knock on the man's door. But he could be anybody.

It occurs to me that nobody knows I am here.

My heart is galloping now. I feel queasy. Finn's sobbing, at least, has subsided now that I'm back in the car.

There will be other B&Bs. Surely. But my phone battery is almost drained. If I go into Google, it's going to die.

"Okay love." I turn and smile through the gloom at my tearful boy. "Everything's okay. I'll get you up in a minute. In a minute, love. Okay?"

He is shattered. His eyes are red-rimmed and puffy. He has had no nap today at all. It's a miracle he hasn't exploded before now, after the excitement of the port, and the ferry ride. I dig in my bag and find a juice box crushed at the bottom. "How about some juice?"

I fumble around, putting in the straw, then give him the carton. He stops crying, and squeezes it so apple juice spurts out of the straw across his red suit, and the gray upholstery of the rental car. He starts to cry again. I steel myself—I can't get him out here, in the middle of this freezing street. I start the engine.

Susannah's house is about five miles west along the coast. The route would probably be quite straightforward without this fog. But there can't be more than one Isabella Point on the island. I have a number from the gallery website. My phone will probably hold out for a short call.

The gallery phone rings and an answering machine clicks on. I hang up. Of course, she wouldn't be there at this time of night. Then I remember that the gallery opens in March or April. The truth is I never fully expected to meet Susannah Gillespie. She could be anywhere in the world right now.

I want to call Doug.

But no. I definitely can't call Doug. Doug is the very last person I can call right now.

I could call Alice, but clearly that would only worry her. I have to stop wanting to call people. I have to think for myself and sort this out. There will be a bar somewhere. Or a restaurant. I'll find that; then someone can tell me where the nearest B&Bs are. If all else fails I can always go to the police—though I can't imagine how I'd explain to a police officer how I came to be here with a toddler and nowhere to stay. They could probably arrest me for criminal incompetence.

I decide to drive through town. If all else fails, I'll circle this god-forsaken island all night until it's light, and we can get the ferry back to the mainland. I glance at the gas gauge. Half full. I have no idea how much gas a person would use up if they drove all night.

I start the car and pull out, slowly, through the fog and back to the main street.

I crawl along, squinting through the windshield and fog. There are a few shops—a bakery, a drugstore, a health food store, a clothing store, then *The Fisherman's Catch*—a bar—but no lights. No signs of life. The bar is closed, presumably only open in season. This is a ghost town.

Then I see the sign through the fog: *Susannah Gillespie Gallery*. I'm right outside it. The windows are dark. But for a moment I feel a thrill. It is real. She is real. I did not make this whole thing up.

I've looked at the map enough to know that I just have to follow the coast road west to get to Isabella Point, so I keep driving.

"Up?" Finn says. But it's halfhearted and I can hear the sleep in his voice now.

"In a little bit, love, soon. We just need to find . . ." I hear myself waver, then clear my throat. "We'll be there soon, and then we can get you out, okay?"

Clearly I need to tell someone where I am. It is insane to head off into the wilderness without telling someone. I stop the car and pull out my phone, praying that the battery will last. Then I dial Alice. It goes straight to voice mail: "This is Alice MacKenzie . . ." Of course, she is asleep. I need to text.

My phone beeps, and dies.

I pull out again, slowly. We're at the top of the tiny main street, and the street lamps just stop. The world shrinks to the patch of road directly in front of the car.

If I'm lucky, I'll find a B&B at any moment. If not, maybe I'll get to Isabella Point and Susannah will be there. I have a vision of myself, and Finn, knocking on doors, asking people to take us in. Doug would rightly be livid if he knew what I was doing right now.

"Mama up?"

"It's okay, love. Everything's just fine." My voice has the artificial smoothness of the true lunatic. "Not far, now."

I crawl along with my eyes on the curb, the low beam bouncing back at me. There are no other cars, because clearly no locals are unhinged enough to drive in this soup at night. There are no houses—my headlights show tall pine trees on both sides of the road. It is like being in a submarine, creeping through gray water.

Somehow, I am going to have to find the turn to Isabella Point. I pull over again and the fog edges eerily around the car. I try to picture Google Maps. It really wasn't far. Maybe three miles? I make myself breathe. I have to stay calm.

Slowly, I pull out again.

As I crawl along the road, I start to sing.

"*She'll be coming round the mountain when she comes, she'll be coming round the mountain when she comes . . .*" I don't know where the urge to sing this song came from, but out of nowhere I find a memory of my mother stroking my hair and her voice— "*She'll be riding six white horses when she comes. She'll be riding six white horses . . .*" I'd forgotten that she used to sing to me. But now her voice floats up so clear it's as if she's in the back seat next to Finn.

I have edited out so many of the good bits of her as a mother. The rows and hurts are the more tenacious memories. The good bits must have faded into my subconscious. I search for more good memories.

We made a honey cake once. That's one. We mixed whole wheat flour and butter and spoonfuls of honey and when it came out of the oven it fell apart, and we ate anyway, it in warm sticky chunks at the kitchen counter.

She read to me. That's another. She read Grimm's fairy tales about dogs with saucer eyes, evil godmothers laying curses, needles jabbing into pale fingers, the sinister baby-stealing Rumpelstiltskin who must be named. I'd rest my head on her belly, and feel her voice vibrate beneath my ear. But I remember the anxiety too—the fear that at any moment she'd get up and go. Once, I reached up a hand and touched her hair, and she looked down at my face and her expression changed, her features contorted—she burst into tears.

She could make me feel so good when she chose to, but I could never touch her sadness. I just felt it there, squatting between us with its saucer eyes fixed on my face. Sometimes, just looking at me seemed to cause her pain.

"Again again!" Finn says. I realize I've stopped singing.

"Singing ay ay yippee yippee ay" I peer through the windshield, trying to remember the other verses. *She'll be wearing pink pajamas . . . Oh we'll all come out to meet her . . . Oh she'll have to sleep with grandma when she comes.*

I sing on, and on. Every time I stop singing, Finn says "Again again!" so I keep singing. *She'll be comin' down a road that's five miles long.* And somehow the singing makes me feel less afraid. It works.

I glance at the mileage counter and slam my foot on the brake, peering through the windshield.

"Mamamamamama."

"Wait a minute Finn. Wait. I have to think."

Fog swirls over the hood. I have to be close to the turn because we've come three miles now.

I edge forward, five or six miles an hour, braced to slam on the brakes if a car should pull out of a side road.

Oh we'll kill the old red rooster when she comes . . .

I imagine a vehicle plowing into our flank, crumpled metal.

I crawl along like this for maybe ten more minutes. I've missed it. I've missed the turn. I'm about to stop and turn back when a sign—carved on a log—looms in the headlights: *Isabella Point.*

The arrow points left. I turn down a single track road, bumping over potholes and lumps of broken tarmac. If I can find Susannah—if she's in—I can explain myself, and ask her for the name of a nearby B&B.

It's better than dying of hypothermia in January in the car, plunging off a hidden cliffside in the fog, or knocking on a psychopath's door.

The headlights bounce off something white—a mailbox with a red flag. Next to it, fog swirls around another wood-carved sign: *Isabella House.*

Finn had gone very still. I glance over my shoulder at him. His heart-shaped face is blank but his eyes are still open.

It is impossible to see anything of the house through the fog, but I think I can see a slight glow and my heart gives a bounce. Please let her be home. Please. It's only just past eight. Not really late. Please let her be in.

I get out and suck in a lungful of freezing, salty fog. I can hear the sea crashing onto rocks not too far off and a bitter wind bashes my ears. I zip up the parka, pull the hood up and go around to get Finn out. He is still wearing his all-in-one suit. He is bundled up, stiff-limbed, but thank goodness, in this freezing air. I bury my nose in his neck for a moment, inhaling his sweet, sleepy, apple-juice smell. "What an adventure," I whisper. "What an adventure." He looks at me with big eyes, clearly unconvinced.

I beep the car locked as I climb the icy steps with Finn. Somewhere in the house dogs begin to bark, savagely. There are lights. The lights really are on. There's a deck running across the front of the building but it's impossible to see anything beyond a few feet. The waves sound louder up here and the wind howls in trees. The fog is damp on my face and I can taste the sea.

I stand by the front door listening to dogs, and I feel as if I've climbed up to a high cliff and am about to plunge off, not knowing if there's water below.

Then the door opens.

Two golden retrievers burst out. I lift Finn higher. The dogs weave around us, huffing and growling.

"Get back, stay."

The voice is low and authoritative. She steps into the light and for a moment we look at each other in silence.

She is tall, a few inches bigger than me, wearing a fisherman's sweater and old jeans. I recognize her from the picture on her website, though she is more angular and tired-looking. Her shoulders are broad and straight, her hair is twisted up behind her head and there is a deep frown line between her eyebrows. But the thing that really stands out is her eyes. They are an extraordinary pale blue color.

She is holding the door open with one hand and I see thick silver rings, one on her thumb, and a couple of silver bangles. A pair of reading glasses dangles from a beaded chain around her neck. I realize she is waiting for me to speak.

"Hello," I say. "I'm so sorry to just show up on your doorstep like this. I—I—I e-mailed you and I tried to call you earlier—I'm Kal MacKenzie. I think you may have known my mother? Elena Halmstrom? I'm Elena's daughter, from England."

Her eyes widen. She glances at Finn, blinks, and then looks back at me. "You're *what*?"

"Elena Halmstrom—I think she was your old friend who went to live in England? You sent her . . . Elena . . . I'm her daughter. I'm Kal. I'm Kali."

She takes a step back, as if I've threatened her—the color drains out of her face. Her eyes fix on Finn again, then back on me. Then she squares herself, seems to raise herself up even taller.

"Kali?"

One dog circles us, pushing me from behind so that my knees buckle. I wrap both arms around Finn. The other dog joins the first and they barge, as if trying to knock me off the deck. She doesn't notice, or try to stop them, she just stares.

"Look, I'm so sorry to just knock on your door like this."

"Kali?" Her voice is hoarse. "You're Kali? Elena's Kali?"

"Yes, yes, well, Kal. I know this is . . ."

"And this—him," she swallows hard. "This . . . little boy . . ."

"This is my son, Finn."

"Shit." She covers her mouth with both hands. "Holy shit." She backs away, staring at Finn as if he is a terrible apparition.

"I'm so sorry. I know I should have gotten hold of you first, but I was rather stranded . . . the B&B I thought I'd booked turned out to be shut and I couldn't find anything else—I just didn't know where else to go."

She takes her hands away from her mouth. Her face is still very white. But she opens the door wider. The dogs bundle back in. She steps aside, and I see her take a big breath.

"Well Kali," she says. "I guess you'd better come inside."

It's warm and beautiful inside—pale wooden floors, off white walls and a pleasant smell of essential oils, cooked onions, and wood smoke. I feel myself relax, just a tiny bit. This is civilized. This is okay.

The lights are soft, and I can see a log fire burning at the end of the corridor in what must be her sitting room.

Susannah doesn't speak.

"I won't . . ." I begin but she shuts the front door and passes me without a glance; then she just walks off down the corridor, taking long strides, not looking back. She clearly assumes I'll follow. So I do.

The hairpin that roughly holds her hair off her neck has a big silver wasp on it. The pin comes out of the wasp's body—an oversized sting. It flips gently as she strides down the corridor. Finn grabs the neck of my sweater with one small fist and keeps his other arm wrapped tight around me. I hug him close.

The fireplace is medievally huge. In front of it is a thick white rug. Two large brown sofas, with plenty of cushions, face one another, and on one there is a crumpled blanket and a biography of Barack Obama, spine cracked, face down.

Finn clings, silently. I hold him away from the dogs' noses, praying that he won't start to scream again.

There are books and plants and paintings everywhere and above the fireplace hangs a huge abstract in swirling blues and greens. Susannah turns to face me, with her back to the fire. Her eyes really are a peculiar color—a light blue-gray, as if the pigment has been bleached from them; wolf's eyes. The dogs stop by her feet, one on each side, looking up at me.

"Well," she takes a breath. "You look exactly like her, and your son . . ." She stops. "Your son is so much like . . ." But she stops there. Again, she looks shaken.

I have never thought about whether Finn looks like my mother but I suppose he might. He has the same half-moon eye shape and our heart-shaped face. But he also looks like Doug. He has Doug's chocolate brown eyes and a dimple on his chin, like Doug, not on his cheeks like my mother and me.

I glance at my feet. I probably should have taken my boots off at the door. I'm making dark wet stains on the rug. I move back a few steps, away from Susannah and onto the wood floor. Finn is heavy and my arms are getting tired now, holding him so tight.

"I'm so sorry to just show up like this," I say, again. "I just wasn't sure where else to go."

"Yeah, well. I'm amazed you found your way here in this fog, at this time of night. That's quite an achievement."

"I drove very slowly."

She stares at me for a beat too long. Then she thrusts out her arms. "Okay. Why don't you take off your things and give them to me? I'll hang them up."

I look around, unwilling to put Finn down until I know that the dogs are safe. She seems to understand this and whistles them to her side. They flank her. I turn around, and unpeel Finn's hands from my neck. I sit him on the sofa, and, with my back to her and the dogs, I unzip his snowsuit. For once he doesn't struggle to get up and run off. He looks at me, and I can see the doubt in his eyes.

I kiss his head. "It's okay, sweetheart. I'm here. Mommy's here. Are you a bit sleepy? What a long day it's been, eh?"

Then I take off my own boots and coat.

Beneath all this weather gear, our clothes are warm and dry, though Finn's hands are chilly, just from the brief time outside.

I pick him up again and he doesn't object, and with one hand I try to gather up our things. She doesn't move or try to help. She is just watching.

When I hand everything to her, she still doesn't move, and I feel, for a moment, as if we are an art exhibit that she's assessing. I see her take in Finn's face, his hair, his hands, then she looks up and down my body, just briefly, from my feet to my head. Finally, her eyes meet mine and I see something in them that is not irritation or shock at an unannounced visitor. It is suspicion. And then she looks away, and for a moment I wonder if she is afraid.

But of course, she can't be. This is her house. I'm the uninvited visitor. If anyone is scared it should be me. I wonder what my mother would have said to her about me over the years. If they really were in touch then Susannah probably knows about my explosive adolescence, the running away to France, my failure to go to India; my feckless year waitressing in Brighton.

I have an irrational urge to defend my past self—to tell her that whatever my mother has said, I did eventually put myself through A-levels, and undergraduate and graduate degrees. I have a career, a husband. I wonder, for a moment, who Susannah thinks I am. What version of me does she think she knows?

"What are you doing here, Kali?" Her voice is icy. It makes me jump. "Why have you brought this . . . child . . . this little boy to my house?"

She is absolutely right of course. It is incredibly rude, and odd, to show up like this. I suddenly want to seize our belongings out of her arms—and run.

"She sent you, didn't she? She told you not to call first."

"What? My mother? Oh. No. No. God no. She didn't."

Her head flicks to look at something behind me. I glance around, but there is no one else here, just the empty corridor leading back to the front door.

"I did call the studio—I don't have your number here. There was a bit of a mix-up. I booked a B&B, but I suppose they didn't get my reservation, and the ferry was late—well, it didn't show up, then the next one left early then . . . I just didn't know where else to go. I'm so sorry. I e-mailed—did you get my e-mail? And I left a message on your gallery answering machine. I just need . . . If you could give me some numbers of Bed & Breakfasts . . ."

I can see a kitchen through an archway behind her. The fire crackles and a log falls with a thud but she doesn't flinch. The dogs turn in unison to look at the log, then back to look at me again, slightly accusingly, as if I made it fall.

"Elena didn't send you here?"

"No," I shake my head. "No."

I can't just blurt out that my mother is dead. I don't know what that will mean to her and it seems tactless to announce it within minutes of entering her house. It is possible, I realize, that I'm about to deal this woman an awful blow.

"Then," she raises her chin, "how did you find me?"

"Oh. I came across your name and—well, I was on a sort of trip to Vancouver and I just thought I'd . . . it was a bit of an impulse really. I meant to speak to you first of course."

"An impulse?"

"I'm really sorry. Look. You're completely right. I only came tonight, like this, because I was stuck. If I could just borrow your phone . . . My phone's run out of battery."

She holds up her hand. "It's all right, Kali," she says. I want to ask her to call me Kal, because nobody calls me Kali, but it seems unwise to correct her at this point.

She turns and walks down the corridor. She opens a closet and I watch her hang up my coat, then hang Finn's red snowsuit on a hook. She rests both hands briefly on the downy fabric of his hood. Then she bends from the knee, keeping her spine straight, to put my boots on a shoe rack. She stands back up, and kicks the door shut with one leg.

She seems less frosty now that the coats are dealt with, more relaxed, as if she's decided to be nice. "Well. This is kind of a surprise, Kali, I've got to tell you," she pauses. "Your mother is an old friend."

I try to smile.

"Okay, so you're here. You're here. And of course you're exhausted. What can I get you? Is the little guy hungry?" She looks right at Finn, and smiles, but only with her mouth. Then slowly she reaches out a hand toward him. He sees it coming, and shrinks into me, burying his face in my chest.

"He's a bit shy," I say, "and very, very tired."

"Would he like a cookie?" she asks. "Some milk?"

"I'm sure he would like milk, wouldn't you love?"

But again, she just stands, without moving, her eyes fixed on Finn now. She is tall, erect and broad shouldered. Her irises really are disconcertingly pale.

"What did your mother tell you about me, Kali?" She uses that harder voice again.

"Actually she didn't say much at all."

"Really?"

"Yes, nothing really."

"But she told you where to find me."

"Actually I just googled your name."

She seems confused by this, her brows knit as if she's thinking hard. I stroke Finn's hair out of his eyes. Maybe I should just come right out with it as she clearly isn't going to let it go.

"Well, I don't get many visitors out here in January. No one comes to this island in January. Most of the locals aren't even here in winter. You can come here for a whole week at this time of year and not see further than the end of your nose. But you're here. You're here. So, hey, Kali, sit. Sit. Don't mind the dogs—they won't hurt the baby. Sit. Right there, you sit on the sofa. I'll get cookies and milk, and a glass of wine. I guess we could both do with one, huh?" She looks at me intently. "This really is kind of a shock."

The dogs stand and watch her as she goes into the kitchen. They smell of seawater, almost fishy and they pant rhythmically as if they've been running. They are indistinguishable, twins with amber eyes and matching blond coats. I realize they are guarding me, like two shiny jailers, keeping me on the sofa but watching the archway into the kitchen, where Susannah is moving around.

I can see hanging pans and a white range cooker, but she is out of sight. I hear a cupboard open, then shut. Finn wriggles himself into a more comfortable position on my lap and I kiss the top of his head, "There, love, you get sleepy now. It's okay." I need to get the number of a B&B before it's too late to call. And I need to charge up my phone. But the charger is in my bag in the car outside.

A gust of wind comes down the chimney making the fire flicker and smoke billow briefly into the room. I stroke Finn's hair again. He has relaxed a bit, now that she's gone. The warmth from the fire is calming and I can feel from the way he holds his head, as if the ligaments in his neck can't quite do their job, that he is not far from sleep. Gently, I ease it against my shoulder, and he doesn't resist.

I think about the ocean stretching and heaving out there beneath the fog, thousands of miles of it. I remember the magazine article saying how exposed this house is, perched on a high rock. I cup Finn's cheek in my hand, and decide to focus on the room rather than on what's outside it.

Art books, newspapers, and magazines spill over the low table— *The New York Times*, *The New Yorker*, the *Vancouver Sun*, *Time* magazine, *National Geographic*, a coffee table book about Dale Chihuly, a Seattle glass artist; another about whales.

I remember seeing an exhibition of Chihuly once at the Tate modern, absurd glass concoctions in gruesome psychedelic colors. There is a globular sculpture behind the sofa opposite me; a striking deep red glass orb, like something from a dream of blood. I wonder if it is a Chihuly. It looks familiar, as if it has materialized from my own subconscious.

Then something whacks against the windows behind me with a thud. I jerk and spin around. Finn's head flies up, and, wild-eyed, he lets out a cry. The room reflects back at us and it is a moment before I realize that I am looking at a pair of hungry yellow eyes, pressed to the glass, fixed on us. I scramble to my feet, clutching Finn against me. The dogs jump up.

"You okay?" She comes back in, carrying a glass of red wine and a small plate. "Down!" she growls at the dogs. They lie down.

"I . . . I saw . . ." I point, wordlessly, toward the window and a sort of hissing sound comes out of my mouth. Finn starts to sob. I search for the eyes again, but they have vanished. And then I realize that—of course—it must have been the reflection of one of the dogs. The noise was a gust of wind. I hold Finn close, swaying gently side to side. I really do have to calm down. "Shhhh, it's okay. Silly Mommy. It's okay. Just the wind. Everything's okay." His cries subside quickly.

Susannah hands him a cookie. He slowly reaches out a hand and takes it from her. His face is blotchy, and his eyes are red-rimmed. His fleece, I notice, is stained from the ketchup he splattered over himself at the ferry port, and from the juice box in the car. His hair is knotted and wild at the back. His fingernails are filthy. I see Susannah notice all this, as he takes the cookie. A look of profound sadness, perhaps longing, passes across her face as she watches him nibble. I remember the article mentioned that she has a grown-up son.

I look down at the dogs, and they both turn their eyes up at me without moving their heads.

"Pretty cruel weather, huh?" She hands me the glass of red wine. I put it on the coffee table, and then sit down again, positioning Finn on my lap. "We get crazy wind storms up here."

She goes back into the kitchen and comes out with a mug, and a glass of wine for herself. She hands me the mug. "I warmed his milk up just a little," she said.

"Thank you," I hesitate. "Actually, I should just probably put the milk into a sippy cup." I rifle in my bag. "I have one—he'll make a terrible mess if I give him milk in a mug." I am not sure how I'm going to pour the milk from mug to sippy cup with one hand. Plus, the sippy cup really needs washing, it's been at the bottom of my bag all day and has old milk in it, or juice, I'm not sure which—maybe both.

"Oh. Sure. Of course," she says. "It's been a while since I had a little one in the house. Here, that thing needs a wash. Give it to me." She thrusts out her hand for the sippy cup, and mug, and takes them back to the kitchen. I hear her washing the cup. I wish I had done it myself—she'll think I'm negligent to have such a filthy cup. I wonder if I should go through and help, rather than just sitting here. But Finn is getting very sleepy and if I get up, he will start to complain.

"Thanks!" I call after her. "Thanks a lot."

A few moments later she comes back, and hands the clean cup of milk to Finn.

"So, welcome. Welcome to Spring Tide Island." Standing above us, she lifts her glass. "Cheers."

I take mine from the coffee table. The wine smells like vinegar.

"Have you lived here a long time?" I ask.

"Thirty-odd years." She sits, at last, on the sofa opposite mine with the red orb behind her. "Almost your lifetime I guess. How old are you now? Wait . . . thirty-nine in February, right?"

"Yes, actually, wow, that's right." I can't imagine how she would remember my birthday.

"I can't believe it's been thirty-eight years," she blinks. "It doesn't feel any time ago."

I want to ask her more, but it is too soon of course, to go into any of that. I want to ask why my mother was always so unpredictable on my birthday—was my birth that traumatic? My birthdays seemed to make her so sad and withdrawn, even when she tried to be cheerful. Alice's birthdays, in contrast, were uncomplicated and joyful. Susannah is watching me. It's too soon to roll out my own psychodrama.

I pick up the wine again. My body feels a bit odd, as if my cells are all beginning to tilt the wrong way. A shiver trails across my back like the fingertips of a ghost. I am, I realize, profoundly tired. I put the wine down again.

Susannah has tucked one leg under her. She sits upright and the hand holding her glass rests on the arm of the sofa. Nestled in my lap, Finn sucks loudly at his milk cup.

She looks younger than sixty, if that's how old she is; solid and toned. My mother, who gardened and walked in the countryside every day, was fit until the cancer hit, and always strong, but Susannah's edges are somehow harder.

"I've got to tell you, Kali, it's kind of a shock to have you just turn up on my doorstep—with this . . . this child." Her pale eyes meet mine. "Why didn't you call? Did you think I wouldn't see you?"

"I did call," I say, yet again. "I just suppose you never got the message. And then the B&B was shut and . . ."

"Yes," she cuts me off. "You said."

We look at each other for a moment or two and I am sure she thinks I'm lying about the B&B—though I have no idea why. The wind slams against the windows again and I jump. Finn's head jerks up. "It's okay," I murmur. "Shhhhhh. It's just the wind." I want her to stop staring at us.

"It's a long way to bring such a small child."

"I know. Look, I really didn't plan to be doing this—coming here like this, I mean, if you have the numbers of some B&Bs . . . I should call one."

"Kali," she interrupts. "Why don't you just tell me why you brought . . . the . . . him here."

"It's just Kal, people tend to just call me Kal," I say. "I've never really been Kali. Anyway—well, I just—I think I already said this—I came here because I was in Vancouver. I wanted to meet you and thought it would be fun to see the island. I'm . . . I'm curious, I was hoping to find out more about my mother, and who she was before she had me and I thought the two of you were probably good friends at one time."

"Oh," she nods. "We certainly were."

"Well, great." I feel a rush of excitement. "That's great. She never said much about her time in America. And I'd really like to know a bit more about that, and her childhood, and what it was like, when she had me."

She narrows her eyes. "You came because you want to know about your *birth*?"

"My birth? Well, yes, among other things—I suppose so."

"And you can't ask your mother about any of this?"

We look at each other and I feel my face get very hot. She tucks her chin in, as if she's been slapped. She nods to herself, sharply, twice. As she looks at her wine glass the corners of her mouth drop.

"Elena died," she says, quietly. "Didn't she?"

I nod. Then out of nowhere, I think I might cry. I straighten up and look down at the top of Finn's head. I can't allow myself to fall apart. Not here. Not with this woman.

She holds herself upright and her expression is glassy. I can't work out whether she's also struggling to keep herself together, or whether this is just a routine sadness at the loss of someone she once was close to.

Eventually she looks at me. Her pale eyes glisten. "I'm sorry for your loss, Kali. And for Graham too . . ." She forgets to mention Alice.

The dogs get up and go to her. They settle, one on her foot, the other alongside the sofa.

"I'm really sorry—I honestly didn't intend to just blurt it out like that. I wasn't planning to . . ."

Her nostrils flare. "So you came because you wanted to break the news in person?"

I wonder why she'd think that I would bring my toddler eight thousand miles to tell her, a complete stranger, that a friend she hasn't seen in thirty-eight years has died. "Well no," I say. "I just thought it would be interesting to meet you."

"Interesting?" she looks as me as if my word choice is preposterous. "How did she die?" she snaps.

"She had breast cancer."

"Oh." She strokes a dog with her foot. "I have three friends with breast cancer right now. How is Gray doing?"

"My father? Oh, he's okay. He's very sad, obviously, and quite lost, but he isn't one for talking about his feelings much so . . ." I hesitate. "Did you know my father well, then?" I have never heard anyone call him Gray. Not even my mother, who always called him Graham, though I remember that he signed himself Gray in that letter.

"I knew Gray a long time ago, in California but I haven't spoken to him in years. But you know all that, right? That's why you're here." There is that icy tone again. She takes a gulp of the wine. "Shit. She was so young."

I nod.

She launches herself from the sofa, and goes to the fireplace, bending to chuck another log on the fire. Sparks fly but she doesn't brush them off herself. She leans one hand against the fireplace. I can see her taking long, slow breaths.

"My husband died of lung cancer." Her expression becomes momentarily wild, her eyes too round, straining in their sockets.

"I'm so sorry."

For a few moments, neither of us says anything. The only noise in the room is the crackle of the fire. Gusts of wind bump, intermittently, against the windows and the walls of the house like big, angry fists.

I can feel a headache creeping in behind my eyes. I can't just sit here like this. I have to find a place to stay. It'll take at least forty minutes to get back to the town in this fog.

The dogs look at me from her feet as if urging me to leave. I am so incredibly tired. Finn really needs to get to bed. She is staring at Finn, as if mesmerized by his sucking.

"I'm really sorry," I say. "But I should probably try and find a bed and breakfast."

"What?" she shakes her head, just once, and looks at me again.

"I need to find a B&B. I . . . Do you think you could give me a number of a few near here? Would it be okay if I borrowed your phone?"

"Seriously? You actually do have no place to stay?" I can feel the accusation in her voice. I wonder if she hasn't listened to anything at all that I've said. She stares at me and suddenly, it's as if the oxygen isn't right in the room. My whole body tells me to get up, to go— every instinct says "get out." But I am so exhausted. I swallow and blink. It's dehydration and jet lag. Finn stops sucking. I stroke his hair and kiss the top of his head.

"Kali. You've gone kinda pale," she says, slowly. "Are you always this pale? You look like you need to lie down."

"Can you just . . . can I call a nearby B&B? I really must go."

"Oh Kali. There *are* no B&Bs here. I told you. It's not that sort of place in wintertime. The nearest B&Bs are back in town. There's only one who bothers to stay open year round, and she flew to Turks and Caicos yesterday. Besides, I can't possibly let you get back into a car in this weather. Part of the road goes right along the cliff top. It's a miracle you got here alive."

I feel panic bloom in my chest. "But . . ."

"You're Elena's daughter. You'll stay here, of course. That's why you came here, isn't it? I don't have a crib but we'll work something out. Honestly, I wouldn't think of letting you go back out in this, and nor should you—you have a child to think of."

I stiffen. "I didn't intend to . . . this was not the plan. I actually need to head back to Vancouver." I glance down at Finn. His eyes are half-shut now.

"Yeah, well, that's not going to happen tonight is it?" She is standing above me. She lowers her voice again. "You look kinda peaked, Kali."

"Kal," I say, faintly. She's obviously thought of me as Kali for almost four decades and plainly isn't going to stop now. There is a distant thumping in my ears and the crackle of the fire, the wind, her voice all sound a bit muffled. It occurs to me that I might be about to faint.

"We'll talk in the morning. You need to get some rest—look, the little guy is almost asleep. No reasonable mother would even dream of taking a baby back out in this."

She is right of course. Then again, no sensible mother would bring their child to the edge of nowhere and bed him down in a stranger's house. I wonder what my father would say if he knew I was planning to actually stay with Susannah Gillespie.

She lays a hand against her forehead and closes her eyes. I see her take another long slow breath. Then I realize that she actually wants me to go to bed. She wants me to take Finn away so she can absorb what I've just told her about my mother. She, too, looks distinctly pale.

As I get up the room tilts slightly to the left. She steps across and puts a firm hand under my elbow.

"Did you guys even eat?" she asks.

"No, no we're fine. We ate at the ferry terminal. Endlessly. All day. We were there for hours. There wasn't much to do but eat. I'm just a bit off balance. Very tired. I haven't had much sleep lately. Jet lag."

Finn is heavy against my chest and I can tell from the feel of his limbs that he is asleep. She steers me away from the sofa and guides me past the fire through a door into another corridor. She walks ahead of us. The sippy cup falls out of Finn's hand and I stop and brace myself to kneel and pick it up without jolting him awake, but the dogs are right behind me, and I don't want his head near them, so I decide to just leave it where it is for now.

The house, I realize, has no upstairs. The dogs' claws click on the wood floor. Ahead, Susannah is holding a door open. She doesn't smile. She just watches me. For a moment I feel as if I'm being led to a prison cell. Again, I feel panicky. I try to breathe. This is fine. She is an old family friend.

"Okay, so, the bed's clean," she is saying. "But can he sleep in the bed with you?"

"Yes, yes, that's fine, of course. Thank you."

"All you have to do is get in and sleep then. You're all set."

There is a huge, furry white rug and a low double bed, along the wall under a window. "Bathroom," she points at a bathroom door. "There's shampoo, soap, shower gel, toothpaste in there—let me know if there's anything else you need, for you or . . . the little guy." I wonder if she's forgotten Finn's name. She stares at him for a moment, then looks away at the blank window.

Her profile is striking—a firm chin, high cheekbones, a definite nose, and that impeccable posture, as if she's suspended by a string from the crown of her head. "I'll go get your bags—you have a car outside? Is it locked?"

I nod.

"City habits, huh?" She holds out a hand. "You want to give me your car keys?"

I lie Finn gently on the bed and look around. There is a fern in a big pot in one corner, and a whole wall of books. A colorful Mexican blanket is folded on the end of the bed, and there are piles of pillows in pinks and reds. A Seattle Film Festival poster hangs on the wall over the headboard. There is a huge white vase, the size of Finn, next to the bookshelves. The room is civilized, normal, tasteful. I turn to say thank you but she is gone.

As I kneel by the bed, my head spins. I ease Finn's clothes off then pull the quilt over him. His diaper is soaked. I haven't changed it in hours and I should brush his teeth, but if I get him up to brush his teeth and change him now he will wake up, and then, God only knows when he'd sleep again. After last night, I can't risk that.

I lie on my back next to him and close my eyes. I can hear the wind gusting against the window but no sea sounds, and for a second I feel the lurch of the ferry pulling out of Tsawwassen to cross this wild sea.

There was just me, Finn, and two other passengers on board—both heavy set middle-aged men who obviously knew the crew. I read *The Cat in the Hat* to Finn over and over until I felt too sick to continue. Then we lurched around the cabin for the rest of the trip, Finn running wildly ahead, pausing only to bash at things with both hands.

Drinking beer beneath the neon lights of the passenger deck, the men didn't talk to us, though they glanced over their shoulders from time to time. I tried not to think about what they could do, if they wanted to, out in the middle of the ocean where no one could see.

And then I'm back outside the Magnolia B&B, knocking on the door, and the gruff man is shouting from a foggy porch. Doug would be appalled if he knew about any of this. I'm going to have to think more clearly from now on; plan things better. Tomorrow I will go back to Vancouver. Finn and I will visit the aquarium and the children's museum and any other safe tourist attraction we can find. Then we will fly home. This quest for my mother is mad. I will never find her here, in this house of gusts and glass. She is gone. Forever.

Then I hear a creak. I open my eyes with a start—I didn't realize I'd closed them. Susannah is looming in the doorway with my bag in her hand. She is motionless, half in shadow, watching me. In the gloom, her eyes are almost luminous. My heart is beating too fast.

Her bare feet are noiseless on the rug as she walks toward us. She puts the case down by the bed.

"I really am sorry," I sit up, "to land on you like this."

It's colder in here than in the front room. I get off the bed—wanting to seem busy and alert—I kneel to open the bag and dig around for Finn's pajamas and a clean diaper, even though I know I'm not going to use them right now.

She watches me. His usual bedtime routine involves bath, three stories, at least ten rounds of "Baa Baa Black Sheep," and his musical car cell. But he is out, shattered from the broken routines, the junk food, the novelty and upset of all this travel.

I feel Susannah move away. I root around for my toiletries bag. When I look up, she is still there, watching from the door. Then I realize that she is not watching me, she is staring at Finn. She becomes aware of me looking at her, and lifts her chin.

"He's a beautiful child," she says. "He has perfectly symmetrical features, classically spaced, like a Botticelli Christ. He's just so much like—" She stops herself. Takes another breath. I wait, but she doesn't go on. We both gaze at Finn's sleeping face.

I am cold, and so tired, but she's still standing there and I'm not sure what she wants. I pull the Mexican blanket off the bottom of the bed and wrap it around my shoulders. She turns and fiddles with a dial on the wall by the door. Perhaps she wants to talk about my mother.

"It'll warm up soon," she says. Her voice is hard again.

"It's fine. Don't worry. Thank you so much." My legs are lead tubes, weighing my hips down. My head throbs, evenly.

She rests one hand on the door frame. "I can't believe she died," she says, in almost a whisper.

"Nor can I."

Our eyes meet.

"I really didn't mean to land on you like this," I say.

"Oh Kali," she says. "I always knew you'd come one day."

Chapter Six

I wake to the distant thud of waves on rocks, and the caw of gulls somewhere high above the house. I'm sticky and hot, curled like a comma around Finn who is sleeping on his back, both arms flung up by his ears, cheeks pink. I want to pull him toward me and breathe in his sweet sleeping smell, but I shouldn't wake him. I turn my head and look over my shoulder at the door. It is shut.

I'm still in my jeans and sweater, on top of the duvet like Finn, though I've kept the Mexican blanket over me. The curtains let in pale light, but the room feels airless. My mouth is furry. I didn't brush my teeth or wash my face last night. I just flopped down when Susannah left, and plunged almost instantly into a dead, dreamless sleep.

I reach for my phone but it is not on the bedside table. Then I remember that it is in my coat pocket in Susannah's closet, the battery dead. There is no way to know what time it is. I kneel up and, inching forward so that I don't wake Finn, I pull back a corner of the blind and peer out. The glass squeaks as I wipe condensation away. The fog has lifted and there is the ocean, stretching messily beneath a washed out sky. A few clouds drift overhead.

Immediately outside the window there is a deck, one or two black rocks, and a lot of pine trees and undergrowth. A big gray squirrel dashes past, leaps onto the railings, and disappears over the edge with a flick of its tail.

I ease myself out of bed, but Finn doesn't stir. I hover by the door but I can't hear anything outside, no movement at all. I open it a crack. Nothing.

I shut it and peel off my clammy jeans, sweater, and T-shirt—all my clothes smell stale. In the shower, the jets of hot water pummel me awake. Susannah's shower gel is called Kiss My Face, and smells strongly of mint.

Back in the bedroom, I pull on a clean T-shirt, some new socks and underwear, and my jeans. I peer at myself in the mirror. It is liberating not to have to deal with hair dryers or conditioners or de-frizzing products. But I don't look like myself anymore; I wonder what Doug will think when he sees me. Then I realize that Doug's opinion of my hair is hardly our top priority. I should text him to let him know that Finn is safe.

My eyes still have shadows under them and they look bigger with my hair like this. I am still way too pale but at least I don't feel unwell. That would have been awful, to get sick here. I actually feel perfectly healthy today—energized by the minty shower—and definitely hungry, starving, in fact.

It's obviously irresponsible to have arrived like this, but it's done and there is no point in spending my whole time apologizing. I must stop groveling to Susannah. She is clearly not the sort of person who'd offer up her spare room out of politeness.

I linger by the bed. Finn is still in a deep sleep. His eyelashes are dark and thick, like Doug's, and with his dirty blond hair and pixie face, he does look angelic. If Doug were here, he'd take a picture. Doug is always taking pictures of Finn. He will be missing his boy. Whatever else is going on, Doug will be missing Finn terribly by now. And though he is too young to articulate it, I feel sure that Finn misses his dad too.

I realize that last night, for the first time since I found Doug's phone, I didn't have to try not to think about him. At the very least, this trip is a good distraction. Finding the texts feels slightly unreal now. I think about Doug, trying to talk to me on the phone and then me cutting him off, over and over again. Is it possible that I have somehow misread the texts? This could be a huge mistake.

But then I remember the guilt in Doug's voice. I know him. I know everything about his voice; everything it carries. And I heard the guilt.

I have to stop doing this. This trip is not about Doug; it's about my mother. I'm going to find out everything I possibly can about my mother's past. This is my one chance to know what went before—what she was like before she had me. Maybe if I understand her past better, our relationship will make more sense. It is too late to make amends, but it is not too late to understand.

I'm desperate for a coffee and I'm so hungry. Finn could easily sleep for another hour or two. I decide to let him—the house isn't huge. If I prop the door open, I'll hear him when he wakes up—he always lies for a bit when he wakes up, singing "Mama, mama." I'll hear him. I shove the bag between the door and the door frame and walk in socks down the corridor and into the living room.

My feet don't make a sound. There's no sign of the dogs. I generally like dogs but these two don't connect in the way that most retrievers do. They're not normal pets. They seem empty and glassy-eyed, watchful.

The sun is brighter in this south-facing room. I look out the enormous windows at the ocean, flexing to the horizon. For a moment I think about the life that teems beneath that surface—shoals of fish, sharks, octopi. When you imagine being under the sea, you imagine warmth—a hangover from the womb maybe—but it must be bitterly cold under there. There will be Alaskan tides and icy currents rushing off glaciers. That sea is certain death.

I shiver. It is cold in the room and my sweater is too thin. This room feels bigger and much chillier than it did last night. There is a mound of ash in the fireplace, and the sofas look paler in daylight; they are more beige than brown. The glass sculpture is less blood-like in this light, too, more orangey red—but it is still some-how uncomfortable to look at. It reminds me of a blister that is about to burst. It is also dangerously close to Finn-level. If Finn was standing next to it, it would be at his head height and he'd be able to simply reach up and yank it down. I must keep him away from this corner of the room at all costs.

In fact, Finn loose in this room doesn't bear thinking about. There are beautiful ceramics everywhere—on low shelves, on a sideboard, a gray bowl on the coffee table, a tall vase in one corner, about his size. I will have to watch him constantly in this house.

I gaze up at the watery abstract over the fireplace. It looks more eerie in the pale light, mysterious and vaguely threatening—an underwater scene viewed through half-shut eyes.

I head through the archway and into the kitchen. There's coffee in a percolator next to the range cooker; open shelves stacked with pottery plates and bowls—thankfully too high for Finn; a breakfast bar with a big bowl of tangerines, and two white wooden stools. To the right of the kitchen units there is a circular pine table with four chairs, and on the table is a glass bowl full of shiny red apples. The tiled floor is covered with a blue and white striped rug. There are some photos on the shelves behind the table. There is no sign of Susannah. She must be up, because of the coffee. I go across to the photos.

There is a man standing on a rock, in shorts, with a backpack. He has a beard, glasses, and a slightly beleaguered expression as if someone is telling him to stand up straight, move to the right, stop scowling, smile. I pick up the photo next to this: a young boy, six or seven years old, squinting at the camera. He has a chubby, defi-ant little face, and messy hair and a definite look of Susannah, only softer-edged. I put the frame back, next to the man.

The next picture is a beautiful close-up of a whale, in a silver frame. Its vast black and white body heaves up out of the water and droplets fall away, illuminated like pearls. Then there is a black and white land-scape, pine trees and sea, presumably taken around here somewhere. Behind that, unframed, is a photo of a group of women with their

arms around each other. I spot Susannah in the center, younger looking, with a wide smile. Her hair is blonder, in a ponytail, and she's taller
than the other women; somehow she is the focal point even though
she is not in the center of the group.

There's a cluster of smooth stones in a little bowl. I put the photo
back, and run a finger over their smooth surfaces, then over the
driftwood sculpture of a whale that is propped up next to them.
Something moves out of the corner of my eye. I look up, and squint
through the French windows and then, as my eyes adjust, I see her.

She is standing outside, only a few feet away from me, leaning on
the railing of the deck with her back to the view. The dogs are by her
side. Her pale eyes are watching me through the glass.

I raise a hand and let out a half-laugh, "Hello!"

After a beat, she nods, just once.

She has a white coffee cup in her hands and her hair is crumpled
up off her neck—a mix of steel and faded blonde with tendrils that
waver like snakes around her cheekbones. I can't believe I didn't
notice her when I came into the kitchen. The low sun made it hard
to see out but really, I was too nosy, too focused on her things to
see her standing there, watching me. It isn't clear why she didn't call
out. Or come inside.

I walk quickly across to the kitchen area, listening for Finn as I
pass the archway into the living room—silence. The French doors
open onto the deck. The freezing wind slaps my face as I step out.
The sea roars below. I gasp in a breath. The air is so cold it feels as
if it's burning into my lungs. The dogs look at me, ears pricked, but
they don't move or wag their tails. The deck is as slippery as it looks.
I step gingerly toward her, hugging myself. Seagulls caw and the
waves thud. She turns her head away to look at the ocean.

"Well," she gestures vaguely out to sea. "The fog lifted for you."

She doesn't sound angry.

"Wow. It's a stunning view."

She turns back to look at me. Her eyes are sunken with dark
shadows under them, as if she hasn't slept at all. Then again, maybe
she always looks this way in the morning.

"Baby still asleep?" she says.

"Dead to the world."

The sea is more green than gray, and is quite rough, with curls of white surf. There are a couple of pine-covered islands in the distance, and one or two boats far out. There is a huge drop below us, maybe sixty feet down or more. Dark rocks glisten down there, as the waves thud and pull across them.

I glance back at the house and for a second I feel sure that I'm going to see someone standing inside, watching us. But of course there is no one else here, no one except Finn. I have to make sure—at all costs—that Finn does not get out onto this deck.

The kitchen is perfectly visible. She would have had a clear view of me, nosing around. I should say something about the photos to defuse the situation—but somehow anything I could say about them would seem even more intrusive. So I say nothing.

The house is single story, built in unpainted wood. It feels organic, as if it's formed itself from the forest of pines that surround it. We are positioned above the sea on a triangular patch of rocky land. The house must have a view of the sea from both sides. The wind is brutally cold. I'm shivering as I lick the salt off my lips and hug my inadequate sweater tighter around my body. The insides of my ears begin to throb.

She's wearing a thick brown fleece and yoga pants, and a huge gray scarf, but her feet are bare—red and bony and strong. The cold clearly does not bother Susannah.

"So, who was Isabella?" I ask, stamping my feet. The freezing damp soaks my socks. "This is Isabella Rock, isn't it?"

"Isabella Point. It's kind of a sad story actually. She was the young and beautiful wife of an early settler. She died soon after childbirth, leaving a little baby. Then it died a few weeks later."

"How awful."

"Yeah, well, there's also a story that her husband murdered them both in a drunken rage."

"Really?" My voice sounds very English suddenly, and prim.

"The place names up here are one long trail of tragedy," she looks sideways at me. "Those British sailors were pretty overwrought by the time they got this far—you can hear their fear in the names: Desolation Sound, Danger Cove, Cape Caution, Strangers Strait, Hope Channel, Blind Channel . . ." She pauses, looks at me. "Alert Bay."

"Yes, well, it does feel pretty remote here, I have to say." I jiggle on the icy balls of my feet and hug myself tighter, trying to stop my teeth from chattering. "And huge. Everything is just so unbelievably huge here."

"Okay. You're freezing. Coffee." She starts to walk back to the French windows.

She pours coffee into a squat pottery mug.

"Did you make this mug?" I hold it up. "It's really pretty."

"I don't do mugs." She turns away.

"Oh."

"My friend Annie made it. She lives just down the road. She's a potter too. She's the one standing to the right of me in that picture you were looking at a moment ago. Short hair, big smile, overalls."

I feel myself blush, so I sip the coffee. It tastes strong and dusky, but not bitter. Clearly, gourmet coffee beans have made it to the island. This feels reassuring. So does the fact that Susannah has an artist friend named Annie who makes pretty mugs and lives just down the road.

"Sit," she points at a stool. I watch her opening cupboards.

"Bagels? Fruit?" She doesn't stop to hear whether I want them or not, but takes a kitchen knife and slices into a sesame bagel. Little seeds scatter. Her wrist is smooth and hairless, lightly tanned despite the season. She doesn't look pale at all now. In fact, her face is quite golden, as if she has recently been somewhere sunny. I realize that she really must have been in shock last night. I wonder what my mother meant to her.

She pushes up the sleeves of her fleece—chunky veins run up her forearms. She puts both halves of the bagel into a clicking toaster that shunts them along on a treadmill then pops them out at the bottom, perfectly browned.

While this happens, she is slicing bananas. There is a calendar above her, with a Rodin sculpture on it, and though I can't read any of the scribbles it's clear that she keeps busy out here, even in winter. I notice the clock above her head. It's 6:45 a.m.

"My God, it's early."

"I generally get up around five," she says. "So this isn't actually particularly early for me." She pushes a plate at me. "Butter there, blueberry jelly—Annie's again—there." She points to the pots in front of me.

I bite into the bagel and it's so delicious—fresh and soft inside, with a chewy crust and nutty seeds that stick in my teeth. The buttery jam oozes over my fingers and I lick it off. I could eat and eat and never stop. I have to force myself to slow down, to breathe and chew.

I think about what Finn and I ate yesterday—fries and ketchup and greasy grilled cheese that tasted like plastic. No wonder I felt ill. I imagine what the mothers at Finn's playgroup would say about that particular festival of chemicals. It occurs to me, that I can't stand Finn's playgroup. I really can't. Why do I do it to myself? I can't stand all the Boden-dressed mommies with their snack boxes of rice cakes and their multi-pocketed diaper bags. We have nothing in common except our babies. I will never, I decide, set foot in that church hall again. It is surprising how clear things become when you step outside your boundaries.

"Will we hear the baby," Susannah asks, "if he wakes up?"

"Finn?" I say his name, pointedly, between chews, "We'll definitely hear Finn. He isn't quite as docile as he probably seemed last night. In fact, he's very active and extremely loud most of the time."

She slides another half bagel onto my plate. "Well, eat up while you can then. I remember when my son was that age it was a luxury just to sit down."

I feel myself relax. Friends who make jam. Chats about motherhood. This is all perfectly safe.

"How old is your son now?"

She turns away, as if she didn't hear me, though I think she must have. I take another bite. My jeans are digging into my stomach and while her back is to me I undo the top button and pull my sweater down to hide it. My body is slowly warming up, but my hands still feel stiff from the cold wind. She pours more coffee for herself, but doesn't sit down. She unwraps her scarf and walks around the breakfast bar toward me. As she thrusts a hand at me I flinch away.

"Here, I won't bite you. Take this—you're still cold." But she doesn't put the scarf into my hands, she wraps it round my neck, once, then again, tighter.

The scarf is so soft and I know the smell now, the scent I noticed in the living room: it is jasmine, my mother's favorite scent, mixed with something else, slightly acidic, like damp dogs and clay. I mutter a thank-you through a mouthful of bagel. I want to tell her that the jasmine smell reminds me of my mother but it feels too intimate to have noticed her scent, so I keep quiet. And I don't want to bring up my mother, not yet. Not until I've eaten properly. I drink some more coffee.

"So, I'm going to walk the dogs." She leans back against the range, holding her cup with two hands and watching me eat. "Then I'll work. You guys can hang out here, then we'll have lunch."

She seems to assume we are staying.

"I'd love a walk," I say.

"Yes, well, I need to get moving," she says. "I'd like to be in my studio by seven thirty."

"Sure. Okay. But, I should head off when Finn wakes up. You've been very kind, but . . ."

"All you've talked about since you arrived, Kali, is leaving. Are you always this restless or do I make you jumpy?"

"No, God, no, not at all. I just didn't mean to impose on you like this, that's all. You have to work."

"If you want to go, go." She doesn't take her eyes off my face. She knows I won't go. We both know that she has something for me.

"Well, maybe I should charge my cell up first, so I can make a few calls."

"There's no cell reception up here." Her voice is even. "No Internet either."

"Really?"

"I like to keep the house clean of all that."

"Oh, right."

"You can use the landline though. And I have broadband in my office at the gallery, if you need to get online."

"No, no. It's fine," I sip the coffee again. "I'll be fine."

I finish the last of the bagel and wipe my hands on my pants. "That was absolutely delicious," I say. "Amazing. Thank you so much."

"My friend, Maggie, runs the bakery in town." I dimly remember seeing a bakery sign in the shape of a giant cupcake, looming above me as I drove through the fog. I wish Susannah would stop staring at me. Her pale eyes are unsettling and I don't know where to look. I remind myself that she has friends who bake and make jam. Friends called Maggie and Annie. There is nothing alarming about any of this. She's right: I am jumpy. But she is still staring at me.

"I'm embarrassing you," she says. "It's just that you look . . ." she takes a breath. "Almost exactly as I remember your mother, apart from the hair." She touches her own cheeks.

"Well, yes, people always say how much I look like her."

"She was so lovely," she says, and there is heaviness in her voice. "Like you. Same heart- shaped face, but with hair . . ." She gestures, vaguely, as if stroking imaginary hair.

My hand flies to my head. "Actually, I just got all my hair cut off. It was sort of an impulse thing. I'm still not quite used to it myself yet, I keep forgetting it's gone."

"You're into impulse things, aren't you?"

"No, actually I'm really not, not usually," I say. "Usually I'm quite a planner."

"Well, the Audrey Hepburn thing suits your face shape." She says this without flattery, as a professional judgment, and I feel myself inflate, just a little. I imagine that this is the sort of effect her approval has on her chosen artists.

"I remember being very envious of your mother's hair," she says. "I wanted her hair and she wanted mine. In those days, my hair was blonde and I grew it right down to the base of my spine. Nobody tells you that going gray changes the whole texture of your hair but it does. Mine used to be like silk and now—anyway. We were quite a pair, back in the day, me and your mother."

I can't imagine my mother expressing girlish wishes about hair. I can't quite imagine Susannah doing so, either. But for a second she looks younger, just for dipping into these memories. Two spots of pink have appeared on her cheekbones and her eyes shine like washed pebbles.

"Well, yes, she did have great hair." I'm not sure why we're talking in so much detail about hair when there are so many other things to discuss, but I can't seem to stop either. "She didn't go very gray."

"Did her hair . . . ?" she stops. "When she had treatment . . . ?"

"Fall out?" I shake my head. "She wouldn't have chemotherapy."

Susannah nods to herself, as if she'd expect nothing less of my cantankerous mother. Her eyes fade and the line appears between her brows again. "I should have known she was sick."

"Were you two in touch regularly?"

She looks at me, sideways, as if I may be messing with her. "Did she . . . she didn't . . ."

"Sorry—she didn't *what*?"

"Oh never mind. Never mind. How did she . . . did it . . . was it very long?"

"The illness?"

"Was it long?"

"Her cancer was quite advanced by the time they diagnosed it. She actually didn't go to the doctor for a very long time after she found the lump. So when she did finally go, it all happened quite fast, really, just a few months," I have to work hard to keep my tone even, but somehow I manage it. "She wouldn't have chemotherapy because I suppose she didn't want to prolong it. I suppose she didn't want to suffer for longer than she had to."

"Were you with her when she died?"

The food lies heavy in my stomach. "Actually, I was. I got there just a few moments before. But I don't know if she knew I was there, or . . ." I stare at my mug. It is almost a relief to be saying this out loud, even to this slightly hostile stranger. I think about my mother, shrunken in her bed. When I arrived everyone was running around fetching towels. I don't know why towels were needed right then, at that last moment of her life. Why towels? I still had my coat on, Finn in my arms. I dropped my bag, and the smell hit me—an ancient smell that I shouldn't recognize, but somehow did. As I approached the bed, my mother's hollow face lit up and just for that second I thought it was because of me.

But she wasn't looking at me. Finn was tucked against my shoulder, but I'm not sure if she was seeing him, either—she was already somewhere else, and then she gasped, like she was sliding under the water, and her eyes widened, as if she'd seen something surprising and longed-for beneath the surface. She died just as Alice rushed back in with an armful of towels.

"Hey—you don't have to talk about it," Susannah says, "if it's too raw."

"No, it's okay. She died at home and she, well, it was . . . she looked sort of pleased at the very last moment, as if she'd seen someone . . . I know that sounds weird."

"She saw you."

"No. It wasn't that. Maybe it was Finn—but really, I'm not sure if she even knew we were there. And we weren't . . . I wasn't . . . my sister had been caring for her a lot, and they were very close. It's all much harder on Alice, all of this."

"Your sister?" Her eyes flick back to my face as if I've said something else that is confusing.

"Yes, Alice. She took leave from work the last couple of weeks. The two of them were very close, and I—we—well, my mother and I had quite a difficult relationship. Maybe she told you all this? I suppose I was a bit hesitant to go and see her. But you don't need to know all this. It's just messy family stuff."

"Death and guilt . . ." She looks down, twirling her silver thumb ring with an index finger. I wait for her to elaborate, but she doesn't. Then she looks back at me again. "My God, Kali. You're so like her.

Your voice—you even have her gestures when you talk. It's like she's right here, in my kitchen."

"Well, I didn't get her eyes. Alice got the beautiful green eyes."

"Yeah. You have your father's eyes exactly."

"Really? No. I don't think so, not really. Dad's are more grayish blue."

Her whole face flames scarlet and she turns her back on me, putting her mug in the sink.

Then I hear a crash coming from the other side of the house, and a dull thud, followed by a long, distant wail.

"Oh shit!" I leap off the stool, and sprint through the living room and down the corridor to the bedroom. The door is shut and I can hear him crying inside. He must have dislodged the bag and it shut itself. "Finn?" I try to open it but it won't budge. "Finn?" I call. "Sweetheart? I'm here. It's okay."

"Mama!" he howls.

I shove the door with my shoulder, and whatever is blocking it shifts. Finn is standing in his spaceman pajamas, with his arms by his sides, looking up at me, eyes wide and filled with tears. Beside him the big white vase is on its side and there is a large chunk out of its rim. The broken-off shard is by Finn's leg. I swoop and pick him up, checking him for cuts. He's fine. But the vase definitely isn't. The suitcase was blocking the door.

"Oopsie." Finn looks down at the vase. He has stopped crying now that he's in my arms. He just looks shocked.

"Just an accident," I smooth his forehead as if I can actually stroke away the fear and shock. "It's okay love, it's okay."

He must have woken up, and then somehow knocked the suitcase so that the door clicked shut. Then he couldn't reach the door handle. It looks as if he was trying to climb onto the upside down vase to reach it. He is nothing, if not resourceful.

"My poor little love," I say. "You got stuck in here didn't you? The door shut and you got stuck. But it's okay now." I realize that my hand is shaking. Silly. He's fine.

"Mommy's here and it's okay."

His face lightens, then, and he struggles to get down. I know he'd like to go and tug a few more sharp bits off the vase, now, to see what will happen next.

"Here, look! Over here! Let's get you dressed. Breakfast time!" I try to redirect him to the bed. Susannah appears in the doorway.

"Is he okay?"

"God Susannah—I'm so sorry. I'll pay for that—I'm really sorry. Finn got stuck in the room, somehow, and he must have broken the vase trying to get out. I'm so sorry."

Her expression is closed-off, her mouth small. "You shut the child in here?"

"What? No! What? Of course not. I didn't... The door must have..."

But she isn't listening, I can tell. She goes and bends over the vase, straight-backed as always, picking up the large broken piece.

"Look, Susannah. Please let me pay for it." I think about the Chihuly in the front room—what if this vase is by a world famous potter? "Do let me replace it, please."

"It's not a problem," she snaps, her back to me.

"Seriously, I'd like to replace it."

"I don't care about the vase, Kali." She looks over her shoulder at me. To my surprise, she doesn't seem angry, just cold. "Toddlers break things. The main thing is that the baby is okay. Don't you think?"

I wish she'd stop calling him "the baby," "the little guy," "the child." "But he's fine!" I say. "Totally. Aren't you, Finn?"

He wrestles himself out of my grip and runs, with one pajama leg on, the other flapping, toward the bathroom. "Ba' time!" he shouts.

"No, no bath now." I hurry after him.

Susannah takes the broken vase away. I wrangle Finn back onto the bed, put a clean diaper on him, and finish dressing him in his warmest fleece and the jeans with the dinosaur on the pocket, as he wriggles and protests and babbles. The incident is forgotten. He has moved on already.

As I walk with him through to the kitchen again, his small hand tucked inside mine, I realize that I've eaten too much too fast.

Maybe it was the shock of hearing his scream, or the anxiety about the broken vase, but the bagels are lodged at the top of my stomach now, like big lumps of lead.

"So, if you want to come for a walk, I'm going to go now." Susannah is clearing up the kitchen. "But I guess you'll need to give him breakfast?"

I desperately want to be out in the fresh air, under that high bright sky. "Actually, we'd love to come for a walk, if you don't mind some company? Finn can have some bagel to chew while we walk—I'll just put him in the backpack, I have one that I carry him in. It's in the car . . ."

"Oh. Sure."

She whistles and the dogs leap to the French windows, wagging and turning circles.

"I'll just get my coat and boots—and the baby carrier. Would you mind watching Finn just for a second?"

"Of course," she says. I hesitate. She looks at Finn who is holding onto my leg. Then she peels her lips into a smile. She kneels down so she's at his level. "You want a banana? You look like a banana lover to me."

To my surprise, he smiles up at her. She nods. "Okay. So, why don't you come sit here, on my very best chair, and then you can pick the biggest banana of all?" Her motherly tone is unexpected. But it works. He reaches up, trustingly, and takes her hand. Before he notices, I duck away through the archway and into the living room.

I go out into the freezing morning and get the baby carrier from the car, then I go to the hall closet and find Finn's snowsuit and the parka and my hiking boots. I get into my coat, zipping it right up. It takes me a while to find my hat—she's taken it and put it, folded, on a shelf up above the coat hooks. I still have her scarf around my neck and it feels too tight but I keep the coat zipped right to the top anyway. I pull on my hiking boots, then, and clomp through the house again, wondering vaguely if I shouldn't be wearing my boots inside.

The kitchen is empty. There is a half-eaten banana on the counter. Susannah and Finn have gone.

I haul open the door and rush out onto the deck. The sun blinds me for a second, and then one leg slips from under me on the icy wood. I almost crash down backward, but I grab the railing and wrench myself upright. I hold onto it with both hands and peer over the edge, my heart pummeling my chest, wind battering my ears. There she is. I see her far below on the rocks, with waves crashing behind her, and Finn standing by her leg, holding her hand. They are both looking up at me. He doesn't even have a coat on. He is standing on the icy rock in just his woolly socks. Vast waves lash the shore, not far behind where they are standing.

"Hey!" I shout. "Wait! I'm coming. I have Finn's snowsuit! And the carrier! Wait a second!" He will freeze. I want him in the all-in-one suit right now. He looks tiny on the big rock, and the waves are too close, and too tall.

It is bitterly cold.

I hook the baby carrier onto both shoulders and spot a gap in the railing, a little further down the deck. I pick my way across the wood so I don't slip again. There are some steps nailed into the rock face with just a thin railing to hold onto as you wobble down them. I can't even think about her getting Finn down here. Did she carry him?

I begin to climb down, hanging onto the banister with both hands. I can't think about them, teetering on the cliff face like this. At least she is strong. She probably comes down these steps every day of her life; she knows every inch of them. The steps are covered in a sheet of ice and they creak as I climb down, and I pray that whoever hammered them into the rock face knew what they were doing.

The black and gray rocks shine under a white sun and as each wave hits, foam fans into the air behind them. I slip and jump over the rocks to them. Susannah's mouth is a thin line and her eyes are narrow, watching me. Finn's hair is illuminated on the ends, lifting this way and that. He beams at me, yanks his hand out of Susannah's, and starts off in a stumbling run over the slippery rock toward me.

I leap across the gap to him and whisk him up, just as his foot slips and he begins to tumble head first toward the crevice. "Wow! Whoopsie! Hello!" I haul him into the air. He laughs.

"It's so cold out here! Look at the sea, Finn. Look at the big waves." I stuff him into his downy red snowsuit while he protests, and I zip it right up. Then I wedge his boots onto his feet. "There you go. All warm now." His limbs stick out, padded. I realize I haven't got his new gloves and hat. I left them in the suitcase. I pull up his hood—he looks like a small red astronaut.

"Dat!" he shouts, pointing at the sky behind me. "Dat!"

I look where he's pointing, above the cliff and the house and I see it too—a huge bird of prey riding the wind tides with glorious hooked wings outstretched, its body and white head perfectly still. I can see the tips of its feathers fluttering. Its head is perfectly still.

"Bird," I say. "That's a big bird."

I turn back to Susannah. She is looking the other way, out to sea. When I look back at the sky above the house the bird of prey has gone.

I persuade Finn to get into the backpack and I strap him safely in. His hands are red and freezing already. I pull up his hood again, and pull the sleeves down over his hands. Then, unsteadily, I heave him up onto my back. The straps dig into my shoulders through the parka. I clip it around my waist. He really is getting heavy.

I clamber over the rocks toward Susannah. "We just saw this huge black bird back there, like a vulture." I am out of breath already. "A great big thing with dark wings and a white head!"

But she seems to want to get moving. "I usually go around the rocks," she says. "And then there's a longer beach. You up to it, *Elle*?"

"What?" I wonder if I heard the slip right. The wind is so strong and the waves are loud. "Yes, definitely." The bagels are heavy in my belly. I swallow a mouthful of saliva and my ears buzz. The sun is very bright and the wind is so cold it makes my face feel immobile.

"Is he warm enough?" She glances at Finn.

"Don't worry, he'll let us know if he gets cold." I try to smile. "He isn't one to suffer in silence."

"Needs gloves," she says, disapprovingly, and starts to walk.

I want to point out that it was her who brought him down here without even a coat, and in socks—socks!—but I don't say anything. It occurs to me that my mother's disengagement, when it came to her grandson, might have been something of a blessing.

I follow Susannah over the frozen rocks. Her thighs are solid and strong as she leaps from one to another and I have to work hard to keep up, with Finn weighing me down, and the added instability of his weight on my spine. I lurch and slide over the slippery surfaces, arms out for balance.

We round the headland onto a long shingle beach. The dogs bound ahead, their glossy coats rippling. The coast is nothing but forest—an ocean of pines, different hues, some dead, some sprinkled with snow. The big flat rocks along the shore remind me of a magnified picture of the epidermis, layer upon gray layer. I see a flash of white between the tree trunks and a tall animal leaps and vanishes, a deer or maybe even a moose. Ravens circle overhead and I spot a wisp of smoke rising from the pines, and further over to the left, another smoky line.

Susannah walks fast, a few steps ahead. Her feet know every nook and hollow. She is staring out to sea as she goes, as if expecting to see someone in a boat, skimming toward the shore. My thighs and shoulders are aching and I wonder how far and fast she is planning to go.

"See the harbor seals on that rock." She stops and points to a peninsula just ahead of us, raising her voice over the wind. I catch up and stand close to her, breathing too hard. She is pointing at an enormous black boulder further over to the left of the bay. It seems to undulate. I blink hard. Then I realize that the rock isn't undulating. It's covered in living things—seals.

"You get transients up here, hunting them."

"Transients?" For a moment, I picture shabby people with spears.

"Orca?"

"Oh. Right. Killer whales?"

"Yeah. But I guess you know all about this, don't you?"

"Well, no," I shrug. "I don't know anything about killer whales actually." I have a vague image of black and white creatures in Florida theme parks. I remembered a news story a few years back, where one dragged a trainer under by her ponytail and held her there until she drowned, while officials ushered away the appalled spectators.

She looks at me. "Seriously? You don't?"

It's not clear what she's trying to imply. She blinks, looks away, and then looks back at me again. "Really?"

"I'm very ignorant, I'm afraid."

There was another incident, I remember, on the news—a man seized by the ankle and dragged into the tank by the whale during a performance in some aquarium somewhere in America. She dragged him under and up again for what seemed like hours. In that case it turned out that the whale had heard her two-year-old baby crying just before the performance began, and was upset. "Do you see a lot of killer whales up here then?" I ask.

She is staring at me and once again I get the feeling that she thinks I'm not telling the truth. We've stopped on a rock, and waves crash just ahead of us, throwing up spray. I feel it on my face—but we are just the right distance not to get too wet.

"You're honestly telling me you know nothing about whales?"

"I'm sorry," I shrug, trying not to let my irritation show. "I've seen them in theme parks on TV but apart from that, no. There aren't too many killer whales in the English Channel."

She stares down at me, but doesn't seem amused. Then she takes a breath. "In spring, the transients—the carnivorous orca—they come right up here at breeding time for the seals. People around here have seen them try to scoop a dog off a beach, or wash a trapped moose off a rock. I've seen a transient swipe a seal right off that promontory there."

"Whales eat dogs?"

"Well, it's rare, obviously, but transient orca can. Friend of mine had her terrier taken by a transient, just up the coast from here. The killer whale is top of the food chain," she straightens. "Nothing can touch it. You really don't know this?"

"No!"

"Well, they have no predators at all—unless you count humans."

"I always assumed whales ate plankton or maybe fish."

"Baleen eat plankton, orca don't. Resident orca eat fish—and that's the bulk of the population around here, actually. Residents eat things like kelp and sockeye and herring. They're in trouble, now, because salmon stocks are so corrupted thanks to fish farms introducing sea lice. There are also all sorts of toxins out there now that affect the food supply. Then there's noise pollution from all the ships. It gets in the way of echolocation so the whales can't find food or communicate. It's criminal what we're doing to the orca's environment. But anyway. Yeah. Residents are peaceful pescatarians. The 'killer' bit is more a reflection of human fears than a biological reality."

"Like the explorers, naming the land," I say. "Human fears written on the landscape—or on whales."

"Well, yeah, I guess so. It's what we do, isn't it? Name the terror in order to conquer it. The only problem is," she glances at me, "We *are* the terror."

"Do they really come right up to the shore and eat dogs?" I look around for her retrievers. They are sniffing around the rock pools further up the beach. She doesn't seem concerned about their safety.

"Well, I guess mainly they stick to sea creatures. Last year I watched three of them separate an adult male harbor seal from his family on that rock right over there." She points to a flat rock, a bit like a stage, to the side of the cove. "It was like a mafia hit. Fascinating. They stunned him and dragged him out to sea. His family—his whole seal clan—was watching from the rock as they slowly beat him to death. It's a sport for the orca. They could kill him instantly, of course, but they prefer to take their time and have some fun with him first." She looks back at me. Her pallid eyes glimmer against her ruddy skin.

"It sounds gruesome."

"Yup. Well. Nature is gruesome, Kali. They tossed him around like a beach ball, slowly battering him to death."

I feel as if she's testing me, pressing to see at what point the ignorant townie gets squeamish. I can feel her eyes on my face and I look firmly into the waves, determined not to give her the satisfaction of seeing me flinch. Finn drums his palms on the crown of my head and kicks his legs.

"After that, they take the kill back to the matriarch," she continues, planting one foot on the rock next to her, as if it is a step. "Orca society is matriarchal."

"Really?"

"Uh huh. Sure. You get mothers, sons, sisters, brothers, aunts and uncles in the same pod, but no fathers. The males go off to mate in other pods but they always come back to mommy. Each pod—the extended family—revolves around a matriarch, and she can live to be eighty years old, maybe more. She makes all the decisions about where they go and when. She gives all the orders—and they obey her. Maybe because of this tight structure, they have these really powerful family bonds: loyalty, love, devotion, trust. They're highly civilized— they celebrate and play, they socialize, they have traditions, they even grieve when a family member dies."

"It all sounds very human."

"Well, yeah. It is, kinda. Though, frankly, they're a step ahead of humans, with the matriarchal thing, and their peaceful life," she glances down at me again. I smile but she doesn't smile back. In fact, her face is stony. She scrapes some strands of hair away from her mouth. "In the early days of orca research all those male scientists just assumed that the big bulls were the bosses—the massive whales you see, with those intimidating six-foot dorsals? It took them a while to realize that, in fact, the mothers were in charge. Even those great big males stay with their mothers their whole damned lives, doing what they're told. But you're right, Kali. In some ways they aren't too different from us: it's all about mom for them, too."

She's staring out to sea and I can't tell whether she is teasing me or simply stating a fact of life.

Finn drums his legs against the sides of the carrier, like a rider, urging his horse to leap into the waves. I picture a killer whale matriarch rising out of the sea right here, in front of us—jaws agape, towering, ready to sweep us under.

"So you get a lot of killer whales up here then?"

"Oh, sure. This region is known for them. There are a couple of pods that really own this particular stretch. But there are about two hundred northern residents out there, and researchers know every single one, now, literally by name—thanks to your mother, and . . . the others. It's amazing what they started."

Her eyes are the same color as the palest ice-slicked rock behind her and she has them fixed right on my face.

"I'm sorry—did you just say my mother?"

She looks away again, across the gray sea. "Every single orca has a name and a detailed entry on the database. The researchers know all the families, now; they understand their relationships, ages, personalities, medical histories, everything. They can identify every single whale out there by its markings and the shape of its fin. Every dorsal is a unique shape—with specific scars, scratches, nicks or marks. And the researchers have records of them all. They have unique saddle patches too—those gray patches; they're like whale fingerprints. But yeah, it's incredible, really, what they started."

I shake my head. "Wait—you said my mother a minute ago? I don't understand. Started *what*? She was here? What do you mean?"

But she's walking away from me, hopping effortlessly across the rocks, and my words are lost on the wind.

Finn shouts "Go!" And kicks his legs to and fro. He used to wind his fingers in my hair but he can't now, so he slaps the back of my head. "Go, go."

"Susannah? What do you mean?" I call after her. I struggle to catch up, my boots slipping on the sheet of ice. I have to slow down. I can't fall with Finn on my back.

I pull off my hood to hear her better but all I can hear is the howl of the wind and the thud of waves on granite. "Please Susannah. Please wait—what has my mother got to do with all this? I don't know what you're talking about!"

She looks back at me and I think, but I'm not sure, that there might be a half smile on her lips. She lets me catch up.

"Oh? The orca-mapping project?" she says. "It's a very big deal. So, I guess Elena was pretty pleased by that, huh?" She reaches up, behind me, and I think she takes Finn's fingers in hers as she speaks. "I assume she at least kept up with the developments, back in the UK? Did she stay in touch with anyone at all from those days?"

I shake my head. Freezing gusts of wind thump my ears. "I really don't know what you're talking about. Are you saying she was up here? On Spring Tide Island? Studying these whales?"

She lets go of Finn, "The baby's hand is very cold," she says. And she hops onto the next rock.

The heavy feeling in my stomach has turned to a sharp triangle of pain. I try to step onto the rock after her, but I slip, and one leg shoots down. My boot dips into a rock pool, so cold it sends shock waves through my body and I only stop myself from toppling by shooting both hands out to the rock face in front of me. My elbows jar with the effort of keeping my body, and Finn, upright. Susannah leans down, and hauls at the backpack's metal frame, pulling us up and out.

"You okay?" she says. "You have to be careful with a baby on your back. It's slippery here."

"She was up here?" I shout. "My mother was here?"

"Your foot's wet," she says. "Kali, take it easy."

"I'm fine, I'm *fine*." The urge to scream in her face is overwhelming, but I make myself lean over slightly, pressing at my belly with both hands. "Look. I just don't know what you mean about my mother and the whales."

She turns and walks away. For a moment the sun bursts through some clouds and she is standing in a patch of almost white light, her wavy hair lit up from behind.

"Wait!" I yell. "Christ Susannah! Just stop will you?"

She stops, and now I know that she is enjoying this. She's toying with me.

"Oh? Oh. She really did tell you nothing, huh? She never even told you about her work up here? The orca mapping?"

I get, more carefully this time, onto the same rock as her. My stomach feels unstable and there's too much saliva in my mouth.

Susannah smiles down at me. "So," she raises one eyebrow, "She really did cut off when she moved to England didn't she—from everything? It makes sense, I guess. But wow. Anyway, look, Kali. You should know one thing, at least, about Elena. You can be proud of her. You can be proud of what she did up here. Whatever she turned into, over there in England in that cozy country cottage of yours, she once contributed something important to the world."

"What did she do?" The salt wind whips past my face and the force of my words is lost again. "Tell me!"

Susannah reaches up and I think she is pulling Finn's hood up. "Your mother was involved in the very early days of a Canadian government research project to survey the orca population. Mostly in Puget Sound. She and . . . she joined some other researchers who'd set out to photo identify every single orca. The whales were being captured by sea parks and the project was a huge turning point in marine conservation up here. The researchers discovered that the southern residents were being basically wiped out by theme parks. They managed to get that banned, but then they wanted to assess the damage. There's a whole institute built on all this now, there's amazing orca research underway still, and conservation laws . . ."

I open my mouth to ask if this was what my mother's abandoned PhD was on, but she just keeps talking, looking out to sea, knowing she has me now. Finn is slapping the sides of the baby carrier with his hands and making "OOOObaba" noises. I will him not to lose patience.

"Killer whale capture was big bucks in the seventies," she is saying, "The theme parks only wanted the babies—the yearlings. They still do—they get them in Iceland now I think. Anyway, it was a military operation. They'd literally use explosives and harpoons to separate a baby from its mother. Most of them died within weeks of captivity. There was a famous capture, down in Puget Sound, years ago, where they took five or six in one round up. Only one survived—in fact, you might have heard of her even in England—a whale called Lolita? She's still alive, down in California somewhere, and there's this movement now to return her to the wild. They know the exact pod she came from. They know her sisters and brothers and mother. Some researchers played her sound recordings of the pod—they know now that each pod has its own dialect. The other whales in the tank with her didn't pay much attention to the sounds, but Lolita went crazy—she seemed to recognize her family's voices. It's chilling, when you think about, what we've done to these animals. But at least the orca up here are protected now; they're on the endangered species list."

"But, hang on. Just hang on." I can't take this in. "What's my mother got to do with all this? She studied dolphins."

"Orca," she gazes at me, "are part of the dolphin family."

"So, what—you mean, she did her PhD up here, not in California?"

Susannah doesn't answer. She's looking out at the waves again and her face is troubled, but concentrated. She looks as if she's scanning the water for something. She puts both hands up to her temples and her nostrils flare.

"Was she doing research up here?" I say, again. My head is buzzing, I feel as if someone has poured ice into my ears.

"They'd go out on the water in all weathers, all times of year. She had this all-weather suit, bright yellow, an inch thick—she walked like an astronaut in it—with her binoculars and camera slung around her neck, her hair all over the place. And she had a hydrophone that she'd drop down off the boat, to listen and record the sounds the whales made. She was fearless. You get seventeen foot tides up here, hurricane force winds. But she'd always say 'no picture, no proof.' She was completely obsessed with the work—totally passionate and single-minded. I worried about them a lot up here in winter."

"I can't . . ." It seems so impossible that she's talking about my mother. "I just can't . . ." Finn whacks my head with his hand and makes a long, loud "maaaaaa" sound. I ignore him.

"So, Kali," Susannah looks right at me, "whatever she turned into out there in England, her life wasn't ordinary. She did some good."

I squint at her in the bright sun. For a second, I wonder if she has made this entire story up. The triangle of pain in my gut is intense now; my legs feel shaky. Finn is slapping my head with his hands. "Go, go, go, go, go." But then my stomach lurches and I realize that I'm going to throw up. I open my eyes and look wildly around—I must have made a panicky noise because Susannah suddenly steps toward me, with her hand out.

"Are you okay?"

"Gonna throw up." I fold my hands over my lips, lurch away from her over the rock. I throw up a gush of bagels and coffee into a tide pool. I can't bend over too far because of Finn on my back, and I have to hold my legs far apart to stop the vomit from splashing up them.

She is behind me. I want to tell her to leave me alone but I have vomit coming out of my mouth and nose and I'm hideously ashamed of the sounds, of the stench. But as I throw up again, I feel her standing behind me. She doesn't speak. She doesn't touch me. She just stands and waits. Maybe she is distracting Finn in some way.

Afterward, she hands me a tissue. She looks at the sea while I wipe my face and blow my nose.

I start to apologize.

"The little guy's hands," she says, "are blocks of ice. We should get back to the house. Give him to me. I'll carry him." Without waiting for me to agree, she reaches both hands around my waist from behind, unsnaps the belt, then hooks the carrier off my shoulders with Finn still inside, and lifts him onto her back. Then she sets off.

Back in the kitchen, she swings the backpack down as if Finn weighs nothing. She bends to unstrap him, blocking me with her body, and lifts him out.

His cheeks are scarlet and his eyes shine and he wriggles to get down. She puts him down and he toddles off to the stool, still in his red snowsuit. I follow him.

"Kali, you know what, why don't you just go rest for a bit?" she says. "You look like you need it. He'll be good with me. We'll get to know each other. I'll give him some breakfast, then we can hang out for a while. Huh, little guy? You like pancakes?" Finn glances back at her, then makes for the dogs. They're lying by the door.

"Finn!" I call.

"Oh, they won't hurt him," Susannah says, dismissively. "They're excellent with kids." Sure enough, the dogs actually wag the ends of their tails. Finn kneels down and shoves his hands into their curling wet fur. They continue to wag, gently. One licks his face. I feel my shoulders relax. Maybe it's just me that the dogs don't like.

"Seriously, Kali. He'll be perfectly safe with me."

"But you need to work."

"Oh work can wait."

"He can be quite a handful . . ."

"Kali," she says, "I have done this before you know. The two of us will just hang out for a bit, get to know each other. You need rest. You look kinda sick to be honest—and you don't want to get any worse, do you? We don't want you stuck up here for days, do we?"

I realize, then, that the offer might be less for my benefit than for hers. The last thing she wants is me loitering here for days in a sickbed. And she's right. I do feel depleted, and queasy, and extraordinarily tired. The thought of someone else having Finn for a bit is tempting.

Susannah is a mother—she'll know how to keep him safe and distracted. I can easily leave him with her for half an hour while I rest. I'm in the same house after all.

I brush my teeth and crawl into the bed. I can't keep my eyes open, despite the long sleep the night before. My throat feels as if someone has rubbed it with a scouring pad. The spare room is warm and the mattress is soft. The sheets and pillow smell of fresh laundry detergent. The past ten days really have taken it all out of me. I feel the tension in my body release, just a bit, as I lie down. But the emptiness deep in my belly is more than just the result of throwing up.

I hear Finn laugh, somewhere in the house, a piping noise of pure delight. He hasn't even noticed I've gone.

My brain begins to float, and images skim behind my eyes: my mother on a little motorboat, fearless of winds and tides, teetering on waves with the six-foot fins of killer whales slicing through the water beside her; her hair streaming out, her eyes as green as the sea. And I know Susannah isn't lying. This remote, wild place feels like hers. It is her.

I smell jasmine, very faintly, and for a moment, I feel as if she's here, standing somewhere in the shadows of the room, just out of sight, watching me even though I can't see her. I think about Susannah's description of her work and I feel as if I have been handed something precious: a tiny window to the woman my mother once was.

I drift into sleep, resurface into the room, then drift back again, and as I sink I feel my mother's hand on my hair. She is here, with me, next to me, so close that I feel the warmth of her body, and I can smell her, properly now, jasmine and soil and salty winds. And then I hear her voice, crisp, next to my ear. "*Kali*" She only used my full name when she needed my attention. "*Watch out.*"

I snap open my eyes. My heart thuds against my chest.

The room is chilly, divided by sharp clean lines: bookshelves, poster, bathroom door, window frame. I breathe in and out, waiting for my leaping heart to calm down.

I've heard that people do this when they lose someone; they hear that person's voice—they feel their presence. But I don't want a voice, or a feeling—I want her. I want my mother. I want her back in all her complicated, infuriating flesh and blood. This is the reason for the emptiness deep in my belly: this is my sickness. My mother is gone. She's gone forever and I didn't say sorry. I didn't tell her I loved her. I could have made everything right but I didn't.

As I bury my face in the pillow, I realize that I want Doug too. I want to hear his voice, to feel his arms around me and to tell him what I've just discovered about my mother and the whales and the photographic database. I want to smell his skin and feel his broad body and hold onto him as I tell him what I know.

I sit up and crawl across the bed, leaning over to yank his sweater out of the bag. I curl on one side and bury my face in it like a pillow. I can smell him, faintly, in the scratchy wool, and there is a comfort in the simplicity of his smell.

For a short while I let myself imagine what it would feel like to lie here with Doug. These sounds would be different if he was here. The wailing wind would not sound so hollow and bereft; the chimes on the deck would be less eerie, more musical.

I wipe my eyes and nose on Doug's sweater. The persistent moan of the wind up here reminds me of something I had completely forgotten about. One Christmas, years ago when I was just a teenager, my mother asked for a cassette tape of wind sounds—and my father actually found one for her. She listened to that tape for months and we all laughed at her, as if there wasn't enough wind in the Sussex countryside. But she said she found it relaxing. I couldn't stand the tape—it sounded haunting and empty and I'd switch it off if I came into the kitchen to find it playing. It made me feel lonely; it made me think of death. But she really loved those wind sounds. Her favorite track, I remember, was a blizzard in Cape Cod. I remember how, beneath the hoarse rush and moan, you could hear a barn door slamming intermittently.

The wind in this place is definitely not comforting. The gusts are so powerful they shake the walls, as if they might scoop the house—and all of us in it—off this rock and fling us out to sea.

I have to stop. It's just weather, nothing more. The wind only feels threatening because I am exhausted, and alone, and very far from home, and I am in shock too—this is grief, one of Alice's stages. Everything in this place feels so gigantic and inhospitable. Everything is on a different scale here. The trees tower so much higher, and the birds and rocks are so much bigger. But none of this will hurt us. I need to sit up and pull myself together, and stop being so pathetic: I am stronger than this. I know I am.

Do I really want Doug here, right now, in this bed? Do I really? I remind myself how stressful our bed at home had become. For the first sixteen months of his life Finn woke up several times a night. Because Doug had to work the next day, I would usually get up for Finn. Then even on weekends, I'd get up, because Finn was used to me at night, and not Doug. And I did this night after night to the point of lunacy. Often, I'd come back to bed having finally gotten Finn back to sleep and Doug would be lying on his back, snoring.

I'd twist and turn for a bit with a pillow over my head, aware of the minutes of precious sleep time ticking away before the next wake up. Then eventually, I'd shake Doug and he'd take himself off to the spare room so we could both snatch a few minutes of sleep before we had to get up again. Most mornings I woke in a cold bed, with Finn babbling next door and Doug in the attic room above us.

This is how marriages unravel. It is a creeping process. Each night Doug and I added another brick into the invisible wall that was growing between us, and we didn't even know we were doing it. We were just so tired all the time. All we wanted was some sleep.

But I wonder, now, whether Doug was lying in the spare room all those nights, thinking about her. Was he trying to work out how to leave me and be with her? Or have I got this all wrong? He was trying to tell me what happened and I wouldn't let him. It all feels bamboozling, like a dream where you are being given complex information, but none of it makes sense. I just need time. I will be able to face him, and listen to whatever he wants to tell me. But not now.

I can't sleep now. I sit up and hug my knees. This is agony. If Doug has had an affair then nothing in the past—no memory or feeling—has the same meaning anymore. Doug was good, solid, true, and now maybe he isn't. Maybe I don't know who he is at all. But of course I know who he is. It's Doug. He would never do this to me.

I shove his sweater off the bed, lean over, and find my phone. The screen is blank. I get the charger and plug it in. I have to talk to him.

This is insane. For a moment I see myself with complete clarity: I have been acting like a lunatic child. Running away with my hands over my ears—"la, la, la, I can't hear you."

The phone flickers briefly to life but there is no signal—and I remember that there is no reception out here. I put it down, slump back, and shut my eyes.

When I wake up, my mouth is dry. I stare at the ceiling and listen to the far off crash of the waves, wind thumping like flat hands on the windowpane, and the spooky sound of the wind chime. Then I think, "Finn!"

I hurry through the cold living room to the kitchen, dragging my inadequate pullover over my head. The kitchen is clean and tidy, no sign of life. Susannah's boots aren't there by the French windows and the dog baskets are empty. The deck is empty too. Grayish clouds scud across the sky.

She wouldn't have taken him down those steps again, to the rocks, would she? Surely not. I wrench open the doors and the waves and wind are deafening for a second—overwhelming, blaring. I run out onto the deck, slipping, and righting myself, like before, heavily against the wooden railings. I peer over. The tide is in and angry waves beat at the black feet of Isabella Rock.

I look around. The cold is biting into my bones already. A path runs around the back of the house and disappears into the pine trees. I have never seen trees so colossal. They seem to be powering themselves skyward, stabbing at the clouds. "Susannah?" I go to the edge of the deck. "Susannah!" The wind howls in through the treetops and sweeps my voice away.

High above the house, a gull cries, emptily. I have to stop panicking. They'll be inside. I didn't even check the rest of the house. And if they're not inside, she probably has him out front. She's a mother. She knows how to keep a toddler safe. She'll know to hold his hand, and not let him run on off along this slippery deck, or go anywhere near those steps. She'll know to watch him every second. Not to turn her back, even for a moment.

I hurry back into the house and down the corridor to what I think might be her bedroom. I knock. "Susannah?" Nothing. I try the handle, "Susannah? Finn?" I peek in. A big white bed. Huge windows. I close the door again.

I don't know if I slept for minutes or hours. But it's okay. They'll be around here somewhere. I open the coat closet, opposite her bedroom door. His snowsuit isn't there. Right, so they're outside. I go and open the front door and stand at the top of the stone steps leading down to the driveway. The rental car is parked behind an old Subaru.

"Susannah?" I bellow. My socks are wet and my feet are freezing. The seagulls call above, and the wind thrashes at the pines. Far off I can still hear the waves crashing on the rocks. The house is completely hemmed in by trees. "Susannah! Finn?"

My wet socks slither on the icy deck. It seems to run all around the building. I follow down the side of the house.

And then I see them.

Finn has his back to me, and is standing right in front of big windows, bundled in his red snowsuit, boots on this time, and gloves, and a hat. He is looking off down the deck, standing completely still, staring intently at something low down. Susannah crouches by his side, her arm protectively around his belly. She is looking at the same thing. I don't think I've ever seen my son stand so still. Then I spot what they're looking at. Just feet away from Finn is a large gray squirrel. It is giant, cat-sized. It has a nut or something in its paws and is nibbling on it, tail tip twitching.

At home, Finn has a *Squirrel Nutkin* board book, an awful dumbed-down version that would make Beatrix Potter spin in her grave, but he loves the pictures and likes to point at them and get me to say the names. He must feel, right now, as if his book has burst to life in front of him.

I want to go to him, but I mustn't spoil the moment. Then Susannah notices me. She turns her head, unsmiling, and her eyes are the color of the palest sea glass. At the movement, the squirrel shoots off and Finn lets out a shout—part objection, part thrill.

Susannah stands up and takes Finn by the hand. He turns and sees me.

"Mama!" he pulls away from her and runs toward me and I hug him and pick him up, his definite weight in my arms brings relief flooding through my body. My feet are numb, and the wind eats into my back but Finn is warm as a blanket. He presses a cheek against my face.

"Squoll," he says, his brown eyes bright. "Squoll!"

I kiss him. "I know! That was a really big squirrel. And it was eating a nut, wasn't it? Like Squirrel Nutkin."

Susannah comes up behind him. She holds herself stiffly, and there is something hostile in the tilt of her chin, as if she has been thinking about me while I've been asleep, and has found me wanting.

"Thanks for looking after him," I say. "He's obviously having the time of his life."

"Yeah. Feeling better?"

"Much. Thanks, Susannah. It's so good of you to do this. I'm not sure what time it is—did I sleep for a long time?"

"Almost two hours."

"Oh my God—two hours!" No wonder she is angry. "But you should have woken me up. You wanted to work!"

She stares at me for a second, her head slightly on one side, and then she reaches out a hand as if she's going to touch my face. Instinctively, I lean away from her hand. She drops it to her side.

Finn wriggles to be put down, then runs back to where the squirrel was. "Squoll!" he calls, in an old-fashioned "cooee" voice. "Squoll?" He squats, holding the railings with both hands, and peering into the trees, his hair blown this way and that.

She watches him, and a gust whips a few strands of her silvery hair across her cheek. It is the look of a grandmother—tender, proud, tinged with longing. Then she turns her eyes back to me and the warmth drains from them. "Go back inside, Kali. We'll come in, in a second. Put the kettle on. Go on—you're cold—go."

I glance at her, then at Finn. He is still squatting, hands on the deck railings, still calling "Squ-oll?" He'll have a fit if I try to drag him inside. This is exactly what he should be doing, breathing sea air, discovering wildlife. I shiver and wrap my arms around myself, but still I hesitate, moving from one frozen foot to the other.

"Go inside, Kali," she snaps, and I can tell she means it. She wants me gone.

There isn't an electric kettle, just a green enamel one that goes on the stove. As I put it there, I see a little Post-it, on the countertop, next to the range.

Outside,
S

I stand there for a few moments, staring at the Post-it. Now I feel silly, rushing around like that, with panic rising. What did I think she was going to do to Finn?

Her cramped writing is familiar from the postcards in my mother's drawer back in Sussex.

"Thinking of you today,
Susannah."

But why? Why on earth was Susannah thinking of my mother every year on the same day in May? I haven't asked. She isn't an easy person to question. But of course I must ask. Before I leave, I must find out what else she knows about my mother.

Through the archway I can see the tall windows on the other side of the front room, and through these I can see Finn's bright red snowsuit out on the deck, with Susannah bending next to him.

She really is remarkably good with him. It's really not what you'd expect. She seems like the kind of woman who would be impatient and dismissive of small children but she is so intensely focused on Finn, as if she really does have some biological claim to him.

Perhaps there is a grand-maternal body clock too. If so, then hers is ticking like a time bomb. And she is right to disapprove of me: What sort of mother has a moment of lunacy and gets on a plane to Canada? What sort of mother turns up with her toddler unannounced at a stranger's house on a winter's night? What sort of mother sleeps for two hours during the day, leaving her child on a cliff edge with someone she barely knows? No wonder Susannah is hostile. Then again, if she is that annoyed at being left in charge of Finn for so long, why did she send me inside? Why not just hand him back? Perhaps she feels he needs protecting, from me.

I realize that I'm doing it again—it's the old fear of inadequacy. From the moment Doug and I decided to try for a baby I began to be afraid that erratic mothering is passed down in the blood. And I have certainly been distracted here—I think about the vase, Finn's panicky wails, and the slammed-shut door. I really haven't been properly tuned into what he needs, not really. Maybe this is how it starts: little moments of neglect that multiply and join up and swell into full-on bad mothering.

But I'm being ridiculous. I may not be the perfect mother but I would never—ever—allow myself to treat Finn the way she treated me—loving him, then turning away; being there—then not. Right now, I am his fixed point; I am his, completely. And just for these few years, while he is small, he is mine, too. The image of a yin-yang ball pops into my head: the two of us curled around each other, forming one smooth sphere. I will not ever abandon him the way she abandoned me.

It suddenly occurs to me—genuinely for the first time—that Doug might have felt a bit left out. I've been trying so hard to be there for Finn, to be a better mother that I have sealed Doug out of our little sphere. I have given all my constancy to Finn and left Doug out in the cold. If anything, I loved Doug more after we had Finn—but day to day I have failed to show him this. Instead, I have resented him for working. For sleeping. For still having a career. Whatever has happened between us, I've definitely played my part.

I need to talk to him. When they come back in, I'll ask to borrow the house phone.

While the kettle heats up, I wander through to the living room and look at the shelves behind the Chihuly sculpture; big white cubes filled with books and objects. A ficus trails down from one of the highest shelves. Most are packed with books, but in one cube there's just a wooden Buddha and a framed Tibetan prayer. Another cube contains only three large, smooth, white pebbles, an oil burner and a carved wooden box, containing essential oils: bergamot, lavender, jasmine. In another cube there is a beautiful pottery plate decorated with blue fish.

I browse the cubes that contain her books. There are novels, many in hardcover, Pulitzer Prize winners, household names, mostly women—Nadine Gordimer, Margaret Forster, Toni Morrison, Maya Angelou, E. Annie Proulx. There is a large section of art history: two big cubes of it. In another, there's a whole chunk of poetry, everything from Milton to Sylvia Plath. One slim book, low down, catches my eye because I've seen it so recently. Its pale blue spine leaps out at me.

I pull it out. And then I just sit for a moment, and stare at it in my hands. It's the exact same edition. I turn it over. There is a piece of paper marking a page. Before I even open it I know what page it will be.

You Left Me.
You left me, sweet, two legacies,—
A legacy of love
A Heavenly Father would content,
Had He the offer of;
You left me boundaries of pain
Capacious as the sea,
Between eternity and time,
Your consciousness and me.

Not a eulogy from a daughter, and definitely not a wedding poem.

I flick to the front of the book. *Susannah Gillespie.* There is no date.

I re-read the poem. I wonder if Susannah sent this book to my mother, or the other way around. I look at the back. It's the same edition as the one in our house in Sussex, and it's Canadian. So, yes, Susannah must have sent it to my mother. And then I realize what I've been missing—of course. I can't believe I didn't work this out right away. They were on a California campus in the seventies surrounded by protests, feminist consciousness-raising groups, love-ins, streaking, psychedelic drugs. They were lovers.

It's like staring into a kaleidoscope, twisting the end, and waiting for the tiny fragments to shift and clatter and roll into their final coherent pattern. And yet, this pattern doesn't quite feel right, either. Or does it? I just don't know.

I'm just going to have to ask Susannah outright.

I hear movement by the front door, then the dogs' scuffling claws. A shriek rises from the kitchen and for a second I think it's a bird, trapped inside the house; then I realize it's the kettle's panicky whistle. And then I hear the front door open. The dogs burst past me to their food bowls, and Susannah is talking to Finn about squirrels. One dog laps water noisily in the kitchen.

"Hi!" I shove the postcard back in its place, thrust the book back on the shelf, and leap up. "The kettle's just boiling!" I run over and take it off the stove, and I hear Finn's voice, chattering nonsense back to Susannah as they open the closet to put away his red snow-suit and rain boots.

Southern California, Spring 1976

On the surface the only thing that changed was her routine, because, of course, she didn't go to Sea Park anymore. She heard the baby orca died after five days. It couldn't work out how to feed. They moved it to a separate tank and tried to feed it mashed up cream and fish through a tube but it starved to death within earshot of its distraught parents.

She couldn't discuss what had happened. Gray was away, which made it easier, and she simply told Susannah that she didn't need any more data on the dolphins. Susannah seemed to accept this as an explanation for Elena's sudden presence in the condo.

She told herself that she needed to think it through, rationally, before making any firm decisions or telling anybody, but really, her mind was made up as the film rolled to a close. In just under two weeks she'd be heading north to British Columbia. The researcher—Jonas—had offered her a ride, and a place on his friend's house boat for the summer. She could meet the others up there, and become part of the orca-mapping project. Really, there was no dilemma: she still had her small inheritance—she was going.

She spent a lot of time in her room, reading everything she could find about orcas. She read that their bodies were black and white to trick their prey—in the murky underwater world only the white part of the killer whale's body shows up—so they appear far smaller and less threatening than they really are. After reading a paper about the structure of the dorsal fin she realized that Orpheus's dorsal had collapsed, not through sickness, but through lack of use. In the wild, orcas constantly use their dorsal—they dive deep and often—and so the cartilage is strengthened and bolstered. Swimming circles in a shallow tank was nothing in comparison to the workout of swimming in the wild. It seemed likely to Elena that Orpheus's six-foot fin had simply atrophied in captivity.

She read that the orca survey researchers had already established that Pacific Northwest orcas were divided into two distinct races—residents and transients. Transients had more pointed fins, traveled in smaller groups, and ate marine mammals, whereas residents ate mainly fish, and socialized in large groups. Looking at the illustrations, it looked like Bella and Orpheus were resident orcas. There were, the survey estimated, about two hundred and eighty resident orcas left in the Pacific Northwest. Orpheus had been taken from the waters off eastern Iceland, but Bella was captured in Puget Sound. This meant that her family was among the counted whales—somewhere out there, right now, in the Salish Sea.

She read all the reports she could find from the Orca Survey and as she read them she understood what Jonas had been trying to tell her: this was far more than a population study. Identifying individual whales was going to allow for longitudinal studies into social relationships, travel patterns, habits—and communication. It was a way into this hidden world. The scientific potential was huge. She could become one of the first scientists—if not the first—to study orca communication in the wild.

When her head was packed with information, she'd walk down to the beach, and sit in the sand, watching pelicans swoop across the sky, or pods of pacific white-sided dolphins cut along the coast. She'd walk through the sand, digging her heels in to find Pismo clams or gather mussels from the tide pools. Then she'd take them home for Susannah to cook in garlic and butter. She had a growing list of questions for Jonas. The questions now filled half a notebook. He said he'd be back, and around campus for a week before they went north. She tried not to think about Graham, still in Europe, unaware. She found that she couldn't remember where exactly he was, or why he'd gone there. She had no idea how she was going to tell him about her decision. He might understand—she could explain it, and the rationale behind it, and he'd let her go because he had to, but it would hurt him.

The odd thing was that she couldn't bring herself to talk to Susannah about any of this. A couple of times, when they were swimming together, she thought she'd try to explain what was happening, but then she couldn't work out how to begin. After a while she realized what was stopping her from talking. Her instinct was telling her that Susannah wouldn't just disapprove; she would be angry. She would take this as some kind of personal affront or rejection. Lately, the friendship had taken on a confusing shape—she felt as if she did not fully understand its rules or parameters. The last thing Elena wanted was a messy confrontation with Susannah.

Elena hadn't spent much time in the condo before, and she was surprised to find that Susannah was hardly ever at the university. The guys rolled out of bed at nine every morning, blearily grabbed bagels or drank juice from the carton, and, leaving trails of crumbs and coffee, disappeared to their labs. But Susannah was always around. Her teaching commitments were obviously minimal—she only ever spent a couple of hours at a time in the studio. She said this was because every creative urge had dried up since she'd been in California; the light was all wrong, she needed dampness, clouds and drizzle; the dry heat and brightness made it impossible to work. But she didn't do much else, either.

She didn't seem to have other friends, or anywhere else to go. She seemed to be perpetually lingering: in the kitchen brewing another pot of coffee; chopping up a cobb salad for lunch; sitting on the patio with a sketchpad; or holding out a cold bottle of beer at the end of the day. Sometimes, Elena would come across her just sitting at the breakfast bar, preternaturally still, staring into space. It occurred to Elena that Susannah might be around all the time because of her. Lately, she had begun to feel waited for. Whenever she went into a room she half expected Susannah to step out of the shadows.

On the surface, everything was pretty much the same. At the end of every day, they'd walk along the road together and climb down the stone steps to the beach. They'd clamber over the rocks to their cove *and swim, and then they'd lie for a bit in the sand, chatting as the sun went down. Back at the condo, Susannah would cook.*

But one day, when she'd been down at the beach alone, Elena got back to the condo to find Susannah hurrying along the hallway toward the kitchen. She looked over her shoulder, sharply, as Elena stepped through the front door.

"Hi." Elena threw her sunglasses onto the table.

But Susannah didn't move, or speak.

"Are you okay?"

She said nothing. Then she turned, and walked, slowly, into the kitchen.

Elena went into her room and tossed her book on the bed. Then she saw that her journal was open on the duvet. She had hidden it, as always, in a box of tapes, before she went to the beach. She went into the kitchen, determined to confront Susannah, but she wasn't there. For once, she didn't come back 'til late. The next day, nothing was said. They went to the beach in the evening, as always. Though this time they swam more, and talked less.

The problem was that Elena just wasn't used to being around another person this much. During her whole time at the university she'd always lived on her own; even as an undergraduate she managed to get herself a single room. Her entire childhood had been solitary. This situation would be unbearably claustrophobic if it wasn't for the fact that in less than two weeks she'd be gone.

They'd probably stay in touch. Maybe they'd even visit each other. No doubt they'd write. They'd always have these shared memories of the condo and their evenings on the beach, and they really had connected; perhaps because of the parallels in their childhoods they had recognized something in each other that normally stays beneath the surface. But over the years that would fade too. They'd forget the uncomfortable stories, or the moments when they'd looked at each other, and understood, and not needed to say anything else. Elena wasn't sure how sustainable a friendship like this could ever be in the real world.

* * *

It was late afternoon, the day before she left, when it finally came to a head. Susannah knocked on Elena's bedroom door. "Hey—I made iced tea. You want some?"

"Well . . . actually . . . I'm kind of . . ." She dragged herself off the bed, and opened the door but Susannah was gone already, assuming she'd follow.

It was still very hot on the patio. Susannah had her eyes shut and her face tilted skyward. She was in cutoffs with her athletic brown legs stretched out, crossed at the ankles, barefoot as usual. The soles of her feet were dun-colored and dusty. Behind her, the branches of the apple tree burst with flaky pale blue petals.

Susannah didn't move or open her eyes as Elena approached, but her lips curled into a smile. On the wrought iron table the iced tea sat in two identical glasses, with stalks of mint. Elena felt the garden close in.

She didn't sit down. She had been intending to just slip out at dawn the next day, leaving a note. But there was something about that smile.

"Listen," she said. "You know what? I have some news: I'm quitting my PhD. I'm leaving town."

Susannah's eyes snapped open.

For a moment, all the garden sounds—a buzzing bee, chirping birds, the breeze rustling through the apple blossom—seemed to pause. Susannah slowly drew her legs in.

"I'm heading up to British Columbia. I've . . . well, tomorrow, actually."

"You're leaving tomorrow?"

"Well," Elena pushed her hair out of her eyes, scooping it all up behind her head and tying it there with an elastic band from her wrist, too tight. "Yes. I guess I am."

"Oh. How long for?"

"A while. I'm not sure."

"You're not sure?"

"I don't know."

"What are you saying, Elena?"

"I'm saying it's all wrong here—this whole thing, my life here, my work—Sea Park—it's all deeply wrong. I shouldn't have been a part of it in the first place."

"*Your life here is deeply wrong?*" *Susannah's face froze.*

"*At Sea Park. I can't be a part of that anymore.*"

"*You aren't a part of Sea Park—you're just an observer.*"

"*Observation is participation.*"

"*Yeah?*" *Susannah's lip curled. "And who told you that?*"

"*What? Nobody told me anything.*"

"*Well,*" *Susannah took a long breath in. "This is kind of dramatic, Elle, I've got to tell you.*"

The air between them tightened a notch. Maybe it was because Susannah had been in the condo first—standing in the kitchen that day, doling out the eggs—but she'd always assumed a sort of unspoken dominance. Elena realized that, since they met, she had been tiptoeing around Susannah, not wanting to stir anything up, unconsciously, perhaps, making sure to be even-tempered and calm. Well, this was the end of it. Elena looked right into Susannah's furious pale eyes. "It may seem dramatic to you. Susannah. But it seems perfectly sensible to me."

A sweet, fresh smell drifted from the apple blossom. Warblers sang in the trees. A breeze rustled the leaves and lifted a few strands of Susannah's golden hair. Petals drifted down between them, like confetti.

Then Susannah said, "Tomorrow? You're leaving tomorrow?"

"*I've been offered a ride . . . one of the researchers is heading.*"

"*So when were you going to tell me?*"

"*I'm telling you now. I really only just decided. I'll honor the rest of the rent, don't worry . . .*"

"*The rent?*" *for a moment, she looked confused. Then she straightened. "You only just decided? Really?*"

Elena remembered her journal. She opened her mouth to say something about it, then decided not to. In a way, Susannah's prying made things easier.

"*So, what exactly are you planning to do up in British Columbia?*"

"*I'm going to study killer whales in the wild. There's a photo identification project going on—a survey of all the orcas in the region—and I'm going to help.*" *She began to pick a small scab near her thumb. She could feel Susannah staring at her, rooted to her chair. "But ideally, I want to listen to them too. I want to record them. Maybe I'll see if I* can get funding." She picked the scab again, it was coming loose. "But I'm not sure about the practicalities yet."

"It all sounds admirable, Elle. But what's the rush? Why not finish your PhD? You can't just quit. You have . . . you have commitments here."

"But I don't want to finish my PhD. That's the whole point. That's what I'm telling you. It all feels artificial. I don't want to understand dolphin play behavior if it's just evolved as a response to captivity. I'm not even sure I know what play means under those circumstances . . . it's just . . ." She looked up at the sky, at the blossom swelling behind Susannah's head. "This all feels like a great big lie."

"A lie?" Susannah tilted her head to one side, with her lips thin and tight. Her irises were almost the same shade as the blossom. It occurred to Elena that they were both talking about different things. "You know what's a lie, Elle?" Susannah continued, "This whole conversation. That's what's a lie. This isn't about whales, or your PhD, is it?"

"What are you talking about?"

"You know what I'm talking about."

"I really don't," Elena said. "I really have no idea."

The scab had begun to bleed, a little red bubble that quickly turned into a streak—way too much blood for such a tiny scab. She sucked at it.

"What about Gray?"

"Graham will be fine. He's busy—he's in Europe right now. He's applying for some . . . something . . . he's . . ."

"You haven't told him either have you?" Then suddenly, Susannah sat up tall, her eyes brightened. "Okay. Wait. I get it. I get it!" The tension in her face melted. "I get what's happening here. You're afraid. You're freaking out about the marriage proposal—."

"Actually, no—no. I'm not freaked out about that. And this isn't about fear. I'm not running away from him—or anything else. And I've never been less afraid in my life."

"Then you're totally deluded."

Elena dashed the blood on her jeans. "Deluded—how?"

"Wait—you're bleeding." Susannah reached out a hand. "Look— you're bleeding everywhere."

"It's just an old scab."

"But there's blood all over your hand, look at it." She reached across the table and her thumb ring caught the light. It hovered in the air between them for a second like a glinting silver weapon.

Elena swiped her hand away. "It's nothing. Stop! Okay? Just stop this." Her T-shirt was sticking to her back. The sky was too blue, and the sunlight made her eyeballs ache. The smell of the apple blossom was becoming sickly.

Susannah stood up, holding out her muscular brown arms. "You can't just leave. You can't just go away like this, on some crazy impulse." Elena smelled the mustiness of Susannah's armpits. She stepped backward, out of reach.

"This is not a crazy impulse. This is completely right. This is what I'm for."

"What you're FOR?"

"Jesus! YES."

Susannah dropped her arms back down and leaned on the table, with her head bowed. "Why can't you just be honest?"

"I am being honest!" Elena heard herself shout. "And . . . and this— and everything else in my life—has absolutely nothing to do with you Susannah! Nothing at all!"

Susannah's chin snapped back as if she'd been punched. "Fine," she muttered, "but what about Graham?"

"What about him?" She should have done what her instinct told her to do, and just gone, at dawn. This was exactly what she'd wanted to avoid.

"Have you told Gray?"

"I told you, he's away. Listen, I'm not expecting you to understand this, okay? I can see it probably does seem impulsive to you—but it's the right thing for me."

"Finishing your PhD is the right thing."

"You are not," Elena growled, "my mother."

Then before it could disintegrate any further, she turned and walked off, through the kitchen and into her room, shutting the door.

She half expected to hear Susannah's feet thunder after her. She wished the bedroom door had a lock. She sat on the bed. She could hear the warblers outside, and far off, the waves. The condo was eerily silent. Susannah must have stayed in the yard. She ripped the elastic out of her hair, and scratched at her scalp with her nails. Her hands, she noticed, were actually shaking. Somewhere in the condo the phone rang. She really had no idea why Susannah was being so intense. So possessive. It was crazy. They'd only been friends for a few months.

She looked at the tapes and notes in unopened boxes around her. There was all the rest of it, too, in her office on campus: stacks and stacks of dolphin research. Perhaps Susannah was right. If she stayed, then in six months, maybe nine, she'd have a PhD. Then she could get a job and funding to research whatever she wanted. She could see why all this would seem lunatic.

But her life here was over. She didn't want a PhD. She couldn't spend any more nights in this condo. She needed to go north and listen to wild killer whales.

She got up off the bed, grabbed the chair, and hauled down her backpack from the top of the closet. It smelled stale inside. She began to shove things into it: her two thick winter sweaters, barely used since leaving Seattle six years ago, all four pairs of jeans, cutoffs, sneakers, her only pair of wool socks and walking boots, all her T-shirts, underwear. Telling Susannah had been a huge mistake. Susannah couldn't be expected to get this. Nobody could. Nobody except maybe Jonas, and the others up there in British Columbia, people whose names she didn't even know yet but who would understand.

At one point, as she stuffed handfuls of notes into a box, she heard Susannah call through the door—nervously, softly—with a light tap.

"Elle?"

"Yeah?"

"I'm sorry."

"It's okay. It's fine. I'm sorry too."

"Can I come in?"

"Maybe later, okay? I'm just packing right now. I'll come find you in a bit?"

There was silence, then she heard Susannah's bare feet move away down the hall.

She'd leave everything in the garage and deal with it when the lease ran out. She got out a roll of trash bags, ripped one off, and began shoving her files and tapes into it—and as she filled each bag she felt a sense of growing lightness.

Graham would be okay. Better than okay. Without her, he would lead a successful and orderly life. She pictured him with a pretty English wife and several well-spoken children, a steady career in London or Edinburgh. Without her, his future would unfold as neatly as one of his architectural drawings.

When he had proposed, lying in his bed with his long arms around her, and his breath warming the crown of her head, he'd said, "We should get married because I'll be in London next year and I don't want to be without you."

It sounded like an arrangement, but when she looked up she saw the hope in his fine, gray eyes, and she said, carefully, "I don't think I'm ready for marriage, Gray. Nor are you. We're too young."

"Then I'll wait—as long as you want."

For a moment she thought he might be about to cry, but of course, Graham never cried. He just looked at her, with his jaw set in determination. She closed her eyes and kissed him.

Telling him face-to-face would only make this harder for him. And she couldn't wait—she needed that ride. She needed to go. She kept the letter brief and factual.

She would mail it as she crossed campus at sunrise. Nothing else mattered now—not Graham, not Susannah, not the boxes stuffed with years of research, or the wasted rent money, or the abandoned office. Her tipping point had been reached: she was already gone.

CHAPTER SEVEN

Susannah washes her hands then puts on a striped apron. She rolls up her sleeves and I notice a rub of clay on her forearm as her silver bangles clink. Her face is ruddy from the fresh air.

Finn is on my lap, chewing a chunk of bread, and attacking a notepad with a pen, mainly jabbing holes in it. Susannah takes a large steel chef's knife and begins to chop chives.

"Are you sure I can't help you?"

She looks up at me, briefly, but doesn't reply. It's as if she's somewhere else, not even seeing me.

She looks more masculine in the daylight. She has a straight nose, broad shoulders, and a very firm chin. She is looking down, and the lines at the corners of her mouth make her look profoundly sad.

The dogs are in their beds by the window. One is sleeping, the other lies with ears half-pricked, big eyes watching her in case she drops something edible. The hopeful expression suddenly makes me think of Max. He was always in the kitchen with my mother, saucer eyes fixed on her hands as she cooked.

And then I remember how we dug the hole that awful spring evening. Alice was inside—maybe too young to cope with this grim task. I was about twelve years old. It was rare that my mother and I should do something without Alice. I remember, despite the awfulness of what we had to do, feeling glad that she chose me to help her, and not Alice.

My parents got Max when they first arrived in England so he had been there since I could remember. In the earliest picture I've ever seen of myself, I'm about one, sitting on the floor next to Max as a puppy, both of us looking up, enthusiastically, at the camera.

My mother and I were both crying as we dug, carelessly shoveling through sprouting bulbs, slicing into daffodils or crocuses. But then, as we removed more layers of soil, her tears began to escalate. Then she sank onto her knees and her crying became a sort of rage—sobs vomited up one after the other, faster and faster, and I stopped crying then; I put a hand on her back but she just kept sobbing as if I wasn't there. Things were surging dangerously out of her, spiraling noises I'd never heard before, and I knew this couldn't be about Max anymore.

I thought about running to the house and getting Alice, six-year-old Alice, or calling Dad at work, or maybe banging on a neighbor's door. But then, abruptly, she stopped. She straightened as if someone had injected her spine with metal. She got up, and without even looking at me, she walked away, back into the house.

She left her spade in the dirt, and our dead dog, wrapped in a towel, by the half-dug hole. I finished digging the hole as best I could, and rolled him in. His body made a deep, echoey thud as it hit the bottom, and some of the towel came off so I could see the tip of his blond tail, and I had the urge to leap in and unwrap him again, to check that he wasn't still alive, that this wasn't all a dreadful mistake. But I didn't. I scraped soil over him with the spade. The tip of his tail was the last thing to disappear. I went back into the house, took off my rain boots, and washed my muddy hands in the downstairs sink. My own tears had gone and my mind felt dense and heavy, like clay.

She wasn't in the kitchen. There is a stable door into the living room and the bottom half was shut. On tiptoe, I peered over the top. She was on the sofa with her back to me. Alice was in her lap. She was stroking Alice's silky hair with one hand. Alice looked up. She had a chocolate digestive biscuit in one hand. Our mother's face was buried in Alice's neck. There was chocolate around my sister's mouth.

Susannah's dog has given up hope of scraps. It has put its nose back onto its paws again. I have no idea why I'm sitting in this woman's kitchen, with these painful memories rising up in my mind. I should say something. It is rude to just sit here and watch her make us lunch, but I can't think of anything to say and anyway, she doesn't seem bothered by silence.

I wonder, again, about the things she must know about my mother—and maybe about me. Did she know me as a baby? I have never even seen a picture of myself as a newborn. I suppose my parents lost any pictures in the move to England. Maybe Susannah has a picture of me somewhere. I should ask. I should also, of course, ask her about their relationship. Why not?

As an interviewer, I should be able to find the right questions. I should be able to put Susannah at ease, open her up, get her to tell me more about my mother's past, their relationship—those California days. But I can't quite work out how to start. There is something deeply forbidding about Susannah, an invisible carapace. I should be able to crack this of course—I interview people for a living, but the people I interview have volunteered to tell their story. They want—need—to open up. Instinct tells me that if I ask Susannah directly about her relationship with my mother, I will get nothing.

Finn has finished his bread, and is now eating the pen, wriggling to get down off my lap.

"Okay." I put him on the floor and take the pen out of his hand.

"Mine!" he cries. "Mine!"

"Hey! Look at the dogs." I point at them. "I think they're hungry."

"Dog." He toddles toward the sleeping retriever.

I get up and hover behind him as he waddles around the kitchen island, past Susannah's legs, and over to the dogs. He hurls himself face down on them, diving into a mound of fur. I am left standing next to Susannah.

"He really loves your dogs."

She says nothing.

The sky outside has darkened. The pines thrash as if trying to escape the murderous clutches of an invisible giant.

Then she looks at me, suddenly. "You eat eggs don't you?" she says. "How's the stomach?"

"Fine. Thanks. Fine now. I'm starving actually." I sense that it will irritate her if I offer to help again, but I feel as if I'm standing too close to her.

"Shall I make us some tea?"

"You English and your tea."

I suppose she's right—it's obvious that I am filling an awkward gap with tea. She gestures with the knife tip at a cupboard above the sink. I go and open it, and move boxes of Yogi and Tazo teas around: Peppermint. Zen. Chamomile. Calm. Chai. Jasmine Green. "Do you want some Susannah?"

"Nope."

I decide against tea, and go and sit on the stool next to the island. I am not going to let her intimidate me. I think about asking if I can use her phone to call Doug. I imagine her shrug "Sure" and the gesture to the phone that's on the wall by the fridge. It would be impossible to talk to him with her in the room, and Finn running around. Even in the living room she'd hear everything—and I'd have to keep Finn off the ceramics in there. Her back is to me and she is reaching up into another cupboard with one strong arm.

Finn is still rolling around in the dog basket, giggling.

There's a bowl of almonds on the counter. It is wide and white and decorated with swooping, moss-colored birds. I take a few and crunch on them.

"I did make that." She nods at the bowl.

"It's beautiful."

She goes across to the fridge. She moves as if wading through water with an urn balanced on her head. It is odd that someone with such hard edges can make such a beautiful bowl, and move with such grace. Her wasp hair clasp is coming loose, slanting in a mass of graying waves.

"Susannah," I take a breath. "I've been wondering, about you and my mother. Were you very close?"

I see her jaw tighten. She gets out cheese and eggs.

It takes all my willpower to leave the silence hanging.

She puts the food down on the counter and comes over to the breakfast bar. Then she rests both hands on the edge of it. Her back is to Finn, which is good as he has his hands in the dogs' water bowl now but I don't want to stop him, because I don't want her not to speak. I can't look right at her because I know if I do I'll feel smaller—and then the balance will shift, and she won't talk to me the way I want her to. I gaze past her, at my son as he tips the water slowly onto the kitchen tiles, watching it pool and spread.

I can feel her eyes on my face.

I take another almond and crunch into it with my front teeth, very slowly, and then look at the remaining half in my hand.

"Yes. Your mother and I were very close, Kali," she says, at last. Her voice is low, and slightly spooky.

"Hmmm?" I nod, and chew some more. Behind her, Finn opens a cupboard.

"She *is* my dearest friend."

I decide not to pick her up on the present tense. "Were you . . . ?"

"What?"

But I can't do it. I can't ask directly whether they were lovers. "It's just odd that she never talked about you at all. Did something happen between you? Did you fall out over something?"

"She didn't tell you a thing about me, did she?" She sounds pleased, as if stating this to herself, rather than asking me a question.

"No, nothing at all. Not that I can remember anyway."

"Huh. Yeah, well, I guess Elena's better than me at cutting off." Her voice is brittle and suddenly loud, and with a harsh laugh she reaches out and picks an almond off the plate. It is disconcerting, the way she keeps referring to my mother in the present tense. The light glances off her silver thumb ring. I force myself to keep quiet. First rule of interviewing: shut up. But she doesn't elaborate. Behind her, Finn opens and closes the cupboard door a few times.

"But I wonder why?" I say, eventually. "Why did she cut off like that?"

She turns the almond around between her thumb and forefinger, as if weighing up how much to give me. "I guess," she says slowly, "she needed to put everything behind her—me, friends, research, everything. She needed to make a new space for herself in the world. It was easier that way. She had a new life out there in England, and maybe that was the only way she could handle it."

This seems extreme, even for my mother.

"But you wrote to each other? You were in touch?"

She opens her mouth, as if to reply, but then her face falls, as if someone has let go of the strings. For a moment, she stares at her hands. "Constantly," she says.

I think about the drawer full of cards she sent, year after year. I should ask her about that. But instinct tells me that if I go there this conversation will be over. It strikes me that in this respect, at least, Susannah is a lot like my mother.

She chucks the nut into her mouth. "I always had this image of your home in Sussex," she says. "This little English thatched cottage, with roses and hedgerow and apple trees and sparrows. Is that what it's like?"

"Well, there's an apple tree." An image of my mother with the chainsaw flashes into my mind. She would prune it herself, every spring, after it flowered. She did our neighbor's cherry tree too. My mother actually owned a chainsaw. She knew how to take the motor apart and clean the bits, and put it all back together.

"But it's a thatched cottage, right?"

"No, sadly not. It's a Victorian red brick and flint, directly at the bottom of the village high street, with a roundabout and a signpost outside it and roads going off on either side. I always half expected a car to careen down the street and smash right through our garden wall and into our front room. It's actually amazing that it's never happened."

But she isn't listening anymore. She is staring at her hands. "I miss her," she says, "every day."

"Did you ever consider visiting?"

She laughs, as if this is preposterous.

"I suppose you were very busy," I try to keep to my neutral interviewer's voice. It doesn't work. She gives me a dismissive look and says nothing. Finn is taking things out of the cupboard now, plastic bowls. He looks very serious, squatting, with his bangs in his eyes. If I go over to stop him, he'll object, and we'll all get diverted.

"So," she says, "she only lived in one place then, after she took you to England?"

I nod. "The house my father bought, before she came."

"Yeah, well, I guess she wanted stability. She'd had a lot of . . . a lot of . . . disruption in her life. She couldn't handle any more change."

I sit up straight. "Really? What disruption?"

But that's it—her face snaps shut. "We should eat," she says. She picks up a whisk. There is a loud bashing noise, and glass shatters. I leap up. Finn is standing, horrified, staring at his hands, swaying slightly. And there is blood. On his hands. Shards of glass lie all around him, a silver frame at his feet. He opens his mouth and wails. I hurl myself across the kitchen.

*

Susannah cracks eggs, sharply, one after another into a big ceramic bowl. She only uses one hand, and as she cracks each egg she swoops the hand up and lets the yellow yolk trail its mucus then fall—slap— into the bowl. It is almost two o'clock.

Finn is sleeping on the sofa, now, with cushions on the floor in case he topples off. It wasn't a deep cut, just a surface scratch on the soft skin of his palm. He screamed for a bit while I washed it, dabbed it dry, and put antiseptic on it, and then covered it with a Band-Aid from Susannah's first aid kit. But he stopped crying when Susannah gave him a chocolate chip cookie.

There was glass everywhere. The frame was ruined. As I dealt with Finn's scratch, Susannah swept up the debris with a dustpan and brush. The black and white photo—it looked like a whale—lay reproachfully on the countertop.

For a while, Finn fussed and whined and wouldn't be put down—but wouldn't be held—and his eyes became red-rimmed, his movements more and more jerky. I paced up and down the kitchen, but he wouldn't settle and eventually I realized that it wasn't about the scratch; he just needed a nap.

It took half an hour, sitting by the sofa, patting his back, singing "Baa Baa Black Sheep," but he fell asleep eventually, with his cheek on his bunny, his butt in the air.

I watch her break the last egg and toss the broken shells in the garbage can.

"I'm so sorry," I say, "about the picture of the whale. Is the photo itself damaged?" It isn't on the counter anymore.

She stops what she's doing, but she doesn't look at me. She just stares at the pan, and then she pours the eggs in.

"I feel really bad that I let him break something else. Obviously, I'd like to replace the frame."

"Weren't you watching him?" Her voice is dry. "Didn't you see what he was doing?"

"Well, yes. I mean, I could see him by the cupboard. I thought it was a Tupperware cupboard—I thought he was just playing with plastic tubs, and we were talking. I didn't think there would be a silver picture frame in there—"

"No," she interrupts, still staring oddly at the pan. "Well. I guess you weren't watching him closely enough, huh?"

I can feel my shoulders stiffen. Who is this woman to lecture me on how to look after my own child? But of course, I'm in her house, and he just broke another of her belongings. I force myself to sound deferential. "I'm really sorry, Susannah. You're absolutely right. I should have watched him more closely; it was silly of me. I didn't see him pick up the whale picture." Then I realize that the picture Finn just broke is the one I was looking at this morning—the photo of the orca launching itself out of the water. It was on the sideboard with the other pictures. She must have put it away to keep it safe, though she didn't put any of the other pictures away. Just the whale.

"No," she hisses. "I guess you didn't see, did you, Kali?" She still isn't moving. She is holding the spatula and her knuckles, I notice, have turned white. "He could have slashed himself right open on that glass. He could have given himself a terrible injury."

"Please," I try to sound unthreatening, placatory. "Please let me pay for a new frame." She doesn't respond—just stands there, gripping the spatula. She probably put the photo in the cupboard because it's precious, and she didn't want him to pull it down. No wonder she's angry. "Please," I try again, "It would make me feel a lot better to replace it."

"Oh Kali," she turns her head, ever so slowly, and fixes her bleached-out eyes on mine. "I don't want your *money*."

Chapter Eight

The omelet oozes cheddar and chunks of fleshy tomato; it is flecked with chives and black pepper. I make myself eat more slowly this time, pausing for sips of water. Neither of us speaks. I try to see all this from her perspective. She's right. I have been distracted, definitely. I haven't been as vigilant with Finn as I should have been. This is a house full of expensive breakables and I have brought a toddler here, and then failed to watch him closely. I have to be more alert. I need to watch him every second. The notion of Finn near the Chihuly makes me feel positively ill.

She has obviously hidden the whale photo again, already, but I can't see how breaking the glass would damage the actual photo. And the frame must be replaceable. But I can see that this is not just about a silver frame.

She has had enough of us. That's what this is. I can't blame her. We should leave. I want to leave. But I also want to know what she knows about my mother. It's obvious that she's hiding something. If I go without finding out what she's hiding, I may never know.

I think about her hand gripping the spatula. She probably won't ever tell me the truth. Perhaps this is futile. Maybe when Finn wakes up, I should just pack our things. We could get the last ferry back.

I fork some omelet into my mouth. At least now I know where my mother learned to tie nautical knots.

I can hear Susannah chewing her food. I can't bring myself to look, but I can feel her eyes on me.

"So," I force myself to raise my head. She is, indeed, staring at me. "Susannah, I'd love to hear more about my mother before I head off. I should get the afternoon ferry back to Vancouver—but I'd love to know what she was like when you knew her."

"Oh you don't have to leave," she says. She sounds suddenly friendly, as if the photo incident is trivial. "I was upset about the child back there, but you don't have to run away now. You've come such a long way. Stay another night, at least."

"Oh. Well. That's kind. Thanks."

She chews on, slowly, very straight-backed, fork in one hand, the other splayed next to her plate.

I suddenly have the feeling, again, that she is toying with me—a push-me, pull-you game. But why? I am tying myself up in knots here. I blink and rub my eyes. I am tired, still, despite the long sleep this morning. Behind her, the sky outside the French windows is growing heavier and darker. Maybe she's right. I could stay another night, get over the jet lag, maybe find out some interesting things about my mother, and then leave first thing in the morning. I try to smile.

"Susannah, how long did my mother live up here?"

"Here?" She puts down her fork, wipes her mouth with a napkin. "Oh she never lived here."

"But you said . . ."

"She was living farther north mainly. She never came here, to Spring Tide. I didn't even live here in those days. I lived in Vancouver."

"Oh? Oh. You were living in different places?"

"We were roommates in California. That's how we met. There. Not here. You really didn't know anything at all about your mother's life did you, Kali?"

"No." I don't know why I have to keep persuading her of this. Does she think I'm pretending ignorance?

"I can't believe she never said a word." She's looking at me, but she sounds as if she's talking to herself.

"I never even knew she studied killer whales."

"She didn't keep up with the latest research?"

"I have no idea. I don't think so. But maybe she did, and never told me."

"Well then, Kali," she sits back. "How about we start with what you *do* know about your mother's past?"

"What I know?" I push away my almost-empty plate. "Very little. That's why I came to find you. She absolutely hated talking about the past. She wouldn't tell me anything, in fact. I just know the bare bones. I know she was an only child, and that my grandmother died when she was little." As I talk, I realize our roles have reversed—she's the one asking questions and I'm opening up. "In fact, I was sort of hoping you might be able to help me piece some things together, if you know anything? Did she ever talk about her childhood with you?"

She looks at her fork, picks it up again, and stabs a tomato with it.

"She wouldn't even let me ask questions," I continue. "She'd just snap at me—'I don't know' or 'I don't remember.' On a good day she'd say, 'It makes me sad to look back.' I suppose I stopped asking pretty early on. Then, as an adult, when I should have pushed her for more information, I didn't because we just didn't have conversations like that. It felt too . . . risky . . . We had managed a sort of truce, we were reasonable and polite to each other—and I probably didn't want to risk that."

Susannah swallows her food with a gulp as if she's just thought of something. "You have a sister? Alice, right? Did she talk to your sister?"

"They were much closer." I take a sip of water and force myself to stop talking. "Oh."

"But Alice says she didn't tell her anything either."

I can see the relief in her eyes, now, but I'm not sure why.

"So," she says, in an almost friendly voice, "You want me to tell you about your grandparents? Is that it? Fill you in a bit on your family history?"

"Yes, well, God—definitely. Can you? If you know anything, I'd love to hear it."

"It's not a pretty story, Kali."

For a moment, I wonder whether to tell her about my visit to Harry Halmstrom. Then I decide not to. She'd only think I was unhinged. I lean forward, "No—that's okay—please—I really want to know everything you know about my grandparents."

"Sure. Okay. So. Your grandfather was violent. A wife beater. He beat your grandmother, but not your mother. He was a drinker."

I feel as if she's leaned over and punched me. I don't know what I was expecting, but it wasn't this. "Oh god. That's . . . that's . . . horrible."

"He was drunk and at the wheel of the car when the accident happened."

"What accident?"

"When your grandmother was killed?"

"My grandmother died in a *car accident*?" I realize then that I'd always imagined that my mother's mother died from some tragic and somehow old-fashioned illness, like tuberculosis. In absence of facts, I have apparently invented a family medical history.

"Wow," Susannah says. "She really told you nothing, huh? Your grandparents were coming back from a night out in Seattle and he'd been drinking; he veered across four lanes and smashed into a tree. Your grandmother was thrown out of the car and died instantly. He staggered out with a few scratches. Your mother was eight years old at the time."

"Jesus," I sit back. "This is horrific." I don't want to ask the next question, but I make myself. "Was my mother in the car too?"

"No, of course not. She was home alone. She told me it got really late, and they didn't show up, and then the police came to the house. She hid in her mother's closet, because she was scared she'd done something wrong."

For a moment, I can't speak. I picture my mother as a terrified, abandoned little girl, cowering in a closet on the night her mother died and it is unbearable. This, presumably, is what my father wanted to tell me about, when he cornered me on the stairs. This would certainly explain my mother's erratic behavior, her sadness about the past, her unwillingness to talk about it. She would have been badly damaged by such a childhood trauma.

I wonder if I have found the root of our issues at last. Perhaps something dark and unconscious was going on for her—maybe I reminded her of herself as a child—we looked so similar. Maybe that was it? Or maybe I looked like her father. These things would explain, to some extent, why she couldn't cope with me, but was always such an uncomplicated mother to Alice, tall, blonde, calm Alice. I suddenly want to call my sister. Does Alice know any of this? This is ghastly.

Worst of all is that my mother is gone and I will never be able to ask her about this or tell her that I understand, and I'm sorry. This explains why she leaped at the chance to marry my father and become English, and live in a Sussex village and paint and make shepherd's pies, and never, ever go back to the States. I look up at Susannah. She is watching me. She sinks her canines into a hunk of granary bread.

"Thank you for telling me. This actually explains a lot," I say.

She shrugs and chews. Then something occurs to me. What if my mother just pretended that her father was dead. What if he is in fact still alive? Could Harry Halmstrom be the man that Susannah has just described? Maybe he changed his name to Harry. But, I'm being silly—how did he end up in Vancouver? Of course, Alice is right. I have to stop filling the gaps with my own stories.

"What?" she says. "What is it?"

"Nothing. It's just that, before I came here, I went to this old people's home in Vancouver. This probably sounds crazy to you—but I went to meet this old man because I thought he might be a relative. He's ninety-three years old, and his name is Harry Halmstrom and Halmstrom is a very uncommon name—so I wondered . . . But of course it couldn't be him because my grandfather is dead, isn't he? And his name wasn't Harry it was Theodore. So I don't know why I thought . . ."

She puts the bread down. "You did *what*?" Her face has gone the color of construction paper.

"I know. It was a bit silly of me to think that just because of the name . . . I don't know why I went but I suppose I was curious, because Halmstrom is an unusual name and . . . no, but really, the truth is I just needed an excuse to leave England."

"Your mother's father died," She fixes her eyes on mine. "He died."

"Oh. Right. Well. Yes, I thought so. But the slightly disturbing thing was this old man seemed to recognize me—but maybe he didn't. He also said lunatic things about drowning and murder. My sister thinks I must have given him the name and he picked up on it. He was pretty senile, and extremely old."

Susannah looks stunned, as if I've leaned across the table and slapped her.

"Yes, well, I suppose it was a bit mad of me to go there."

She closes her eyes and her nostrils flare. She is breathing deeply and slowly. I see her belly rise and then fall again. Yoga breathing. Lines bracket her mouth, her brow remains creased in a frown, and her neck is very straight. Her face is severe, even in repose, as if her features are lodged in their defensive positions. Then her eyes open again. "Your mother's father died just before she went to college, Kali."

"I know," I say. "Anyway, can you tell me anything more about my grandmother? What was Katherine like?"

She leans forward, elbows on the table. "Terrified of your grand-father I'd imagine. Your mother told me he'd drink, come home, and hit her—on the body, not her face, so nobody saw the marks—people knew, of course—neighbors, friends—but no one did a thing to stop him. They just accepted that this was what some men did. Your grandmother sounded like a frightened person, but kind and loving. You know what, though, Kali? When I met Elena she was actually okay—despite all the crap. She'd been through it, but she was an incredibly resilient person. She was so strong. Some people can do that—they can defy the past. Your mother was one of those people. She was determined to live life and follow her heart and be afraid of nothing. I loved that about her. It made her pig-headed, but she was so fearless."

This doesn't sound like my mother at all. I think about her daily life—the school run, walking the dog, painting the sea again and again and again. Her life was all about routine, repetition and pre-dictability. In fact, this drove me wild as a teenager. I wanted to push at her boundaries and break her boring rules. It was a pretty stan-dard adolescent rebellion but now I know she came out here and chased killer whales across a wild ocean; took massive risks when she was not much more than a teenager herself. Why did she allow her life to get so small and domestic?

I think about my life in Oxford: my ever-shrinking job. Play-group. Sainsburys. Mommy and Me Music. Fishfingers. I never did get to India. Despite everything, my life has become as domestic as my mother's.

Then again—where am I now? On the rim of a new continent, facing out.

I suddenly remember my father in the stairwell—his talk of "secrets." And I make myself ask it because this is the only chance I'll ever get to know the truth.

"Did my grandfather abuse my mother, Susannah?"

"Oh no." She looks at her hands on the table. "Not physically, if that's what you mean. It was more neglect really. He was old-fashioned, strict, and away a lot—he sold logging equipment, you knew that, right? He left her with strangers; sitters, neighbors. Then, from the age of about fourteen, he left her to fend for herself when he went away. He didn't drink so much after the accident but she sure as hell didn't like him. He had no idea what to do with a sad little girl. She told me that when he died she felt relief. I guess it's impossible to forgive the person who robbed you of your mother." Her eyes suddenly flick to my face. She looks startled—guilty—as if she's said something appalling, and behind her eyes I glimpse the same twitching fear that I saw when I first walked into her house.

I wonder what has happened in Susannah's life to make her this way. Maybe all this—the beautiful house, the art, the thriving gallery—is her defiance of some equally nasty past. What sort of a mother did Susannah have? And what sort of a mother did she then become?

She pushes her hair back up into the wasp clasp at the base of her neck and glances over her shoulder, through the French windows. "There's a storm coming." She closes her eyes and takes a long breath as if drawing the storm toward her. When she opens them, she does so slowly, her eyes rising up beneath slowly lifting lids.

"Kali," she says, almost lazily, "why did you have such a hard time getting along with your mother?"

"Oh? I don't know. I really don't. It's hard to explain." It's always like this when I try to describe my relationship with my mother—there is really no way to document it clearly, probably because I have never fully understood it myself.

"Well," she says, "how about you give me some examples."

"Oh. I don't know . . . Okay. The thing is, she could be great; she really could be a great mother. When she was on my side it felt amazing. When I was about fourteen, I was suspended from school for writing rude things about my geography teacher. My mother and I sat in the principal's room together, and she had to read this thing I'd written. I was quite scared, waiting for her to get angry. The principal said some sanctimonious things, but my mother still just sat there. Finally, she looked at him and said, 'If you're going to teach them this sort of language you should at least teach them how to spell the words properly.'"

Susannah's face lights up. "Yeah, right. She was never very good with authority figures."

"Yes, well, what I mean is—she was complicated. We were complicated together. She could be on my side, like that, totally an ally. But it never lasted. I just never knew where I was with her. We could be fine and then this cloud would descend and she'd withdraw as if I'd committed a horrible crime and she couldn't bear to look at me, or be anywhere near me. That was undermining. It felt unsafe. It probably made things harder that she and Alice got along so well. The two of them were completely harmonious. But I suppose we just clashed. People do, don't they? We brought out the worst in each other."

"Huh," she nods. "So that's why you're obsessed with her then? You thought she didn't love you enough?"

"What? No. I don't know if I'm *obsessed*. And I don't think she didn't love me enough. I know she loved me. It's just . . . it's a lot more complicated than that." But I feel the old resentments begin to surface. It all seems worse now that I am a mother myself. Even if I had ten children I can't imagine ever allowing Finn to believe that I preferred one of his siblings.

Susannah is still looking at me, eyebrows raised. I feel as if she is rather enjoying watching me wrestle with all this at her kitchen table.

I make my voice lighter. "I really was a vile teenager and Alice was angelic, clever, pretty, talented, helpful—much, much nicer. I don't blame her for preferring my sister. Frankly, *I* prefer my sister too."

"Oh. Sisters." Susannah wipes her hands, gets up, and picks up the plates. "Fucking poisonous things. I have one myself. Haven't seen her in nineteen years." Her tone is brutal. I look at her, probably with horror, and she stares back at me, chin up. Instantly, I feel the need to defend Alice.

"None of this is my sister's fault," I say. "She didn't ask to be the good girl. She always tried to include me and smooth things over. She was always quite protective of me, in a way, even though I'm the big sister and it should be the other way around. It must have been a nightmare for her to be stuck between me and my mother all the time." My voice wavers. Behind Susannah the sky is almost dark.

"Huh, well, I guess there are worse things in life than not being your mother's favorite." She walks toward the sink. She obviously doesn't get any of this and I can't expect her to. But I wonder, again, what sort of childhood Susannah had.

She is completely right. This makes me look like a spoiled, middle-class whiner. I have to stop chasing my mother like this. It's too late—manifestly too late.

Susannah is filling the sink with water. I realize that, once again, she is in control. She's getting information out of me, and not the other way around.

"You'd be really good at my job." I get up and gather our plates, fighting the urge to slam them together. And then, of course, she asks what I do for a living. I follow her over to the sink. After I've told her about the website, she asks questions about my social psychology degree, interviewing techniques, the research behind the website, the funding. When she hears that it is partly funded by the National Health Service and Oxford University she looks impressed. "I guess people like hearing about other peoples' sicknesses," she says.

"Ultimately," I say, "everybody just wants to tell their story, no matter how awful that story is."

"Well I don't," she says. For a moment, our eyes meet. This time she's the one to look away. She squirts in dishwashing liquid and plunges her hands into the boiling water. "You like your work?"

"Actually it's become a bit frustrating since I had Finn. It's impossible to do it properly. I only work one or two days a week now, so I tend to get given things that no one else wants to do. And I don't even feel like I do those properly."

"Well work more then."

"It's really not that simple. I mean, I want to be there for Finn too. I want to be a good mother for him." She doesn't say anything. I'm sure she's thinking I'll never be that.

"Where's the baby's father in all this?"

"Oh." I glance at my wedding ring. "Oh, well, I . . . I don't really want to talk about Doug . . ."

She turns to me, wiping her hands, watching my face. I can feel her taking in my features, lingering here and there. Her eyes soften, and it suddenly occurs to me that when she looks at me like this, she's looking at my mother's face and not mine: or at least, at the echoes of my mother's face in mine. My mother would have been younger than I am now when Susannah last saw her. I feel a shiver pass over my skin as if she has reached out to stroke me.

"When you look at me like that I feel a bit like one of your exhibits," I laugh, and turn away to hang up a saucepan.

"It's just kind of curious, to see you all grown up I guess."

"So you knew me as a baby?" I blurt it out. She doesn't answer.

Somewhere far off, thunder rumbles. A gust of wind bashes against the French window and one dog, in its basket by the range, looks up, sharply. "It's just, I don't know a single person other than my parents who knew me as a really little baby, before I came to England. . . . I've never even seen a picture of myself as a baby."

"Huh? Is that right?"

"So, what was I like?"

"As a baby? Oh, you cried all the time. They said it was colic, but I always thought you were just objecting to being born. I used to walk you around outside to give your mother a break. You sure had some lungs on you."

She says it so casually. I must be staring at her because she gives a harsh laugh. "What can I say?" Her eyes are wintry, the pupils sharp and black. "You were a screamer."

"I just . . . you're the only person I've ever met who knew me then. This is completely weird."

"Well, your mother knew you then."

"And my father."

She shrugs and turns away again.

"Do you have any pictures of me as a baby?"

"No." She washes a glass.

I take it from her, carefully. "Oh. I just thought you might have . . ."

"Well, I don't."

"I've always wondered, Susannah, whether my mother resented me in some way. She had to stop her PhD because she got pregnant, and give it up and move to England. Maybe that was the root of our issues. I mean, I basically ruined her life, didn't I?"

"That's a little simplistic, don't you think?" There is a clap of thunder, louder, flatter, but no lightning. I peer through the archway at the sofa. Finn doesn't even twitch. "Women did have careers and babies in the seventies you know," she is saying. "In fact, I happen to know that your mother read *The Female Eunuch* because I gave it to her myself."

"Yeah, but not many women had a career chasing killer whales around the Pacific Northwest. You can't exactly get day care for that can you?"

She goes over and begins to brusquely wipe the table.

"So am I why she gave it all up?"

She keeps wiping—making big jerky movements. I wonder if she's angry.

"Susannah?"

She walks past me, throws the cloth into the sink, and begins pulling on her boots.

"Where are you going?"

"I have to get something in before it rains."

I look through the archway into the front room. I can see the sofa. Finn's bum is in the air: his best sleeping position. There are cushions all around him. He'll sleep for at least an hour. Susannah is wrapping the gray scarf around her neck. This is turning into a conflict, and I have no idea why. But I don't want this conversation to end yet. For the first time, I feel like I'm getting somewhere with her. She steps through the French windows with the dogs behind her.

I yank on my boots and follow her into the icy air. The sky roils overhead, and another clap of thunder makes me jump. Waves thrash at the rocks below. Three rooks or maybe crows—fat black birds—circle the treetops behind the house, jet black against the troubled sky. She is walking away, fast, down the path along the side of the house toward them. I hurry along the deck.

It is not clear why she is so reluctant to just tell me things. Why can't she tell me everything she knows about my mother? What's the big secret?

I jump from the deck onto the path that leads into the massive pines. I run faster, catching up to her. The wasp hair clasp is almost out, and the veins on the side of her neck bulge. I can hear her breaths as she strides along. The path leads us deeper into the forest. A few quick drops of rain tap down through the prickly branches above us. Another clap of thunder—lower, closer, louder. I mustn't leave Finn—not with a storm about to break over us. Not in the same room as a Chihuly. I'll have to go back—I'll turn back in a moment.

"When I was little, my father was away a lot," I half shout at her, though I'm not sure she can hear me, or is listening. "He set up his own architectural firm in London; he's a total workaholic. My mother was basically a single parent. Even when he was there, on weekends, he was mostly working. She ran the house—she did everything, she was very practical. She even fixed the plumbing. And she had her art—but you'd never know she'd studied marine biology, or researched killer whales up here. I don't know why she never told me any of this. What I want to know, Susannah—are you listening?" I know she is. "Susannah, what I don't understand is why she didn't say anything about all this. Why was it such a big secret?"

There is a clearing up ahead. It's raining now, droplets coming through the prickly branches, soaking into my hair, so cold they sting my skin. The chill slices through me and I hug myself as I stumble along behind her. I'm going to have to get back to the house for Finn. I can't leave him there.

Susannah, in her brown fleece and big scarf, seems unconcerned by the cold, the storm, or my voice. There is a sharp crack above us, and I hunch, rabbit-like, and then lightning illuminates the patch of land we're standing on.

She doesn't even flinch. She strides toward a wooden building. It is Swedish looking, built in light pine, with large windows and solar panels on the roof and outside. Spread out on the ground, are three paint-stained sheets, no doubt set out to dry earlier. She picks one up and begins to fold it. I run across to her. The rain is getting faster, dripping down my neck.

"Are you planning on leaving that baby alone in a thunderstorm for long?" she shouts.

"I'm about to go back! But just tell me one thing. Just one thing. I just want to hear it for sure. She gave up her PhD because of me, didn't she? Because she got pregnant with me?"

Susannah tosses the folded sheet onto the small deck of the studio, where the dogs huddle, and scoops up the next one. I can't see inside the building because it's dark in there, and the door is closed, slat blinds down, and the windows are streaked with rain. She doesn't seem to notice the weather, even though the wind lashes the tops of the trees above us. She just keeps folding. I have to go back.

"Susannah?" I yell. "Can you just answer me?"

"Holy shit. You really don't give up do you, Kali? Not even with that baby alone inside a . . ." I don't catch the words—I think she says "strange house" but it might be "stranger's house."

"He's sleeping!" I yell through the rain. But I know she's right. "It's been five minutes! And I'm about to run back! As soon as you answer me—"

"Quitting the PhD had nothing to do with you," she snaps. "She quit to come up here."

I wipe the freezing rain out of my eyes. "You mean the mapping project wasn't her PhD?"

"Her PhD was on the play vocalizations of the Sea Park dolphins in California."

Another clap of thunder cracks through the air, right above us. My jeans are sticking to my thighs and the rain is soaking into my sweater. I'm shivering violently. Susannah tosses the sheet with the others, but instead of going toward the studio, as I expect her to, she turns and walks away, back toward the trees.

"Wait!" I run. The dogs bound after her, tails whirling like propellers. Lightning flashes, shifting a whole patch of air above me and I freeze, involuntarily. She disappears into the pines.

*   *   *

As we peel off our boots in the kitchen, I slide the French window shut. I can see Finn, oblivious to the thunder and lashing rain, his bum still in the air.

"See," I nod toward him, breathless. "He sleeps like a log. When he was nine months old he slept through an entire fireworks display that shook the walls of the bedroom he was in. He didn't even twitch."

The rain was closing in now and there was no visibility outside at all, just layers of falling water. I'm soaking and very cold. But I'm not giving up now. "Susannah, I'm confused . . . I don't really understand the timetable—what she did, and when—and why, come to think of it."

She pushes her hair back with both hands. Looking down at me, close up, she seems taller, her bones sharper, the lines on her wet face like carvings; her forehead was high, like a priestess. "Fine," she snaps. "Your mother's research was in Southern California, near the university." She grabs a tea towel and throws it toward me, and then takes one herself and wipes rain off her face. "This was before you came along, a long time before. You want to know what happened to make her quit her PhD? Okay. Sure. I'll tell you. Sit down." She points at a stool. "Sit."

I sit.

"She got interested in the two captive orca at the park where she was studying the dolphins." She dries the straggling ends of her hair. "The female orca was due to give birth, and Elena persuaded the park authorities to let her record the sounds it made during labor. It was one of the first captive killer whale births ever to happen in the States. Your mother put a hydrophone in the water and sat by the pool throughout the labor, two days. She watched the orca give birth, recorded all the sounds, and then she watched as everything fell apart.

"When an orca is born it swims right away—the mother noses it to the surface for its first breath, then they swim together. They surface and dive together, and breathe in synch—the mother alters her breathing pattern so the baby can mimic it. And she feeds it as they swim. But this baby at the Sea Park didn't have the motor control to cope with swimming around and around a tiny tank so it kept bumping into the sides. The mother was worried that the calf was going to hurt itself. She was so busy nosing it away from the tank walls that she couldn't feed it. In the wild, the other female whales will help a new mother, kind of like village midwives, they point the calf at her mammaries, they nudge and shepherd the baby until it can feed reliably on its own, and they support the new mother—but in captivity she didn't have any help, she was on her own. I guess the instinct to protect outweighed the instinct to feed."

I am struggling to understand why Susannah is telling me this, but I nod along, hoping that the point will emerge.

"So, the Sea Park guys eventually yanked the starving baby whale away from its mother and put it in a separate tank to try to get it to feed—and then of course the mother went crazy. Imagine, a killer whale hurling herself against the side of the tank, yowling—barking—for hours on end. The Sea Park guys had no idea what to do. They tried, pretty ineptly, to force-feed the calf with a tube, but it starved to death after a few days. The mother never recovered. She wailed, screamed, and bashed herself against the tank nonstop for two days—and then she just gave up. She lay still, not feeding, moving only in slow motion to breathe. She died not long after."

"That's a horrible story."

"Yeah, well. I'm telling you this because it changed everything for your mother. It altered her outlook. And that's when she met . . . she met the others, the conservationists, who were involved in the orca-mapping project. They introduced her to the issues with the wild orca. She quit her PhD, dropped out overnight, and came up here to join them."

"So, dropping out of university had nothing to do with me?"

"You weren't even *born*, Kali."

I hug myself tightly. My damp clothes stick to my body and I have goosebumps though I'm not sure whether they are from the cold or from Susannah's words.

I look at her. I wonder if she has any idea of what she has just done for me. It's as if this restless, hungry thing that has been inside me all my life has vanished; someone has opened the doors and it has galloped away. I think about what she's said: my mother, dropping everything, furious with the Sea Park, upset, but clear-eyed, certain of her future.

"And what about my father?" I say. "They were together, right? What did he think about her change of plans?"

She gives a chilly laugh. "Oh Gray didn't really have a say. None of us had a say. That's Elena for you. Totally single-minded."

"She left him in California?"

"He was finishing up his scholarship at the time, looking for a job. He was in London I think, interviewing—he didn't see it coming. Neither of us did."

She is agitated, now, pacing between the stove and the French window. A flash of lightning fills the room and for a second the lights dim—I glance through at Finn but he still hasn't moved. There is a pause, then a clap of thunder that seems to shake the glass. Susannah doesn't seem to notice.

Then something occurs to me. "What was my father like in those days?" I watch her face closely.

"Gray?" Her voice comes out high. She stops moving. Then she shrugs. "Oh, he was nice: serious, very proper, very clever, lovely Scottish accent. But, well, I . . . hardly knew him. Your mother was an excellent compartmentalizer." She looks at me, blankly, then spins around and strides out of the room.

Now I've got her. It's like pressing an injured limb until you find the fracture point—and I think I have it. I must have it. I lean against the range. The warmth spreads up my back. It is obvious: Susannah didn't have an affair with my mother. She had an affair with my father.

She is behind the letter he sent my mother before he brought her to England—she is the source of the guilt that was there, behind every word he wrote. Susannah was the reason my mother hated America and wouldn't talk about the past. No wonder my mother cut her off.

The scenario isn't hard to imagine: my mother takes off with a bunch of obsessed orca researchers, leaving my father and Susannah on campus together, both feeling abandoned and lonely and hurt.

I just have to get her to admit it. Then I'm done here.

Rain lashes the windows but the thunder and lightning seem to have swept back out to sea. The dogs are in their beds, noses down. Finn is still motionless. Behind him, over by the big windows, Susannah stands with her back to me, staring out at a wall of rain.

I walk slowly into the living room. Rain drums against the roof and lashes the glass. A rumble of thunder sounds in the distance. I stand by the arm of the sofa. The rug is stained under her feet where rain has dribbled off her clothes. I can see her face, reflected in the darkened windows. I realize she is looking right at me.

"Susannah. Was my mother very in love?"

She stiffens. "Who with?"

"What? With my father, of course."

She laughs, throwing her head back. It is a weird, barking sound. "Shit!" She spins around. "Holy shit Kali! Didn't she talk about any of this to you? I mean, nothing at all? Seriously?" She wipes her hair off her face. "This is NOT my job."

Finn sits up with a start. He opens his mouth and the wail is like the buildup of a long, slow siren. I go to him, bend down. He looks at me, baffled and sweaty. I hug him tight, and over his head I say to her, "She ran off, leaving you and my father together, didn't she? Why can't you just tell me what really happened? It was years ago, it doesn't matter anymore. I won't judge you. I just want to know."

I heave Finn off the sofa. He wraps his arms around my neck and sobs into my ear.

"It's okay, love." I pat his back. "It's okay. Just silly shouting. It's okay." But I don't take my eyes off Susannah.

"I thought nothing woke him," she says, nastily.

I ignore this. "My mother is dead Susannah! I just want to know what happened in her life to make her who she was. Can't you give me that much? Did you have an affair with my father, Susannah? Or was it my mother?"

The windows reflect the room and I see the dogs coming from the kitchen behind me. For a moment I think they've heard the aggression in my voice and are coming for me. I brace myself, hanging onto my sobbing child, and wait for their teeth to sink into my calves. But they go straight past me, over to Susannah.

And she just walks away with them, down the corridor, toward her room with her chin up like an empress.

I am trembling as I try to calm Finn down. The poor little boy. First we shout and wake him up, then we snipe over his head. Poor, jet-lagged, disoriented little boy. This is no place for him. There really is no point in this. It's futile. Susannah is only going to give me what she wants to give—and that, apparently, is almost nothing.

I hug him, and kiss his wet face. "Shhhh, shhhhh. It's okay, love; it's okay." His sobs subside. He smells milky and sweet—always more babyish when he just wakes up. His hair is soft and static. I smooth it off his forehead. But then Susannah reappears. She stops at the entrance to the living room.

"This isn't any of your business." She leans a hand on the door frame. "But I'll tell you anyway just so we're clear here. I did not have an affair with either Gray or your mother. Gray loved your mother very much. He was," she pauses glancing upward as if searching for exactly the right word, "a fucking saint." She turns, again, and stalks away.

So, she won. If this was a battle, then right now she's standing over my corpse, waving a bloodied machete. I look down at Finn and he hiccups. We should just go. We might make the last ferry—if it leaves when it should. Though, granted, that's a pretty big "if."

But here she is again, striding up the corridor toward us. This is becoming positively farcical. I brace myself for another announcement but she walks right past us, through the kitchen, and out the French windows—I feel a blast of cold air. The dogs follow her into the rain. She slams the doors shut. The handmade plates shiver on their shelves.

My head throbs. Finn hiccups again, just once. I stroke his hair out of his eyes again. "Let's go, love," I say.

He looks up at me with Doug's chocolate brown eyes and I kiss the end of his nose. I need to change his diaper. Pack up our stuff. Give him some milk. I seem to spend my whole time leaving these days.

Then I force myself to stop. This time, I have to think. I've done far too much running from this to that, bouncing across oceans, standing on freezing doorsteps. I have to make a proper plan this time. Am I really going to drive Finn through a thunderstorm across this god-awful island only to miss the ferry, or to find that it left six hours earlier than it was supposed to—or not at all? Then we'll have nowhere to stay, and I can't imagine having to crawl back here and beg Susannah for her spare bed again. It would be far more sensible to stay tonight, make amends like a rational adult, then leave calmly in the morning. This, undoubtedly, is what Alice would tell me to do right now.

I shift Finn onto my hip. I am still damp and cold, I need to change my clothes—but as I start to move, a blackness rushes from behind my eyes and my ears buzz. I quickly sit down on the sofa before I fall over.

Something is wrong. Something is off-balance deep inside me. I shut my eyes and the world spins. Only Finn's body on my lap is firm and solid and warm and definite.

But of course something's wrong: I'm jet-lagged. This is stressful. I'm confused. My mother just died. My husband may or may not be having affair with his glamorous ex-girlfriend. I've blown all our savings on a plane ticket to the middle of nowhere. It would be frankly abnormal to feel normal at this point.

I feel Finn's hands on my face, patting my cheeks. "Mama?"

I hug him tight. I want to talk to Alice. I need to tell her what I've discovered about our mother's awful childhood and the orca mapping project. Perhaps she already knows some of this. But I don't think so. I'm sure she would have told me about this if she'd known. Alice is as much in the dark about our mother's past as I am.

The two of them were harmonious and happy, but it seems that my mother's past was unbreachable, even by Alice.

Finn slithers off my lap and toddles away chatting to himself, "Bah, bah. Dat?" Then I realize he's making for the Chihuly. I launch myself after him, sweeping him to the right, so his legs fly up toward the bookshelves. I whisk him into the kitchen and put him down. My head wheels.

"Again! Again!" He starts off again—a tripping, lurching, full-diapered run toward the French windows.

"Come here you cheeky monkey." I grab him from behind and whoosh him up again and my head whirls as if I'm the one in the air, not him. I hug him to me. He laughs, and reaches out his hands. He holds my chin. "Bah." He smiles. "Again!"

My legs feel very weak. We look at each other for a second.

"How about some nice warm milk?"

"Again! Again! Up! Up!"

"Milk first, okay?"

He takes the cup and shoves the spout into his mouth. He gazes up at me and his eyes glaze over a little as he sucks. It takes so little to comfort him, really. He doesn't care whether we're in British Columbia or Oxford High Street. He doesn't care about the big sky or the waves crashing onto the slimy rocks below. He just cares that I'm here every morning when he wakes up, that I pick him up when he's hurt, that I swing him through the air to make him laugh, and give him milk and food, and sing him to sleep with "Baa Baa Black Sheep" every night. I think about the black and white pictures I used to show him as a tiny baby; the endless playgroup conversations about "stimulating" our babies, "cultivating" their musical tastes, "developing" their linguistic skills. How did motherhood become so fraught and extreme? This is what matters. Just being here. This is all he really needs from me.

I carry him back into the living room and sit on the sofa again, Finn on my lap, his chubby legs sticking out, both hands on the handles of his cup. I have to make a plan. But the truth is I don't know where to go next. I certainly have no interest in visiting the Vancouver Aquarium.

There is a book called *The Magnificent Orca* on the coffee table. It is heavy and glossy. I lean over, with one hand, and flick it open.

There are pictures of black and white whales, leaping through stormy seas against a snow-capped mountain backdrop. The male dorsal fins, I read, can be more than six feet long. Taller than Doug.

No. I can't think about Doug now. What good would that do?

The first chapter is called "Myths of the Orca." I read over Finn's head. The name is down to the Romans: *Orcinus: "belonging to the kingdom of the dead,"* and *orca* from *"orcus"*: *Roman god of the underworld.* I scan the names the whales have been given through-out history. Like the landscape up here, each name represents a little pocket of human fear: *killer demon, feared one, Blackfish, Sea Wolf.*

I skim a section on the stories told by the indigenous people of the Pacific Northwest. One tribe had killer whales living in houses and towns beneath the ocean. One believed that orca ruled the under-sea world. Another believed that the orca embodied the souls of the tribe's dead chiefs. Others thought the whales were the spirits of their men who had been lost at sea: when an orca was seen near the coast it was the dead man, coming back to check on his loved ones—or his enemies.

One Alaskan tribe did see the orca as benevolent though—a gen-tle benefactor, watching over the tribe and keeping its people safe. In fact, the author says, this myth is closer to the truth. The only incidences of killer whales harming humans have taken place in theme parks. He goes on to describe moments when captive whales seem to "snap," dragging a trainer down to the bottom of the tank and crushing them against concrete. One seized a trainer by the leg, then whipped him around and around underwater like a rag doll, eventually pushing him to the surface, semi-conscious, moments from death. One orca killed her trainer, after being forced to per-form while her young calf cried for her in a nearby tank. Given the decades of torment these animals have undergone at the hands of greedy theme parks the really astonishing thing is how kind these animals are and how deeply tolerant. It only ever happens, the author says, when they are pushed to the furthest edge of their sanity. Perhaps, he suggests, killer whales feel a sense of responsibility or even kinship toward humans. There are reliable accounts of orca pods guiding lost ships to safety through the fog, of saving our drowning pet dogs, or befriending us as we sail across their seas. If this is the case, then we have sorely let them down.

Finn has finished his milk, but is content to sit for a moment, sucking on the spout. It's rare, I realize, for us to just sit together like this. Normally, I'm rushing around, cleaning, making food, or dragging him out somewhere. We hardly ever just sit together.

I stare at the cover of the book—the beautiful black and white body of the whale. If you take a killer whale out of the water it will self-destruct. After a while its body will simply collapse under its own weight. It strikes me that there is no truth about killer whales. There is just layer upon layer of stories, memories, and opinions; of fears, hopes, and beliefs. The whales are our story keepers; they exist in another realm, always out of reach, imploding if we get too close. The whales are fiction.

Unless you are a scientist. If you are a scientist then killer whales are raw data—black and white tubes of sound and behavior and markings to be documented and decoded. If you are a scientist all the stories don't matter. What matters is data. What was it Susannah said? *No picture, no proof.*

CHAPTER NINE

I decide to stay.

The ferries are too unreliable, and I shouldn't leave like this anyway. I have to smooth things over. Presumably, Susannah has gone to her studio. I'll bundle Finn up in his snowsuit and rain boots and get outside for a bit. The rain has almost stopped. It's no doubt freezing, but he'll be happy outside, and he'll sleep better tonight if he gets fresh air.

When we come in again, after a long time poking at wet stones and throwing sticks at tree trunks, it's almost dark. We walk up the corridor to the living room and the dogs are sitting by the sofa. They watch as we come toward them but they don't move. Their amber eyes are fixed on my face. Suddenly, my skin prickles. I scoop Finn up.

"Good doggies," I say.

They stare at my face in the half-light, their glassy, teddy-bear eyes unblinking. "Bloody hell. Good boys." Their tails don't twitch.

There is no sign of Susannah. I edge past them with my back to the window. They keep their eyes on me and their noses turn to follow as I creep away down the corridor. Finn senses the threat too—instead of wriggling to get down and play with them, he holds onto me with legs and arms, in a baby chimpanzee grip.

In the spare room I shut the door tight. She said the dogs were harmless. Even Susannah wouldn't be nutty enough to allow dangerous dogs near a toddler. Would she? They were probably just tired. Maybe hungry. It's not clear where Susannah is. I wonder if she is actually okay. Maybe I should look for her.

I go to the toilet, turn on the shower, and peel off my clothes. Then I undress Finn and take off his diaper. In the shower he splashes at my feet as if he's at the beach, and I turn my face up and let the warm water run over my eyes and mouth, and down my body. I look up, through the sheets of hot water. There is black mildew on the limestone grouting in one corner.

We come back into the living room from opposite ends, at the same time. The dogs are wagging their tails, turning circles around her, begging to be fed. They look like normal attractive pets, completely harmless.

I realize that I have been here nearly twenty-four hours and I don't even know their names. She interacts with them, wordlessly, never fusses over them, or talks to or about them. They're a little pack, the three of them, with Susannah as Alpha dog.

I follow her into the kitchen, holding Finn's hand. She flips on the light and pours kibble into the dogs' bowls then washes her hands. Their heads bob and they slaver, as if attacking a fresh kill rather than a bowlful of Pedigree Chum. Finn tries to run toward them and I kneel down and hold him. "No, you can't touch dogs when they eat. The might bite you."

He looks at me.

"Dangerous," I say, again, in my most shocked voice. "Dangerous! Don't touch the dogs when they're eating. No. Dogs can bite you if they're eating."

He looks back at the dogs, plainly wondering whether he should touch them, to test out this intriguing theory.

I lean my back against the warm range, and hold him firmly between my knees. He watches the dogs.

"Susannah. I just wanted to say sorry about earlier. If you want me to go . . ."

"No!" she says, sharply. "NO." Then she gives a dry laugh. "I mean, where to? Where would you go? The last ferry left at five."

"Okay, but I'm sorry. I was completely out of order before. We'll go tomorrow. You've been very kind."

Finn is trying to grab at the almond bowl now, on tiptoes. I stand up and move the bowl out of his way.

"I had no right to ask you all those things," I say. "It was none of my business." He goes over to the chair at the round table, and bashes it with both hands.

"Finn," I say pointlessly. "Be gentle." I need to give him something to eat, or he's going to get very grumpy very quickly. He hasn't eaten anything for hours. His routines are in tatters. It's the first thing the childcare books tell you: keep to a routine.

Susannah opens and shuts a cupboard above her head. She pulls down a bottle of vitamins and takes two without water, throwing her head back and closing her eyes briefly. I see the lump in her throat move up and down.

"Would you mind if I made Finn something to eat? A boiled egg maybe?"

"He must be hungry," she says, eyes still shut. "Help yourself."

Without toys, or a TV, it's going to be almost impossible to keep him occupied while I cook even a boiled egg. I look around. "Would you mind if I gave him something to play with? He likes bashing pots and pans."

"I have a headache." Her eyes are still shut. I think she is doing yoga breathing again.

"Okay. Sorry. No. Of course."

Finn is making for the sideboard with the photos on it. I run over and whisk him away—he squawks—"Come on, love, come over here with me." Susannah is watching. It's as if she's just waiting for me to mess up.

"Do you have any frozen peas by any chance?" I ask.

She turns and opens the freezer drawers, beneath her fridge, and pulls out a packet of organic peas. She holds it out to me without moving away from the fridge. Then, as I come take it, she turns her head away, and looks out the window.

I am not sure if she's still angry, or whether it's the headache. I get out a plastic pot from the Tupperware cupboard and tip a handful of frozen peas into it. This is Finn's favorite distraction. He will sit for ages in his high chair while I cook, picking the peas out, one by one, and sucking on them, as if they are sweets. I show him the pot and he grabs it with both hands. Peas fly into the air, then bump and roll like mercury balls across the tiles. I bend over, scrabbling to scoop them up. He is already shoving some, along with some dog hairs, into his mouth. I can feel Susannah, looking down, watching.

"No!" I say, too sharply, grabbing his hand. "Dirty."

He jumps, startled.

"Okay. Wait. I'm going to get you clean peas. Those are dirty peas. Dirty. Yuck." I scrape them out of his fist and his face clouds over. Quickly, I pour more peas into the pot and hand it to him. He looks at me steadily, from under his bangs, then tips them over onto the floor. He whooshes his hands through them, sending them spinning in all directions.

"FINN! No!" She is just standing, staring, as if this is the most incompetent mothering she's ever witnessed. I feel my throat tighten; I want to cry. I cannot possibly allow myself to do this.

"Okay. No peas then," I say. "Not on the floor."

Finn sweeps peas across the tiles and shouts "No!"

I pick him up and he starts to yell.

"Stop it," I bark. "Stop shouting!"

Susannah straightens. "Give the child to me."

"What?"

"Give him to me."

"It's okay, I can manage, thanks."

"Just give him to me, Kali." She reaches over and pulls Finn out of my arms. He is red-faced, mouth open. His wails intensify as she pins him to her body. As she walks off with him, he holds out his arms to me over her shoulder, "Maaammmaaaaa!" It is a panicky cry.

My instinct is to run after her and grab him back. Who does she think she is, whisking my child away? But I also know, on some level, that she's right. Things can only escalate from here. If I take him back I won't be able to cook his egg and he'll shout and wreck more of her belongings. Without a high chair to strap him into, it's hopeless. But I can see his little star hands, reaching out for me over her back as she carries him away, and his fearful face—open-mouthed, round-eyed—"Maamaaa!"

"It's okay, love," I call after him, slavishly, guiltily. "I'm just going to make you a nice egg. Look. I'm right here. A lovely boiled egg! You have a story with Susannah while I make the egg. Okay? I'm right here."

"Maaaamaaa!"

I force myself to turn away from him and go to the stove. My hands are shaking; I rest them on the sink. It won't kill him to cry for a minute. And after a moment or two, his wails subside. He's just hungry, that's all. Tired and hungry. The quicker I feed him the better. I peer through the archway. She has him on her hip, by the bookcase, and is showing him a bowl of smooth wooden balls.

I fill the pan with water and look for the knife to cut bread into toast soldiers. Coming here really was an appalling idea. You can't ever know a person completely, even your own mother—perhaps especially your own mother. Susannah isn't going to help me here. Maybe nobody could. What I really wanted, when I jumped on the plane, was for my mother not to be dead.

I realize that I still haven't established when I booked the return flight. The time around the funeral is a bit of a blur now. I need to get on the Internet to check, but of course Susannah has no connection here. And I have to call Doug. He'll be worried about Finn and missing him. He'll also be furious by now, about the credit card. I need to call Alice too. But it's the middle of the night in England now. I can't call either of them, or anyone else.

Suddenly, the geographical reality of where I am hits me. There are miles and miles of the earth's crust between me and my home. And nobody—not a single person in the entire world—knows that I am here, in Susannah's house.

*

Susannah bends over the fireplace, stacking up logs in a tepee shape. Thick veins worm across the surface of her bare feet; the knobs of her anklebones beneath her rolled up jeans are smooth and white as beach stones. I hear her knees click as she reaches for the matches. Like my mother, Susannah seems to avoid footwear, even in January.

Finn is finally bathed, fed, changed, and asleep. This time I've wedged the bedroom door open with our heavy bag so he can't possibly pull it out of the way. It's eight-thirty now—four-thirty in the morning British time. I am light-headed, washed out.

"Okay," Susannah straightens as the fire takes. She turns to face me. Behind her, flames lick hungrily up the logs. "You find yourself a drink and put some spaghetti on to boil, while I take a shower. Then we'll eat."

Obediently, I go to the kitchen and dig around in the cupboards; I find wine glasses and the opened bottle of red wine from the night before. I pour two glasses. It's a Washington State Merlot but I wonder if it's been open for a long time because it smells very vinegary. I leave the wine, take a pan from the metal hooks above the stove, fill it with water, and put it on the range.

Susannah's bedroom must look out to the side of the house. It probably has a spectacular ocean view. There is a sound of pipes and water rushing. I smell wood smoke. There is whole-wheat spaghetti in the store cupboard, alongside glass jars of brown pasta, dried pulses, macadamia nuts, dried blueberries, flax seeds, lentils, lima beans, mung beans, evening primrose oil, multivitamin, flax oil, fish oil, sunflower seeds, iron tablets, glucosamine. No wonder she looks so robust. I take a couple of handfuls of spaghetti and slide them into the bubbling pan. The boiling water spits in my face.

What I can't understand is how my mother gave all this up—this wild ocean, the snow-capped mountains, and the orca that needed her protection. That leap—from wilderness to hedgerows, from killer whales to the school run, hydrophones to oil paints—is just unfathomable. I suppose she was damaged by her childhood, whatever Susannah says; perhaps she knew that what she really needed was the stability and order that my father offered. But she must have felt so hemmed in. The Sussex countryside, with its tight, knitted hedgerows could not be further from this colossal wilderness. Then again, she did spend a lot of time by the sea.

I suddenly remember a massive fight we had—our last, in fact. I was about seventeen. We were in the kitchen. I was by the kettle and she was next to me, at the sink, peeling potatoes for a shepherd's pie. I'd just told her I wasn't going to do A-levels, I was going to drop out and work on a French fish farm with my new boyfriend, who was twenty-three and had a motorcycle. We were going to earn money, then go to India.

She put down the peeler, slowly. "Just tell me one thing." She turned her green eyes on my face. "Without an education, what do you intend to do with your life?"

"What's so great about an education?" I snapped back. "You got an education and it didn't do much for you, did it? Are you saying I should slave away at university so I can become a housewife and spend my days making bloody shepherd's pie? Anyway—isn't this just a tiny bit hypocritical? I mean, you dropped out didn't you? I'm just saving myself several years of hassle by doing it now."

Her lips went white, her face tightened, and her hands bunched into fists—and for a moment I thought that—for the first time—she was actually going to hit me. But she didn't, and the contempt in her voice was worse than anything physical she could have done. "You have no idea what you are talking about Kali. You have *no fucking idea.*" She turned, and walked away.

I wanted her to forbid me to go to the fish farm. I wanted her to order me to finish my A-levels and ban me from ever seeing the boyfriend again. I wanted her to reach out and hold onto me and tell me that she loved me and wouldn't let me do this under any circumstances. But she didn't. She left the peeler on the draining board, and walked away.

I finished making the shepherd's pie, but she didn't come back until late at night, and by then my bag was packed.

I never lived at home again. I never went to India, either. A few months later, when things didn't work out with the boyfriend or the fish farm, I came back to England. She said I could come home, but I was too proud. I moved into a dismal student apartment in Brighton and became a waitress. Doug is right: it was never one-way. And I didn't even say sorry.

I look up. Susannah is in the doorway, half in the shadows, just watching me with a disconcerting, blank face. I don't know how long she's been there.

"Oh!" I jump up. "Hi."

She doesn't move or speak. Her hair is wet and combed back. Her forehead is high and hardly wrinkled except for the deep crease between her brows. Her mouth is a long line and her colorless eyes are fixed on my face.

Then I notice that the spaghetti is bubbling away, and its water is thick and pasty. I've made nothing to go with it. I haven't set the table, even, or gotten plates.

"God, sorry, I sort of stalled . . ."

She flares her nostrils, takes a breath, nods once, briefly, then walks past me and opens the fridge.

A moment later she has me chopping onions. "We'll make clam sauce," she says. "It's pretty good." She doesn't sound angry. Just neutral, calm, as if she has made a decision, and is happy with it.

The tears stream down my cheeks as I chop the onions. She's standing right next to me with her pile of tomatoes, but her eyes aren't affected at all. She slices into the tomato flesh with her chef's knife. Her hand is fast and efficient as she chops.

"So, I'm curious about something," she says. "What is going on with your husband?"

I stop slicing the onion.

"You might as well tell me, Kali. Get it off your chest," she shrugs. "It's eating away at you. I can see that. And you'll probably never see me again—so why not?"

I don't want to stay in touch with her either, but it seems distinctly brutal to just say it, outright.

"So?" she asks. "Tell me."

My first instinct is no way—no way am I going to discuss Doug with this woman.

But then I realize that she has a point—I do have nothing to lose. I'll never see her again after this and if I open up a bit, maybe she will too. I take a breath. "Well, I think he might be having an affair." I pick up another onion and wipe tears out of my stinging eyes with the back of my hand which only makes it worse. "I'm not sure though, really. He tried to explain on the phone but I couldn't—wouldn't—let him. To be honest, I'm not sure what's happening between us."

She starts to chop herbs, rapidly, like a professional chef. "Huh? I wondered what made you run all the way out here. So, are you leaving him?"

"No! Well, I don't know, I don't think so. I just found this . . . and then my mother died the very next morning . . . and I just couldn't face confronting him."

"So how did you find out about his affair?"

"The woman—his ex-girlfriend in fact—sent him some text messages." I feel my face growing hotter. It sounds tawdry. Texts. Infidelity. It doesn't sound like Doug.

"Huh? What do they call that these days? Sexting?"

"No. No—No. Nothing like that. She just, well, she texted to say she missed him . . . in a particular way."

"She *missed* him?"

"She missed him, 'Spiritually, emotionally, and physically.'" Spoken out loud the words lose some of their power. They are just words. Slightly Mills & Boon words, at that.

"Is that all?"

I pause, knife in the air. "Well you can't miss someone you don't have a relationship with, can you?"

"Can't you?" Our eyes meet. She doesn't blink. "I think you can."

"How?" I look down at my hands, red knuckled from raw onions and cold winds; my wedding ring shines back up at me. "You can't. That doesn't make sense."

"So, who is she? Do you know her?"

"Not really. She's his ex-girlfriend."

"There you go. They are connected."

"But she was his college girlfriend fifteen years ago. She can't have missed him for fifteen years!"

She looks at me again. I know what she's going to say.

"Anyway," I say, quickly. "They'd been seeing each other recently for work, so the missing thing was obviously recent. And she sent him another text saying *have a great day, gorgeous*. You don't say that unless . . . And he'd obviously deleted other texts. I looked for them . . . anyway. He was guilty. He sounded guilty, when he tried to explain. It's . . . can we talk about something else now?"

We chop again in silence. I realize that Susannah may have a point about the missing thing, but all the same, I heard the guilt in Doug's voice. If he hasn't slept with her, why would he be guilty?

"I'm sure you'll work it out somehow," she says, brusquely. "My friend, Maggie, who runs the bakery in town, says we are never given anything in this life that we can't handle."

"Actually," I put down the knife and blow my nose on the paper towel, wiping away onion tears. "That's crap, because I'm not handling any of this very well at all."

"You came, Kali. You found your breathing space. You're doing your thing."

"No I'm not, really. I just came here on an impulse after a horrible loss and not enough sleep—and to be honest, Susannah, I'm not really sure what I thought I'd achieve except a humongous credit card bill. I mean, I thought maybe you could help me understand my mother, and our relationship. I want to feel connected to her, but right now I feel pretty much disconnected from everything.

Sometimes I feel like I can't possibly even be here, in your house, on this island. It's like being awake and asleep at the same time. It's . . ." I pick up the wine and sniff it. "Sorry. I know I probably sound a bit unhinged."

"Killer whales sleep and move at the same time," she says, conversationally. "They shut down one hemisphere of their brain but the other stays awake, so they can keep moving, breathing, and watching for dangers as they sleep. You see them sometimes out at sea, side-by-side, all of them sleeping—they surface together and take these long, slow dives—they'll go on for miles and miles, sleeping and moving together. It's a beautiful thing, kind of mystical."

I picture the whales with their loved ones tight around them, synchronized, protecting one another even as they sleep. "I just feel," I say, "very alone."

"Oh Kali," she says, "you are alone."

I look at her. She chops on, nonchalantly. "You've lost your mother and possibly your husband," she says. Then she turns her head, and her bleached out eyes settle on my face. "That's why you need to stay here for a bit longer. That's why you came."

"Oh, no," I look down at the mess of onions, "honestly, Susannah, I couldn't stay any longer here. I mean, we really do have to go first thing tomorrow, to get back to Vancouver. I've imposed on your hospitality quite enough."

"No you haven't." She touches the tip of her knife against her glistening index finger. "And anyway, you shouldn't be dragging a young child around like this. You owe it to that baby to stay here at least one more night. You're here for a reason. You need to accept that. And you need to learn to accept help, Kali. Especially in your condition."

I look at her. I have no idea what she's talking about.

She takes the board with my onions and garlic, and tips them into the frying pan.

She picks up a spatula. "Does your husband know about the baby?"

"What baby?" I look at her and she looks at me. "You mean Finn?"

"No. The one inside you"

I let out a wild laugh. "What? You think I'm pregnant? God no. No. I'm not pregnant." I glance, involuntarily, at my belly. We both do. I stop laughing. "Why . . . why on earth would you say that?"

"You just seem pregnant to me . . ."

"Good God. Why? Because I threw up?"

"That, and I don't know—you just seem pregnant, Kali, that's all. I've been around pregnant women plenty of times. I've been one myself in fact. You can't touch your wine and you're very tired; you're kind of out of it, not noticing things. You threw up. But it's more than that of course. From the moment you walked through my door you just seemed pregnant. You *feel* pregnant. Your aura feels pregnant."

"My *aura* feels pregnant? Well, I'm definitely not," I consider introducing Susannah to the four years it took me to conceive Finn, the diagnosis of unexplained infertility, the eventual mind-blowing success—and the fact that Doug and I have only had sex about four times in the past six months. But of course, I would never go there with her, never in a million years. "Well, whatever my aura is telling you has been lost in translation because I am categorically not pregnant," I say. "I'm jet-lagged and . . . discombobulated."

"Discombobulated?" she laughs and shakes her head. "Okay."

She cooks the onions for a bit, then adds the tomatoes to the pan, some chopped herbs, then mixes in tiny fetal clams, stirring until it all thickens to a deep red sauce, with caramel-colored oils on the surface, and flecks of herbs and the globular shellfish bobbling about. The salty, garlicky smell is overpowering.

I turn away and reach for the plates. My hands feel jittery. The plates are thick, hand-made, with a pale blue glaze and a blue whale design in the center. I lower them very carefully from the cupboard. They are heavy.

"So," she takes one and lifts overcooked spaghetti onto it, "we're agreed then. Tomorrow, you rest and I take the baby away for the day."

"Oh no. Really! I couldn't let you do that, no—no. Honestly."

"Kali," she snaps. "I am offering to help you."

"Yes, I know you are. And that's very kind. But Finn would miss me. He hardly knows you, after all, and all this is strange for him—you said that yourself. And, he's hard work sometimes too. No, really. I wouldn't dream of it."

"You must."

"No, really, Susannah. That's so kind of you, but I couldn't lie here while you entertain Finn all day, it'd feel totally wrong."

She spoons the sauce onto the spaghetti.

"And I'm not that bad, honestly." I continue, "I think I threw up because it's all been pretty intense lately—with Doug, and my mother's death, and jet lag, and then hearing all that stuff about my mother's life up here—stuff I had no idea about. I mean, what sort of mother has this past and doesn't mention it—keeps it from her daughters for decades? It was a bit much to cope with." I take the plate. "I'm just, you know, slightly overwhelmed. I probably need to process all this. I'm just not myself right now. I'm really not myself at all."

"Who are you then?"

"What?"

She smiles, and for a moment, I almost like her.

We sit down and pick up our forks. She grates Parmesan onto her pasta and hands the greasy block to me. We eat for a few moments in silence. The food tastes strongly of the sea, it is gloopy and salty. The clams slide over my tongue. I feel like one of her dogs, great lumps forcing themselves down my throat. I rest my fork on the plate.

"What was your husband like?" I say. "Were you together for a very long time? How did you meet?"

"Which question would you like me to answer first?"

"Sorry," I smile. "How did you meet?"

"Well, I was forty and I'd been single for a very long time, many years in fact. I didn't want anyone in my life and I'd decided I'd be on my own forever, but then my biological clock kicked in—wham.

I didn't see that one coming. I guess the universe was telling me to have a baby. I'd started the gallery by then, I had my life in a good place, and my creative work was flowing. But the urge for a baby was . . . powerful."

"And did you meet through your gallery?"

"No, actually. He was a writer—biographies that nobody reads. I was in Vancouver and happened to be in a bookstore where he was talking." She reaches over and fills up her glass again. She leans back on the chair, hooking one arm over the backrest, raising her glass with the other. "I told him I was on the pill."

"Oh."

"Ah. You're one of those?"

"One of whats?"

"A love-at-first-sighter," she smiles, not very kindly, just with her mouth. "Let me guess. You want roses on Valentine's Day. You believe—or maybe believed—that your husband was 'the one'— your destiny?"

She's right of course. I do. Did. Not the roses, but I did believe Doug was the only one for me—I never doubted that I wanted to stay with him for my whole life, not even in our most stressful moments. In fact, I realize, I still do.

When we met, introduced over dinner by the only people I knew in Oxford, he offered to show me around the city. I'd been single for a long time—I felt safer that way. All my friends were married by then and I was thinking about working for a year or so at the new job, then maybe going to India at last. I thought I would be alone forever.

It was the last Sunday in March and we met in Christ Church meadow. It was so cold but the daffodils were out—egg-yolk yellow splashed down the riverbank. I was wearing a green woolen hat and no gloves, and Doug had on his big overcoat and the navy blue wool sweater that is, right now, in Susannah's spare room.

It seemed astonishing that this meadow could exist in the center of a city, tucked away from the buses, tourists, and *Big Issue* sellers. Doug told me there were cows in the meadow in summertime.

That, he said, was the thing that convinced him he wanted to take his job—the city cows.

As we walked along the Cherwell, he told me about getting his college position, and his mixed feelings about it, and I felt the bright egg yellow swelling inside me until I was bursting with it.

So, yes, Susannah is right: I did know. I knew instinctively from that first walk, when the colors of the world turned up and everything was clearer, richer, bigger because he was there. He always said he knew too on that first day. That was our story: the daffodils, the instinct—the knowing.

We were engaged only a month later. My friends all assumed it was a desperate mistake. Alice was polite, though clearly dubious; and my father asked if perhaps I could bring Doug to meet them. Only my mother got it—unquestioningly. I remember the vibration of happiness in her voice that I had never heard there before. She, alone, believed that I could know after such a short time—and she'd never even met him.

Then again, maybe I didn't know. Maybe all that was in my head. Perhaps Doug went along with the story for me. If he has had an affair then our story is twisted and stained now, like everything else.

"Sore subject, huh?" Susannah's voice startles me. I find I can't answer.

"You want to talk about it?"

"No." I sit up straight. "No. Really. So, anyway: your marriage lasted, didn't it? You and your partner made it work."

"We were hardly love's young dream Kali. My son needed a father. And Marc was a pretty good father actually. For a while he lived on the island but not with us, and then I had the studio built and he moved in, and we were all kind of together for a bit. Then he died."

I can't read any sadness. Just a statement of fact.

"So, where's your son now?" I don't even know her son's name. It seems rude to ask now.

Her face clouds over. "Oh, that's enough about my life." She picks up her wine and takes a slug. The Merlot has stained her teeth a brownish red. I realize she may be a bit drunk. "You had a good father too, in the end, didn't you? I'm sure Gray was a wonderful father."

"What do you mean 'in the end'?"

She sips the wine. "You know what," she says, "you're nothing like your mother."

"Yes, I know that."

"Elena was open and trusting. You're the opposite."

"Open and trusting? My mother? You have to be kidding."

"Oh, yeah, well." She tosses up a hand and looks away. "I guess she changed. Of course she would. I knew her a very long time ago. People change. I'm not surprised. Who wouldn't after what . . . we both changed. I did for sure." She drinks again and when she clonks her wine glass down, some spills onto the table, staining the pine. If either of us is like my mother then it's Susannah—I can't pin her down, even for a second.

"So," she leans forward, "tell me about your travel plans."

"Well, I'll head back to Vancouver."

"To do what?"

"I'm not sure. The aquarium?"

"So you do have no plans."

"Well, not really—but—"

"Are you glad you found me at least? Are you glad you came on this great maternal odyssey?"

I try to ignore the sarcasm. The light above the table makes patterns, like jagged trails of frost, across her pale irises. Her hands, I notice, are broad and strong, with mannish veins running across their surface.

"To be honest, Susannah, I don't feel like you've told me very much about my mother, though I'm grateful that you told me what you did about my grandparents. That's helped me make sense of a few things. But there are still some things I'd like to know."

"Like what?"

"Okay. Well, when my mother came up here to do the whale-mapping project, where did she live?"

"Oh. They lived on their boats, mainly. But then she bought the float house and . . ." she stops. A blotchy redness spreads up her neck.

"The what?" I almost shout it.

She clamps her mouth shut.

"A float house? You said she bought a float house? What's a float house?"

I want to leap across the table and shake her.

"Oh. Well. Your mother," she shrugs and takes another sip, "lived for a while in a float house, much further north." She tips the wine into her mouth, again, gulping it down.

"Where?"

"Oh it's just a little chunk of land in the middle of nowhere. Nothing there. Tiny, tiny community, like, maybe five other houses on the whole island. But orca, year round orca, that's why she went."

"But I don't even know what a float house is!" My voice is almost a wail.

"Well. It's a kind of houseboat: a house that's built on a floating platform of cedar logs. You can drag it to whatever location you want. The loggers used to live that way, nomadic, moving whole communities—schools, stores, houses—from job to job." She waves her glass and then drains it. "Not that Elena was a nomad. She only wanted that place because of the orca. She always said the island chose her, not the other way around."

I lean over and pick up the wine bottle. It clinks against the rim of her glass as I pour her a generous amount. I notice that her hand is trembling as she pushes back her hair. She obviously minds that she has let slip about the float house, despite the bravado.

I try to wrestle the pieces of information into a shape: my mother dropped her PhD, shot up here to join some conservationists, lived on boats, photographed and recorded endangered whales. Then she bought a piece of land and a floating house—she must have felt that she belonged here. You don't buy land if you aren't planning to settle. Did she think she would live here forever? If so, what about my father and his scholarship?

"But wait—did my father come live in this float house too?"

Her eyes go round and startled and she touches the side of her head with her fingertips, then she breathes out through her nose. "Gray? Of course not. I told you—Gray was back in California at the university, he had his scholarship to finish up. And really, Kali, can you imagine Gray up here?" She gives an edgy, metallic laugh.

She's right. I can't imagine my father up here. But I can imagine my mother out there on that wild sea.

"Okay. Did something happen between my parents?"

"What? Elena and Graham?"

"Yes! My parents. Did they break up?"

"Okay," she sighs. "Sure. They did break up, yes."

"For how long?"

"Shit Kali, I really can't remember—and honestly, this is ancient private stuff between them." She leans back and holds up her hands. "Ask Gray."

"Okay, yes, you're right. I'm going to—as soon as I get home. But just—just tell me this one thing. Where was the float house?"

"Oh," she waves a hand. "*It's* way farther out . . . way up . . ."

I realize she's using the present tense. "Susannah—are you telling me that my mother's house is still up there?"

She shoves back her chair and rises to her feet. She is a little unsteady and her hip knocks the table.

"Is it still there, Susannah?"

"Just forget it." She looks down at me, then suddenly raises her voice, making me jump: "Just drop it!" She turns away and walks, slightly waveringly, toward the sink.

She has finished the bottle of wine. I don't move. I'm not going to let a bit of drunken shouting stop me now. "The float house is still up there, isn't it Susannah?"

The dogs scrabble off the floor and mill by her legs. Her back is to me and her shoulders are tight and broad. She drains her wine-glass and rests both hands on the counter, swaying gently. I stare at her obstinate torso. Who is this person to decide what I should and shouldn't know about my own mother? Who is she to keep something like this from me?

"Susannah." I get up slowly. "Please don't walk away from me."

She turns. Her cheekbones look more sunken, her eye sockets deeper. A snake-like vein bulges down the center of her forehead. "Shit, Kali, you really need to let this go! This is ancient history. You have *no fucking idea* why you are here! In fact, you have no idea what's happening here at all. So, Kali my dear, I suggest you drop it."

"Everyone calls me Kal," I say, through gritted teeth. "Not Kali. I told you that before. No one ever calls me Kali. I hate it. Only my mother ever called me that—usually when she was angry."

"Seriously? But Kali's . . . it means—"

"Yes, I know what it means: the Hindu goddess of death and destruction," I say. "That's why I'm only—ever—Kal."

"Oh no, no, no?" She throws her chin up. "Seriously?" Then she looks at the ceiling, as if addressing my mother in the heavens, "You didn't even talk to her about her name? You didn't?" She gives a throaty laugh.

"What do you mean?" I fight the urge to look up too. I grip the back of the chair with both hands. I imagine picking it up and hurling it across the kitchen at her, the wood splintering against her muscular body.

"Kali is the mother goddess—she's *Shakti*—ultimate female power. She's the goddess of time and change. She's fierce—admittedly— some myths have her dancing on the corpses of demons she's slain, not realizing that her husband's body is among them. Huh? But she finds the infant Shiva on the battlefield too; she stops slaying people and picks him up to protect him. She nurses him right there in battle, covered in blood. So no—Kali's not death—she's mother-power. She's protection, nurture, defiance. Your mother and I talked about this a lot." She suddenly lowers her voice. "I was getting very into Hinduism at the time. We wanted a strong, fearless, warrior name. Ultimate female power—I mean, who wouldn't love a name like that?"

"*You* loved my name? Are you telling me *you* named me?"

She touches a dog with her bare foot. "Yeah, I guess I did in a way."

"Okay. This is actually getting quite weird."

"I guess I was more into Hinduism than Elena."

"What—were you a Hindu, Susannah?"

She waves a hand and laughs. "Look, it was California in the seventies. Everyone was a fucking Hindu. Everyone was everything! It was all about Eastern spirituality and mysticism. I went Sufi dancing at Big Sur, I chanted at Esalen, I studied the *Bhagavad Gita*— and the *Koran*—and the fucking *I-Ching*, Kali."

I stare at her. My mother never told me any of this. When I asked about my name, she just said she liked the sounds.

"You do know I'm your godmother, don't you?" she says.

That's it. Now she really has gone too far. "No, you're really not." I turn and walk away from her, back to the table. I stand behind it.

"No, seriously, I am." She saunters after me. "Though I guess I've been stripped of that title, huh?"

If she were my godmother, surely my parents would have thought to mention it.

Susannah leans a hand on the tabletop and stares at me, unblinking. "Elena didn't want you to be a scared person. We both liked the power of Kali. We wanted you to be fearless."

"Well, it didn't bloody work! I do not have ultimate female power and I am not fearless. Far from it. I was actually quite scared of *her*." I realize this is sort of true. I was always a little bit afraid of my mother.

A laugh curdles from the back of her throat. "You were afraid of Elena?"

"No. Yes. No! Sometimes. On some level. But I think maybe she was scared of me too. God, I really don't want to talk about this with you. Why am I talking about this with *you*?"

"Well, I guess it was always going to be complicated."

"What? Why? Why should it have been complicated?"

"Oh never mind. Shit. It's late. I guess I've had a little too much to drink, huh?"

"Why won't you tell me anything?"

"Okay. Now, listen, Kali." She shoves her hair out of her face. "We've both suffered a terrible loss. We need to care for ourselves right now. We need to nurture ourselves, and heal."

"Kal!" I snap. "And what have you got to heal? You hadn't seen her in years!"

We stare at each other across the table. Then she takes a long breath. She blinks, slowly. "Wow," she says. "Holy crap. Losing people is tiring."

"You lost my mother decades ago, Susannah."

"You know what? Neither of us has lost her, Kali. Because she isn't really gone, is she?" She leans both hands on the table. Her boney eyes are fixed on mine. She takes a long breath in through her nose, as if summoning my mother's spirit. "Don't you feel her with us? You must. You must surely sense her. She's right here, Kali. Right now. She's with us right now. Can't you feel her? Can't you? I know you can: she's here. She's in this room with us, right now."

"For chrissake Susannah! You have to stop this! Stop this right now! My mother is bloody dead. I watched her die."

"Oh, you need to go to bed." She waves a hand as if to dismiss me. "I guess we both do."

"What I need," I grit my teeth, "is to know who my mother was."

"Actually, you really don't." She straightens, hands on hips. She suddenly seems very tall and broad.

"Yes I do."

"You know what, Kali? The thing that really gets me right now is that this actually isn't about your mother at all. This isn't about you chasing down Elle's secrets. This is about you distracting yourself from the humiliation of a straying husband. Look at you!" The sinews in her neck stick out like wire and she seems to raise herself up and inflate, like a cobra. "You come here like a spoiled little girl with your questions—demanding answers, answers, answers. Instead of caring for your baby boy you ignore him—you neglect him—and you sit there and fuck with my head. Shit!" She slaps one hand on the table and I jump. "I was wrong about you, you know? You are so much like her it hurts. It's agony to be in the same space as you. You're completely fucking single-minded—driven by intuition and impulse. You force me to dredge up all these things—things you can't even imagine: painful, awful memories and you don't even understand why you're here. You don't have a fucking clue! This is not about you at all. So stop asking all these questions!"

"Who are you to tell me what I'm here for?"

"This is my house you're in right now, Kali, and believe me, I know why she sent you and it wasn't for this shit."

"What? Why who sent me?" I stare at her. "What are you talking about? Nobody sent me here."

She looks at me, unblinking.

"Jesus Christ Susannah. You know nothing about me!"

"Oh Kali," she shakes her head. Her voice is suddenly flat and hard. "I know *everything* about you."

She spins away from me and stares out the French windows, at the cold blackness and the rain falling onto the deck.

Our eyes meet in the glass, and for that second I see the demons lurking inside her. I don't know what psychodrama I've stumbled into here, but I need to get out of it. I need to leave.

I turn and I walk out of the kitchen, through the living room, not looking at that fat red orb, not looking at the dogs—though I know their amber eyes will be fixed on me. I half expect her to thunder after me, hair flying, dogs baying by her side, but she doesn't.

Back in the room I shut the door. There is no lock.

I kneel by the bed where Finn is sleeping. Adrenaline is pumping through my body, making me hot and trembly. I try to slow my breathing down.

Finn is on his back, hands thrown up, surrendered, head to one side, lips slightly open. He is so beautiful and perfect, and so very little. He always seems to shrink when he's asleep, as if he is reverting to his baby state. I put a hand, very gently, on his stomach and feel it rise and fall beneath my palm, warm and tight under the soft quilt of his sleeping bag.

Susannah may be positively deranged but there is also some truth in her accusations. She's right that this isn't just about my mother—I am running away and I'm scared. She's also right that I have not been the best mother lately. I didn't wedge the bedroom door open properly, I let him break that frame and cut himself, and I lost it over peas and a boiled egg. What she doesn't seem to realize is there is nothing more important to me than Finn. But why do I care what she thinks of me? Tomorrow, we'll be gone. And we are certainly never coming back here.

I stroke his head with my fingertips. Maybe this trip is unfair to him. The lack of routine and the strangeness can't be easy for him. But then I think about his utter delight at the squirrel today. And again, outside, this afternoon, stomping through puddles in his red rain boots, grabbing things, poking sticks into mud, bashing rocks, and laughing at his own breath in the cold air. Finn is fine. There's more to life than routines. I'm not going to let Susannah undermine me. My child is perfectly happy.

And this is not just a distraction. This is real and important.

As I watch Finn sleep I realize that this is not over. My mother is where everything begins. She is what makes me who I am, the mother that I am. Like an orca matriarch, she is influencing absolutely everything, even now. If I never know what happened to her up here then I will never be able to make sense of myself, and I will always be afraid—and running.

Susannah may think I am weak and afraid and distracted but she's wrong. There is something in my mother's past that she knows. I can feel it, lurking like a burglar in the shadows. Maybe I will stay tomorrow because I have to get it out of her. We can get the last ferry of the day—I need to know what secret Susannah is protecting.

British Columbia, Late Spring, 1976

As they motored up the coast one day, they came across an old claw-foot bathtub that had been abandoned on a shingle beach. The three of them hauled it into the boat, then squashed themselves around it, and motored back to base.

They pushed, dragged, and heaved it up the steep path to the campfire. There was a mound, overlooking the bay, over to the left of the fire, surrounded by tall, skinny pines. "Bathroom with a view," said Dean.

The guys got shovels and began digging a fire pit where they planned to put the bath. Elena went and got firewood from the tarp on deck, lugging it up in three loads—one to them, two to the main fire pit, where that morning's embers were still glowing beneath the green branches Jonas had put over them. She crouched down to try to revive them, blowing at an angle as the guys had shown her. None of them had eaten anything since a peanut butter sandwich at lunch. Her arms and legs felt stringy, and each time she turned her head it was as if the world took a second or two to catch up.

The sun began lowering itself toward the horizon. Jonas and Dean were like kids, messing around together in the dirt.

Elena took Jonas's sharp, curved fish cleaning knife and sliced into the Chinook's belly. She tugged the blade along in a swooping motion, the way he'd showed her, and opened the fish up. Then she scraped out dark, twisted, fish stinking entrails into a bag before cleaning out the cavity with patient strokes. She tied the guts tightly in their bag. Then she made her incisions under the pectoral fin, and snapped *off its injured head. When she looked up, the men had heaved the bathtub over the pit, and were filling it up by lugging buckets of sea-water from the shore. She went back to the salmon, drawing the knife along its spinal column, concentrating hard to keep her hand steady.*

She washed the heavy salmon fillets down and lay them on the cedar plank as Jonas had shown her—the Native Canadian way. She had watched him spear the fish with a Swiss Army knife corded onto a branch that afternoon in a stream that was teeming with Chinook. He stood very still on a rock, halfway out in the rushing water, hold-ing the spear point below the surface. After a bit, he eased the knife toward a fish and then, with a sharp downward stab, he pinned it there. But he didn't lift it out right away—he went into the freezing water, up to his thighs, and dug down with one hand to grab it. He came wading out of the water with an enormous salmon on the end of his spear. His eyes shone and were deep blue, like the sky behind him. She saw his Viking ancestors in his broad shoulders, the big fish in his hands and his solid, wet thighs coming over the rocks toward her.

He slapped the fish down, heavily, then eased the spear out of its neck. The fish was the length of her forearm, a shimmering mixture of silvers, and she felt suddenly sorry that it had to die for them.

"It must be cold in that water," she said.

"If you lift the spear up," he said, "she slips off and she's gone." The fish was still impaled on his knife. The blade had gone into its skull from above, right through its brain. Death, at least, would have been instant.

"How do you know how do to all this?" she said. "Who taught you this stuff?"

"Various people. Myself. When I was eighteen," he said, "I decided to come up here and survive a month with nothing—in the end I was up here three months. I didn't want to go back."

"Don't listen to his wildman routine. He looked like a skeleton." Dean was lying on a rock, just above them. She'd forgotten he was there. He spoke from under his baseball cap. "We all thought he'd died up here."

"Your poor mother."

A shadow fell across Jonas's face, and he knelt down to the salmon ducking his head as he tugged the blade out of its skull. It made a crackling, suctioning sound. From under his cap Dean said, "His mom had just died."

She flattened out the burning logs and balanced the ends of the plank on stones on either side of the fire.

Jonas's reaction to his mother's death seemed, in some way, to demonstrate the essential difference between men and women. When her mother died, she had frozen. For a long time, she was afraid to go to school, or to leave the house. But when his mother died, he had headed out into the wilderness. Then again, perhaps the two reactions weren't so different—they had both retreated. And she was only eight years old. The only wilderness she could find was inside herself.

She wondered what losing someone she loved would do to her now—would she freeze and become afraid again? She didn't think so. But it was hard to imagine what it would be like to experience that level of pain again.

The art was to cook the fish through without setting fire to the plank, which they left soaking at night in seawater. You had to find the exact right spot on the fire; too hot and the whole thing would go up in flames; too cold and the fish would be raw. Just right and the cedar smoke infused the fish, bringing out its most delicate flavors.

Jonas and Dean had finished filling the bathtub now. They'd got the fire going under it and smoke drifted around them, obscuring their faces. They were talking about the orcas, something about charts for tomorrow, but she couldn't hear what. The clearing was saturated with rich golden light, but the evening chill made her wish for another, warmer pullover. She was dog-tired now and couldn't bring herself to go to the boat and get one.

Every single thing she owned was damp anyway—every piece of clothing, even the pillows and the sleeping bags. The inside of her backpack felt as if a family of sea slugs had recently crawled through it. The pages of the books and journals she'd bought in Victoria—anything *she could find about orcas—were already sticking together. And now the stove in the boat was broken so they had to build up the fire at dawn just to fill the thermoses of coffee for the day.*

The smell of the cedar roasting salmon made her stomach growl, but at the same time she felt slightly sick. In fact, she'd felt off-color a lot recently, probably because, when they weren't eating salmon, they were eating peanut butter. She craved collard greens and kiwifruit. At night she dreamed of black California grapes. Jonas and Dean assured her that vitamin C sources were abundant up here—they spent one long, irritating afternoon on the Zodiac outdoing one another with plant names. The berries alone had gone on for a good hour—fairy bell, cloudberry, bear berry, hairy manzanita, Indian strawberry, chokeberry—until Elena was sure they were just making words up. "There's a whole grocery out there," Jonas said. "Burdock leaves, nettles, wild ginger and garlic, nuts, licorice." But they never seemed to be on dry land long enough to forage. Dean's wife had packed him a big bottle of multivitamins to ward off scurvy and when they remembered, they each swallowed one. But Elena was dying for a good crisp apple.

"Ladies first then." She looked up. Jonas was grinning down at her. "The water will be warm pretty soon." The sleeves of his checked shirt were rolled to the elbow, showing strong, tanned forearms. He still had oil smears on his arms from fixing the Zodiac's outboard motor when it broke that morning. His jeans—which had never really dried from the river—were soaked down the thighs again, from carrying buckets of seawater. They were smeared with dirt from the earth and the tin bath. For a moment or two, she just gazed up at him.

Then Dean came over to the fire and poked at it with a stick. He was filthy and bedraggled too; the dirt had darkened his hair from flame to gingerbread. She couldn't see his eyes but his mouth looked sad. Sparks flew up around the salmon. Jonas went off to throw the fish guts out to sea.

Dean must be missing his wife and baby. She wondered what his wife thought of him coming up here with his old high school buddy to spend two months chasing orca—his second summer in a row.

He wrote her letters most evenings, which he'd send back to Victoria with passing kayakers or any fishermen who happened to be headed south. She wondered what proportion of the letters actually made it home.

On the journey from Victoria, Dean had told her that his wife was a University of British Columbia anthropologist. Her specialty was First Nations oral storytelling traditions. It was her passion, he said, but she stopped six months ago when their son, Daniel, was born. Elena imagined a woman with Inuit-style hair, baking bread and telling her baby stories in a sing-song voice.

"So, does your wife go back to work this fall?" she asked him now.

He turned his head. His face was tired, but placid. She realized that it was just in profile that his mouth looked sad. "Nah. Her job involved field trips half the year—and mine involves field trips half the year—and they're not always different halves of the year. So, she's at home now with Danny."

It took a moment for Elena to realize that he meant his wife had quit her job permanently.

Jonas came back, wiping his hands down on his jeans. "Okay, so— I'm serious—you want to get in that bath first, Elle? That water's not going to be pretty after it's had me and then Deano in it."

She glanced from one filthy man to the other, and got up.

"Just be sure to sit on the wood planks," Dean said. "You don't want to scorch your butt."

She walked, with as much dignity as she could muster, up the little slope to the tin bathtub. Below them, she could see Dean's big long boat, and the Zodiac next to it. Dean's boat was their base for the next two months. It was huge and cumbersome, stank of oil and mildew and, faintly, of fish. The engine had broken several times on the journey north from Victoria but each time, the guys fixed it after only a short battle. It guzzled oil and left trails of inky smoke against the gray sky, but it was warm inside, with narrow cabin beds, a rudimentary toilet, and most importantly, no rain. Jonas's Zodiac was their daytime home—just twelve feet long, inflatable, with an outboard motor and no shelter—a boat to chase whales in.

Beyond the boats, the ocean glowed in the last light. The waves, which had been choppy and unsettled all day, were calmer now, as if someone had soothed them with the promise of a good night's rest. The sun had swollen into a fat gold orb and was easing itself behind the shadowy islands that lay between the bay and the open sea.

She glanced around. The little clearing where they'd built the main fire was hugged on all sides by tall firs, spruce, and pines. There was no need to feel exposed here. The tiny canning town was filled with commercial fishing boats, but it was right around the headland. The fishermen, many of them Native Canadians, would be sitting on the dock chewing the honeyed strips of sockeye they called "Indian candy" or throwing back beers in the shack bar—but they were half a mile away. Nobody could see her here, except the two men by the fire. And only one of them was looking.

She peeled off her damp pullover, then her T-shirt. Goosebumps sprang up on her skin. She glanced over her shoulder again. Dean, a gentleman, had turned his back, and was crouched on his heels over the salmon. Jonas looked steadily across at her. She felt blood rush to her cheeks. She turned her back again, tugging at her jeans. She touched the water with fingertips. It was murky, salty, but perfect— almost hot from the fire beneath—but not boiling. They'd put two planks along the base of the bathtub. She stuck her hand in and prodded them. They seemed secure enough.

Taking a breath, she eased her underwear off, and, feeling his eyes on her body—the sensation as vivid as any touch—she lowered herself into the water. She closed her eyes as the heat eased her tired, chilly limbs. She leaned her head back and let out the long breath that had been coiled inside her.

The last time she'd sat in a claw-foot bath like this was in Seattle as a child. She could picture the white hexagonal tiles on the bathroom floor—the grout was always dark—and the graying walls, the brass sconce lights, the single window with the blinds always down. Just visualizing the bathroom made her feel hollow. Bath times were the worst at first because her mother always used to help her wash her hair. She wished that she could go back, and tell her sad childhood

self that it would all work out because, one day, when she grew up,
she'd find herself in another claw-foot bathtub, but this time it would
be perched over an ocean full of whales—all waiting to tell her their
secrets.

She moved her hands slowly through the water and despite the tired-
ness, she felt herself grow full again, just at the thought of the whales, as
if someone had turned on the heat and lights inside her.

It had been a long, damp, chilly day; the third in a row with no
sightings. They'd slept by the campfire last night—too despondent
and tired to bother climbing down to the boat—and she'd woken that
morning, freezing, and stiff, in a drizzle, with her eyes sealed shut.
There had been a moment of exquisite panic as she realized that her
eyelids really weren't working—she probed the sockets with her finger-
tips, feeling a strange, marshmallow puffiness. She scrambled up and
felt her way to the water container hunching down to splash handfuls
of cold water on her face. This allowed her to open her eyes into slits.
She grabbed the speckled mirror from her pack and in the dim first
light, she could just make out her reflection: she let out a strangled
scream.

Dean sat up, took one look at her, and laughed. His ginger hair
stuck up at all angles, like a madman.

"No-see-ums."

"See what? What the hell's wrong with me? Jesus Christ! My eyes!"

"No-see-ums—invisible bugs, gnats. They can get you in the night
if you aren't close enough to the fire."

Jonas turned over, opened his eyes slowly, and peered at her. He
gave a throaty morning laugh. "Holy shit, you've been mauled."

While Dean built up the fire for coffee, Jonas grabbed a small bottle
from the boat. He knelt in front of her and dabbed at her eyelids very
gently with the pad of his finger. The lotion smelled strongly of pine mixed
with lavender, and something else that she didn't recognize. "I get it from
my friend, Thayer," he said. "She's lived up here all her life, three genera-
tions of her family—she makes it herself. It's better than hydrocortisone."

Her eyes were puffy but okay now, but the mosquito bite on her
ankle that she'd been scratching all day felt weirdly stiff. She peered

down at her foot. Through the greenish water, the ankle looked huge and distorted. She laid back, gingerly, and shut her eyes again. If she slipped off the plank her butt would hit red hot tin. The wood smoke from the fire beneath the bath filtered up around her—at least it would fend off gnats. She hoped the mosquito bite wasn't infected. That had happened to her once on a trip to Big Sur with Graham and she'd had to go to a doctor for an antihistamine shot. But she could not think about Gray. It was best not to. Her childhood had at least given her that skill: she knew how to draw down the blinds in her mind and move on. She was expert at it.

She had no idea what getting to a doctor involved up here, but it was unlikely to be straightforward. She'd ask Jonas for more of his friend's remedy to put on the ankle and hope for the best.

She really was exhausted. Her muscles felt like melting wax. All day, they'd scanned the horizon, motoring from one possible sighting to the next. Jonas and Dean had tried to train her how to look for blows or fins.

"Your eye naturally fixes on immovable objects," Jonas stood next to her, looking through his binoculars as she looked through hers, "See? Your eye wants to fix on things—it wants to jumps from one object to the next—that rock there, the harbor seals over there, that sail—the white triangle—see—right there." She followed his gaze, and her eyes did, indeed, take great leaps. "What you need to do," he explained, "is retrain your brain and eye. You have to look at the spaces, because that's where the whales are. They appear in the spaces between the things our brains tell us to look at."

The sun had vanished, now, into the sea behind the island, and stars were appearing, first one or two, then handfuls, as the darkness closed in on the camp.

"Elena?" Dean's voice cut into her half-sleep. "Food's ready."

"Okay. You guys go ahead." She wasn't even hungry anymore.

Her whole body felt loose. She watched the sky thicken to silver-studded velvet above her. She could hear the rumble of Dean and Jonas talking, but not the words.

She thought about the orcas they'd seen in the first week, before this lull, and it struck her that the whales were in control. They decided when they'd reveal themselves, and when they would vanish. The first day, out on the Zodiac, they'd found a pod early on—a floatplane pilot had called in a sighting and they'd been given the location, close by, over the VHF. They were motoring along, scanning the horizon when the whales appeared from nowhere, slicing through the water, maybe thirty feet from the stern. Jonas cut the engine and for a second there was silence and she felt that same first moment of awe—almost terror—at the sheer size and grace of these slow beasts. She counted seven, eight fins.

Three of the orca started to show off. They zoomed through the water then leaped out, in synchrony, with a twist of their bodies in midair. Elena tried to take photos, but she never seemed to press the shutter fast enough to capture the fins and the markings on their shining black and white bodies. Sea spray flew off their flanks as they leaped. But Jonas and Dean were an expert team—Jonas photographed the left side of the fins, while Dean, with binoculars and the laminated catalog, scanned for distinguishing marks in the couple of seconds that the body of the whale was visible. They identified the matriarch, and two of her sons and three juveniles—the whales responsible for the biggest leaps and splashes. Each one had a name, as well as its own Pod ID—a letter followed by a number.

And then, after just ten minutes, they vanished. All the whales submerged in unison and that was that. Jonas and Dean hunched over the catalog, scribbling notes about what they'd seen but Elena sat in silence. Her limbs felt jittery, her heart banged in her chest, and her head buzzed. She stared at the ocean, willing them to come back, wondering where they'd gone, and why. How had they communicated this change of plan? Had they heard a call from far across the sea? Or had the matriarch instructed them to stop goofing around and move on? She needed to listen.

Then, bobbing on an ocean full of wild orcas, she suddenly missed the Sea Park whales. Being here felt almost like a betrayal. Bella had been taken from these waters. The mapping guys had established that pods traveled hundreds of miles up and down the coast. This meant that Bella's family was out there. She could have just been watching Bella's brothers and sisters, or cousins, nephews, nieces, uncles, aunts. Maybe one of the older females was Bella's mother.

She wondered if whales hold memories like humans. If so, there was a whale out there somewhere that would remember the day her baby daughter was ripped away in bloodshed and panic.

The men had finished up their notes. They patiently talked her through the findings—the nicks and propeller cuts, that slightly twisted tip on the big male's dorsal—and the importance of getting a clear picture of the saddle patch. She listened carefully.

She'd get better at this, she wasn't worried. But she knew now that she needed to know what was going on beneath the surface too. She needed to record the sounds these whales were making as they leaped and spy-hopped and tail-lobbed. That, in fact, was all she wanted to do.

She'd explained her dolphin work to the guys on the journey north. They had listened, and nodded, and asked good questions, but she could tell that for them it was a distraction from the real, conservation job of cataloging the orca population.

She needed to bring the hydrophone. She'd prove to them that she could do both. Once she became good at identifying the whales and photographing them, she could do it with headphones on. And, then, with the hydrophone dropped into the water she could begin the enormous task of mapping wild orca behaviors to vocalizations. It might take a lifetime to decode killer whale language, but she had a lifetime to give.

If she could amass enough preliminary evidence to make a grant proposal, then there was a future in this work. She didn't have the patience to spend the summer watching and learning from the men. She could do both. She needed to start listening—right now.

The smell of wood smoke and roasting salmon mingled with the forest scents. The night symphony was starting up and the waves had passed the sunset lull and banged rhythmically on the rocks below. In the forest behind her a wolverine barked relentlessly, and, further away, answering barks bounced back across the mountain slope. An owl's lonely hoot cut the rumble of the men's voices.

Then out of nowhere, a huge "kwoooof" echoed up from the bay. It bounced off the trees and the mountains and the rocks and expanded to fill the sky.

Dean—or maybe Jonas—whooped.

"Hey!" Jonas called up. "You hear that blow?"

She smiled, but she didn't open her eyes. Another "kwooof" echoed again, and she felt the sound vibrate through her blood and bones, up and down her spine, right through her heart, into the place that had been locked shut since she was eight years old.

Lying in the claw-foot bathtub on a little mound above the Pacific Ocean, Elena knew that this was where she belonged. It seemed incredible that she'd made it here—blindly following her instinct north, like the salmon swimming home. Whether it was chance, serendipity, luck, kismet, karma, or grace didn't really matter. This was where she belonged. She'd found her spot on earth and she'd never leave.

CHAPTER TEN

A rap on the door jerks me awake.

"Hey Kali. You want me to take the baby into town? I have to run a few errands. He can come along for the ride while you get some rest."

Susannah is standing in the doorway. I am still half in the dream where Doug is shaking me and saying, "*You're not listening to me.*"

I rub my face and glance at Finn—fast asleep on his back—and then at my phone—7:55 a.m. We are all out of whack. After the scene last night, I can't even think about handing her my child. Finn stirs and opens his eyes. I do need her Internet connection though.

"Can we both come?" I croak.

"But you don't need to get up. Go back to sleep. I'll take the baby—give you a break. Where's his diaper bag?"

"Oh no!" Suddenly I am wide awake. "That's okay, really. I'd actually like to see the town," I stroke Finn's sleepy face. "We'll both get up."

She is silent.

I blink a few times. Finn sits up. "Just give us a minute to get ready."

"Take your time," she growls.

We drive through steady rain and mist. Susannah's Subaru stinks of dog and mud. I have to clear damp papers, empty Vitamin Water bottles, and spilling packs of nuts and soybean snacks off the seat so I can put Finn's car seat in. The dogs are in the back, behind a metal barrier, panting in unison. We bounce down the single track and onto the wider road that leads back into town. The wipers squeak and the mist makes any view impossible.

Susannah hums. There are tiny, glistening droplets of mist on her silvery hair. It's not clear whether she has forgotten about our argument, or whether this is her attempt to make peace. She looks somehow decisive, with her chin up, as if she's made up her mind about something important.

I dig my face into the collar of the parka. Finn, packed into his red snowsuit, is chewing on a bit of bagel with one hand, his sippy cup in the other. He looks pink-cheeked and bouncy, happy for the novelty of a drive.

This is my third day on the island and as of yet we have encountered no other humans. I have seen almost nothing of British Columbia but the inside of Susannah's house. Driving away from Isabella Point I realize how odd this has been. The two of us have been brought together because of one person that neither of us—quite obviously—really knows. No wonder things got out of hand.

My head aches and I'm hungry and I realize I forgot Finn's diaper bag. Obviously, I'm not going to tell Susannah this. I'll have to buy some more in town. "How do you get through a whole winter of this weather?" I say. "Doesn't it make you claustrophobic?"

"It's not always like this. Sometimes it snows and it's magical. Winter can be the most beautiful season up here. Sea fog is always a possibility and it's called the 'Rain Coast' for a reason, but you'd be used to that, huh? It rains all the time in England, right?"

"Not like this. At least, you occasionally get an actual view of the world through the rain."

We don't talk after this. She is pale. She has to be nursing quite a hangover. I should apologize for all the shouting, but my frustrations with her seem to have solidified. I wonder if her critique of me as a mother comes from something in her own childhood. I wonder what sort of a mother Susannah was. Is.

But it's true that I don't have the rights to my mother's past. And Susannah has been generous in many ways, taking me in, looking after Finn, offering to let me rest.

"So," I say. "I'm going to head off later today. I've stayed much longer than I'd planned."

"I thought you didn't have a plan."

"Well, okay, if I had *planned* to stay, I'd have stayed one night at most so I've already overstayed."

"You're free to go whenever you want, Kali."

I look at her. "Yes," I say, "I know that."

"So. Vancouver."

I look away, out the window. My face is reflected back at me. My hair is sticking up. I smooth it down. "Actually," I say, "I thought I'd go north, and try to find my mother's float house." I say it casually. I don't mean it of course. I just want to see her reaction. It would be truly insane to take Finn any further into this wilderness. And I have no idea what the float house is like—or where it is—or even if it's still there at all.

She stares straight ahead, chin up. Her jaw is tight. I can see the sinews under the skin. It's no good. I just can't read her.

"What? You think that's irresponsible of me?"

She still says nothing. I think—but I'm not sure—that she's angry. Maybe she's angry with herself, for letting it slip that there is a float house. What's not clear is why my plans should bother her so much. I realize I am onto something.

"So do you?" I say.

"I do what?"

"Think I'm a bad mother to consider taking Finn off to find the float house?"

She doesn't answer. We are driving downhill into the tiny fishing port. Clearly, I am not going to goad her into telling me anything. Susannah is not the type to be goaded into anything.

We drive past a street of pretty, low-slung wooden buildings and brightly painted storefronts. We pass the Rock Salt Bakery. It has shocking pink door and window frames, and an enormous model cupcake sign with a cherry on top. There is a clothing store next door to the bakery, and an old-fashioned toy store. It all looks more civilized than I'd imagined when I drove up here in the fog. We stop to let a bearded man cross the road and he waves at us from under his raincoat hood. Susannah lifts a hand, but doesn't smile. Other than that, the place is deserted.

"It's very quiet here," I say. "Extremely quiet."

"Yeah, not much happens November to March, except weather. Most people shut up and go. But spring and summer get real busy. I shouldn't complain; it's good business. But really I prefer silence."

She sounds calm but I can tell that things are boiling under the surface. I can almost hear her brain fizzing and popping. Then I realize what's going on here: it's the float house. She uses it herself. She probably appropriated it when my mother left and it's her house now. I imagine a weekend cabin, far away from the summer bustle of the gallery. She thinks of it as hers and she's threatened, now that I know about it, because I might reclaim it.

Then again, she's so hard to read. And what am I going to do? I can hardly tow it back to England with me. Maybe my comment about the float house didn't bother her after all. She probably knows I won't be able to find it—how would I? Maybe it's long gone. And she's right. I wouldn't go even if I knew where it was. With a little boy, heading further out into that wild sea in January would be madness.

We park outside her gallery. It's smaller than I remembered from the brief look that first night—painted dove gray with a window showing a couple of pots on plinths. It occurs to me that I'm about to bring my fuel-injected toddler into a room full of priceless breakables. I'll just ask to use the computer to check my flights, then I'll get out. I need to call Alice and Doug and I don't want Susannah listening in.

The gallery is cold and smells of fresh paint. Our feet echo on the polished oak floor as we come in. The main gallery room is to the right, and goes back a long way. It seems mainly empty, except for a few shelves of bright ceramics at the beginning. The dogs mill about at the base of a steep flight of stairs, wagging their tails. The walls are white. The light is muted.

"Feel free to take a look around—there are a few pieces here still. I'll be upstairs. I have a few things to see to up there. Don't let the baby touch anything, though, okay?" Then she disappears up the stairs followed by the dogs, before I can ask if I could bring Finn up and borrow her computer. Like most people who have lived alone for a long time, Susannah only knows her own agenda. I hear a door slam shut. I wonder what on earth she was planning to do with Finn if she'd brought him here alone. Then I wonder if my comment about the floathouse has done this—is she retreating to lick some invisible wound? Or make a plan?

Then I realize that my phone will work, of course, now that we're back in town. Hanging on tightly to Finn with one hand, I rifle around in my bag for it.

Susannah moves about overhead. I hear the wheels of an office chair slide across a wooden floor. She may look like a Californian baby boomer, and have a kitchen full of green tea and mung beans, and fold her legs into the Lotus position at dawn each day, but there is nothing Zen about Susannah. She has the soul of a ruthless executive.

Finn tugs at my hand, leaning into the gallery. "Dat?" he says. "Oh?"

I walk him inside, holding his hand very tightly. The room is empty except for some ceramic fish on one shelf—mercifully above Finn's level. I let him go and he toddles away, fast, toward the end of the room, his feet echoing on the floorboards. He is heading toward the back of the gallery and I can see out through a wall of sliding windows onto a patio garden. There are three or four round bistro tables and chairs, painted light green. I wander after him and gaze out. He presses his nose on the glass, and slaps it with both hands. "Dat," he instructs, looking up at me.

"It's locked, love. I can't open it."

I can imagine the empty ceramic pots that are piled at the base of the wall bursting with summer flowers. I turn and look back up the empty room while Finn bashes the glass. There are skylights and the tall front windows let in light too. The room is broad and L-shaped, and there is a red velvet sofa along the wall at in the foot of the L.

It's easy to imagine this space displaying beautiful art and that little garden with vines covering the trellis and flowers bursting from pots, the sliding windows open, gallery visitors coming and going, seagulls coasting across the evening sky above it all. I imagine private views where guests spill, clutching glasses of wine, into the salty night, voices filling the air. Somewhere upstairs I hear a thud, as if a heavy book has been dropped, or a big flat foot stamped down.

I look at my cell. There is no signal in here. I zip up the parka. "Let's go out, love. Shall we go and have a walk around?"

I pull up Finn's hood and pull his mittens on—I finally remembered to get them out of the case. "Okay. Let's go." He barrels off up the room, in a stumbling run, his small legs moving comically fast, as if struggling to keep up with his toppling body.

"We're going for a walk." I whisk him away from the shelves, toward the front door, shouting up the stairs. "Back soon."

No reply.

"Can I get you anything, Susannah?"

The office chair slides again across a wooden floor and I think I hear her mumbling—maybe she's on the phone.

We step out into the mist again. Somewhere out to sea a ferry horn echoes, and in the port, down below the street, masts clatter and clank. But all the sounds feel slightly muffled—as if I'm wrapped in plastic wrap. Droplets of rain tap the top of my head and soak my face, but they feel light, far off. Finn reaches up and takes my hand—one touch that does feel solid. He goes down the front steps sideways, holding onto me, putting both feet on the smooth surface before dropping a leg down for the next step. When he reaches the pavement I pull up his hood, and he becomes a small gnome, toddling busily next to me.

We head across the road to a railing overlooking the port and watch the fishing boats for a few minutes, but it's too cold and damp to stand here for long. I pull out my phone: a signal at last—just a few bars, but enough. I quickly text Alice.

Tons to tell you. All well. Staying with that friend of Mom's on Spring Tide Island. Found out all sorts of *amazing* things. No phone reception at house. Can u talk?

Then I dial Doug's cell. It only rings twice.

"Kal?"

"I'm just calling to say Finn is fine, really happy. There's nothing to worry about."

"Nothing to worry about? I'm glad Finn's fine but—seriously? You have to be kidding me! Look. I want you to listen to me now and I don't care if you're ready or not. I'm going to talk and you have to just shut up and listen and not hang up. Okay? Just listen to me without hanging up. This has gone on long enough. What you saw on my phone—it was completely one-sided. I told her to stop, there were other texts but the reason I hid them from you is that I knew I was in the wrong to allow her to send them—she'd been sending them for a while, and I didn't stop her. The truth is in some way I probably didn't want her to stop—you were so focused on Finn—as you should be— and bottom line is it felt good to be wanted by someone that badly. It was an ego-boost. I'm ashamed of myself for letting it go on but I did not reciprocate. I did not encourage her. Nothing else happened between us. Okay? Can you hear me? Kal? Are you there?"

I can't speak. I can't seem to let his words sink through the shell of panic I have created about our marriage. I can't process what he is saying. You don't just get texts like that. Is that what he's saying? That she just sent them, unbidden? Why would she just send them? He must have done *something* to encourage her.

"Say something!"

"I can't," I croak. "I have to . . . I can't get my head around this Doug . . ."

He must have done something. You have to do something to make someone send passionate texts. You have to kiss them at least. Or confess an attraction. Or sleep with them first.

"That's okay," he is saying. "That's okay. I know. Just—please could you just come home now. Okay? Just come home and we'll talk about all this properly."

"I can't talk now, I've got Finn, there's a wind—it's so cold—and I can't . . . I don't know what to think. I . . . We'll be home in a few days. I'll text you my flight details."

"Can you call me later?"

"There's no reception where I'm staying."

"Where exactly are you staying?"

"I have to go."

I hang up.

We make our way up the main street, toward the Rock Salt Bakery. Doug's explanation doesn't stack up. Is he really saying he allowed an ex-girlfriend to send him love-texts—but didn't encourage it? How could that be? And even if he did do nothing, it's still a betrayal. Nothing like the betrayal of sex, admittedly, but he turned away from us. It's . . . the problem is, I don't know what it is. I don't know what has happened anymore. I know he's not a liar. Or is he? It's as if, when I try to think about this closely, something goes blank in my head.

It's possible that I've been ludicrous, overblown, mad. But then again, maybe I haven't. There's too much going on here, with Susannah and this wild island and this big ocean with killer whales, and echoes of my mother's secrets in the hissing of its waves. I can't think straight. I need to get away from here—away from Susannah's creepy house and her moods and half-truths. But I want to find out what she's hiding, too. If I run away from this I'll never know.

Finn stops every few paces to poke or investigate things. He is singing to himself, but I can't hear the song. My ears and face hurt from the bitter wind but for once I have remembered Finn's hat. He is bundled up and warm. I peer at my phone again—no response from Alice—then with stiff fingers, I get into my e-mails.

Among some messages from friends, and work—work!—all of which I ignore, there is a new mail from my father.

From: G.K.MacKenzie
To: Kali
Subject: re: Sorry

Do NOT go and see this Gillespie woman.

I have tried your number several times, but am unable to get through, maybe it is an old number I have for you. Do not go there. I will explain everything when you get home. I am anxious to know that you and Finn are safe. Please respond immediately.

G

As I walk, I type my reply.

To: G.K.MacKenzie
From: Kali
Subject: re: Sorry

Why? I've just stayed two nights with Susannah—there was a prob with B&B—but everything is fine. Sorry if I worried you, Dad. I agree—she's quite something. But she did know an awful lot about Mom. Is that why you didn't want me to go? I know about the whales—why was that such a secret? I know about Mom's childhood too. These things are huge. Don't families usually talk to each other about things like this? I know she owned a floating house. I know the two of you split up for a bit. But what else don't I know? Vancouver later today, Finn loves the boats and wildlife up here. We **really do** need to talk now. love K

I press "send" with a numb finger and put the phone away and look down at Finn. A jolt of electricity goes through me: he's no longer next to me. I spin around.

*   *   *

It's fine. It's okay. He's right there—kneeling by a pile of wet leaves near a drainpipe about ten feet back—poking them with a stick. I run back down to him, glancing around to see if anyone has witnessed this shameful display of bad mothering. There is no one around. His jeans are soaked and mulchy. He sticks his hands into the leaves.

"Come on, love." I kneel next to him. "Goodness me. What are you up to?"

He keeps poking, intent on finding some treasure in the muck.

"Come on Finn. That looks really dirty love. Let's get to the bakery! Let's get cake!"

"Dat!" still squatting, he points across the street to a red pickup truck.

"That's a truck," I say. "Some kind of big truck." He grins up at me, his bangs pressed down by his bobble hat. I stroke it out of his eyes. "You really love trucks, don't you? What color is it?"

He looks at it. "Daddy."

Our eyes lock. I have to grit my teeth because the tears are rising. "We'll see Daddy really soon, okay? I bet you're missing daddy. He's missing you too, love. He really is. You'll see him soon though. Come on! Let's get a great big cake."

An elderly man in a navy blue fisherman's hat is chatting at the counter to woman about Susannah's age. Finn and I wait, hand in hand. The bakery smells sweet and yeasty and it's very warm in here. I look at the inflated scones and muffins in the cabinet. Giant cupcakes. Cinnamon rolls the size of salad plates. Enormous, squashy bagels. It is as if the baked goods, like the landscape, have been magnified—or we have shrunk. I pull Finn's hat off and unzip the top of his snowsuit.

I probably shouldn't be eating cakes yet again. The button of my pants is definitely digging in. Then I remember what Susannah said about my pregnant "aura."

I take a few breaths and close my eyes for a second. And there it is—the sly queasiness that has been edging its way around my body for what seems like weeks. It is as if my blood is slightly off or my inner ear needs recalibrating.

But this is daft. I could be bloated because my period is coming. I'm still jet-lagged. I try to think back but I can't remember when my last period was. I recall buying tampons in Boots, maybe a few weeks ago. But did I use them? I have no idea. It seems like another life, when I'd push the carriage into town and buy tampons and diapers in Boots pharmacy, underwear in Marks & Spencer. Diapers—I have to buy diapers for Finn. There is a drugstore just down the street from the bakery. We'll go there next.

The old man shuffles off, holding a baby-sized sourdough. The woman behind the counter is giraffe-like, her slender neck sprouts from a midnight blue shirt; a curly bob, dyed a vibrant wine color, clashes with her red glass necklace. She gives me a pleasant smile and then does a comedy double take: her eyes widen.

I smile on, steadily, trying to pretend that she is not staring. I am sweating in the parka. I unzip it, and order an Americano to go, and then I bend down to Finn and fuss with his zipper. He is mesmerized by the cakes. She turns away to the coffee machine, but then spins back around. Her mouth has curled into a smile and the nostrils of her long, nose have swollen.

"Now I've got it!"

I try to keep smiling, "What?"

"You're with Susannah, right?"

"How did you know?"

"Well you just have to be Elena's daughter!" she cries. She peers over the counter at Finn. "And I guess this beautiful little angel must be her grandchild."

I can't keep up the smile.

"All the way from England! I couldn't quite place your face at first, I think it's the hair, but then when you spoke, with your accent, and I looked at you properly it's unmistakably . . . but Susannah never mentioned a thing about your visit! Is your mother finally here?" She looks behind me, as if my mother is about to materialize by the baguettes. "I can**not** wait to meet her."

"No! What? No. My mother isn't here."

"Oh. Shame. You came alone with the little one?"

"Yes?"

"Well. Well—welcome! How long are you staying?"

"Actually, we're leaving later on today." I hand her a bunch of dollars. "But, sorry—sorry—do you *know* my mother?"

"Oh sure—well, I mean—we've never met, but you sure look just like her. You couldn't be anyone else, even with your cute short hair."

"No, wait. I'm sorry." I give my head a quick shake. "I just . . . How do you know what my mother looks like if you've never met?"

"The sculptures of course. Did she show you? Oh my goodness. Get Susannah to show you her Elenas! You'll *love* them. When she and your mother went to all those places she never took photos but she'd come back and make these beautiful ceramics of your mother's face. They go back a few years now, and they're just beautiful. Honestly, I knew you right away just from the Elenas. So beautiful! Such a bone structure—both of you! Beauties!"

"Wait a minute—Susannah and my mother *traveled* together?"

Maggie nods, but her smile is fading. The sinews in her neck look very taut, as if struggling to keep her head from drooping downward. "They were down in Oaxaca just last month weren't they? I do think it's wonderful to have a friendship that's lasted all these years over such a great distance. You mother sounds like a wonderful person."

"Sorry, no. I mean. I think you've got that wrong. My mother never traveled anywhere with Susannah." I consider adding that a month ago, my mother could not have been in Oaxaca, since she was in bed on a morphine drip.

Maggie's frown deepens. Her cheeks turn carnation pink and one hand flies up, patting at her curls.

"Never mind." I try to smile, again, to cover the embarrassment we're both feeling. "It doesn't matter. Those sculptures sound amazing."

"Well, yes, they're beautiful, they really are. Get Susannah to show you them, she has them in her studio I think, or maybe she's storing them now at the gallery. She doesn't like people to see them generally. Lord knows why as they're stunning pieces, but she will show you, I'm sure. She just has to."

She turns and bustles with the coffee. As she hands me the cardboard cup she is still smiling, but it looks very strained. She turns away and pops two muffins in a paper bag. "And how about a cookie? Would this little guy like a cookie? I have oatmeal raisin. Or chocolate chip . . ." She takes one, and leans over the counter with it. He reaches up, eyes round. "There you go honey," she says. "Oh no—no—keep the money," she waves away my dollars. "It's on me. And you have to try my poppy-seed muffins, here—Susannah loves them. No, please, they're on me too. Tell Susie I said hi." She hands me a bag. "Is she down at the gallery?"

I nod, ask if she's sure I can't pay, thank her, and then take the bag and the coffee.

As I close the door I glance back. Our eyes meet. She blinks rapidly. There is a look of plain confusion on her face.

There is a drugstore opposite the bakery but it is closed—it's only eight forty. I peer through the window and a white-haired man leaning over the counter sees me. He comes over and unlocks the door.

"Sorry," I say. "You're not open yet."

"Oh sure, come on in. Always happy to open early for a pretty lady." He steps back, smiling gallantly.

We go in and find the diaper section. I buy a small pack, some wipes, and let Finn choose another sippy cup—he picks one with a yellow duck on it. We pass down the aisle to the checkout and I see the pregnancy tests. I should just do it. Now that she's planted the thought, I have to just do it.

The shopkeeper is chatty, asking if I'm Australian, then telling me about his aunt in Liverpool. Then my phone pings as a text comes in. I apologize, and pull it out of my pocket while he bags the things up.

There are six new texts. They must have come in since I got the signal—all from Doug. I can't read them. Then one pings in from Alice. I open it.

Call u in a mo—in mtg—Did U call Doug?

I type a quick reply.

Yes. Call me soon! No reception where I'm staying but am in town briefly.

I take the bag from the shopkeeper who looks slightly less friendly. I suppose it's very rude to be texting in front of him.

I'm actually not sure if we really are flying back on Saturday. I realize that I don't quite know what day of the week it is—Monday or Tuesday I think. But better that Doug should have a sense of security about Finn. He needs a narrative for this trip. He needs to know that I haven't abducted our child—it doesn't matter if the day is technically inaccurate. I'll send him the real flight details later.

"Come on, love," I say to Finn. "Time to go."

"No." He squats by the sweets.

My phone pings—I glance at my e-mails. My father's instant reply.

To: Kali
From: G.K.MacKenzie.
Subject: re: Sorry

Dear Kali. I am relieved that you and Finn are leaving the island. You have clearly discovered a lot about your mother and I suppose you felt you needed to do that. Please be aware, however, that Susannah will only ever give you one side of the story and I doubt she will ever tell you the truth. Being someone's daughter does not give you the right to know absolutely everything about them. Our pasts are not public property. Your mother chose to keep some things in the past, and you should respect her wishes, especially now. I know it's the fashion these days to rake over every little detail, but I was brought up differently. My mother said "least said soonest mended" and I find that to be a helpful adage. Perhaps that's old-fashioned but it served your mother and I very well indeed for almost 40 years. Having said this, there are now clearly many things that we must inevitably discuss. Since it would not be appropriate to do this through e-mails please let me know the details of your return flight.

G

I step to one side and hunching away from the shopkeeper, I type furiously:

To: G.K.MacKenzie
From: Kali
Subject: re: Sorry

YES we do need to talk! I know you have every right to your own secrets or whatever—but I'm not the "public." And these aren't LITTLE THINGS. Mom's past is mine too—these things travel down generations, even when the secrets aren't told. I don't want to know any painful details about who did what in your relationship but I do have a right to know some things about Mom because of how she was with me—ie. her past is, in a sense, my past too—and my present. I just want to know who she was! Why is that so bad? Not sure what flight we're on, but will let you know—am sorry this has upset you but we are safe and well—Kal.

Finn is singing to himself, again, nonsense words, and pulling packs of Altoids off a child-level shelf. I kneel and shove them all back on. Then my phone rings. I pull it out, apologizing, aware of how appalling I must seem to the shopkeeper, who is staring me, stonily, now. But it's Alice—I can't not answer.

"Okay. Where are you?" she says.

"I'm in this place called Spring Tide Island, in the middle of nowhere. But I can't really talk properly; I've got Finn here, we're in a shop, and he's pulling things off the shelves and I'm trying to get him to leave."

"What are you *doing* there?"

"Okay, quick version—no, love, don't do that." I try to maneuver Finn away from the Altoids, "I'm staying with an old friend of mom's called Susannah; they were friends at university. I've found out so much, it's mind blowing. Our mother was a whale researcher off the coast of British Columbia. Did you know this? She photographed and recorded wild orca—Finn. Put that—no—put it down now—yes, now—she was part of this massive conservation thing up here, and she left Dad—they split up—she bought land up here— Finn, NO—in the middle of bloody nowhere . . ."

"Kal, could you slow down? It's quite hard to hear you."

"I know. It's a lot to take in—I've actually just been e-mailing Dad—who is being completely infuriating—he says we'll 'talk'—but honestly, I mean, you should see it up here. It's unbelievable. It's so remote and big and wild. Finn—put it down love—come on. Come on!—And she lived here—she owned a floating house somewhere on an island, a cabin type thing—a house built on floats. I think it's still up there—on some island in an archipelago somewhere. She lived there while she studied orcas. And our grandfather, Mom's Dad, was an abusive drinker who killed our grandmother—he rammed their car into a tree when he was drunk. Mom was eight years old. Christ Alice, did you know any of this? Did she talk to you about any of this?"

"Kal—it's almost impossible to—"

"Our mother was a killer whale expert! She owned a floating house in British Columbia!"

"What? This sounds . . ." Alice pauses. "Are you okay, Kal?"

"I'm totally fine! It's all true. Dad has confirmed the stuff about our grandparents. And Susannah told me all about the whales—I don't see why she'd lie." Finn tugs at a box containing ChapSticks and the man leans over the counter, wagging a finger.

"Finn—no." I reach for his hand. "Uh-uh." He shakes me off.

"What?" says Alice. "You're breaking up."

"Listen," I say. "I've got to go. Finn's destroying the shop. But this feels huge, Alice. I think it may explain why Mom was always so difficult with me and not with you—I think she probably had to leave all this behind—and she loved it—because of me. So, I don't know, I reminded her of that, or whatever. Look—Finn's—I've got to go— I'll call you later okay? There's no Internet at Susannah's house and no cell reception but I'm heading back to Vancouver later today so I'll call you when I'm back in civilization. Okay?"

"Listen," she says. "Surely Mom would have told us about all this? Are you sure this Susannah person is reliable?"

"I'm sure," trying to unpeel Finn's fingers from the box. The shopkeeper is walking around to our side of the counter. "Sort of. I don't know. Look, I'll be in Vancouver tonight, back at the same B&B—and I'll call you from there."

"But I want to know what else you've found out."

"The whales and her parents are the main thing, but we can talk properly later. Okay?"

"But I didn't know any of this," she says. She suddenly sounds about eight years old.

"Me neither. Now aren't you glad I've come here? Because I am. Look, it's okay. I really do have to go now—I'll call you from Vancouver. Don't worry."

"Okay." For once my little sister doesn't tell me to be careful, or question the wisdom of my actions.

I hang up, and start apologizing to the shopkeeper who is plainly appalled by me. I try to scrape up ChapSticks with one hand, while preventing Finn from getting back to them with the other, all the time aware that mine is just the sort of behavior that I can't stand in other people. Eventually, I wrestle Finn—now kicking and howling—out the door. As it shuts, I see the man staring after me with a look of contempt on his once-kindly face.

My phone is in my hand and before I put it in my pocket an e-mail pings in. I can't not look.

From: G.K.MacKenzie
To: Kali
Subject: Enough.

Yes we cannot possibly have this conversation via e-mail. Please phone immediately on getting home.
   G

He is right about that.

Back in the gallery I call up "Hello!" There is no reply, but I think I can hear her muffled voice up there.

Maggie's comments make no sense. I wonder if she has mistaken something Susannah said. She must have mixed my mother up with another old friend. Or maybe Maggie is not so reliable. She certainly seemed flustered. Living here could make anyone lose touch with reality. Then again, she could only have recognized me if she'd seen my mother's face.

I sit down holding Finn between my knees. Fortunately, the cookie keeps him occupied and he munches on it, then holds it up to offer me a bite too.

"Yum." I bite the soggy cookie. It is outrageously sweet and tastes as if it's been rolled in cinnamon. It is only nine in the morning, and I'm feeding him cookies.

"Num, num." He stuffs more into his mouth. It is so vast but I have a feeling he will not stop, even when he's full to bursting—he can't believe his luck. For a moment I imagine the playgroup mommies with their Tupperware snackboxes of organic rice cakes. Unsalted.

"That," I try to smile at Finn, "is a truly huge cookie."

His brown eyes are enormous beneath his bangs, looking steadily up at me as he chomps. I can see the doubt behind them. He is thinking "when is she going to take it away?" He is preparing to defend that cookie with his life. I take a sip of coffee; it burns my lips. Then I look down at the drugstore bag in my hand.

I need to do it now I've bought it. It's a waste of $15 otherwise. I might as well. "Let's go to the toilet, love," I say. "Come on, come with Mommy." I put down the coffee, take his hand, and we go into the bathroom. I lock the door. The automatic fan comes on. The room smells of lavender. There is soap and hand cream on the wall, both Aveda, and a little scent diffuser with aromatic sticks pointing out of it. I know that I shouldn't let Finn eat a cookie in the bathroom, but if I take it away he'll howl, and clearly I can't leave him outside with the ceramics. I imagine him climbing up the shelving, a deft little mountaineer.

"Don't touch anything in here, okay? No touching." He munches, ostentatiously, then bashes the garbage can with one hand. It makes a satisfying clank. He bashes it again.

I leave the stall door open so I can see him.

"We'll do your diaper in a minute, okay? After I go to the toilet."

"No," he says, through a mouthful of cookie.

I pull the packet out of the paper bag. This is Susannah's fault—the comment about "feeling" things the moment I walked through the door. This is her fault.

When I come out of the toilet, Susannah is at the window, looking out at the rain. Her hair is looped and twisted in its silver wasp clasp and she is upright and broad-backed. She turns as she hears the bathroom door.

"Everything okay?" She looks down at Finn, at the half-demolished cookie. I know she's wondering what sort of mother gives her child a cookie that size at breakfast time, then lets her child take that cookie into a toilet. But I can't feel my feet on the floor. I am floating.

"You okay?" she says again.

"Fine thanks." Astonishingly, my voice sounds relatively normal.

"So you guys went to the bakery?"

I nod.

"Did you . . ." she raises her chin, "did you meet Maggie?"

I nod.

"What did she say?" Her eyes are fixed on my face.

I lean down and slowly pick up the bag of muffins. "She gave me these for you." I hold them out.

She takes a muffin. I take one too and bite into it, but I can't taste anything. The seeds are gritty and my mouth feels dry. The whole room seems to have shrunk and I am hovering, now, very tall and straight, a few feet above the floor.

Susannah turns away, munching, and points to the ceramic fish. "So, this is by a young Vancouver potter," her voice is bright and efficient. "Huge talent." I haven't experienced this version of Susannah yet—the gallery owner, the expert, the authority. I follow her over, holding tight to Finn's sticky hand.

The fish are rounded like tangerines and they shimmer, each scale delicately glazed in silvers and blues. I examine them from all angles. Their scales catch the light and glint as if they are twitching.

"Look at the fish," I say to Finn. He looks up at them, not terribly impressed. He has cinnamon whiskers.

Susannah explains something about glazes and firing methods, oxidizing clay.

Above them, on a shelf, is a bigger, fatter fish, this time with blue-gray scales. It is hollow, and there's something inside it. I lean closer. It is a light blue speckled egg. For a moment, we all just gaze at it. And I think of the tiny thing inside me, right now, its busy cells multiplying, expanding, swelling.

Then I remember my mother's bone carving—the fish with the leering man inside its belly. It is still in the jewelry box, back in my suitcase at Susannah's house. I'd forgotten all about my mother's box. I forgot I even brought it.

The floating feeling stops abruptly. I look at Susannah and she glances sideways at me. Her eyes, I notice, are the color of the lightest, most iridescent scale on the biggest mother fish.

British Columbia, 1977

She didn't make it to the hospital. When her water broke she was on her own on the boat, at the sink, scrubbing burned milk off a pan. "Shit," she looked down. "No. Not yet." She felt wet warmth spreading down her legs and then her bare feet were soaked. It was three weeks too soon; he wouldn't be here 'til tomorrow. This could not happen now.

She forced herself to think rationally. It was going to be hours before anything happened. She would get her coat on and go to the boat next door; Ted would call the midwife. She wasn't alone really. The dock was full of people who would do anything to help out.

But then it became obvious that this was not going to be like the baby books said it would be. The first pain seethed around her lower belly almost as soon as she'd turned away from the sink to dry her hands. She leaned against the counter gripping the edge as pain radiated out from her pelvis, round her back, down the fronts of both thighs. Then it passed. She stood up. She went toward the bed for her pullover, but before she got to it, another one came, even stronger than the first.

This shouldn't happen. It was supposed to start slow. It wasn't supposed to hurt like this at first. If this was early stage labor she was not going to survive the pain later on. They seemed to be rolling in, one after the other with almost no break between. Perhaps it was because she was in the belly of the boat—this dark, safe, primitive cave. Perhaps if she got up on deck, in the cold night, they'd stop. But then she forgot about her coat or getting to the boat next door because it took over—she met each pain on her hands and knees with her head down, swaying and bellowing like a cow. The only way to survive this was surrender. In a semi-lucid moment she glimpsed what the whale must have felt, giving birth in that small tank—and it was a sort of liberation. It wasn't like being trapped at all because with each pain, the walls of the boat, the rain on the roof, the clink of the mooring ring and the sea against the hull faded to nothing—there were no boundaries or walls anymore. Her body—and what was happening inside it—expanded to become the whole world.

She had no idea how long this went on for, but suddenly, she felt the energy shift—for a few minutes, nothing happened at all. She may even have slept. Then a force gathered inside her, and she began to push with a strength she didn't know she had. There was a wild burning and she put both hands down there and, with a shock, she felt a hard, round, wet bulge between her legs. She lost all awareness for a bit, something rushed through her and then she was propped up against the wall. She looked down at the streaky baby in her arms—a cord trailing between her thighs—so much liquid all around, like the sea. She gazed at it—a real baby—her baby—the color of a pale bluebell, streaked with curds, festooned with blood.

She wrapped herself around the little body and there was a yowl—ten tiny fingers shot up, making star shapes in the air and she felt herself fill up with oxygen—she heard herself, laughing and crying at the same time—and then she started to shake. Violently. She shook so hard she was afraid her baby would slip out of her arms.

Ted burst down the steps. He paused in the doorway, "Holy mother of God Elena you had the damned baby." He came and knelt down, grabbing a blanket from the chair to cover them up. His platter hands were shaking too. "You had the damned baby Elena!"

"Ted," her voice came out bizarrely normal. "I need you to call the midwife. The number's by the stove."

Sandra came down as Ted thundered up to go to the call box. She instantly became practical—mother of four herself, grandmother of two, she found towels. There were deep worry lines on her forehead but she moved calmly around, getting things.

"It's okay, Sandra," she said. "Don't worry. We're fine." But she still couldn't stop shaking.

The midwife arrived and suddenly there was a boat full of people, all bustling and talking at once. The midwife was a thin woman, wrinkled and creased, with long, clean fingers and didn't waste any time—she checked the baby, over, then took Elena's wrist and counted seconds on an upside down watch before gently examining between her legs.

"Came fast huh?"

Elena nodded.

"Couldn't even wait for daddy."

Elena smiled, weakly. Her teeth chattered.

"You're okay. It's shock," the midwife said. "You'll be fine, but you need to deliver the placenta now."

She laid out towels and a sheet and gave instructions—as if busing, at this point, was really necessary. But Elena couldn't take her eyes off her baby—pink now, smelling like dew on grass and fresh air—the midwife said something about the power of endorphins. "There you go," she murmured. "There you go. One more push."

Everything calmed down eventually. Ted made toast and butter, muttering through his grizzled beard, while Sandra cleaned up. The midwife helped Elena to get up off the floor and onto the cabin bed. Before, she'd felt nothing, but now there was a burning, battered feeling. Her legs were still shaking. Someone put a mug of hot, sweet tea next to her.

The baby was diapered and in a white pajama and hat, and wrapped in the blue blanket that Susannah had knitted, completely certain of a boy. The midwife arranged Elena on one side, firmly arranging her limbs and then the little mouth suctioned, around her nipple.

In the days and weeks after the birth, each time she breastfed, Elena felt the walls close in. It wasn't possible to move; she just had to sit there until the feeding was over. It was torture. She wasn't used to being immobilized this way, or to having this much time to think. Sometimes, sitting alone in the cabin for what seemed like the hundredth time in just a few hours, she felt as if she might explode into thousands of shards of glass, each one sharp and vicious.

She soon realized that the problem wasn't the baby or the need to feed the baby, apparently constantly—the problem was that now their baby was actually here—this perfect little being—she couldn't picture a future anymore. There was no future that worked for all three of them. And there was far too much time to think about this.

One night as she sat up in bed in the dark, feeding and feeding with waves slapping on the sides of the boat and the wind howling outside making everything creak and rock and bend, she realized that this might be the end. And she felt a flood of panic wash through her.

She had been ridiculously certain of everything during the pregnancy. Looking back the naïveté was staggering. Or maybe it had been hormones or pigheadedness. Or maybe they'd just been too busy to think it through. Despite the speed with which her life had changed the pregnancy had felt right. But now it was as if someone had switched on the lights to reveal that an apparently serene room was, in fact, a shambles.

They both believed in living in the present, and pursuing their own thing—he still did. But now there was a very real and pressing baby to care for, to plan for. He seemed to be able to carry on living in the moment, but she could not.

He was right that, for now, nothing much needed to change. Babies are portable. They don't really care where they are. When the weather improved, she could probably carry on going out on the boat. Back at the boat she could work on her sound data during nap times too. The coming summer would be manageable. She thought back to last year, on the boat with Dean and Jonas, going out all day on the ocean, sometimes camping out by the fire. They could do all that with a baby.

By the time the fall storms closed in she'd become adept at photographing and documenting the whales—she could even recognize a few individuals from a distance by the shape of their dorsals, or their particular style of play. She understood the pods and the matrilines, and could remember many of the whales' names. But most of all, she had begun to listen. And she needed to get back to that.

It was only February now but in a couple of months people would start filtering back up to the islands again. By the time the orcas gathered for the salmon runs there would be the little community of marine biologists, photographers, whale enthusiasts, kayakers—even the odd film crew—up there. These orca-pilgrims were her tribe now. She couldn't imagine not joining them again this year. And she could— this year, at least, she could.

But after that the future was a looming blank, and it scared her.

She had to be realistic of course, about the summer—the damp, the bugs. Even in midsummer there would be filthy days when they'd huddle with flasks of coffee in heavy rain gear, waiting for the radio to crackle to life, staring at marine charts, growing more chilled and damp and frustrated. But they could rig up a rain shelter on the Zodiac. She'd wrap the baby in layers and layers of insulation. Weather was not the deal breaker.

But growing up just might be. With a crawling baby the picture became more complicated. You couldn't keep a crawling baby on the twelve-foot Zodiac for ten hours a day, in all weathers. Or could you? A toddler? A school-age child?

There had to be a solution. She had only just discovered what she needed in order to live. Her future had seemed so definite from the moment she ran across campus that day, with her backpack and dawn spreading pink across the sky. She thought of Dean's placid face by the fire as he told her that his wife had given up her career as an anthropologist to stay home and raise their child.

She looked down at the little head at her breast. She could not give up. Without her research what sort of a mother would she be? Without her work motherhood would become a slow strangulation. She needed both.

She had to think rationally, because there had to be a way forward. But a voice in the back of her brain told her there was a reason that all the main orca researchers were men.

Maybe they could find a conventional house in one of the larger logging communities up there. At least, she'd be close to the orcas. But she could not imagine washing diapers while the others followed up sightings and collected data. Going back to California—or even Seattle—was out of the question. Her life was here—up there—out there—skimming across this distinctly un-baby-friendly ocean.

Maybe she could find help, but even if that was possible, they didn't have the money to pay anyone. She thought, for a desperate moment, about Susannah. It wasn't clear why Susannah had taken the job in Victoria—it was a whole pay grade down and she said herself that the art department was poor.

Susannah knew about babies; she raised her own twin brothers. Elena remembered her saying that when the twins started school they believed that she was their mother; they'd forgotten there had ever been anyone else. She was sixteen years old at the time. Elena had the feeling that if she asked Susannah to quit the art department and move onto the boat to help with the baby, she might actually say yes. But of course that was completely out of the question. They'd kill each other on a cramped boat.

She'd been a poor friend. Susannah was dedicated to keeping in touch, but Elena hadn't even written to thank her for the care packages—hand-knitted socks and chocolate bars and pajamas. The journey from the university was long, uncomfortable and lonely but Susannah had done it twice already, for short, tense visits.

No. Susannah could never be the answer.

But if she couldn't come up with an answer then the research would fall apart. The grant proposal was in, and someone Dean knew at the Canadian Department of Fisheries had indicated that it was likely to succeed. Three years funding for a study into acoustic and behavioral correlations of killer whales. She had to be out, gathering data.

Lately, she had missed the orcas so intensely that her stomach actually ached with longing when she thought about them. It was already clear to her that the repertoire of killer whales in the wild was rich and complex—there were the echolocation clicks for foraging and to locate one another, and a whole range of pulsed sounds that could travel for miles through the ocean. She'd already identified a particular whistle—she heard it again and again—that seemed to say "I'm over here." But there were so many other sounds to identify and decipher. It was possible that some of the vocalizations were unconnected to any behaviors—and this was where the real story lay.

It was wrong to think of the sounds as "words"—but it was possible that there were vocalizations to convey emotions or social bonds—or maybe something alien to human experience. And how did these whales learn language? Did they learn it from their mothers? If so—at what age did they start to "speak"? There were just so many unanswered questions. No—she could not possibly stop this now.

She slid a finger into the tiny mouth on her breast, and readjusted the suck so that it didn't pinch her nipple. She was so tired—it wasn't just sleep deprivation or the relentless feeding, it was her inability to stop gnawing away at their impossible future. One arm was going dead. She shifted her body, stuck another pillow beneath her elbow and settled back again.

She needed to be farther north where the whales gathered in the summertime in great numbers and where it was remote and quiet—far away from shipping sounds. But was it even possible to raise a child in such a remote part of the world? She'd seen a few children clambering up rocks or splashing in tide pools as they passed along the coastline and through the islands much farther north. There were communities up there, made up of float houses, with smoke trailing from their chimneys. Some even had little yards with flowers or vegetable patches.

She thought about the float houses; they were real family homes, not narrow, stinky borrowed boats that leaked and belched oil and smoke. Though small, they had proper rooms and were part of real—if microscopic—communities. She suddenly remembered one of the orca guys saying, once, that a few of the islands further north shared a school boat. It went around picking up children each morning, then depositing them back at the end of the day.

If she could find a small community, like that, somewhere without noise pollution, with plenty of orcas, where there were other families *and access to a school—then maybe there was a future that could work for everyone.*

She sank back against the wood panels. The float house was the germ of a plan. She had to have faith in that this would grow into something feasible. She closed her eyes and as her baby suckled on, Elena fell asleep. She slept deeply, propped up by pillows, in the narrow cabin bed, but her arms stayed tight around her baby because, even as she slept, a part of her was always alert now, to her baby. And she would never let go.

CHAPTER ELEVEN

Back at the house, I offer to help her put away the groceries. She stopped at a general store on the way home, but instructed me to stay in the car with Finn. She came out after only a few minutes, carrying two paper bags of food, which she threw into the trunk. We drove back in silence. It was clear that she did not want to talk though I wasn't sure whether she was cross, or just tired of company. Now she is at the kitchen sink, scrubbing at her hands, with her back to me.

It's only just ten o'clock. This is what happens when you get up at dawn. Like everything else in this place, the day feels extravagantly oversized. I peer into the paper bags. There is a surprising amount of canned food and also a packet of animal crackers that she must have picked out for Finn, even though we're about to leave.

"Leave that," she says. "I'll do it later." I jump, looking up at her, feeling almost like a guilty child, but she will not meet my eye.

There is another bag on the floor by the stove and I turn to see Finn staggering under a glass jar of pickles the size of his torso. I swoop over and seize it from him before he drops it on the tiles.

"You two go sit." She stands, bare feet apart. Her gaze is fixed on something just to the side of my head. It is disconcerting. I notice a box of Cheerios in the open bag. She doesn't seem like a Cheerios person—more the homemade granola type. She is smiling, now, slightly oddly, still not looking quite at me.

"I bought English breakfast tea," she says. "I'm going to make some for us both."

"Would you like me to make it?"

"No," she snaps, "Just sit down with the child. I'll get him some milk."

I wonder if she saw the pregnancy test box in my bag. Maybe that's what this is about. I have the feeling that she knows. But the last thing I want to do is tell her. She might think that her crazy aura thing was right.

I take Finn to the round table. There is a magazine open on the table top—*Ceramic Review*. I pull him onto my knee and we look at pictures of pots—one is in the shape of a frog.

"Dat." He glances up at me, pointing at it.

"Frog." I make a "ribbit" noise.

He belly laughs. "Again!"

Susannah comes over with tea. It's proper strong tea with milk. I thank her and hand Finn the sippy cup she has filled with warm milk.

"No." He pushes it away. "Nuther cup."

"But this is a nice cup. This is your cup."

His brows lower. "No. Nuther cup."

I think about arguing, but I know this look, so I get up, putting him on the seat, and find the new Duck cup in my bag. I then pour the milk from one to the other while he watches, eagerly jiggling his legs. Susannah is leaning her back on the range, her cup of tea in both hands.

"Phthalates," she says, abruptly.

"I'm sorry. What?"

"In the plastic."

"You mean the cup?"

She nods. "Toxins. Carcinogens, in fact."

I look at Finn, sucking on the duck's beak. He is sitting on the dining chair, pigeon-toed, his legs barely reaching the end of the seat.

"You should at least wash it with warm soapy water first," she says. "But personally, I wouldn't put a plastic cup like that anywhere near a child's mouth." Then she looks at me—this time right at me—and there is that smile again. "But you're trying your best, huh?"

I want to throw the tea at her, but instead, I close my eyes and sip it. It tastes sweet.

"Did you put sugar in it?" I try to sound as if the sweetness is a lovely surprise. I don't want to seem ungrateful or fussy.

"Dash of maple syrup." She smiles again, showing white teeth. "A Canadian touch. Good for cold weather and fighting the damp."

I'm not keen on the sweet taste, but it does feel fortifying. And I suppose I need all the fortification I can get. This pregnancy changes everything, again. It's like being on the switch-back ride at the fair, flying in one direction, then jerking around to head the other way.

"You look kind of out of it, Kali." She sips her tea. "Drink up. It isn't good to get chilled up here." I wonder what has changed, why she keeps smiling now, with glassy eyes. Maybe it's because I'm leaving. She probably feels guilty for accusing me of being a crappy mother. She's trying to be pleasant and make amends. She must be so relieved that we're leaving.

"Okay. So, I should probably have a shower and pack." I push back my chair.

"Go ahead." She smiles, again, and the skin round her mouth ripples like water. I lift Finn down from his chair and hold his hand, then pick up my half-drunk tea, wondering if I can pour it down the sink without offending her.

"No, no. He'll stay with me." She sounds so definite, as if she gets to decide where Finn goes, not me. She holds out one large hand for his. Her silver thumb ring glints.

My grip tightens around Finn's small hand. "No, it's okay," I say, evenly. "He can come with me."

She gives a weird, low chuckle, then shrugs, and turns back to the groceries.

Back in the bedroom, I open the case and find Finn's bag of cars. As I hand it to him, I realize that my mother made the bag. It is blue gingham, with an F embroidered on it and an appliquéd red truck. She made it when he was just born and brought it to us in the hospital with a little blue sweater inside and I remember being so surprised: I never knew that she could do handicrafts. Finn seizes the bag from my hands. "Cars!" He tips them onto the rug. "Cars! Cars! Cars!" Doug was right. Whatever it was that made my mother so distant—and so unable to engage with Finn—it wasn't lack of interest.

"Look at all those cars," I say. "Just look at those cars."

He squats, grinning, and picks up an ambulance. I perch on the edge of the bed and put my hands low down on my belly, across the undone top button.

False positives happen. But every cell in my body is singing—just a tiny song, but persistent—and when I listen I know the tune. I need to phone Doug, and tell him.

It occurs to me that maybe this situation with Doug is all about instinct and trust—like the whirling smoke starlings sucking into the West Pier, if you allow yourself to doubt, then you crash. But it's so hard to separate instinct from fear. Doug lying or having an affair doesn't feel right—it goes against the grain. But—like cows in the city or a killer whale that isn't a whale—maybe it is true anyway. Doug is a good man, but good men hurt people too.

And it is all so feasible. It makes perfect sense that she should track him down again, after all these years; that, pushing forty, child-less in a sea of procreating friends, she should do what many lonely people would—remember her first love and want another chance. It must have been flattering for him at first. Who wouldn't be flattered by the attention of such a beautiful and intelligent woman? And I certainly can't blame her for wanting Doug.

I go and turn on the shower. "Finn, do you want to come in the shower with me?"

"No."

"You can play with your cars in the shower."

"NO."

He makes car noises, chugging one up the side of the bed. "I'll be right in here, then, okay?"

I peel off my clothes, and, leaving the door open, I step in. For a moment, I let the hot water take over. I feel as if I've been chilled for days and days now. I shut my eyes and my head spins gently—I feel the heat spread under my skin, down into the parts of me that have not been warm since it all happened. After a while, I open my eyes and—for the first time in ages—I look down at my body.

I can see now that my breasts have swollen; my nipples are darker; they seem to have melted and spread. And a faint brownish line has appeared, like a child's crayon mark, linking my navel with the top of my pubic hair. My belly is definitely rounder than before. My body must have been signaling up at me, frantically, for weeks.

I need to work out the dates but I can't remember my last period and my brain feels very slow, as if it has changed pace and is edging toward sleep. I force myself to think back about six or eight weeks—before Christmas. Doug was away for a bit in Madrid. I saw friends in London—there was a dinner in Hammersmith—the night on Sarah's sofa bed when Finn didn't sleep at all. Was I already pregnant that weekend?

I look at the fragile blue veins beneath the skin on my breasts. These are new too. They look like intricate blue pencil lines. I touch them and my hands seem to be moving too slowly, almost floating. I try to I count forward: a summer baby? Just for a second, I allow myself to go there: I feel tiny plump fingers curled around mine, a baby's weight in my arms—the fresh, sweet smell of a newborn's head, the pinch and suck of a small, hungry mouth.

I close my eyes—the water seems to be falling so slowly and peacefully on my head—I rest both arms against the wall and then I remember a conversation Doug and I had in the Cricketers Arms the night he got back from Madrid. His mother had come, and for the first time in months, we actually went out. He said we should try for another baby and I agreed, even though I thought there was no chance. Who were we kidding? I was almost thirty-nine and last time it took four years. We held hands over the table and agreed to try harder to connect with each other. We said we needed to make more time for each other, and talk more.

"I miss you so much," he sounded almost bereft. "I didn't know it was possible to be living with someone, and actually miss them."

But maybe he said the thing about the baby to try to convince himself—or me—that everything was going to be okay. Maybe, beneath the table that night, his phone was busy receiving her texts. Maybe it wasn't distress in his voice but guilt. Maybe as we held hands across the table, he was trying to convince himself not to sleep with her. Or had he already slept with her by then? But no—I open my eyes—I make myself stand up. My legs feel a little weak, as if I've been running—No. He has not slept with her. He wouldn't lie to me about that. The water tumbles onto the crown of my head—the heat is making me so groggy. I force myself back to the thought: he said nothing happened between them. But he must have done something to encourage her. What, exactly, did Doug's "nothing" consist of?

I rest both hands on my belly and try to breathe, but the shower feels suffocating now—the water is too hot, there is too much steam—and I feel so tired, as if my energy is draining down the plug hole with it.

I am going to have to go through childbirth again. It was nearly twenty-four hours with Finn: being sent home from hospital twice, four hours in agony in the hospital corridor, before finally a room—a drip, ventouse, stitches. And then the midwife said, "well that was good—for a first birth." Doug was there, all the time, holding my hand, stroking my face, not saying much, but we were somehow connected throughout the birth—even in the wildest part of it, when I hardly knew where, or who, I was anymore. He left the delivery room twice and both times the contractions just stopped. It made the midwife laugh.

I look for shampoo. There is none. I can't bring myself to move. I can't even lift a hand to open the shower door and look for the shampoo. It is as if all the panicking has sapped me now. When I saw those texts, I panicked—and in some way, I've not stopped panicking since then. I thought I'd shaken off the mistrust from my childhood but it turns out it's not as simple as just deciding to be strong. You have to know your demon—examine it up close, become familiar with every boil on its twisted face, with the peculiar stink of its breath, and then grow strong because of—not in spite of—it. For eight years I have been looking to Doug for reassurance instead of finding the strength in myself.

But I do feel weak—physically weak. I realize I've been in the shower for ages—not even thinking about Finn in the bedroom— "Finn?" I shout. My own voice wakes me up. I open my eyes. "Love?" I wrench the lever and step out, grabbing a towel. As I leap into the bedroom, the walls of the room seem to sway in, then out again.

He is fine. Still squatting on the rug, running his cars in circles and chatting happily to himself.

"You okay?"

He doesn't even look up. The hair on the crown of his head is sticking up crazy with static and sleep knots. I should brush it. I don't think I've brushed my son's hair in days.

I dry myself off, my hands feel slightly disconnected from my brain. I have to stop being so panicky all the time. Not everything is a catastrophe. Susannah has got to me—it's this house, and the wind wailing constantly around it—and all the expensive ceramics and breakables—this place has made me nervous. I have to calm down. It's fine. We are leaving.

I dry my feet and as I bend, my head spins again—at some point in the next six months I won't be able to reach these feet anymore. There will be that awful moment when I look down and my stomach will be so vast and then it will hit me—the physical reality of what has to happen in order to get this baby out. I remember last time, when I was huge and getting scared and I made the mistake of asking my mother what giving birth was like.

I was maybe seven or eight months pregnant. There were left-overs from a meal, I remember that—maybe it was my father's birthday—we were in Sussex. But my father wasn't there. Alice wasn't either. I'm not even sure where Doug was. It was just the two of us at the kitchen table.

I saw panic flicker across her face when I asked her, as if I'd caught her in some massive lie. For a crazed moment, I thought she might be about to tell me I was adopted. She stared at her hands.

"I've read that first births can be bad."

The color had drained from her cheeks. She couldn't look up at me.

"So—it was really bad, wasn't it?"

"No. No. It wasn't bad at all." Her voice was hoarse. "I always gave birth very fast. They even have a name for it—'precipitous labor.' You should look it up—it might be genetic." We both looked at her fingers, always with the lines of dirt beneath the fingernails—soil from the garden, paint. They were such straight, strong fingers. The landscape of nicks and creases on her hands was still so familiar to me, despite the distance between us: they might have been my own hands.

"What does it feel like?"

She looked up and what I saw behind her eyes wasn't fear—it was something much more awful and disturbing—a sort of haunted panic; a mess of frantic emotions.

"Mum?"

"Completely overwhelming." She put her hand over her mouth, pressing her lips shut, sealing it all inside. She closed her eyes.

"Oh—look. It's okay." I leaped up. "Don't worry. Let's not go there. Forget I asked. God it's late. I really should get going. The M25 will be awful . . ."

I don't remember anything about what was said after that. I suppose I must have gone and I am not sure, now, if I ran away because I didn't want to hear her birthing horror story, or if I just couldn't cope with the fact that the memory of giving birth to me apparently caused her nothing but anguish.

I asked my father about my birth once, too, years before—when I was not even a teenager. I remember asking him if he was there when I was born. He was silent for a long time. I began to worry that he was angry. When he was angry, he tended to go frighteningly quiet. He never shouted, but there was something about that white-hot silence that was much more alarming than shouting. Eventually he said, stiffly, "In those days, Kali, men had absolutely nothing to do with childbirth."

But I knew this wasn't true because he was there when Alice was born, in the Royal Sussex, only six years later. Each year on Alice's birthday my mother told the story of how the midwife turned away at the crucial moment and my father scooted round the bed, and caught Alice himself.

A gust of wind thumps the window and I remember where I am—perched on the rim of a rock, high above an unfathomable ocean, teetering on the westernmost edge of a tiny crumb that has wrenched itself free of the vast coastline. Sitting here, so tired and lethargic, I feel as if I am not quite in my body. I turn to face the window and lock eyes with my wavering reflection—and then it's as if I'm out there, with my nose pressed to the wet glass, looking in on this crop-haired person slumped there in a towel, unmoving, and at her feet a beautiful boy, crouched over his ambulance and crashing cars.

Inside me the cells are busy dividing, over and over. No wonder I feel so vague and out of it. Finn will not be an only child. By next summer, I could have a two year old and a newborn. I find that I can only imagine another little boy. I am suddenly certain that I will have sons. I will be able to say "my boys" and they will grow up to tower over me and make me proud, terrified— both. It's ridiculous that I didn't realize that I was pregnant. Could my terror and paranoia—my flight—this whole, lunatic, unreal journey be down to something as mundane as hormones? I suddenly think of the big fish in Susannah's gallery, the one with the egg in its belly. This state I am in seems simultaneously breakable, and transcendent.

I need to wake up. The tea Susannah made me is on the bedside table, I haven't even drunk half of it. It's lukewarm now, and revoltingly sweet, and the maple syrup gives it a slightly grainy texture, but I make myself slug it down—and I feel better, almost immediately. I need to drink more and eat regularly. I have to think about this baby now. I have to do my best for this baby too.

I dig around in the bottom of the bag in the hope that I'll locate something clean to put on. My skull suddenly feels very full, as if someone has pumped air into it, rather than blood. My fingers close around my mother's old jewelry box. I pull it out and sit up. The pressure inside my head lessens. I open the soft lid.

At my feet, Finn crashes two cars together then makes "wee-owww" ambulance noises. I hold the carving up to eye level and look at the leering face inside the belly of this fish thing. Maybe it's the angle of my head, or bending down and sitting up—but I feel woozy. I need to eat. I haven't eaten at all today.

I wobble to my feet and drag on my shabby gray sweater and jeans again. They smell damp and stale. I need to wash things, urgently. Vancouver—I'll wash things there.

"Shall we go and find Susannah?" I say to Finn.

He glances up at me. Then he looks back at his cars. "No."

"How about we take your cars with us?" I kneel next to him, so slowly. It's like moving through water. "We can show them to Susannah. Here, let's put them in the bag."

"No." He pushes the bag away. "No."

"Okay. You hold them then. Which one would Susannah like best?"

He thinks about this.

"Shall we put the best ones in the bag and ask her?"

He tries to shove the ambulance into the small chest pocket of his jeans. I try to help him. "Not like *dat,*" he says. "Like *dis.*" He has never said this before, and I grin at him: his first proper sentence. I must remember to tell Doug. Doug is missing things already.

"Like *dis*" he is saying, thrusting the car at his jeans pocket, making the dinosaur picture bulge. But of course it won't fit. I sit on my heels, unable to muster the energy to help him. Eventually, we make our way back down the corridor with the cars stuffed in the back pockets of my jeans.

As we walk, the walls of the corridor press in, then pull out again. I give my head a little shake and glance down at Finn. His hair is shiny and messy. The crown of his head seems a long way down.

On the shelf in the living room the glass bowl glimmers under the overhead lights. It is a raw red in this light and seems to vibrate at me, insisting on my attention. I steer Finn carefully around it, and for a moment I imagine it opening up like a huge mouth—becoming jaws that bite.

Susannah is kneeling by the cupboard under the sink, poking among cleaning products. There is a big cardboard box on the counter top. The French window behind her is open and the air is freezing. I can smell the sea. The dogs are huddled in their basket, noses under their tails. I can hear waves thudding on the rocks below the cliff. She's wearing the brown fleece, the big gray scarf and her boots. Her head snaps up as she hears me come in. A bitter gust whooshes through the doors and I feel so light—as if it could blow me down. She peels her lips into another smile. The smiling is odd. But at least we are going to part on good terms.

"So," my voice, too, feels strangely far off. "We'll head off soon, and leave you to work."

"Oh no. The ferry doesn't go 'til later."

"But I thought there was one at three?"

She hauls her mouth back into that smile. "Winter schedule." Her teeth look vulpine, surprisingly white. I hadn't noticed them before, probably because she hasn't smiled much. I feel as if I'm staring at her mouth, but can't quite move my eyes to look away.

I don't care about the ferry times; I have to get out of here now.

"We'll head off now anyway," again—the far-off, almost whispery sound of my own voice surprises me. "We'll let you work, we've disturbed you enough." Then I remember the carving. "Can I just show you something before I go?"

She stands up and wipes her hands down her legs. "What is it?"

"I found this in my mother's things." I hold it out. The room sways away from me, then back again. I know I should sit down. Or eat. Or both.

She looks at it and the crease between her brows deepens. She doesn't move or speak.

I have to think carefully to form words "Do you know what it is?" I say.

"It's a First Peoples' carving."

"Like Native Americans?"

She doesn't answer.

"An old woman gave it to her."

"Is it," I say, "a fish?"

"No, of course not—it's an orca, look, see the markings. That's the saddlebag. See those, the white patches. Right there. It's carved out of whalebone."

I peer at it, trying to focus—and I can see now that, of course, it's a whale.

"She lived in a little shack. She talked to your mother for a long time, about the orca mainly. Then she went into her shack and brought this out and gave it to Elena."

"What island?" I need to sit down. My shoulders feel too heavy for my torso.

She stretches out her hand. I put the carving onto it. She points at the grinning beast inside the belly of the whale. "That's the demon, Scana."

"Scana?"

"In some First Peoples' legends the killer whale is the demon of the sea and also the guardian of it—there's good and evil in one body. This probably belongs in a museum." She shoves it back into my hand, almost pushing me over. "You should take it to someone; take it to the museum of anthropology in Vancouver." She looks at me closely. "You find anything else in your mother's things?"

"Just a few bits and pieces in a jewelry box."

"Bits and pieces of what?"

"Oh, nothing . . . bit of my baby blanket . . . old study notebook . . . little . . . this little . . . heart shaped rock."

"Susannah." My mouth feels dry and my tongue has thickened so it's hard to get the words out. I need to drink water. I swallow. "Maggie, from the bakery, she recognized me."

"What?" Her head snaps up.

"She said you'd done some sculptures of my mother's face. She said you and my mother traveled the world together."

Susannah stops moving. She looks like an animal in the path of a predator. The cotton-ball feeling in my ears thickens. I have to stay upright. I know she's going to tell me something.

"Oh Maggie's been on anti-anxiety medication for years." She waves a hand in the air and turns away. "She gets terribly confused poor thing." She laughs, an odd, tinkling, off-kilter sound.

"Your 'Elenas.' Are they here?"

"They're in storage, I'm afraid," she snaps.

I step backward and sit, heavily, on a stool. I should ask her about the postcards but I'm just too tired. I can't think anymore. I can't do this. She's going to give me nothing. My arms feel as if I've been doing push ups. The back of my neck is oddly tight. I rub it, but can't quite feel my own fingers. Finn squats at my feet, running his car up the cupboard door. He might scratch the paint, but I can't move to stop him. Susannah is watching him. She doesn't seem worried about the paintwork. I close my eyes. The world spins again, more violently this time. If I'm going to get ill, I need to get ill away from here. I can't let go—not here. I have to leave.

I have to call Doug. Doug needs to know. I need him to know.

"Kali?" Susannah's voice is very far away, as if she's standing in a cave, out of sight. "Kali? Kali? Are you okay?"

My eyelids are sealed, and my throat feels as if someone has stuffed a small sock inside it. I try to swallow but then I feel hands on my elbows. "Kali?"

I try to say tell her I need to go—but I am not sure if the words actually come out of my mouth. I manage to open my eyes a crack as she helps me through the living room—Finn toddles behind us—and onto the sofa.

"It's okay, love, I'm just really tired," my voice slurs—and I try to hold out a hand to him, but Susannah's legs are in the way and my arm feels so heavy.

Finn is next to me now, his new duck cup in one hand, his ambulance in the other. His eyes are so big. I can see he is worried.

I feel my eyelids close and I can't get them open. "Everything's fine, love." I am not sure if I say it out loud.

I feel a soft hand pat the top of my head and Finn's voice, close by, so clear "Night night. Mama."

Then I hear Susannah's voice, calm, but chilly. "Let mommy sleep now."

CHAPTER TWELVE

When I wake up I am freezing cold, and stiff as an eighty year old. The light has changed—the room looks blurry and washed out.

I haul myself off the sofa. There is mist inside my head and I feel deeply sick. What time is it?

"Finn?" I croak. "Where are you, love?"

I walk, unsteadily, through to the kitchen. The clock says 1:15. But it can't possibly be right. If that's the time then I've somehow slept for three hours again. Why didn't she wake me? Where are they? I lean back against the sink. My legs are unreliable, like the stalks of a young plant. "Susannah?" I rasp. "Is Finn okay? Are you there?"

I turn and gulp water straight from the tap. I wipe my mouth with the back of one hand. My head feels as if it's been stuffed with a wet cloth. I splash water on my face. I'm aware of it on my skin, but I can't quite feel it. It is as if I'm wrapped in an anesthetizing blanket.

Her boots aren't by the French windows and the dogs are gone. They must be outside looking at squirrels again. But it's raining steadily. The deck railing is hardly visible, let alone the path to the studio. The house is so cold. I touch my belly with both hands.

Droplets run down the glass like tears. A chill spreads from my stomach, up toward my heart.

I look around the kitchen for a Post-it. My eyes move slower than they should, as if the muscles that anchor them in my skull are weakened too. I can't see any Post-it. But I remember last time. She'll have left one somewhere. Maybe there's a note by the sofa where I was sleeping.

I walk unsteadily back into the living room. There is nothing on the coffee table or the sofa. I move across to the large windows and press my nose to the cold glass—I can see the deck, slicked with rain, and the pines crowding toward the house but no sign of them. It's too wet to be outside. She must have taken him down to her studio.

I suddenly have to pee. I walk toward the bedroom and push open the door.

Finn's cars are still scattered on the rug. The sight is reassuring, as if he is bound to come back for them at any moment. I go the toilet, pee, splash more cold water on my face, gulp at it—I am intensely thirsty. It is freezing in here too. I grab Doug's navy sweater and haul it on as I come back out to the corridor. The overhead light buzzes faintly as if it contains a trapped wasp.

"Susannah?" My voice echoes back at me. All I can hear is the distant moan of the wind, rain drumming on the roof, the gurgle of the toilet cistern and the persistent buzz of the light bulb.

Then I hear something, down toward the front door, a sort of faint thud.

There they are! Finn will need a diaper change if she hasn't done it. Lunch too. I am impatient to hold him, now, to feel is warm body snuggled against me again and hear what he's seen this morning while I've been crashed out on the sofa. There's still plenty of time 'til the ferry. I hurry unsteadily through the living room. The corridor is empty and gray. The front door is shut. I sway, gently by the sofa.

"Susannah? Finn?"

I rub my head. It's like moving through liquid. I remember pregnancy tiredness. With Finn I'd fall asleep at eight every night. But I never slept like this during the day. Then again, I have to factor in jet lag. And stress. It all adds up.

I walk toward the kitchen again, hugging myself. She should have woken me. It occurs to me that they could be in her bedroom—in there with the door shut, playing a hiding game—that might be where the noise came from earlier. They might spring out "Boo!" when I come in. I spin around to go toward the corridor, but then I pause on the rug: something is wrong in here. I scan the room, afraid, suddenly, of what I might be about to see. The quilt where I left it, folded on the sofa arm. The art books and magazines on the coffee table are still in piles. The fireplace has been cleaned out since last night. The abstract painting glows, rich greens and blues, above it.

And then out of the corner of my eye, I see the thing that is wrong. There are splatters of deep red coming out from behind the sofa. I put my fingers to my lips and take in a sharp breath.

But it is not blood. I walk around the sofa, blinking, and I realize that I'm looking at chunks of deep red glass. I stare at the wreckage. It looks as if a fist has crashed down on the Chihuly orb. Curls and shards litter the floor behind the sofa, and smaller fragments have sprayed over the boards, like droplets of blood. Shit. Shit. I step backward. Something stings my heel, a wasp sting. I bend and peer at it, then dig a sliver of glass from my bare foot. A bubble of blood follows it. I dab at it with my fingertips, but several more tiny drops plop onto the floor. The sharp pain follows.

I stare at the scattered red shards and then I think of Finn, reaching up to tilt it from its plinth. Shit. I press my heel down, and wince, but I need to wake up. I press it down again. I blink.

But this doesn't make sense. How could this possibly have happened while I was sleeping? There must have been a humongous shattering noise as the bowl hit the floor. I couldn't have slept through that. No way. I stare at the glass. The puncture in my heel throbs. I shake my head, just once. My mouth is very dry still. I press the sleeve of Doug's sweater onto my heel, pressing the little bulge of blood. Something is happening here, but I have no idea what.

Her bedroom is off this corridor, opposite the hall closet. I knock. Nothing. I knock again. I run a hand over my hair. I am probably going to have to pay for the Chihuly. I have a feeling that they cost thousands. I could be paying for that Chihuly for years.

I imagine him yanking it down with both hands. She must have been angry. Would she get angry with Finn? Would she have shouted at him? She can't have or—surely—I'd have woken. Was he hurt? I think of him, surrounded by sharp pieces of red glass. I'd definitely have woken up if he'd cried in the same room. Where the hell are they?

I can't think about Finn crying without me, or Susannah being angry with him. I push these thoughts to the back of my mind.

"Susannah? Finn?"

The wood floor is cold under my bare feet. I touch the handle with my fingertips, and listen. Rain drums on the roof. There are gusts of wind against the side of the house, and the crash of the ocean on rocks far away. I'm very thirsty still, despite all the water. The walls of the house shift and creak like a ship's hull. I turn the handle.

Tall windows along one wall let in a gray light. They must over-look the ocean but of course nothing is visible through the rain. There are long white curtains, half open. The linen duvet, in a knot, has insects embroidered on it. There are books everywhere, piled by the bed, stacked on shelves, and of course ceramics, too, placed between books, or fixed to the wall. Above the bed is an oil painting of a woman, a seated nude, seen from behind. I look for the light. Above the switch there's a plate with a woman's angular face peer-ing out from it, three-dimensional. I look closely, but it is not my mother's face.

My feet sink into the rug as I step into the center of the room. It is bitterly cold in here—so cold that I can see my own breath, faintly, as I move across the floor. There's a South American wall hanging above a chest of drawers with a stack of colorful African-looking bangles in a woven basket. There are perfume bottles and a tree stand with silver necklaces looped over it. Clothes spill from a laundry basket. A pair of plain black underwear lies by the bed.

Okay. So. They must be at the studio then. They are waiting for the rain to ease off before they come back to wake me up. I should not be in here.

There's a closed-up writing desk next to a door which I assume leads to a bathroom. It is one of those old-fashioned bureaus where you open it up to make the writing surface. There are framed photos along the top. I glance behind me.

Then I go across the room. I push the bathroom open—there are Moroccan blue mosaic tiles all across the walls and floor and a deep bath. The sink is a mess of combs, and clasps and toothpaste oozing out of its tube, a toothbrush face down on the stained enamel, a ball of gray hair on the shelf where silver rings are scattered.

I glance at myself in the mirror. I look sunken-eyed and white and a bit puffy. I splash some more water on my face and dry it with a stained white towel.

Then I peek in the cabinet: a hairbrush with curling gray tendrils in its bristles, a pair of silver hoop earrings, Band-Aids, Advil, insect repellent, and three or four more bottles of pills. I pick one up. The label says *Seroquel.* I have never heard of this or the names on any of the other bottles.

Perhaps Susannah is sick. She looks healthy, but what if she is living with something awful, like cancer? A serious illness would explain her reaction to the memories I've forced her to confront. I've seen this before in people I have interviewed. Their life-threatening illness forces them to face painful memories that they have never come to terms with, and sometimes it's as if they're experiencing the emotions all over again. It is yet another cruel side-effect of ill health.

But illness, of course, wouldn't explain Susannah's invention of travels with my mother, or her creation of my mother's ceramic face, aging through the years. But maybe she was telling the truth when she said that Maggie was mixed up. Maybe there are no Elenas.

I shut the door, hugging Doug's sweater around me. One of the photos on the bureau is of the man I assume was her partner. I recognize him from the photo in the kitchen. He's unshaven and rugged, looking at the camera with weary, lined eyes. Then there are shots of her son as a baby, as a long-haired toddler. I need Finn. They have to be down at the studio. In a moment, I'll go down there and get him.

There is gold trophy from a soccer tournament six years ago and a photo, in a silver frame, of a good-looking teen in a baseball shirt with a skateboard tucked under his arm. Next to it is an unframed snap of a whale, breaching out at sea—a bit blurry and far off.

They must be sheltering at the studio until the rain eases off. I have to stop panicking. There is still plenty of time for the six o'clock ferry.

The desk has a key in it. I turn it and open out the lid.

The first thing I see is a pot of pens and a glass paperweight with a wildflower trapped inside, but then I begin to take in the rest.

I am looking at a gallery of framed photos. And every single one is of my mother.

In one she's at a desk—maybe this desk—holding a pen. Her hair is long and curls over her shoulders, center parted; her expression is surprised, but pleased, as if the photographer has caught her in a good mood. There's a black and white shot of her on a boat looking lean and fit in cut-offs, beaming and holding the mast, leaning out from it, making a triangular shape with her hair in waves streaming over one shoulder.

In a third, a close-up of her face in color—she looks sideways at the camera as if her name has just been called and she's about to turn her head too. This one takes my breath away. She looks so young, but it is so like her—there is disapproval in the eye, a look of masked irritation.

Tucked into this frame is a smaller picture of a toddler in a life jacket, standing on a boat, with his chubby legs planted inside red rain boots.

For a moment, I'm confused. I rub my face. It's Finn.

But no—of course it's not. This child's hair is different, darker, and this photo is obviously old—it is slightly blurry, and the colors have that saturated seventies feel. Perhaps Susannah has a nephew? He really does look like Finn—probably because he's a similar age, with the same chubby knees and rain boots. But there is something deeply familiar about the little heart-shaped face. I feel as if I know it—intimately.

In the next photo my mother is holding a baby. With a start, I realize it must be me. There I am. Me. She is smiling, her face rounder, bright, her dimples deep, eyes very green. She looks happy. My face is almost covered by a little bonnet and I am looking up at her.

My eyes fill with tears as I stare down at the photo.

When I asked Susannah if she had photos of me as a baby, she must have forgotten about this one. This is the earliest picture I have ever seen of myself. It is the only one I've ever seen of my mother holding me as a new baby. And I want it so badly. Maybe she'll give it to me. Maybe I could just take it.

The last photo is black and white again, and it's my mother with a very youthful Susannah—just their faces, laughing. They are girlish and beautiful—one dark, one golden. My mother is looking at the camera and Susannah is looking at my mother. And there it is, is written across Susannah's face: a huge and unmistakable passion.

I stare at the two of them. So, my question is answered: Susannah is unmistakably in love. She was—maybe still is—completely in love with my mother.

This explains why she has acted so oddly, withholding things, getting furious and upset. She can't talk about the past because when my mother left her for my father she never got over it. She held onto her longing—her passion—for forty years.

I gaze at the other photos inside the desk. I realize that I am looking at a shrine.

Poor Susannah. It is so sad to nurse an unrequited love, like this, for your whole life.

Then something else catches my eye—an ancient looking book is tucked behind the photos—browning at the edges and all curled

up. It looks like it's been dropped in a bath. I peel it open and I can't
believe what I'm seeing. It is my mother's handwriting, the same
girlish cursive I know from the notebook. Pages of it. Pages and
pages. And it isn't scientific notes.

This book is in far worse condition than the scientific notebook.
Many pages are welded together, others have disintegrated entirely;
on some the writing is blurred and washed to illegibility. But it's
unmistakably hers.

And, standing barefoot in Susannah's bedroom, with my heart
pulsing, blood swishing in my ears, and the longing for Finn tight
in my belly, I begin to read my mother's words.

Asking S to come was an epic—epic—mistake.

I guess I lost it tonight. We were eating dinner downstairs—some
watery stew thing—quite late, both so tired. She pushed and pushed
at me, telling me I'm being exploited, saying the balance is all wrong
and asking dumb things about payment and finances. Finally I lost it—I
guess I let out all the pent up frustration at her. I yelled something like
"That's enough! If you can't accept my choices then I don't know how
we can carry on being friends." She put her fists on the table and said,
real mean and nasty, "Thing is, your choices, Elle, are just so shitty and
misguided." So that's when I blew—I got up and screamed, "From the
moment I told you I was leaving California you've been jealous. Admit
it! You're just fucking jealous, Susannah. It's pathetic!"

What happened next was kind of unsettling. I saw this rising rage
coming up from inside her—she literally seemed to swell and grow. She
got up slowly, her face went very white—her eyes kind of bulged out of
her skull. She stood very still for a moment, then leaned across the table
and pushed her face right over at me. This big vein was pulsing down
her forehead and her jaw was clamped shut. I think I put up my hands
because I suddenly had the feeling she was going to lean over and bite a
chunk out of my face. There was something vicious and off-kilter about
the way she was looking at me. But she didn't move. After a moment,
she pulled back, slowly, turned around and walked out. I heard front
door slam.

I ran straight upstairs—I don't know why because rationally I knew she'd gone out front—but I just had to go check. All fine. I sat on the floor by the bed. I was shaking and I felt quite sick. It's taken me a half hour to calm down—and I still feel unwell. In fact, I realize I have felt off color more or less the whole time we've been up here. Stress? So much is at stake.

I think what I just saw was all the violence of her childhood balled up into a fist and pointed at me. I kind of always knew it was there—that's why I tiptoed around her for so long. But I'm glad I've seen it now. She's gets this monotone when she tells me horrible things about her family, like "none of that can bother me anymore—I've dealt with it." But of course she can't possibly have—you don't grow up in a house like that and come out intact. At least, with my parents I didn't actually see anything—though I heard it, I think. Maybe. I don't remember much. I realized the other day that I can hardly remember Momma at all— just snatches—a dress with pink flowers, and that necklace with the piece of amber in it, like candy. I guess Father got rid of all her things because there was nothing there at all when he died. When I think about it, I don't remember much before my 8th birthday: I shut off all the memories—which I guess was for the best.

But sometimes I think I don't know what's going on in Susannah's head at all. And the truth is she doesn't know who I am, really, either— we're just two people who were roommates for a while, and told each other stuff. I should never have asked her to come here. But then, I couldn't have managed this on my own. And she wanted to come. She almost wasn't going to take no for an answer anyways.

I have to calm down. I'll go drink some water.

I should probably have distanced myself from her when I got the chance—but when I think about it, she didn't let me do that either— writing intense letters, sending gifts, moving up to Victoria, inviting herself to stay.

Drank water. Took a bath. Fixed with Ana to have another picnic lunch for tomorrow. Calmer now. Ana is a very calming presence. Still tired and a little queasy, but not so riled up. I feel bad for her now. I've no idea where she's gone—it's raining out there, and dark. Must be in the bar.

I have to be more tolerant. She's been through so much. I need to focus on the good things about her. She can be great company—funny, crazy, thoughtful, thought-provoking. Here's what I realized in the bath: she's like Gray. I can't expect her to really understand why I need to do this. I can't possibly tell her about the sense of duty that I have. Somewhere out there Bella has a mother and every time I see a female of the right sort of age, I wonder. I do feel it—like a duty. I have a duty to find her mother, and I will, one day. But if you tell someone you feel a sense of obligation toward a killer whale they're going to look at you like you're a crazy person. It's more than that though. I couldn't tell S about the first day on the boat last summer when I looked into the whale's eye and felt the connection—it was like an electric shock to the heart. You can't explain these things without sounding like you should be institutionalized. But J gets it, and so do the others, because they feel it too. We're a tribe of believers—fanatics to the outside world. S doesn't get this because she feels no connection to the whales. She thinks this is about grant proposals and funding.

Ana told us this morning that in the old days the float houses up here belonged to loggers. They'd tow a whole community—houses and shops, even schools—wherever the next logging claim was. Now there are still loggers, but also fishermen, and draft dodgers, hippies, and anyone escaping or running or looking for an alternative life. So surely I can find a place here too. Shit—footsteps on stairs. She's coming back!

The next few pages are stuck together. I am breathing too fast and my limbs feel shaky. My mouth is very dry. This is incredible. Proof. Though I don't know what of. I flick to the early part of the diary. It seems to be all about chasing orcas—there are several pages about a "matriline" and exhaustive descriptions of pods—the J pod, K pod, and L pod—and the individual whales, each with its own letter, number and name. My mother loves initials. Researchers—I assume they are researchers—are D and K and C and J. Sometimes MB. She seems obsessed with a "catalog."

I read a short section where she is talking about "The guys" and "the boys" and I think she's referring to more researchers but then I realize the "guys" are whales. They are three brothers and they have distinct personalities—or she thinks they do—the little one is shy, then there's the joker middle brother and the more aggressive eldest, who occasionally swims right at the boat then ducks under at the last minute. There's a baby, too—and she's obviously entranced with him. The way she writes, it's as if they are people—not friends, but people in whom she has a focused, obsessive interest. Like an anthropologist inserting herself among a kindly and fascinating tribe. Then she describes something obviously whale-like—"pec-slapping" or "breaching" or "spyhopping" and they're animals again.

I flick forward but a whole bunch of pages are clumped and stuck and I know if I try to pry them apart they'll tear. I can read a fragments of sentences here and there and they mostly seem to be about acoustics—"*that . . . burst pulse again—the creaking, wooden sound*" or "*. . . and she gave a whistle: 'here I am'*"—"*. . . heard them echolocating . . .*"

I lift my head and listen for the sound of Susannah and Finn bursting through into the kitchen, the dogs' claws, Finn's little voice. Nothing. The house is still empty. I really need to go and look for them—he'll be hungry. He needs his lunch. And I need him.

But this journal is unbelievable. Alice has to see this. This is incredible. Susannah has my mother's diary right here and she didn't show me—it proves, at least, that she has been telling the truth. But clearly she left out some of the crucial details. I have to take this home—this is evidence. I have to show this to Alice. This is vindication. It was not so mad, after all, to get on a plane and come here. Maybe it was instinct.

I need to call Alice as soon as I get a phone signal. I was right that my mother resented me for her lost career. When she got pregnant, all of this had to end—Dad probably insisted that she come to England where I would be safe and well-schooled. I basically ruined her life.

* * *

This information is important for Alice, too. It can't have been easy to grow up with a sister like me. Alice had to witness all our fights and live with the constant tension. She must have felt guilty that she and my mother were so harmonious—being the favorite daughter brings its own pressures. She was always trying to make amends. It isn't surprising that she grew up to be so focused on rules and laws and making everything fair. But is my sister happy? I don't think so. Alice, I realize, is as imprisoned by our past as I am. She needs to know the truth about our mother as much as I do. In some way, this could liberate Alice too.

I flip forward: a couple of pages describing how they came across a group of orcas that were rubbing their bellies on some stony beach. A description of the guesthouse . . . *Ana, who runs this place, always seems calm, even when her boys are running around like wild things . . . and those boys really are wild, cute, but wild . . .*

> . . . lovely clear blue eyes, pale lashes, and fine blonde hair that she pulls into a knot on the back of her head. I like her a lot. She told me she's from a family of Swedish loggers and Glen is a fisherman, though I guess he leaves so early and is sleeping when we get back. We haven't seen him, not once. The three of us ate together last night . . . S silent, brooding . . . A and I talked . . .
>
> . . . Turns out they've known each other since grade school. A went to Victoria for a few years to train to be a High School teacher, but "it just didn't feel right not to be here, with Glen." So she came home . . . she said it all so simply, I felt a . . .

The rest of the page is smudged so badly I can't read anymore. I turn over and the letter "S" catches my eye again.

> . . . Woke in the night, last night, maybe 2 a.m. S sitting on the wooden chair by my bed. She was watching me.
>
> The rain had stopped and it was white moonlight, and with that hair, her nightdress, and pale eyes—she looked spooky. I don't know

how long she'd been there—I guess I sensed her and woke up. I sat bolt upright and said something like "what are you doing?" She said, in this low, catatonic voice, "just watching you sleep." I told her to quit it and go lie down. She did. So did I. We both lay there, but I did NOT sleep after that. Even when I heard her breathing slow, I just couldn't. I was still awake when the ravens started clamoring and cawing in the trees, at five thirty.

Now—after another day motoring round the coast, finding nowhere remotely suitable—I'm tired like someone's opened me up and taken my bones out. That's the real problem here: am so damned tired I can't think straight. I feel sick again. I guess S is upset by our argument. She's been monosyllabic today.

She's in the bath right now. It's peaceful in here without her—hiss of the water through pipes, this sleeping angel, the patter of rain on the roof. I never have been any good at friendship, all the intensity women require—the to-ing and fro-ing and unspoken needs and all the little offenses. It's just all so complicated and tiresome. I keep getting this feeling that I'm missing something really obvious, like there's a big list of rules just beyond my field of vision and I'm breaking every one of them, and that's why she's so mad and frustrated. But I don't know what they are.

I need to sleep but have to stay awake but don't want to sleep while she's still pacing around. If I keep writing, then I'll stay awake.

Sometimes, lately, I picture her as this wolf, following at my heels, ready to savage anyone who comes too close—but maybe also ready to turn on me too if the wind shifts and something flicks in her brain. I don't know. Something isn't right with her at the moment—if it ever was.

J called earlier—he's making progress—CDF is interested in the Institute plan—thought it has to go through some committees so won't know for a while. He'll tell me more when back. D's gone home now—C, K and R going next week. It's going to get lonely. I have to work something out. I have to find a home—but maybe that isn't going to happen up here. It's possible that all this has been a ridiculous fantasy.

Right now, I have this intense pain in my head that won't go away. It's cold in this room even with the heater on. My hand is aching like hell from writing—have to stop.

When she gets out of the bathroom, I'm going to tell her we'll do one more day then go. When she's back in Victoria I might even miss her.

Again, the pages stick but in gentle increments I manage to pry the next couple away from each other and continue to read the faint ink.

... miraculous! Beautiful day. Warm, calm. Anchored for lunch watching a black bear on the shore turning over rocks, very patient and slow. I had the headphones on and the hydrophone was picking up all the sounds of the shoreline—the clatter of shingle, even grunting of rock cod, and out to sea, total stillness—no engine sounds at all. Then the sing-song— bree-fftt-whirreeep. I jumped up scanning the waves with the binoculars but couldn't see anything—then—wolf-whistles, a surface blast from a blowhole. I started the outboard and took us round the headland. And there was this a perfect little bay, sun bouncing off the water, mountains reaching up behind it, and six whales—a couple of adult males, a couple of adolescents and two grown females, just hanging out, meandering through the kelp beds. I didn't recognize any of them, but no catalog—so got out the camera, took three rolls of film—though with S and K in the boat, I couldn't record sounds or make proper notes.

Afterward we moored on the beach, and wandered up round the headland. Met an elderly woman who has a little shack—she claims the orca come year-round—I made her repeat that about three times. Even in winter? Yes. In January? Yes. She told us there's a very small community on the island including a family in a floathouse round the other side. Their kids to go school on—yup—a school boat! There's even a seaplane that brings the mail, and there seems to be zero noise pollution—nothing but year round orca ...

After this, the rest of the pages—almost half the book—are clumped together in a thick, rigid wedge. I will have to take this back, dry it out, try to pry it apart carefully. Not now. The only page

I can make out now is the last one—it has faded to almost nothing. Just a few sentences are legible.

> . . . Tomorrow we head back to the float house, these three days have nearly killed me. Total relief to be heading back. S—regal and prickly, kind of deranged at times. J—hell on earth, furious, barely containing himself. KK—heaven, heaven. Just one more day. Forecast good . . .

*

A sound echoes from somewhere in the house. I slam the desk shut, shove the diary down the back of my jeans and hurry to the bedroom door with a mixture of deep relief that my baby is back, and panic that they'll appear just as I emerge from Susannah's bedroom.

"Hello?" I shout. My head is spinning lightly. "Is that you? Hey!"

Silence. Gusts of rain. Creaking timber. No dogs. No voice calling out "Mama!"

It must have been the wind.

I'm going to have to get my coat on and go down and get them at the studio. I want Finn, now—urgently. And we'll need to eat, pack and then get going. I'm determined to be early for that six o'clock ferry. I realize that I don't need to question Susannah about her past anymore because I now have the document. I'm glad, now, that I didn't force her to relive her unrequited love for my mother. It would have been cruel. I can dry it out, and read everything I need, right there, in my mother's words.

I open the hall closet to get my coat—Finn's red snowsuit is gone, so are his rain boots, gloves and hat, and so is her wrap. At least she wrapped him up. I grab my parka, shove the diary into its inside pocket, and walk up to the living room. I would not have liked her to catch me in her room. I imagine, for a second, the rage my mother describes in her diary—those cold eyes—focused on me.

It's time to go. Finn's going to be hungry. I wonder if I should bring his diaper bag down to the studio and a sandwich even. But maybe she's already thought to give him lunch. She probably has. I just need him. And coffee.

I get to the living room, the shards on the floor. It still does not seem possible that I could have slept so heavily that a glass bowl could shatter in the same room and not wake me up. The thought is disturbing. How could I have not have heard the glass shattering around my baby boy?

My stomach grumbles. I haven't eaten anything today except a bite of the muffin. Maybe that's why I am so fuzzy headed and out of it. But I can't stop now. I need to get Finn and go.

I'll write to Susannah when I get home, and tell her I took the diary. I can read the rest tonight when we are tucked up in a Vancouver B&B. It's not stealing because the journal rightly belongs to my family and not to Susannah. And Alice has to see it. I realize I forgot to take the picture of myself as a baby with my mother. I could go back for it. But no—I need to get Finn more.

I shove my boots on and open the side door. The air is bitter, wind scatters rain into my face, waking me up a bit—but with Doug's sweater and the parka I am insulated. I blink and huddle. The sea crashes far below as I pick my way over the slippery deck, tasting salt. I can see my own breath and the tip of my nose is numb already. The trees are crowded in and so unbelievably tall. Their tops swish in the wind high overhead. I try not to think of wild animals, watching from the undergrowth as I pass. They have bears up here, and wolves, and god knows what else.

I break into a jog. The scent of the pines is overwhelming and I run, faster, as I enter the forest—everything is muffled, the wind high above, the raindrops—something large flickers in my peripheral vision; I speed up and my legs feel stiff, my breaths harsh. The sound of the sea is further away, now, and the carpet of pine needles feels spongy under my feet, as if I am running over the surface of a brain.

I just need to follow the path. It's not far. Thank God I came because Finn would be worried, coming through these trees with Susannah, who, really, he barely knows. He'll be wanting me. Then I'm at the clearing. I can see the studio.

There are no lights on but although it's dim out here it's not dark.

"Hello?" I stumble up the wooden steps. "It's just me!" I wrench open the door. "You should have woken me—"

I am in a large peak-roofed space. My breaths echo. It smells of dried clay and pine. It is empty.

Maybe there's a room out back. That's where they are.

"Susannah? Finn? Hello! Where are you?"

Rain drums on the roof. There are shelves of white ceramics stacked up on each wall. A potter's wheel, and a big iron kiln in a corner, paint-dribbled stools and a workbench, old sheets and pottery knives and sharp tools—dangerous things for a toddler—a pair of Hunter rain boots by a peeling coat stand. An empty wine bottle with a candle stub crumpled in its neck, a low red sofa along one wall, covered in an Indian throw, a CD player layered in dust and paint stains. Clay-smeared overalls, splayed on the floor.

"Where are you?" My too-high voice echoes back at me. The sound is alarming.

There are two doors at the end of the room. I push one and peer in—a toilet. The dusty floor is slippery. I walk across and open the other door. Darkness. I pat the walls for a light. Squinting. There. I flick it on, and blink.

It's a meditation or yoga room. There is a wooden Buddha. Strings of prayer beads. A rolled up yoga mat, a stack of Mexican blankets, some cork blocks. The floor is clean and polished. There are cushions to one side, an essential oil burner on a three-legged Balinese table. I smell stale jasmine and other perfumed oils. A garland made of tiny white paper flowers is draped around a table lamp on the floor.

I back out.

I'm not going allow myself to panic. I've missed them, that's all. Perhaps they're out front with umbrellas chasing squirrels. She is only being kind to occupy him. She knows I'm pregnant and exhausted and she didn't want to wake me. She wanted me to have a break. I have to not be angry. Plus, Finn may have wrecked her priceless Chihuly. She should have woken me up. But it's okay. Nothing bad is happening here. I just have to find them.

Suddenly I want him with my whole body. I want to see his little face and hear about squolls and hold him tight and breathe in his sweet, milky smell. He'll want me too. He won't know why he's with her and not with me. I can control my mind, but I can't control my body—the anxiety makes my limbs shaky and my head feel light. The pit of my stomach feels ice-cold.

I leave the studio and step back out into the rain, shutting off the lights, slamming the door and then I launch myself back across the clearing. The trees are layered in shadowy lines, like straight soldiers. It feels better to run.

I am out of breath and water is dripping down my neck as I open the French windows. On the countertop, I notice Finn's new sippy cup.

With the cup in my hand, I go down the corridor, open the front door and step onto the deck. I peer around, calling them. But they aren't here, either.

The rain seems heavier, dripping off the veranda into the under-growth, falling in dense lines through the pines. From the top of the stone steps that lead down to the drive I can see the rental car but not much else. Pulling up my hood I put my foot on the first stone step and it's like stepping onto a glacier: my foot shoots out to one side and my body sways dramatically backward.

I seize the railing but not soon enough to stop myself from crash-ing onto the sharp edge of the step. The duck cup rolls and bumps away down the steps. It's like hot metal rammed against my lower spine. For a second I can't move. The pain is exquisite. If I move, my vertebrae will crumble. Freezing rain thumps down on my head. I hear the bang of the sea on the rocks behind the house.

My arm, suspending me half an inch from the step, shakes with the effort of holding my weight off my spine. Slowly, I haul myself back up. I can move. I press both hands against my belly. Everything in my body feels as if it's shifted somewhere it shouldn't go.

I crawl down the rest of the steps and shuffle to pick up the cup—it is covered in dirt and pine needles. I wipe it on my jeans. I can see the rest of the driveway now.

The Subaru is gone.

Pain seethes through my coccyx. I think about the tiny baby, floating inside me. I can't do this. I have to look and think and be careful. I wipe the rain out of my eyes, off my face.

She must have taken Finn into town. Maybe she ran out of ways to entertain him in the freezing rain—after he smashed the Chihuly. Was she angry with him? Why in God's name didn't she wake me up? I picture Finn strapped into her Subaru, crying for me. I can't bear the thought that she might have been angry with him. A fierce wave of protectiveness sweeps through me and my entire body goes hot, then cold. You can't just take someone's child into town. It's an almost a forty-minute drive in this weather. You can't do that without waking them up to ask.

But Susannah isn't the type of woman to ask anyone's permission for anything. Even a child.

My spine throbs. The rain stings the crown of my head and I am shivering. Not far off I hear the ocean bang the frozen rocks. Holding the railings I haul myself back to the house.

I need to call the gallery but the number is on the website, and the website is on my phone and my phone has no signal here. I don't know what the Canadian directory inquiries number is.

I have to stay calm. She will have left a Post-it somewhere and I just haven't seen it. My spine pulses as I move through the silent house. Somehow I've missed the note where this woman says she has taken my child into town without asking.

Then I spot postcard with a ceramic fish on it, stuck on the fridge. I turn it over, it's blank, but there it is—*Susannah Gillespie Gallery, Spring Tide Island*. And the phone number. I swipe it from under its magnet and pick up her phone from the countertop.

The gallery phone rings and rings. Then her voice mail clicks in, her cool, in control voice.

I leave a message, trying to sound less angry than I am. "Susannah, if you're there could you please call me? I woke up and you and Finn weren't here. I'm going to come meet you in town."

I hang up. I make myself imagine them in the bakery—Susannah and Maggie together cooing over Finn, feeding him more gigantic cookies. He will like that, but he'll want me too. Some part of him will be worried without me. But there's only one road. I can't miss them, even if they're coming back. I will go. I'll grab our things, then drive into town. It's okay. There is only one place they can be and I'm going there.

The pain in my back is less intense but the thought of sitting down on a car seat makes me wince. I move, stiffly, toward the kitchen cupboards, unzipping the parka. I need painkillers. In one cupboard there is a shelf, high up, with pill bottles on it.

I reach up—more prescription bottles—and I don't recognize any names. She is ill. I should have known. I've been around enough sick people, I should have picked up on it. I wonder why she didn't mention an illness. But why would she? We barely know each other. Someone with all that brown rice and tofu would only have so many prescription drugs if she really needed them.

I'm not sure if ibuprofen has the same name in Canada. My spine howls a protest as I stretch higher to see the names on the bottles. I pick one up: Zolpidem. I put it back. The only name I recognize on any bottle is codeine. But the last thing on earth I want is to feel woozy.

I dial the gallery again. My fingers are clumsy and stiff with cold, a raw red color.

"Okay, Susannah? Could you call me right now if you get this?" I say. "Finn and I need to be on the next ferry so I don't want to miss you. I'd like to head down early, in case it leaves early again. So, could you please call me, right away? I'd really like to know where you are, Susannah. What are you doing?"

I hang up. She's not allowed to do this. This is just not reasonable. Just in case I somehow miss her, I scribble a Post-it note:
"Looking for you"
Then I add *"in town!"*
This is not right.

*   *   *

But it's a tiny town and there's only one route from here to it. So either way, we're going to bump into each other. But I need coffee and painkillers; my coccyx hurts and I still feel slightly groggy. I need to wake up properly before I get behind a wheel in the rain.

I find the tin of coffee and open the filter machine, chucking in four scoops, but filling it up with enough water for just one cup. I remember that you shouldn't drink too much coffee when you're pregnant. For a moment, I dither. But on balance caffeine is probably less risky for the baby than veering off a cliff top road in heavy rain.

I flip the coffee machine on and hurry to the bedroom to pack.

I can't wait to get Finn from Susannah, to hold him close and feel his arms around my neck, kiss his downy cheeks, put him into the rental car, with his blanket and bunny and duck cup, and drive away—away from her, onto the ferry and put this oppressive place behind us, forever. Another wave of physical need crashes through my body, as powerful as any fever or sickness. I need my little boy back. Right now.

I won't tell Alice that I lost sight of him for this short time. I won't tell anyone. Definitely not Doug. This will soon be over. I just have to go and get him.

I sweep up toiletries from the bathroom. I have ibuprofen in my toiletry bag—I forgot it was there—I pour two into my hand and swallow them. My back throbs as I lean over to take gulps of water from the tap. I splash more water on my face. One of Finn's trucks is in the shower, his blue sock is under the sink; there is a packet of wipes on the radiator. I shove it all in. I scoop up his cars, and pour them into the gingham bag. Then I start gathering up the clothes that are strewn about the place—his pants and jeans, the filthy ketchup smeared jeans, the small vests and T-shirts and fleeces. I have to get him back, right now.

I find his bunny under the duvet. For a moment, I bury my nose in it, then I shove it into my messenger bag. He'll be wanting his bunny, too. Then I look around. His sleeping bag is not here.

I look for it under the duvet. Down behind the bed. Under the bed. In the bag—did I throw it in there without noticing? And his

spaceman pajamas. Where are they? I dig around in the case; I probably shoved them in there too—this pregnancy fog—it feels as if I
am still not fully awake, not thinking clearly—missing something
obvious. Maybe Susannah took the sleeping bag to keep him extra
warm in the car. Probably a good idea in this weather. It is reassuring that she is concerned about his warmth. And yet, there's something uncomfortable about her being in here, rummaging through
our belongings as I slept.

I gather the rest of our things.

The diaper bag has gone. Fair enough. At least that means he has
clean diapers today. She's a mother. She's raised a son—she remem-
bers what a toddler needs. I think about his other jeans. Where are
they? And his stretchy striped pants. The dinosaur T-shirt. I look
under the bed again and scan the room in case I've missed them.

His blue fleece is gone too. But maybe it's all in the bag, it must
be. I look at the bag—could take everything out and fold his clothes
and sort dirty laundry and work out what I've left behind, but I
just want to get going because I need him now; it's a physical need
rooted deep in guts and bone marrow. I need to leave this darkening
house and this remote, weather-lashed rock. I throw Finn's bunny
into the bag.

I really, really need my little boy.

CHAPTER THIRTEEN

A single light illuminates the gallery sign but the building itself is in darkness. Through the rain-streaked windshield I can see the windows, shuttered downstairs, dark upstairs. A low, gray sky hunches over the gallery roof. I get out and run to the door, battering on the silver doorknob as I pull my hood up. I peer through the letterbox. "Susannah?" A long, low ferry horn bawls through the rain. Droplets drum on my hood and my lips are coated with salt. Silence.

And this is when the cold knot in my gut really tightens. I look up and down the deserted street and across it, through layers of rain, down to the ferry port: blurry lights, a couple of parked cars, a stray dog—no humans. I look up the street again and then I notice the Subaru. It is parked just up from my car. Relief rushes from my stomach to my head. It's okay. They're here. Of course they are.

I run to the Subaru. It is, of course, empty—no sign even of the dogs. The absence of the dogs must mean something—but what? There is her trash—the Vitamin Water bottles and nut packets; some big Tupperware pots, clay-dusted sheets; old walking boots and a tartan dog blanket. And Finn's car seat. I didn't even notice that it wasn't in the back of the rental car anymore. I'm glad she has it because it means that she is concerned for his safety. I'll find them in a minute. I have to try not to scream at her for taking him like this. It won't do any good to have another conflict before I go. But even if I have to sit around the ferry port for three hours, I'm leaving now. The minute I have Finn in my arms, we're saying goodbye.

I wrench open the Subaru and unclip the car seat, hauling it out. It is dotted with Cheerios and there is a little Tupperware pot of them lying on the floor. She must have given Finn Cheerios as a snack to keep him quiet on the journey. Was he crying?

I slam the door and run to the rental car. I fling the car seat in the back then bleep the locks. Then I jog up the street again to the Rock Salt Bakery, with its huge cupcake, and warm lights wavering through the rain. They have to be there. They must be.

But through the café windows I can see that there is no one inside, only Maggie, sitting behind the counter, head down, with reading glasses on the end of her nose.

"I'm looking for Susannah," I burst in. Maggie has a stack of papers on the counter. There is folk music, and the cloying smell of sugar and cinnamon. "Susannah has my son, and I don't know where they are. Have you seen them?"

She stands up, whips off her glasses. "Oh! Kali! You're here? I thought you were back at the house, resting."

"What?" I put both hands on the counter, breathing heavily. "Listen, Maggie. Susannah is here somewhere with Finn, but I don't know where. Her car is here, but they aren't at the gallery—I thought they'd come here, but—." I glance at the door behind her and wonder if Maggie lives above her bakery. Maybe there's a house upstairs, and Susannah is up there, giving Finn a sandwich and playing ambulance crashes. "Are they here?"

"Oh? No, no. Hey. It's okay," she starts to gather the papers. "You look worried. Don't be. She left you a note, I'm sure. She's taken him off on a little trip, just as you suggested—to give you that much-needed break." She smiles and her eyes crinkle. "It seems like a good idea."

For a moment I stare at her. She meets me with her glassy blue gaze, her slightly vacant smile.

"She *what*?" I say.

"She said you—"

"Where? Where has she taken him?"

"It's okay Kali honey. Really. She came in earlier today to drop off the dogs. She said you wanted a break from the little guy, so she was taking him to give you space. I don't blame you—not at all. Nobody's judging you, here, believe me. I've raised three children myself—I know what it can be like."

"No, stop. Maggie. Please . . . She came here? But I didn't ask her to take Finn . . . I would never . . . where has she taken him? Where did they go? She didn't tell me a thing. She just took him . . ."

"She didn't? Oh honey. I'm sure this is a misunderstanding. She wouldn't just go. And don't worry, your little guy's just fine—goodness he looks so cute in that little hat with the earflaps—he's just darling. Cute as a little button!"

"Maggie!" I bark. "Where has she taken him?"

"Okay, honey. Now, don't worry but she just took him on the outer island ferry for a visit to her little cabin—she has a lovely little cabin tucked away in the archipelago. She likes to go there mostly in summertime. It's a bit rough, but it's not too far. Honestly, there's no need to worry."

"What? She's taken Finn on a *boat*? To another *island*?"

"Oh Kali. It's okay, really. Susie's a mother too don't forget. She won't let anything happen to the little one. She must have misunderstood you, but they'll be back again tonight. I think this is all one great big mistake."

"A mistake?!"

"Look. Come sit down, come on." She comes out from behind the counter. She's wearing an Aran sweater and jeans and clogs, and she is broad in the hip but with a narrow torso and that elongated neck, as if she is being dropped, slowly, through a pipette. She ushers me toward a sofa.

"Now. She told me what a hard time you're having, with your husband, on top of everything else, you poor thing. No wonder you asked her to take the baby for a while. Anyone would find it hard to cope in your situation, being abandoned by your husband . . . Even Geoffrey—you know, the gentleman who runs the drugstore—he understood when I told him . . ."

"What? Who? Who understood what?" I unzip the parka. I am suddenly sweaty.

"Oh, Geoffrey mentioned that you were struggling this morning, with the little one. They can be pretty much a handful at that age, huh? And you with another one on the way . . . Now, honey, you just sit yourself down there. I'm going to get you a drink. You're awfully pale. A nice hot chocolate? You do look peaked, hon."

"No!" I remember the gray-haired man who opened up specially for me, and my phone call and bad manners—Finn pulling things down off his shelves. Could that really have only been this morning? Christ, this is completely insane. "Maggie," I try to keep my voice reasonable. "I don't mean to be rude. But I'm coping perfectly fine. I'm not ill. I just want my son back. You can't just take someone's child!"

"Sweetie, she wouldn't do anything to upset you. She said you were sleeping so deeply, you poor thing. Early pregnancy can be tough enough, especially—well, I know you've been under a huge strain, just huge. I'm sure Susie only wanted to help out in any way she could, since she is such a close friend of your mother."

"She isn't," I snap. "Oh my God. She is not a friend of my mother's."

"But . . ."

"My mother is dead, Maggie. My mother died."

Maggie's face falls. "Oh my lord," she says. "Oh, honey." Then she looks suddenly smug, as if this explains everything about me.

I perch on the sofa. My back throbs dimly. For a moment, I feel totally powerless—she has Finn. On a boat. Out there. Then I feel the anger building. I imagine Susannah telling Maggie about my scattiness—how I let Finn break things; telling her about Doug, the pregnancy—or was that the drugstore owner, reporting back on my purchases? This place suddenly does not feel vast at all—it feels shrunken and claustrophobic and airless.

But this is not Maggie's fault. I must not be angry with Maggie. The woman plainly has no idea what Susannah is really like.

"I can't believe she didn't say anything about your mother," Maggie says, as if she's just realized that something is wrong here. "She must be so . . . She must be . . . But I guess . . . that's why she's helping you out like this."

"She isn't helping, Maggie! I never said she could take Finn. She can't just take my son off to another island without asking me. Jesus Maggie. You can't take someone's baby without asking."

She kneels down next to me and puts a hand on my arm. "Sweetie, you're overwrought. I didn't realize you lost your poor mother. So, here's what we're going to do. We're going to stay here, and wait for them to come back. I know you regret asking her to take him, you feel bad—but we women can ask for help sometimes you know. Yes we can. Grief can make anyone a little—off balance. See that ferry down there—*The Sea Maiden*," she points through the rain-streaked café window.

I shake her hand off my arm and lean to see out the window, but I can't see the port at all, just the rainy street.

"That's the outer island ferry, right there." She sounds as if she's soothing a child. "In a few minutes, that ferry will go out to Raven Bay and then when it gets there, and drops everything off, it'll turn around and come back and that's the ferry they'll be on. So you're just going to stay here with me and wait for them to come back. You're going to curl up right there, have a hot chocolate, a nice grilled cheese, maybe read some magazines, take another nap, and before you know it they'll be stepping off the ferry and you'll wonder why you were ever so worked up. Never feel bad for asking for help."

"I didn't ask for help!" I struggle to stand up. "And I don't need rest." It's all I can do not to scream into Maggie's face. "I just need my son back."

"And you'll get him back, real soon."

"That boat, that one down there—would that boat take me to them?"

"Well, sure," says Maggie. "But, honey, you'll only go out to Raven Island, meet them, then have to turn around and come back here—and it's a fair ride—the sea's pretty rough—"

"Thanks." I stand up. "But I'm getting on that ferry." I pick up my bag.

"Okay. I understand. You need your baby."

But then I stop. For once, I'm going to think things through. "Maggie—if she's not at the ferry port, just by any chance, where on Raven Island is her cabin?"

"Why wouldn't she be at the ferry port?" Maggie blinks. "Even Susie wouldn't want to stay out in a cabin in January with a little toddler."

"I just want to be sure I don't miss them okay? I just want to know where they are in case . . . I don't know. I just need to know where exactly her cabin is."

"Well I've never actually been there myself. Susie keeps it as a refuge, you see—she never lets anyone visit. But you could always ask at Raven Bay. These are tiny communities. You think Spring Tide is small! There's a nice woman called Ana, runs the guest-house up there. She's just opposite the ferry dock—Ana knows everything."

"Thank you," I say. "Thank you, Maggie. I'm sorry to be so—so shouty—I just really need to find Finn now."

"Just don't be too hard on her," she calls after me. "I know she likes to be in control, she doesn't always listen, but she really did think you wanted her to take the baby. And she must be upset too . . ."

I look at her and her gaze still has that blank sheen. For a moment, I wonder what Maggie does and doesn't know. I nod, then, hooking my bag across my body, I plunge back out into the rain and sprint, as fast as I can, toward the ferry.

*

There are a few bundled up people on board, hunched on benches in rows. There is no bar on this boat, it's far too small and it's shabby and stinking—it looks like it was built somewhere back in the seventies. It smells of old fish and cigarettes and has a rough brown carpet. It lurches out of the port, rain slashing at the windows.

I am struggling to get my head around the fact that just an hour or two earlier Finn was on this boat. This cannot be happening. I've felt this feeling before—in nightmares—and that time by the ruined West Pier when my mother walked off and I hurried after her, but my feet slid and pushed at the bank of stones, getting me nowhere.

I need to call Doug now. He'll be appalled that I have allowed this woman—this stranger—to take Finn. If I call I'll panic him. But his is the only voice I need to hear right now. And he needs to know what is happening. I feel nausea rising but there's still a signal on the phone so I take a breath and dial. He answers in just two rings.

"I'm so glad you called—"

"Doug," I cut him off. For a moment I can't speak. It feels as if the planet is rollicking off its axis and I have to find something to hold onto or I will be hurled into space with it.

"What's happened?" I hear it in his voice—his fear answering mine. "What is it?"

"No." I suck in the stale cabin air. "No, no. It's okay. He's okay. But I'm . . . I have to . . . Doug, I've been staying with this woman, Susannah; she's a very old friend of my mother's. She knew me when I was a baby—she owns a gallery on Spring Tide Island, near Vancouver. I've been . . . tired . . . very tired, and I fell asleep this morning, and when I woke up, she'd taken Finn to . . . to . . . she'd taken him on a day trip to her cabin . . . on this other island." I take another breath. "Without asking me!"

"What?" his voice is hoarse. "Where is he now? Are you telling me you haven't got him with you?"

"He's with her. It's okay. She's not a random stranger. I mean, I think it's all fine. I don't want you to panic. It's just—I just wanted to hear your voice. That's all. I wanted to tell you what's happening. I . . . I'm on the ferry, going after them, to find them. She's at her cabin. I think it's a float house, actually, I think it used to belong to my mother but—"

"What did you say?" he shouts. "Kal, you're breaking up. Finn's at a floating house? Where are you then?"

"It's okay, really it is. Susannah's friend at the bakery, Maggie, says she's only trying to help—she's been quite good with Finn while I've been staying. I just—I shouldn't have called you, I'm sorry. I didn't mean to worry you. I just really needed to hear your voice, that's all."

"Tell me exactly where you are right now." He knows, just as I do, that this is not right. Nobody can just go off with our baby. "Give me your exact location, her name, everything you can think of."

"I'm on my way there, I'm going to be there, with Finn, really soon."

"Kal," he barks. "Just give me the information."

"Okay. So I'm just leaving Spring Tide Island. It's to the west of Vancouver. I'm on the Sea Maiden Ferry heading to a place called Raven Bay—maybe northwest of Spring Tide. I think it's pretty close. I don't know, maybe a fifteen, twenty-minute ride." As I say this, I realize I haven't asked anyone how long this ferry will actually take to get to Raven Bay. "The woman I've been staying with is called Susannah Gillespie, she owns the Susannah Gillespie Gallery here—there's a website, you can google her. She knew my Mom at university. My father knows her. She's well-known in the art world I think. She took Finn out to her cabin on Raven Bay earlier today, maybe midday. Listen, I'm sure it's fine but . . ." He is too silent. I pause. "Doug?"

Nothing. Dead air. Then a flatline tone.

"Doug, can you hear me? Doug!"

I look at the phone—*call lost.*

I have no idea how much—if anything—Doug heard of what I just said. I should never—*never*—have called him. What can he do but panic now? And I can't even call him back.

Hearing myself explain all this has grounded me slightly. When you say the facts, it's not so bad, really. It's outrageous that she took Finn off without asking me. It's wrong—it goes against all sorts of unspoken rules, but it's not a disaster—and I'll be there soon. I'll have him back before I know it. I mustn't let hormones and the foreignness, the bigness of this place, propel me into an unruly state. I should never have called Doug.

The boat lurches further onto the rough sea. There is no visibility. It is as if we are being bounced across the ocean in a pod of rain. I rest my head in my hands. The ibuprofen is wearing off and my coccyx aches. My head aches too, from the caffeine, all that heavy sleep. My mouth is still very dry. I have still eaten nothing. The idea of food makes me want to throw up.

Rain lashes against the scratched windows and the boat tips and teeters over the tall waves. Sickness rolls through me. I close my eyes. How are these people not vomiting? This is awful. I make myself open my eyes—there are five or six people on the benches around me—all men—all zipped into weather gear, mostly staring at their knees, or reading papers.

Maggie is a reasonable, sane person. She wears clogs and bakes poppy seed muffins. She has presumably known Susannah for years. She would have behaved differently if there were a reason to worry: I must have missed the note.

Suddenly I feel the anger rising up again, the sheer, impotent fury. She doesn't get to take him away from me like this. You can't do that.

Even if she thought she was doing me a favor, she didn't have to lie about it. She told Maggie that I asked her to take him away. The lie, I realize, is what takes this from deluded to outrageous.

For a moment I imagine screaming at Susannah when I get off this ferry. I picture myself flying at her, grabbing Finn and howling, spitting, in her face. I feel myself getting hot and shaky, as if I'm about to attack her. But I mustn't allow myself to lose it. And screaming at her would achieve nothing. When I meet them at the other end of this appalling journey I must just take Finn calmly and turn around and get away from this woman forever.

The fleeting thought of holding Finn again triggers a physical reaction, a knot of pain and longing in my gut, and an ache in my arms and shoulders. It makes me think of when he was a newborn and I'd hear his cry and my breasts would leak milk—the maternal body overruling the rational brain.

The ferry heaves onward. I glance at my watch. It's been twenty minutes already. I turn to the man on the bench behind me. "Excuse me? Hello?"

He looks up. His face is almost totally obscured by a beard, a woolen hat tugged down over eyes that are small, lined and very weary.

"How long does this ferry take to get to Raven Bay?"

He grunts something that sounds like "half an hour."

"Half an hour?" I say, leaning closer.

He lifts his chin, briefly, out of his zipped up jacket. "'Bout an hour."

"An hour?" I sit back on the roiling seat. An hour! But Maggie said—but then I realize that nobody has said anything about how far it is to Raven Bay. I never asked.

She took Finn on an hour-long ferry ride? In these conditions? On this sea? This is not outrageous. It's insane. What the hell was she thinking?

But perhaps they have different standards for weather up here. For them, this is just a normal winter's day. A bit choppy. Maybe they have a different sense of distance, too. I remember my mother telling me once about a rail journey she took across Canada as a child. She said that as she climbed into her bunk at night the train was just beginning to go around Lake Winnebago. When she woke up the next morning, the train had been chugging all night. It was still going around Lake Winnebago.

I don't remember why she was crossing Canada on a train, or how old she was, or who she was with. I don't even remember why she told me this story—perhaps to keep me quiet on a long car ride. I'll never know now. But the point is that everything in this place has been scaled up—the landscape, the weather, the distances, the wildlife. An hour on a ferry, for these people, might seem like nothing. Towering waves. Lashing rain. Normal.

I fix my eyes on my feet. Despite this rationale, I feel the cold nausea edge toward my throat and I know it is more than seasickness and pregnancy. It is fear.

The ferry would hold about forty people at most, but there are almost no passengers on board. All are men. I want to scream, "Help me! She took my baby!" I look at their blank, tired faces, one after another, and one after another they glance up at me, then look away, as if embarrassed for me.

I stare through the stained window. The sea is angry and swollen, and every few seconds another gray wave hurls itself brutally against the glass. I wonder how Finn would have dealt with this trip. Did he throw up? He would definitely have been scared, and missing me. He will want his bunny too. I dig in my bag and pull it out. It looks forlorn, as if it, too, knows that this is bad. I dig my face into its soft brown fur. He wouldn't understand where she was taking him or where I'd gone or why she couldn't give him his bunny. He would feel abandoned and alone. He will be wanting me badly, and he will think that I've abandoned him.

My mouth fills with saliva and I blink back tears, looking for a bathroom sign.

I try to remind myself that on the ferry from Vancouver he was delighted, running around, bashing things; it was me who felt seasick. Maybe he'll think this is all an adventure too, maybe he'll be distracted and won't miss me. But I know this is not true. He will be confused and frightened. I get up and begin to stagger up the aisle toward the toilets. I have to stop thinking about Finn's distress. It is not going to help get him back. I have to stay calm and if I am going to stay calm I have to not think like this. I just have to focus on the fact that I am about to get him back, and this is about to be over.

The ferry bucks as it moves further out, into deeper, wilder waters. When I peer through the window again the lights of Spring Tide Island are long gone.

I've vomited three times into the reeking toilet before we get there. Every cell in my body feels as if it is turning itself inside out. It's nearly four as the ferry slows and it is starting to get dark. But I made it. I am here and in a moment, I will be holding my baby and I will never, ever let him go again. Never.

My entire body aches for him now. I can't wait to get off this boat and sprint as fast as I can to wherever they are standing and to pull him out of her arms and hold him as tight as I've ever held him.

Presumably she will be waiting in the ferry terminal to get onto this boat. I squint through the windows to catch a glimpse of Finn's red snowsuit, but they're too freckled and cracked and the rain is too heavy to see anything except the faintest blur of lights as we ease into Raven Bay.

Will she have him wrapped up warm? Did she remember to change his diaper? Did she let him have a nap? Has he eaten anything today? As I stagger down the gangplank through the drizzle, clutching his bunny, my legs wobble, my head pounds, and I can taste vomit through my nose. My throat hurts from the dry retching at the end. But of course there is no ferry terminal on this tiny crumb of land. I squint through the rain. There is a slippery looking walkway ahead, and a small hut, and then behind that, a single-lane road and a row of tall, wood-slat houses.

There is no sign of Susannah or Finn.

The men push past me, muffled by their waterproof gear. They trudge away in a line, like the faceless figures in a dream. It is brutally cold up here. I shove the bunny into my pocket and pull up the hood of the parka, yanking the toggles so that it clings to the edge of my face; the chill stings my hands and I shove them into my pockets too. Waves bash against the pier that shelters the dock, throwing wild plumes into the air. All I can smell is salt and fish and something like diesel oil. I search the waterside for a flash of red snowsuit, but even with the rain I can see that they are not here. The ferry must be early. Of course. She'll be coming any moment. She'll be coming round the corner and I'll see them. I just have to wait.

A couple of ferrymen in huge coats are hanging around by the hut. Could I have somehow missed her getting on the boat? I turn and scan it, but, no, nobody could have gotten on yet. The doors are shut, there is a barrier at the bottom of the gangplank and the crew is unloading crates from the hull. And anyway, she would have had to walk right past me to get on.

On the other side of the ferry, fishing vessels bump against the wooden dock, their masts clattering a percussion to the howl of the wind. I'm shivering. I can just make out dense pines sloping up behind the boats and houses toward what may be a snow-capped mountain, but it's hard to tell with the rain and the glowering sky. It seems impossible that she would bring Finn to a place like this.

Waves crash and thump against the sea wall. A ferryman hollers and then I hear the boat engine churn and shudder. I spin around.

The ferry is moving. It is pulling back out into the waves, churning a mess of gristle-gray water in its wake.

"Stop!" I run toward it, my boots slipping on the stones. "Wait! Stop!"

A yellow-jacketed ferryman barks something at me. I skid to a halt.

"Is it leaving?" But I can see that it is. I run over to the man. He is looping rope around a metal hook. "Is that ferry going back to Spring Tide? Is that the last ferry of the day? To Spring Tide?"

He nods and grunts something from beneath a rain hat and continues to loop the rope. I can't see his face—his collar is turned up, peaked hat pulled down. "That's the last ferry?" I shout, again. He leaves the rope and walks up the stones to the shed, which he locks. His work boots are giant and rimmed with salt.

"Shit!" I watch the ferry disappear into layers of rain. "Oh shit. Oh no. Oh no."

Everyone has gone except the ferryman, who is heading off across the road now. Susannah and Finn are not on that boat. I couldn't have missed them. So where are they?

An appalling thought plants itself in the center of my brain: what if Maggie got this whole thing wrong? I think of her vague, bovine face, with its slightly vacant blue gaze. I could have come all the way out here and Susannah is actually at home with Finn, thinking I've just gone and left him. And now I'm stranded. I remember Susannah saying that Maggie was unreliable—something about anti-anxiety medication.

But Maggie seemed completely certain that Susannah brought him here. She didn't seem anxious or confused about that. I look around at the deserted port. Perhaps Susannah missed the ferry. She's about to appear. It could have left early. I remember the ferries at Tsawwassen. She is about to come.

I know that I am clutching at explanations, like someone plummeting from the top branch of a tall tree, grabbing at anything that might save me. I will count to fifty. Just fifty. Then I'll do something.

This is starting to feel genuinely out of control.

I shiver in the rain, counting in my head, but I am freezing and water is beginning to soak through the parka.

At fifteen I realize I have to go to the guesthouse and find Ana. I can't just stand here, counting. I'll ask to use Ana's phone. I make for the road—and I can see the sign—The Raven Guest House. I can see a peeling house front with a black door between other weather-beaten buildings. It seems miraculous that it is there.

I start move faster—jogging across the road and past a tiny closed-up store, *General Joe's*, and then *Cat's Bar*—a corrugated iron building with a boarded-up window, ripped tarpaulin across the roof, and a barrel outside for cigarette butts. A matted ginger cat slinks behind some garbage cans, hissing and curling its wet spine.

I knock on the guesthouse door. After a few moments, a grim-looking woman opens it. She has deep eye sockets, sunken cheeks, and thin hair pulled back tightly on her skull. She is wearing a shapeless pullover, baggy jeans, and Eskimo slippers.

"Are you Ana?"

She nods.

"Please—could I possibly use your phone?" I try to catch my breath, to sound calm. "Maggie told me to find you. I'm trying to find my child. But my phone doesn't work here."

She squints down at me. "Maggie?"

"Maggie at the Rock Salt Bakery, on Spring Tide Island. I'm sorry," I say. "I'm trying to find my son—he's just a baby. He's not even two." My voice wavers. I make myself take a breath. I can't cry. "I just need to use your phone if I possibly could." I half expect her to slam the door but she stands aside, without a word, and holds it open. I step inside. The house smells of wood polish and coffee. The hall is narrow and dark, with a grandfather clock and a steep stairway, with a striped runner.

There is an old fashioned green pushbutton phone on the hall table.

"I'm sorry, but I need a number," I pull my hood down, "of the Rock Salt Bakery on Spring Tide Island—Maggie's number? Do you have it? Or can I call Directory Assistance?"

She looks at me for a beat too long, then opens her address book, and passes it to me. There, in neat handwriting, is Maggie's name. It's the first sign Ana has given that she knows what I am talking about.

"Thank you," I say. "I'm really sorry to barge in. Thank you so much. I'll pay you for the call of course." She is looking at me, intently, as if trying to work out where she knows me from—then she nods.

I turn and dial Maggie's number and an answering machine clicks in.

"Maggie." I force myself to sound calm. "Susannah isn't here—she wasn't waiting for the ferry at Raven Bay and now it's left. Please can you go and meet it, when it gets in, just in case I somehow missed them? It left here five minutes ago and it's, um, twenty past four now. And could you leave a message here at the Raven Guest House? I'm going to go and find Susannah's place now just in case they're still here. But I'm a bit worried that I'm stuck here, or I've missed them and I'm . . . Just call me as soon as you can, please."

I hang up and glance over at Ana who is looking closely at my face. She looks away.

There will be a rational explanation for this. There always is. I hear Alice's voice in my head, telling me to think logically. I must not get dramatic. Then I imagine Doug shouting, "What the *fuck* are you doing, Kal?"

"Thank you," I say to Ana. "The person I was staying with on Spring Tide Island has brought my son up here for the day. But she was supposed to bring him back and I think that was the last ferry and she wasn't on it. Was that the last ferry to Spring Tide today? The one that just left?"

Ana nods. "Next one's tomorrow 'bout noon."

"Right. Oh no. Shit. Okay. So." I press my temples with the heels of both hands. "I need to get to her cabin then because maybe something has happened to them." For a moment, awful images crowd my mind—of Susannah slipping on steps above the sea with Finn in her arms; of her collapsing in a cabin, from whatever illness she has, and Finn toddling out the front door, wailing, looking for me in the rain, with the waves crashing and sucking beneath him. No. I have to stop. It's too easy to make up terrifying scenarios. What would Alice say? Stick to the facts.

Finn is up here somewhere. I am about to see him. They just missed the ferry, it left early. That's all.

"So," I swallow and turn to Ana again, "could you just tell me how to get to Susannah Gillespie's cabin? Maggie says you know it."

"Susannah?" Ana's bright brown eyes fix suddenly on mine.

"Yes. Susannah Gillespie. From Spring Tide Island; she runs the gallery there. Do you know her?"

"You want the float house."

"The float house?" Of course. So I was right. She did take it over when my mother left. "Yes. Yes. The float house. Where is it? Can you give me directions—I'm going to go there right now."

"There's no one will take you up there tonight." Ana's voice is quiet, but firm. Something has changed in her demeanor. It's as if she is now taking me seriously, rather than waiting for me to get out of her house.

"No. I mean, it's okay. No one has to take me there. I just need to know where it is—can I walk? If my son is there, he'll need me—and it's possible that something has happened to them. An accident."

"The float house is out on Black Bear Island."

"Where?"

"Another boat ride from here."

I stare at her. She has broken red veins on her cheeks. "Another boat ride?"

"No one's going to take you up there tonight—almost dark and storm's coming in."

"Wait! No. Please. I think maybe this is a mistake. Susannah—Susannah Gillespie—she has a cabin right here, on Raven Island. Maybe she has both? A cabin here, and the float house up there on what was it—Black Bear Island?"

"No." Ana shakes her head. Her eyes are bright. "She just has the float house."

"Are you sure?"

She gives a curt nod. And I believe her.

"Well then I have to get to the float house, to Black Bear Island. Right now."

"My nephew will take you out in his boat," she says. "But not tonight."

"I'll pay him. Whatever it takes. I've got cash. Please. Give me your nephew's number—please—just let me speak to him."

"Won't take you tonight. No one will."

"But someone has to," I hear my own high-pitched voice. "Look, I don't think you understand—Susannah may have my child up there. Something could have happened to them. I have to get there, right now. If no one will take me I'm going to call the police."

She thinks for a second. "But they could be back on Spring Tide, though, huh?"

"No. I don't know. Maybe. But I don't think so. I have to check the cabin, the float house. I have to check it."

She looks at me, steadily, for a long while, and I can see that she's running through various possibilities. Her pink scalp is visible through her hair. It's hard to tell how old she is. She is very upright and there is an energy to her that is younger than her weathered face and thin hair as she picks up the phone and dials rapidly. She turns her back on me. I can't hear what she's saying, she's mumbling, and her lilting accent doesn't help.

"Please," I say over her shoulder. "Could I just talk to your nephew?"

She hangs up. Her eyes are alert and serious. "Sven's on his way."

"Who's Sven? Your nephew?"

She nods, then walks away down the corridor and into a kitchen. I can see a big black old-fashioned range. I hear her open and close a cupboard.

"Ana?" I call. "Sorry, but can I use your phone again? It's an international call. I'll give you the money."

I dial Doug's cell. It rings, but there is no answer. I leave him a message, in a very calm voice, explaining where I am and giving him the number on the guesthouse phone. I try home, and his work number—and leave messages on both. Then I ring Alice.

"Where on earth are you now?" she laughs.

"Alice. Shit. Shit! You're there." Talking way too fast, I try to explain what's happened. "I'm getting really scared. I think I should call the police. I'm going to call the police."

"Okay. Slow down," she says. "Slow down. Tell me again. This Susannah woman—Mum's old friend—left you a note saying she was taking Finn on a day trip to give you a break?"

"Well no, or I don't know, I don't know if she left a note or not—Maggie said she would have done but there wasn't one, or maybe there was, but I didn't see it—"

"Who's Maggie again?"

"The baker. A friend of Susannah's."

"Wait, just let me make sure I'm clear because I don't think it's time to panic, yet, okay? You fell asleep this morning, and while you were sleeping this Susannah was looking after Finn for you. And then she decided to take him on a day trip to her vacation house to let you rest?"

"Yes. Well. Sort of." I hesitate. "But it's not a vacation house, Alice. It's a cabin—sort of—a floating place that used to belong to . . . that used to . . . look it doesn't matter. I'll explain all that later. But she's got him and now I don't know where they are."

"Does this cabin have a phone?"

For a moment, I feel ridiculous. "Wait . . . I'll ask." I cover the phone. "Ana?" I call out. My voice sounds high. "Does Susannah have a phone at the float house?"

She comes to the door, with a tea towel in her hand. "No."

"No. You should see it up here. It's unbelievably remote. There's nothing here at all. No cell coverage. Nothing. There's lashing rain, and the sea is violent—and it's so bloody cold. It's not like going to the Isle of Wight, Alice. This is far away."

"Okay," she says. "So when you couldn't find a note you panicked, and came after them on the ferry—but you somehow missed them. And now you're stuck on this island and they're either back on the first island, Spring whatsit, or they're at her vacation cabin?"

"But I just found out it's on another island entirely. The float house—cabin—it's another boat ride away. I'm waiting for someone to come take me there."

"Christ, there are a lot of islands up there."

"It's a bloody archipelago, Alice."

"But they're probably on their way home aren't they?"

"They can't be. That's the point. I just watched the ferry to Spring Tide—the last ferry of the day—pull out and they definitely weren't on it."

"It's going to be okay, Kal. Try to stay calm okay? This is just a mix up. I get why you're freaking out, I really do, but losing it isn't going to help. Just slow down and think clearly. Are you 100% sure you couldn't have missed them at the port?"

"Yes, there's nothing here—a small shed. Nothing. And it's a tiny ferry with about three passengers. It seems to be mainly for unloading and loading supplies. If she was getting on that ferry with Finn I'd have seen her."

"Right. Then what if she didn't come to the vacation house after all? She's back at her house, on the first island, Spring Tide. Did you call her there?"

"No," I say. "God. I didn't—I'm an idiot, I can't believe I didn't think to do that first. I don't think I have her number but . . ."

"Fine. There you go! Get her number from the guesthouse—they'll have a local phone book won't they? Try her at home. Honestly, I bet she's there. But if she's not, then go to the cabin because you're up there, and you might as well. But I'm betting they never came out there in the first place and they're at home, and the worst thing that's going to happen is you're going to look like a twit, and you'll have to stay in a guesthouse for the night and apologize profusely to this poor Susannah woman."

"But I can't leave Finn alone with Susannah for a night!"

"I know. I know. But it won't kill him, or you. He'll miss you for one night, Kal. It's not ideal, but he'll be fine. He'll survive. You'll survive. She's, what, a sixty-year-old woman? Does she have children?"

"Yes, one, a grown up son, but . . ."

"So, she's a mother herself. She'll know how to look after him. Just be thankful you're at a guesthouse—you have a bed for the night. This could be so much worse."

"How?" I wail. "How the fuck could it be worse?"

"Listen, I know your mommy instinct says it will kill Finn, or you, or both of you, to have a night apart but it won't. Okay? This is going to be all right."

"But . . ." There is no way to explain to her that any amount of rationale won't really calm me down because I don't know where my baby is.

"I'm sure there's a perfectly benign explanation. It's bloody hard to get Finn anywhere on time isn't it? I know I'd never catch a ferry if I had him. She's probably forgotten what it's like to get a toddler out of the house, and that's why she missed the return ferry."

"Well, they are pretty unreliable up here . . ." Alice is right. I have to think of rational explanations, normal ones, not plunge into terrifying scenarios. "They don't seem to follow a schedule. Getting out to Spring Tide in the first place, from Vancouver, was ridiculous—they were all over the place." I feel my shoulders relax, just slightly.

"There you go. She could have been calling you to say she missed the boat and was staying in the vacation house but you weren't there to answer the phone. She'll be worrying about *you* now."

"I'm going to kill her, Alice, when I find her. You can't just take someone's child like this."

"I know. It's out of order, it really is. And if that's what she's really done then I agree. But you know what? There might be a generational thing going on here too. I believe they weren't as clingy in her day as mothers are now."

"Are you saying I'm being clingy? Jesus, Alice, she has Finn!"

"No. No. I'm not. All I'm saying is, she probably thought she was helping by giving you a break, that's all. She probably still does."

I can't explain that Susannah is a mother, but not the reassuring sort. All these explanations don't stop my heart feeling as if it's going to explode. They don't stop me wanting to call the police and get a helicopter and fly wherever Finn is right now. They don't stop me wanting to kill Susannah with my bare hands—strangle the life out of her—when I find her.

"I know it's horrible that you aren't with Finn," Alice is saying. "You'll find him any moment now. If you don't—if you don't get an answer from her home and he's not at the cabin, or anywhere else, that's when you call the police . . . okay? But you won't have to. I'm sure."

"Okay." I take a breath. "I have to go now. You're right. I have to call her at home. But if she's not there then I've got to get to Black Bear Island."

"I'll call Doug for you now, and try to reassure him. Nothing bad is going to happen. Try not to let gut level maternal panic cloud things."

"That's a very lawyerish thing to say," I try to make it jokey, but can't.

"I'm his aunt," she says. "I love him too. I've just got more of an overview than you have right now. This isn't a catastrophe it's a misunderstanding. Call me as soon as you get back to the guesthouse. Wait—I'm writing it down—Raven Guest house? Raven Bay? Raven Island? Wait—I'm going to google map you right now." There is a pause.

"Alice, I have to go."

"Holy crap, Kal. You really are in the middle of nowhere."

"I know. And I'm about to fall off the map completely."

"Call me," she says, suddenly serious, "the minute you find him."

I hang up. Ana is in the kitchen. I flick through her phone book and there it is—Susannah's home number. I dial.

The empty ring goes on and on. I picture the phone on the wall of her kitchen by the fridge, sounding out through the echoing house.

Eventually I hang up. I tuck a $20 bill under the phone. Ana comes out of the kitchen and hands me a tumbler of whisky. I drink it down in one slug and it burns the back of my throat, but it feels warming. Then I remember that I'm pregnant, and shouldn't be drinking whisky.

"Sven," she looks me in the eye, "will get you there?" There is something about that look that chills me. This woman knows that I should be worrying. She knows.

A moment later, an enormous man gusts through the front door.

*

Sven turns out to be as taciturn as his aunt, though he is twice Ana's size—a bearded fisherman with blue Swedish eyes, maybe not much older than me though it's hard to tell because of all the facial hair. He leads me back out in the rain and down to a fishing boat that has steel cables, and rope and fishing equipment looped all over the deck, and tall metal poles and more cables towering over a windowed cabin. There are three red buoys attached to ropes on the side of the boat, and a life ring hooked outside the cabin.

The deck smells strongly of fish. Sven gestures me into the cabin. It is warm, with benches, and stairs leading below deck, and a big ship's wheel, and a dashboard of complex switches.

"Do you know Susannah?" I ask. "Susannah Gillespie?"

He turns and looks at me. Then he nods, just once.

"Thank you for taking me in this weather. I know it's late."

He turns on the engine. A radio crackles to life.

"How long will it take?"

"Forty minutes in this sea," he grunts.

"What?" I say. "Did you say *forty*? Forty minutes? The float house is *forty* minutes from here?"

He nods, grimly.

"Jesus Christ. Are you sure? Forty? Four-oh?"

He turns and glances at me.

"Oh my God." I say. "Fucking Hell."

I hunch into the parka, fighting hysteria. This lunatic has brought Finn on an hour's ferry ride then a forty-minute boat ride to nowhere. But she can't have. This must be a monumental mistake. If I'd known this at Spring Tide, I would have called the police then and there. This is wrong. On every level. If she has him on an island another forty minutes from here then something is deeply off-kilter. And if she doesn't have him, then what the hell am I doing heading out onto dangerous seas with a stranger?

Sven bumps the fishing boat out of the port. Alice is right: I have to stay rational. If I lose it, I will only make this situation worse. Right now Susannah may be the one calling the police, thinking I've been swept off her rocks by a killer whale. Right now, Finn could be tucked up safe in bed while she tries to find me.

Through the dirty window I can see the shore receding until Raven Bay is just a blurry shadow behind a curtain of rain.

Sven's thigh, encased in a yellow waterproof suit, is thick and broad and I know that if I touched it, it would feel like oak. As we push through towering waves toward a storm Sven's thigh seems like the only solid thing in the world—the only certainty. I remind myself that he knows these seas. He wouldn't do this if he thought we couldn't make it. I want to crawl over and hang onto Sven's leg, cling to it with my eyes squeezed shut.

The boat rolls up and over, up and over; it teeters at the top of each wave then plunges downward like a rollercoaster. I dig my chin into the scratchy wool of Doug's sweater and it grows damp with my breath. I stare at Sven's broad back. He knows what he's doing. He will have fished these seas his whole life. Voices crackle and bark on the radio. Occasionally he clicks and mutters things into it, but I can't make out any words. It is like a foreign language.

I close my eyes, willing this to be over.

When I open them again, we are passing a blip of land, lit up through sheets of rain by the boat's strong headlight.

"Is that it?" I lean forward, squinting through the streaked window. A cluster of snow-dusted pines ringed by rocks—only fifty or so yards away. Close up I can see that while some of the trees are tall and healthy, other are frail brown skeletons.

Maybe I misheard. Maybe he said fourteen, not forty. "Sven? Is this Black Bear Island?"

"Nope."

Above the chug of the engine I can hear the waves crashing against the stern. We lurch and plunge onward. How the hell did Susannah get Finn across this water? Does she own a boat? It was earlier in the day, less stormy, but I can't even think about my tiny boy in a boat on this wild sea. With her at the wheel. Did she even have a life jacket for him?

Don't think about that. Don't. Just do what Alice said. Stick to the facts. But even the facts are unbearable. Whichever way I look at this I've messed up catastrophically, I have let my child down. He needs me and I am not with him.

The waistband of my pants digs in. I slide a finger up inside the parka and undo the top button. Nausea is building. I don't want to throw up in front of Sven but I feel my salivary glands tighten. It can't be good for an unborn baby, all this anxiety. I have to breathe. I have to believe that I am going to find Finn at Black Bear Island and take him—and the baby inside me—home to England. One day, this will be a story I tell my children—the time their mother lost her mind in Canada.

The nausea is overwhelming. But there is nothing in my stomach to throw up—except for a whisky I am empty. I remember my mother telling me that the cure for carsickness is to find an object far on the horizon and focus on that. Perhaps seasickness works the same way. Maybe this is how she knew that trick. She always knew these things. But it is pitch dark out there—a darkness so deep and disorientating that I can't bear to look out at it.

To take my mind off the fear, I try to think of all the other things my mother used to do to make me feel better. I dive into the deepest part of my subconscious for memories—any memories—and I find them there, glimmering at me like white shells on the seabed.

When I was cold on the beach she'd stop and press her lips between my shoulder blades and blow for as long as she had breath and the heat from her lungs would radiate through my body, warming every organ, right down to my toes.

She used mud, rather than dock leaves, to stop stinging nettle pain. She made ginger root tea for sickness, and rubbed onions on our palms and feet for sunstroke. She kept an aloe vera plant in the hall and would snap off a leaf to ooze cool gel over heat rash or insect bites, or bruises or burns. She must have learned all these things up here where there are no drugstores—just this limitless natural pharmacy.

What would she say if she could see me now? How would she stop this from hurting? She would tell me to stop wasting energy with guilt. She'd tell me to stop imagining the worst. She'd say stick with the evidence, the facts, nothing more. She'd tell me to be strong. She'd tell me, in fact, that I *am* strong. Suddenly it's as if she's on the boat, between me and Sven, I can feel her, right here, and then I hear her voice—she whispers "Don't let fear get in the way."

Then she's gone, and it's just the thud of waves on the hull, and the howl of the wind outside, and the engine of the fishing boat straining beneath it all. I squeeze my eyes tight and try to summon up my mother again. But all I hear is the crackling voices on Sven's radio.

There is nothing to focus on to stop the nausea, because there is no horizon. There is nothing out there but rain and this gale and waves that are so vast it seems that the sea is rising from beneath us, as if Moby Dick himself is pushing toward the surface and in a moment we will be teetering on his spout, or swallowed up whole.

I could ask Sven to radio for the police. But what would I say to them? I imagine myself on that crackling radio trying to explain what has happened. Or worse, calling police helicopters out in perilous gales, only to find that Susannah is back on Spring Tide Island.

And even if she has Finn here, on Black Bear Island, she would only say that I asked her to bring him. Her word against mine—the solid local businesswoman against the incompetent foreign mother.

I'm so close now. I just have to get to the float house. My poor little boy. If she does have him up here, he will be so scared.

I have to distract myself. These thoughts are poison. I stare at Sven's broad back. I remind myself that my mother was once out here on her boat, scanning the waves for orca, with a camera round her neck. She was here, so it cannot be the edge of nowhere—this is my mother's place. This sea was her territory. This was her home and so I am connected to this place too, no matter how inhospitable it feels. Or how unlikely. This place is in my blood. It is part of me too.

It seems inconceivable that she lived out here, but then walked away one day—and spent the rest of her life in Sussex raising children, painting, gardening, walking the dog. She divided existence into "before" and "after" with a thick red line that nobody was allowed to cross.

Then I realize that tonight could be my own red line: my own before and after point. If something has happened to Finn then this journey is going to cut through my life, leaving an open wound, forever. I squeeze my eyes shut. Then, for the first time since I was about ten, I find myself praying—even though I don't know what God I'm praying to.

Please keep him safe. Make him safe. Don't let this happen to my baby. Please don't let this happen.

Sven's boat is slowing. I open my eyes. We seem to be rounding a headland—I catch a glimpse of rock momentarily lit up by the boat's headlight—the water feels slightly less reckless, just slightly.

"Are we here?"

"Yep."

"Where's the float house?"

His hand rises off the wheel. I stand up, swaying and bumping with the boat, and peer through the windshield. We're close to the coast again now; black rocks loom through lines of rain, illuminated by the boat's headlight. Sven is pointing to our right. The boat bounces up and over, up and over the waves, but they feel less threatening now that we're in a more sheltered bay. I grip the rail and try to ride the motion by bending my knees as I squint through the streaked cabin windshield. But all I can see are towering ranks of pines that lead down to rocks, where waves smash, one after another, throwing up extravagant plumes of surf.

"I can't see a float house."

He points again, right in front of us.

"Where? Over here?"

The big hand goes back to the wheel. He flips some switches, picks up the crackling radio, and mutters something into it.

Then I realize I'm looking right at the float house. It is nestled behind a protective shelf of rocks, straight ahead. I see its slanted roof. It is a symmetrical two-story wooden house, with a long window on the top, and two smaller windows below. There's even a chimney. We're so close, I can't believe I only just noticed it. It's made of dark wood so it blends into the trees, and it is long and low, protected from the bay by the rocks. But there is a light on. A light: someone is there. I can see a shape at the main window. I lean forward, pressing as close as I can to the streaked windshield.

She's here. She really is here. I was right to come. And I made it—I made it.

We draw closer to the rocks and Sven turns the boat sideways. It rocks and tilts and for a moment I think it isn't going to right itself and we're going to capsize—but it slaps back down.

I grab my bag and hook it across my body. I see, now, that the rocks aren't black; they're speckled and slick—light grayish on top, with a skirt of seaweed around barnacle-pocked sides. I step out into the rain, tugging at my hood. The pine forest smells sharp and alive, and it is as if the trees are breathing their primitive strength into my cells; another wave thuds onto the rock and splatters foam across the boat.

Sven slows the engine to a rumble. It sways and tilts and I cling to the railing, wind thumping at the sides of my head, looking down at the swirling sea between me and the rocks.

Sven seems to be waiting—is he expecting me to jump? I lean back into the cabin. "How do I get to the house?"

"Can't get any closer than this," he flips some switches.

"What? Do I jump?"

"Or swim," he isn't smiling but I glimpse a very bright blue eye between cap and beard. Then he turns his broad yellow back on me again.

I hesitate. "So you'll wait here—you'll take us back, right?"

He shakes his head. "Uh-uh. Can't do that."

"What?"

"Storm's coming and I ain't waiting for 'er."

"But, Sven, please! It won't take long to get my son—and I can't stay here! I have to bring him back with you, to Raven Bay."

"Uh-uh," he shakes his head again. "Can't wait."

"But—please!" I lean both hands on the door frame. "Please. I need to get back to your aunt's house tonight. I can't stay here! What if they aren't here?"

"Either come back with me or stay here. Your choice. But I'm turning her around right now."

A voice grates on the radio but I can't hear words—it sounds like coordinates. He growls something into the radio and revs the engine.

"Sven—please!"

He turns his head. "Get off now or not at all. I won't smash up my boat for you nor anyone else. I'm getting her away from these rocks in the next five seconds."

I peer back at the float house—and then I see her. Just an outline at the window, blurred, but it's unmistakably her: I know that upright posture, the broad shoulders and—yes—it's Finn—she's holding him on her hip, a solid little bundle. He's here. He's safe.

"I see him!" I start to climb out onto the deck again.

He steps across the cabin and grabs my arm, "Go fast or the sea'll have you. Wait for the wave then jump," he pulls me around to make me look at him. "Jump big."

I teeter on deck. The bitter wind buffets me, and rain thunders onto my hood. The sea is so loud—it seethes around the boat, vast and hungry and angry, and wind howls through the treetops behind the house—but all I can think about is getting to Finn. I wait for a wave to hit and then I hurl myself off Sven's deck. For a second I am suspended in the air, then I thud onto rock—the grainy surface bites into my knees and hands as I scramble away from the next wave that is coming; I move as if there is a wolf snapping at my heels. And it hits. It throws up a sheet of freezing water that whacks down just behind me, drenching my back and legs and feet. I gasp—it is bitterly cold. Water runs down my neck as I scrabble, frantically, up the rock toward the float house.

Behind me I hear the boat engine churning as Sven turns it around—getting away from the rock before the next wave smashes it to pieces. But I don't care about the cold or the storm. Finn is in there and I'm about to get him back.

The rock is covered in a sheet of ice. My feet slip as I clamber away from the sea; my fingers are numb and even the parka couldn't keep out the water but I don't feel cold; I can see the window of the float house. I can see it.

She isn't there anymore but in a moment I'll be on solid ground— one more jump. I don't even care that Sven is going and I'm going to have to spend a night with Susannah on this rock in the middle of the ocean. I am about to have Finn back.

I make it to the top. Wind batters my ears and rain slashes at me. Another gust almost knocks me down—and the next wave slaps on the rock below—for a second I imagine slithering back down the ice into the black sea. The roar of the water and wind swallows the sound of the boat engine, but I can see its yellow lights through the rain.

The rock is a kind of protective platform, lit up by the dim float house lights. I can see that it leads all the way to the shore, just to the left of the house. I slide down it, scraping my hands, and then I leap onto the land. My feet crunch on stones and ice. The smell of the forest is overpowering—I am close enough that I could reach over and touch the sides of the house. The wood is shabby—a patchwork of lighter planks and bits that have obviously been tacked on. It is protected from the sea by the rocks and from the wind by the pines, but the floats on which it rests creak and rattle and bump with the rise and fall of the water beneath it. All around, rain tumbles into undergrowth and through the branches of the trees.

"Susannah!" I shout. "Susannah!"

To get in, you have to make a little leap from crumbling land onto a rim that runs all around the house. I shove the door—the wood feels as if it could disintegrate into splinters at any moment, the paint is peeling but I shove at it, turning the handle.

"Finn?" I howl. "Finn?"

And I leap into my mother's dark house.

British Columbia, Late Summer 1977

It needed some work, but it was perfect—a traditional A-frame, one and a half stories high, built on a platform of cedar logs that had been lashed together with steel cable, and held in place with railroad spikes. Her measurements worked; it fit in behind the rocks as if it had been built for the space. After the guys who towed it up from Nanaimo had gone, she went back to the boat with the baby nestled against her in the papoose. The Native Canadian woman on the market stall said you could "wear" babies in it 'til they walked, sliding them around onto your back as they got bigger.

She pushed open the door, and stepped into her kitchen, one arm protectively curled across the papoose. The float house had belonged to an elderly fisherman and it stank of herring, rollups, mildew and wood smoke. Her eyes adjusted to the light. It would need a massive scrubbing with bleach. She'd ordered parts for the Coleman stove from the hardware place down in Raven Bay and had brought up an icebox with her from Victoria. But she'd need to go back to Raven Bay for planks of wood, screws, and brackets—there were no shelves anywhere in the house.

She squatted, carefully, and opened a kitchen cupboard. The doors felt loose on their hinges, but they could be reinforced—she might need hardware for that too; she should make a list. They could do with a coat of paint too. But other than that, it was going to be just fine: a narrow, practical little galley kitchen, with windows above the sink, and room enough for a little table and a couple of chairs.

As she walked into the living room she readjusted the sling so that it spread out around her back more, and didn't tug so much on her shoulders. They'd agreed that she'd stay here with the baby to sort out the float house, while the guys went down to Vancouver and Seattle for the funding meetings—you couldn't sit in meetings with a baby— not if you wanted to be taken seriously. But she didn't mind being left here. In fact, she wanted to be here alone for a bit. It felt right.

The living room was a good space, larger than she remembered, with enormous windows that, when clean, would give a wonderful view of the bay. Ana's sofa was coming up by tugboat the next day along with the double bed. She'd been planning to stay in the bell tent, but now the house was here, she realized she wanted to move in right away, even before cleaning it. The smell really wasn't too bad now the door was open. She might just bring the camp bed and the Moses basket in from the tent tonight.

She looked through the murky window, at the sea. The house shifted with the sway of the water beneath it. She hadn't thought about this— but she liked the gentle motion. She tried to picture fifteen, twenty foot waves powering across the bay toward the little house. But there were the rocks. And she wasn't afraid of the sea, despite Ana's warnings. She felt at home on it.

This last year had changed the way she looked at a lot of things. She used to believe that willpower and determination were all that mattered in life. You had to find your goal then focus on it and make it happen. Maybe it had begun as a survival strategy in a childhood of lonely Saturdays spent poking around on the beach for sea stars and clams while other girls' mothers took them to ballet class. She had made a decision, aged about nine or ten, that she would be a marine biologist and she had emerged from that childhood with a scholarship and a purpose. She still believed that determination mattered, but now she wondered whether it wasn't that clear cut after all. Maybe life was more mysterious than that.

Only eighteen months ago, she was wholly focused on her PhD, studying dolphins at Sea Park. And now she was standing with her beautiful baby in her own floating home looking out onto an ocean

full of killer whales. She could not possibly have articulated this sce-
nario to herself, even a few months ago. But it felt completely right—as
if this had been her goal her whole life and she just hadn't known it.

She knew there'd be storms and hardships ahead—no doubt
many days when this whole endeavor seemed foolhardy, but this was
undoubtedly the right place and the right life. With that baseline so
firmly in place nothing could really go wrong.

It didn't really matter what other people thought. The community
on the dock had plainly believed that it was mad to bring a baby up
here. Ted and Sandra had sat her down one night to ask if she really
knew what she was taking on. She did her best to reassure them—as
if they were the parents she'd never had. But she'd been right, because
summer had worked out just fine.

They'd rigged up a weather shelter on the Zodiac, and constructed
a secure little baby nest of fleeces and life preservers; she even made a
cell of out clamshells and fishing wire. And then they just got to work.
Admittedly, there were more beach stops, and their day packs now
included a diaper bag—and people couldn't believe it when they saw
an infant on board. But nothing had gone wrong.

In fact, she'd become very good at sitting in a boat surrounded by
killer whales, simultaneously breastfeeding, listening to the hydro-
phone, looking through binoculars, and making observational
notes—while Jonas, Dean—and anyone else who had come out that
day—took photos of the whales, and scanned the catalog. There had
been some bad weather days when she'd been forced to stay at base
camp while the others put on all-weather suits and went out; those
days drove her insane, but most of the time she was out there gather-
ing data. She had made enormous progress in just three months. And
they had a perfectly happy, healthy baby.

She turned her back on the windows, and looked around the liv-
ing room again. It was a little gloomy because of the dirty windows,
and the dark, wood-paneled walls, but it would be a lot better with
furniture and a scrubbing. She'd cover Ana's sofa with a bright throw
rug and put it right there, along the wall, next to the wood stove that
the guys were bringing back from Vancouver. She'd scrub the scum off

the windows, fix up this floor, and lay down rugs; she'd put up shelves, hang some photos, and it would be perfect. She'd need to make a start on the logs though—she wanted to master the chainsaw before the guys got back. She didn't want anyone to have to show her how to use it. She'd had enough of being shown how to do things.

The day they put up the bell tent, Eve had appeared through the trees with her wolfhound. "Learn to use a chainsaw," she'd said, without even a hello. Her hair matched her snowy poncho. "That's what matters most up here. You won't last long without firewood when the nights close in," she looked right at Elena. Her eyes were like small black pebbles. Then, without further pleasantries, she turned and walked away again through the skinny pines toward her hut, raising a hand, but not looking back.

Elena imagined sitting in this room with snow on the trees and the mountains and the float house roof; a roaring wood stove, books and papers spread out, baby toys, a pot of hot soup on the stove . . . She smiled to herself, and wandered toward the stairs.

The float house had cost about four hundred dollars less than she'd budgeted, and by her calculations there was enough money left to keep them going for a year if they were as self-sufficient as possible. They could fell a few smaller fir trees for firewood—and cut back the undergrowth, then there'd be room out back for a sizable vegetable garden. According to Ana it wasn't too late to plant kale and Swiss chard—they'd survive the frosts and snows and give a steady supply of vitamin C until spring. And the forest was bursting with berries now—so she needed to get picking. Fall would be hard work even without a tiny baby and her research to work on, but she didn't mind hard work.

Ducking under the low beam at the bottom of the staircase, she kissed her baby's cottony head, and made her way upstairs. With a forest in the backyard, whales out front, and fresh air all around, there could surely be no better place to raise a child. But she wasn't stupid— there was a lot to learn.

In the bedroom, she walked to the great window and peered through its dirty glass. The sky was clouding over, and the waves looked darker, and swollen. For a moment her certainty shrank and she felt how small and insignificant she was in this tiny wooden house, floating on the margins of a fathomless ocean.

Anything could happen up here.

The nearest hospital was a pretty long helicopter ride away. She folded her arms around the papoose and sucked in a big breath. This was what the pioneer women must have felt, as they laid down roots on the unknown land. It felt scary. But the opportunity outweighed the fear.

The low-angled bedroom needed a good cleaning to brighten it up. It smelled stale and several years of salt and rain stains were blocking out the light. But soon it would be paradise up here—the window was the full A of the roof; you'd be able lie in bed and look out at the ocean. It occurred to her that she could drill a hole through the two floors and drop down a hydrophone into the water. The underwater sounds could fill this room, day and night. They could wake up to the sound of the whales, and fall asleep to their voices at night.

She peered through the grubby glass, down at the deck. "Hey," she touched the sleeping head with her fingertips, "that's where we're going to sit on good-weather days." She pictured morning coffee as the sun rose over the bay. They'd be able to spot whales on the ocean and jump straight into the Zodiac. She imagined beers on the deck, too, after a long day on the water. They'd all sit down there and talk about what they'd seen as the sun lowered itself behind the dotted islands.

The float house was sheltered from coastal winds by a towering forest of pine, cedar, and hemlock, and rocks formed a natural barrier against the waves. They'd be relatively well protected when the storms came. Even Eve had admitted that it was a "good spot." The float house belonged here. It was if this little bay and the rocks and the trees had just been waiting for it to arrive.

Out of habit she scanned the water for a triangle of dorsal or a plume of breath but the waves rose and fell steadily.

"We have to be patient," she whispered. "And they'll come." She watched a golden eagle sweep on the wind tides above the trees, its feathers splayed like monstrous claws.

*   *   *

The cleaning took three full days—punctuated by feedings and diaper changes and the occasional "kwoof" out in the bay when she'd drop everything—seize baby, papoose, camera, life preserver—and scoot down to the Zodiac. She never went far beyond the bay and she couldn't listen without a hydrophone, but she took photos and scoured the catalog at night to work out who they were.

Raven Bay was forty minutes away by boat when the tides were right. When she motored down on the third day to buy shelf brackets, wood, screws, paint for the kitchen cupboards, and more nails, she bumped into Ana outside the hardware store.

Ana must be busy, with her boys to look after, and the summer guesthouse to run, but she invited Elena to the house for a cup of coffee.

Her kitchen smelled of baking and was warm, with the boys' clothes draped across the range, and fishing tackle, rubber boots, slingshots and comics strewn about the place. Today, there was a basket in one corner containing a black cat and six mewling kittens, still blind and jerky. An old Swedish clock ticked above the stove, and with the back door open you could hear waves thudding on the dock and the clink of masts.

As Elena breastfed, Ana moved around as if there was no hurry at all. She always wore the same thing—a weathered blue smock that came down to her knees, thick tights, and clogs. She poured coffee for them both, and put down a plate of zucchini bread, still warm from the oven.

"So," Ana said, "You'll be laying down stores for winter I guess?"

"Uh, yes," Elena said, through a mouthful of cake.

"Every spring I can up a winter's worth of salmon, but you've missed that. Now's the time to preserve your fruits and berries though—do you have jars?" Ana's voice was unhurried: each syllable had its own place, emphasis, and melody.

She hadn't thought about jars. She hadn't thought further than getting the float house in place and getting back out on the water with the hydrophone. "You need to think ahead," Ana was saying. "This isn't

Nanaimo—*you can get days on end, up at Black Bear, where there's no way in or out.*"

So, *together they made a list of winter supplies, including powdered milk, biscuits, and porridge for the baby. She should buy big jars of peanut butter, Ana said, as well as canned meats, yeast, and some big bags of flour.*

When it was time for Elena to leave, Ana went to the attic for a box of clothes that her boys had grown out of.

"*We don't get many folks coming to settle up here,*" *she leaned a hand on the doorpost as they said goodbye.* "*Least of all with little babies. The whole community wants this to work out for you guys, you know.*" *There was concern behind the steady blue eyes.*

"*We'll be fine,*" *she smiled back.* "*We know the sea up here—we've been around here most of the year anyway. And we're pretty tough you know.*"

The sink doubled as a baby bath, the gentle movement of the float house rocked the Moses basket, and she strung up a garland of diapers on the deck. Over the next few days, during naptimes, she tackled the trickier jobs. There were rusty nails and splintery edges everywhere so for a whole day she went from one danger spot to another, hammering nail heads down and sanding off corners to make it all safe for soft knees and curious hands.

Quite a few of the floorboards in the front room were unstable, so one afternoon she parked the baby basket in the bell tent, covered it with netting to keep out any curious animals, and spent two hours levering up rotten boards with a crowbar, and sawing, sanding, and hammering the new ones in place. When she'd finished, the floor was a patchwork of worn and new pine.

She'd cover it with the rag rugs she'd bought in the market in Victoria, the day she'd finally said goodbye to Susannah.

Finding the right location at last—and then the float house—had washed away much of the tension of that stressed-out week in Raven Bay; they'd parted as friends. But she was not in a hurry to have Susannah up here; she couldn't forget about the argument over the dinner table, and the weirdness in the air between them. But Susannah had been sweet in the end—eager to please—perhaps trying to make up for it. They'd both been under pressure. It was best forgotten about, really. Best to move on and finally put some distance between them.

On her sixth evening in the float house, Elena painted the peeling kitchen cupboards a sunflower yellow; it had been the only color left in the hardware store, but she kind of liked its sunshine feel.

The next day she got up at five in the morning, when it was still dark. The dawn howls of wolves and coyotes echoed through the trees as she stripped the window frames down to their bare wood. Through the glass—clean now—she watched the first pink rays stretch out across the horizon and the sea turn from gunmetal to its soft morning green.

She pulled on her grubby fleece, and went out to boil a pan of water on the camp stove by the tent. She brewed a pot of strong coffee, taking it out onto the deck. She felt light-headed and a little queasy from paint fumes and sleep deprivation but as she drank the coffee and ate a stale bread roll with jam, she watched the sky lighten to baby blue and she was completely content.

It was hard to picture what was to come in winter. She knew about thirty-foot waves, and hurricane-strength winds, and about the southeasterly storms that could sweep in from nowhere and last for days. But she also knew they'd stick it out up here, whatever happened because this was home now.

She didn't feel lonely during those eight days, but she did feel a growing impatience to get back out there. There was so much work to be done and every time she saw a plume of breath and motored out with the camera toward the whales she was acutely aware of the vocalizations she was missing beneath the surface.

One particular matriline—consisting of seven whales—seemed to "own" the bay. She felt sure that they were curious about her activities. Sometimes they lingered in the bay, close to the rocks, and spy-hopped—their faces peering upright out of the water—as if checking on her progress. Once, when she motored out to them, they *put on a playful display for her. The two younger brothers breached, twisting their muscular bodies as they flew through the air and slapped their flukes on the surface so that the sound bounced off the rocks. They tail-lobbed, plainly relishing the echoes they could create by thumping their tails on the surface of the water. Their elegance amazed her. These creatures were the size of tankers but they rose up from the depths and entered the air like ballet dancers— hundreds of pounds of shining black and white muscle suspended gloriously against the sky.*

She needed the hydrophone. It was agony to watch this and not listen too. She wanted to know what vocalizations went with all this horsing around. She wanted to record the sounds that the matriarch made just before they vanished; she was sure there must be a single command. But she had to be patient. Only two more days and she'd have the parts, fix the hydrophone, and get back out there.

On the day before the guys returned—another bright and sunny sky—she decided to go down Raven Bay again in the Zodiac to get supplies for a special homecoming meal. She strapped her gurgling baby into the papoose on her back, and steered the Zodiac out of the bay, eyes fixed on the horizon.

In Raven Bay, she bought more preserving jars from the hardware store, along with another box of nails, two packets of sandpaper, and twenty more shelf brackets; she was learning that whatever quantity she thought she'd need, she should double it. She also bought more crackers, flour, and yeast so she could bake bread when they got the oven working; some granola bars and coffee; two more bottles of bleach and Milton fluid; and a pint of peanut butter. She longed for apples—to sink her teeth into a crisp Jonah Gold—but there was no fresh fruit in the store. She bought cans of beans and tomatoes and a sack of rice to make a vegetarian stew. There was sorrel and chanterelles in the forest behind the house, and so far she'd picked four pints of blackberries. It would be a feast.

Back at the float house, she moved all the crockery and kitchen things from their boxes in the tent into the newly painted kitchen. With tin mugs and plates, real glasses and cutlery, and cupboards full of supplies, it was complete.

She opened a beer and carried her exhausted baby back out to the fire pit by the tent—chucking on another log and wrapping a tartan blanket around them both. The stars were coming out in great handfuls and there was a chill in the air. She felt tired and a little queasy as she settled down to feed. It was almost a seasick feeling—like she had on the Zodiac the first few times Jonas took her out. She hadn't eaten properly today. It was easy to get depleted when breastfeeding a big baby.

She needed to fix the hydrophone the moment she had the parts, and get back out there. Even if Eve was right, and some orcas really did come here throughout the winter, most would surely be gone by the end of October. That only gave her two months to gather as much data as she could on the matriarch's burst pulse sound—she felt sure it was an instruction. She had a hunch that it was directional—probably to do with food. It could also be a sound that the others mimicked. If she could collect enough data on this one sound by late fall—establish whether it was a stereotype call, or something else—then she had her starting point.

She put the beer down and sat back, gazing up at the stars. As always, at the back of her mind, was Bella. Somewhere out there was Bella's mother. What she hadn't realized, until she saw killer whales in the wild, was the strength of their family bonds. They stuck together, touching each other and communicating verbally all the time. It seemed such a harmonious way to live—older whales were never left out, they were always in the center of the group, and the pod shared everything— childcare, hunting, play. It was wrong to use words like "love," but it was clear that the social bonds in family units were profound.

If this closeness extended to language—if particular sounds were peculiar to one pod or another—then theoretically it would be possible, one day, to match Bella's vocal patterns to her family. That could take decades—of course—and she'd have to go back to Sea Park and gather more sound data from Bella. But maybe one day she'd be able to map Bella's vocalizations to a pod, and find out where she belonged.

Elena hadn't shared this particular obsession with anyone, not even Jonas. She had asked the orca survey guys, last year, if there was any way to trace Bella's family, but although they knew about the two Sea Park whales, they didn't know which pod Bella had been taken from. She'd been captured in the bloodbaths, before the regulations came in. They knew about a couple of other captive whales in Florida—there were records of their captures, and they'd been able to work out their whole family trees. But not Bella.

She sipped her beer and looked down at her baby's beautiful sleeping face, a perfect oval, completely symmetrical. It occurred to her that this need she had, to find Bella's mother, might not be purely scientific. It was somehow related to the darker part of herself, the frightened eight year old whose mother wasn't coming back. But there was no use thinking about all that. She'd boxed it all up and it should stay that way. She never could see the point in introspection or looking back.

"We just need to get back out there," she whispered. "Don't we?"

Her research wasn't something she "did" anymore. It was who she was—as much a part of her as this beautiful baby. She remembered something Dean said about his wife, who stopped traveling among Native Canadian communities to stay home with their son. He said she didn't do anything "by halves." At the time Elena had taken this to mean that she'd made a positive choice to be an at-home mother. But in fact, maybe Dean's wife didn't have a choice: some things can't be watered down, portioned off or rationed out.

It occurred to Elena that without the float house she would be in exactly the same position as Dean's wife. If she couldn't make it work up here she would have to stop completely. A life studying killer whales in the wild was full immersion or nothing. Without this place, she would have to become a different person. There was an awful lot invested in these cedar planks.

She closed her eyes and swallowed the mouthful of beer and for a moment she was overcome with gratitude for her shabby floating house and the rocky corner of land that had allowed her to stay, and be herself.

CHAPTER FOURTEEN

At first I can't see a thing. A powerful smell of mildew hits my throat, and beneath it something rotten and organic. A faint light glows through the doorway up ahead and as my eyes adjust I see that I'm in a galley kitchen. I stumble toward the light.

And there he is, on her hip, sturdy and round and bundled up in his navy blue fleece. She is facing me, but he's looking out the window still—maybe looking for me—the back of his hair is all knotted up. I throw myself across the room. "Finn!" He turns his head. His eyes are huge and frightened.

"Oh love, oh sweetheart! I'm here. I'm here. I've got you!" He opens his mouth and lets out a strangled wail—part surprise, part desperation. He throws out his arms for me, tipping his body after them like a diver launching off the high board, trusting he'll be caught—and I catch him; I feel his weight in my arms and the sobs swell in my chest and throat. I hang onto him, feeling him mold himself to my body again, and cling there, like part of my flesh.

I screw my eyes shut and just for a moment my whole being is wrapped around Finn, breathing him, absorbing him; a sphere again. This is over. It's over. There is no red line after all. I have my baby back. He's safe.

My legs are shaking so I slide to my knees and hold him tight, rocking gently to soothe him. His arms are tight around my neck. I know I have to rein myself back in. I have to not frighten him with the force of this relief.

"I was worried about you, love, but it's okay. I've got you. Everything's okay now. Mommy's here. I'm going to stay with you now, okay? I've been looking for you all day."

This is not a crisis anymore. I have to get a grip and be calm for my already frightened child. I kiss his wet cheeks. "What an adventure you've had," I say. "My poor little love." He looks up into my eyes and then he lets go of my neck and holds onto my jaw with both hands, as if checking that it is really me.

"I was looking for you, love. I was looking so hard and I didn't know where you were, but I found you didn't I?"

Slowly I become aware that Susannah is standing above us. And she is not moving.

But I can't take my eyes off Finn. She has put him in his spaceman pajamas and his warmest fleece. His eyes are startled and red-rimmed—he is so tired—and I can see he's been crying for a long time. But he's not hurt. Not physically at least. I run my hand over his arms and legs. They feel solid and warm beneath the clothes. She has even pulled socks over his footsie pajamas. As least she is attempting to keep him warm—and it's freezing in here. The dampness feels like a poultice. I kiss his face all over, breathing in his sweet smell.

"I'm here. I've got you. It's all going to be okay now."

Finally, I look up.

I'm expecting an apologetic face, guilt, even fear or tears in her eyes. I'm expecting her to run her hands through her hair and say, "Shit, Kali, I'm so sorry! We missed the ferry and I had no way to reach you—"

Her face is a frozen mask.

She stares at us. In the dim light, her eyes look albino. I clasp Finn tighter and stand up to face her. And that's when I lose it.

"What the . . . what do you think you're doing?" I have to force myself not to scream and swear because of Finn and my voice comes out strangled. "What in God's name are you playing at Susannah? Who do you think you are, taking my child like this? Jesus Christ I should call the police! I don't care what you thought you were doing, who you thought you were helping. This is unbelievable. It's unbelievable! You can't just take someone's baby!"

She doesn't take her eyes off my face. She doesn't flinch. She doesn't even blink.

"Well?" I hiss.

Finn whimpers and puts both arms around my neck again. I kiss him, "It's okay, love, I'm a bit cross with Susannah, but it's okay. Everything's okay." I glare at her over his head. My limbs are trembling. "Say something," I grit my teeth. "Explain to me. What the hell did you think you were playing at, bringing him here to this place?"

And then she smiles. She actually smiles. It's just the corners of her mouth, not the eyes: the smile of an aristocrat observing a peasant. One eyebrow rises fractionally. She lifts her chin. Her pallid eyes are settled deep in her skull.

Rain drums on the roof. The house creaks and shifts and sways. The house, I realize, is unsteady beneath my feet. In fact, it doesn't feel like a house at all—it feels like a boat: unstable, perpetually shifting. I realize that the room is so dim because the only light is coming from candles. They are everywhere, on every shelf and flat surface—thick, church-type candles, melting and oozing wax. Garlands sway above her, pale in the flickering candlelight, like the ones in her meditation room at Isabella Point. But this is nothing like Isabella Point. This place stinks and it's so cold. Susannah is still staring at me.

I glare back. "Aren't you even going to *speak*?"

The half-smile vanishes. "Oh I knew you'd be difficult about this."

I give my head a little shake. "What? No. I'm sorry. What?"

"Oh come on." Her voice is flat and somehow off-kilter. It's a voice I've never heard before and it chills me more than the freezing air or the draft rattling the float house windows. "You shouldn't have come, Kali," she continues. "This has nothing to do with you."

"What?"

"She sent him to me. She didn't want you here too."

"What on earth are you talking about? Who sent who to you?"

"She wanted me to know that he's back, that's all. Because she wants me to be free of all this—everything! I mean, my God, just look at him." She gestures at Finn like a proud grandmother. "He's back, isn't he? He's alive."

I cover Finn's head with one hand. "You're not making any sense Susannah."

"Oh, you shouldn't even be here." She sounds impatient. "Fretting, fretting. I'm going to take care of him don't worry. I'm not going to let anything happen to him, not this time. Oh no. And to be honest, he's more at risk with you isn't he? I mean, my God, you can't look after him—you don't want him. You let the child pick up shards of glass, you ignore his cries, you leave him in the dark in thunderstorms, you lock him in bedrooms . . ." She looks at me and frowns. "This time I'm going to save him. And I'm not going to let you, or anything else get in the way of that. You should have gone back to England where you belong."

I stare at her, a chilly feeling spreading in the pit of my stomach. "I don't know what you're talking about Susannah. None of this is even slightly—"

"I have to show him to Jonas," she snaps. "When Jonas sees that his son is back he'll release me. That much must be obvious, surely, even to you?"

"What? Who? Who is Jonas? Release you from what? This is nonsense . . . you're talking nonsense. Are you ill?"

"Oh just stop! Stop—stop!" she puts her hands over her ears and glares at me. "Stop it."

"Susannah, this is . . . you're not making any sense—"

She drops her hands and speaks slowly, leaning down toward me as if I'm an idiot child. "She. Sent. Him. To. Me."

"My mother?"

"Of course."

"But my mother is dead, Susannah!"

"She knows that his father needs to see him."

"Finn's father is in Oxford, Susannah. He's in England."

"Oh no. His father," she fixes her colorless eyes on my face, "is right here."

"Oh my God." I look up at her. My arms tighten around Finn's tense little body. "You're completely insane."

Through the window behind her, I can just make out the flickering yellow light of Sven's boat as it vanishes around the headland.

Chapter Fifteen

Susannah drops her hands and strides across to a woodstove.

"So," she says in that deadened voice. "What on earth am I going to do with you now? You weren't supposed to follow us here. How the hell did you find your way here?"

The glow of the logs through the window of the woodstove casts a reddish light on her skin. She bends down and wrenches the iron handle—the metal shrieks. Her mouth is grim and set. Sparks fly out as she tosses a log in, and smoke billows into the room. She slams the stove door shut again. The wasp clasp at the base of her neck glints as she turns to face me again.

"Susannah, listen. I think you're confused. I think this is—"

"Jonas needs to see him," she cuts me off. "Why can't you get that? He'll forgive me when he sees that his son is safe. She understands that. Only now you're here messing it all up—you weren't supposed to come here."

"You honestly believe that my mother—my *dead* mother—sent Finn to you?"

"Of course she did! It's an act of love, don't you see? To release me from Jonas. That's what's so amazing about her. She understands everything." She glances at the ceiling as if my mother is there, presiding benevolently over this mad mess.

"Who is Jonas, Susannah?"

She stares at me. "You," she says, firmly, "are not supposed to be here." The crease between her brows intensifies.

"No. Actually, I am definitely supposed to be here because you took my child. You took my baby."

She is silent for a moment, staring at me as if I am a puzzle to be solved. Finn grips my neck and I pat his back in circles. "Shhh." I look up at her. Instinct tells me that I have to lose the outrage. "Honestly, Susannah, you're really not really making any sense," I say, in a slightly condescending voice that I don't really recognize. "I think you've . . ."

"Stop!" she barks. "Stop talking. You're making everything so . . . so . . . complicated."

"It's not complicated at all, really. It's very simple. He's my son—and you took him."

She raises a hand and points a finger at my heart. I close my mouth. But she doesn't move or speak. For the first time I notice that the dogs aren't here. I'm used to them being next to her, or nearby. Where are the dogs? I glance around. But of course she couldn't bring them here, on two boats, to the furthest edge of nowhere. Then I remember Maggie mentioning that Susannah dropped the dogs off at the bakery.

She seems to have gone into a trance. She has dropped her hand to her side and is just standing, eyes shut, swaying gently as the stove roars behind her. My jeans are wet from the waves, and it is so cold here. Rain lashes the window and the wind moans outside; I can feel the draft on the back of my head and neck. But Finn seems warm at least. I can feel, just by the hand I'm holding under him, that his diaper has been changed recently too. She obviously hasn't harmed him.

I just have to get us away from her—from this place. But where could we possibly go? Sven is long gone. Maybe there are other people somewhere on this island but unless they are right next door I am not going to find them in the dark with a storm blowing in.

There is a low sofa next to Susannah, covered in some kind of brownish blanket. Above it on the wood-paneled wall is a sort of gallery of framed photos. I remember that this is my mother's house. Surely nothing bad could happen to us here.

I edge away from the window. Susannah doesn't move. I can see the doorway that leads back into the kitchen. Maybe I could get in there and grab a knife or something. If she is dangerous I might need to physically protect Finn. The thought makes a shiver run through my body. I feel sick again. There is no way I could possibly fend her off—she's not only taller and heavier but far stronger than me.

Her eyes snap open, as if she's listening to my thoughts.

"Where are you going?"

I stop. "Nowhere."

"You stay where you are."

I pat Finn's back, and sway with him. "He needs some milk. Has he eaten? Did you feed him?"

"Of course I did! What do you think I am? He just had milk."

"Are you hungry, love?" I say to Finn. He looks up at me with big eyes and shakes his head.

"There," she says, archly. "See?"

A floorboard beneath my foot creaks, and then I feel it give—I whisk my foot off it but for a split second I picture the sucking sea and sharp rocks beneath the floating house. If Finn and I went through this floor we'd plunge into freezing water with our backs against the seabed, and the belly of the house pressed on our faces.

I have to stop being so fearful. I have to think.

"Have you got a phone?" I say. "Because I should probably call my sister to let her know I'm okay. I called her from Raven Bay, when you took Finn, so she knows I'm here. She knows exactly where I am. They all do. Ana, and Sven . . ."

"Huh? They do? Well. Nobody's here now are they? And no, there are no phones." She puts her head on one side, "Well, actually, that's not true. I think Jeff over on the other side of the island has one. But . . ." she shrugs, then looks right at me, with a half smile. "That's a ways away."

A dark shape shoots out of the sofa cushion behind her, scuttles madly through the sofa legs, and into the furthest corner of the room "Shit!" I yelp. "Jesus Christ what was that?"

She doesn't even twitch.

I point at the sofa. "Oh my God there are rats here Susannah. Was that a *rat*? I can't believe you'd bring Finn here. This is a nightmare. It's freezing. It's damp." I look around, at all the candles. "Is there even electricity in this house? There isn't electricity, is there?"

"I've kept it just the way she had it," Susannah shrugs. "Though of course in those days the generator worked. Yes, you do have to be kind of careful here, Kali. Watch your step. The rocks, in particular, are quite perilous."

I look at her. She looks back, steadily.

"But Maggie said this is your refuge."

"Ah. So it was Maggie who sent you here. Idiot."

"She said this is your sanctuary. This isn't a sanctuary, Susannah, it's a bloody wreck—this place is falling apart." I take a step or two closer to the kitchen, and glance in.

There is a candle on a peeling yellowish cabinet, and next to it a box of food—I see the Cheerios logo and a bag of apples, a box of animal crackers, a big glass jar of something—pickles—and a Horizon organic milk carton. These are groceries she bought today. She planned this. She shopped for it. She dropped the dogs off. Took some of Finn's clothes. She must have packed it all up while I was sleeping on her sofa. My sleep. What did she put in that cup of tea?

"You don't belong here," she says.

"Actually this place is probably legally mine," I snap. "But don't let that bother you."

"Yours?" she says. "It's Gray's, technically, but we don't need to get into that do we? This place is the last place on earth Gray would ever want to come to."

I think of my father's warnings.

She stares at the dark window, the lashing rain. I can't make out her expression. She might even be smiling. The shadows have pooled in her eye sockets and I can't see her eyes anymore. Her cheeks look sunken and there are deep lines on either side of her mouth. She turns her head, slowly, toward me.

Instinctively, I cover Finn's head with my hand. But she goes across to the sofa and, leaning one knee on it, she reaches up to the wall and unhooks a picture.

"He was so good looking, wasn't he?" She gazes at it. "That's what hoodwinked her you see?" She steps toward me, holding out the picture. I can see a man with a beard in a woolen hat, standing on the deck of a boat. "She never could see how dangerous he was."

"Who? This man? Who is he?"

"This?" she holds it up to me, smiles, then looks at it again. "It's Jonas, of course." She gazes at him. Another gust of wind hits the float house roof and the whole structure shudders.

"But who is Jonas, Susannah?"

"Oh come on Kali. Jonas started this whole mess."

"Oh. Then . . . but . . ." I squint across at the photo. In the dim light I can't see him clearly, but he is wearing a yellow all-weather suit. And finally it hits me: of course. This has been staring me in the face the whole time. My mother didn't leave my father for the whales, she left him for Jonas—this whale researcher. This handsome bearded man.

I can't believe this has not occurred to me before. "My mother ran off with this man—the whale researcher? Jonas? They were lovers?"

"Oh Kali," she shakes her head. "Are you seriously telling me you haven't even worked that out yet?"

"I've been a bit preoccupied," I snap back. "What with you drugging me and kidnapping my son."

Immediately I regret my tone. She moves rapidly across the room holding the photo against her body. I shrink back against the wall, squeezing Finn to my chest, covering his head with my hand. Candlelight flickers in her white eyes. "Don't give me that bullshit," she grits her teeth. She holds up one finger, close to my nose. "Don't."

I force myself to lift my chin and stare back at her, even though I want to cower, or better still—flee. "What do you mean?" I say.

"Oh you know."

"Actually I really don't, honestly, but . . . okay. Look . . ." I edge sideways. I have to calm her down. Something is misfiring in her brain. "Susannah, it's okay. Listen, maybe you can just tell me what happened up here. I'd really like to get it straight. Are you saying my mother left my father and had an affair with this whale researcher, Jonas, and then it somehow went wrong and she went back to my father? Went back to California? Is that it?"

"Ha. Yeah. Went wrong. You could say that."

"And she left you too?" I try to speak gently, "Is that what this is all about? She hurt you too?"

"Me? She didn't hurt me. She needed me. Someone had to protect you from him."

"Me?"

Her eyes flicker over my face, and she frowns. "No. No. Not you. Of course not. I'm talking about Elena. And you. Both of you. All of you."

"So, you had to protect us from this man—from Jonas?"

She is staring at the picture again. She is breathing hard as if holding all this in her head is a huge effort.

"He was dangerous? Jonas was dangerous?" I think about my mother's safe routines, her Sussex life, her periods of deep depression, her moods. "What did he do to her, Susannah?" I glance into the shadows of the kitchen, half expecting a big bearded figure to appear in a yellow suit. "Where is he?" I say. "Where's Jonas now?"

She doesn't answer.

"Susannah. What did Jonas do to my mother? You have to tell me."

"It's not what he did," she says, "but what he was *capable* of doing."

"So he didn't do anything? He didn't hurt her?" I feel something release in my skull, as if someone has loosened a metal band around it. "Okay. What happened then? Did you persuade her to go back to my father? Is that why Jonas needs—needed—to forgive you?"

Again, she says nothing. I can see thoughts, maybe memories, tugging at the muscles on her face.

"Where is Jonas now?" I try to keep my voice soft. "He's not up here, is he, Susannah?"

The tip of her nose is reddish. Violet thread veins map her cheeks. Her hair is wild and her fingers, clasped around the picture frame, are red raw. There are lines of dirt under each fingernail. She drops one hand to her side, and her fingers begin to tap rapidly against her thigh.

"Susannah? Can you hear me?"

"She upped and left just two weeks after she met him. I mean—who does that? Can you believe that? Two damned weeks!"

"My father must have been really upset."

"Gray? Oh, he was destroyed."

This is hard to imagine. My father has always seemed so unreachable, positioning himself somewhere beyond the petty demands of emotional involvement. My mother's death is the only time I've ever seen him vulnerable. It is hard to imagine him as a young man in California, abandoned and distraught. "So—she really fell in love with Jonas?"

"Jonas was very persuasive." Her fingertips tap harder, faster, and then, as if taking its nervy cue, her leg begins to jiggle. I hug Finn tighter. "He was idealistic. Moody. Intense. Totally obsessed with his orca-mapping project. He had a God complex. He was going to save the world and I guess she was going to be his little handmaiden."

"Okay, I definitely can't imagine her as anyone's little handmaiden."

She stops twitching and tapping. "Well, yes, you see, that's the first reason it could never work," she says this almost anxiously, her eyes searching mine for affirmation. "It really was never going to work out, was it?"

"Did my father just let her go?"

"She'd already gone! She crept out like a criminal while he was away. Of course, it was a monumental mistake. Monumental." She starts the jiggling and tapping again.

"Maybe it was just something she felt she had to do? I mean, she was very young, wasn't she? People do make mistakes don't they? And she made the right decision in the end because she loved my father, they were . . . content." I can't say happy. Happy is not a word that fits my mother.

"You told me you wanted to know everything," she sighs, "But you really don't, do you, Kali?"

"What? No. I do. That's why I'm asking you all these questions." I shift Finn to my hip, keeping my arms tight around him. My back is beginning to ache. I stroke the hair out of his eyes and kiss him. "It's okay, love."

She looks down at the photo again. "I always knew he'd try to hurt her. I always told her he would—that's why I stayed as close as I could. I wasn't going to let it happen, not to you," she's talking to herself now. "Not to my Elena."

"But, you said he didn't hurt her."

She fixes her white wolf eyes on my face.

"What did he do, Susannah? He did something, didn't he? Just tell me what it was. Where is Jonas now?"

"He's dead," she spits. "Jonas is dead."

"He died?" I feel relief flood my limbs. Finn is so heavy. I shift him to the other hip. "Okay, but you said . . . something about you coming up here to see Jonas?"

She laughs—a thin and shivery sound. "You want to know the whole story, don't you? And you won't let up 'til you get it. Your mother's daughter. Well fine. Fine! I'll tell you what happened! They were photographing a new family of orca and a storm came in. It happens all the time up here—like this one coming now—a polar storm just closes in, almost no warning," she claps the frame against her leg and I jump. "Seventeen-foot tides, massive winds. The seas up here are dangerous. *Dangerous!*"—she shouts it—"People die every year out there. Every year. He drowned! Okay? Jonas drowned!"

"Is that what you mean by my mother getting hurt?" I ask, as gently as I can. "Her grief?"

Susannah is muttering something; I can see her lips moving, as if she's consulting an invisible companion.

"Susannah? You mean my mother was hurt by grief?"

So this is why she would never talk about the past: this horrible accident, her dead lover, the grief—and the shame of betraying my father. But something is still missing from this story. "Susannah," I say, slowly. "What has this got to do with you? Why did my mother refuse to speak to you for thirty-eight years?"

Her face darkens and her body seems to inflate. Her eyes bulge and the vein running up the center of her forehead begins to pulse. She throws the photo, like a Frisbee, across the room and it smashes on the wall behind me. I jump. Her hand shoots out and I think she's going to punch me over Finn's head—I lurch backward, but she hits her own forehead with a flat palm. It makes a loud smack. She does it again. And again.

"Susannah . . ." Finn starts to cry. I press his head against my chest. "Stop! Please. Stop."

"That's enough." She screws her hand into a fist. "Enough!" She punctuates each word with a thump against the side of her head. "Leave—me—the—fuck—alone."

Finn's cry is escalating like a siren, his mouth baby-bird wide, his whole body rigid. But she continues to shout over his cries. "You've undone thirty-eight years in three days." Her face is turning scarlet. "And now you follow me up here to—what—torment me? Hadn't you done enough? Why are you doing this to me? You're not meant to be here. You aren't here. Why can't you just GO AWAY?"

"It's okay. It's okay. I'm not doing anything to you, Susannah." I stroke Finn's hair, trying to calm him. "I'm not trying to upset you, I promise. And I didn't bring Finn to you—you took him from me. Remember? I just came up here to get him back. I won't ask you any more questions, okay? Please, please try to calm down."

Her shoulders slump. She looks crestfallen. It occurs to me that she may actually be more of a danger to herself than to me, or Finn.

"It's okay. Let's get some sleep, eh, Susannah?" I coax, "You look really tired. It's been a very, very long day. Finn's exhausted. He really needs to sleep now. Let's sleep. I'm going to go away, first thing in the morning, okay? As soon as I can. And everything will be all right again. Please. Let's just . . . let's see if we can just sleep."

She turns and flings herself across the room and up the stairs.

As I soothe Finn I can hear her stumble to the top, and then crash around for a bit. Little bits fall off the ceiling like confetti. Gradually Finn's sobs subside.

"There you go." I kiss him again. "Silly Susannah, all that shouting. It's okay. Silly old Susannah."

I walk with him into the freezing kitchen and try to open a drawer but the wood is swollen and warped and nothing will budge. My hands are stiff with cold. I try another. From a corner, a spider the size of Finn's fist flexes its legs at me. I grab the bottle of water, wrench it open by balancing Finn on one hip, and gulp at it, keeping one eye on the spider. It doesn't move. Icy water trickles down my throat.

I don't need a knife. People only get kitchen knives in Hollywood movies. This is not dramatic—it's just sad. She's plainly unwell. I just have to get through the night, then leave the moment it gets light.

I walk slowly back into the room, testing each board before I put my foot down. The photo of Jonas lies where it landed, half propped up against the wall, shattered glass around it, the frame half off. His features are very definite: a strong nose, a big chin. For a moment, I feel as if he's looking right at me, across time; as if he wants to communicate something important. I shiver.

"Let's go and warm up next to the stove, because it's nice and warm to sit by, isn't it? We just won't touch it." I carry Finn, gingerly, across to the stove. Suddenly, I really am exhausted. My legs are stringy. I wonder what all this is doing to the baby inside me—tranquilizers, whisky, stress, panic. It's not exactly what the pregnancy books recommend for the first trimester. If it is the first trimester. Who knows? Rain lashes against the window and the wind roars over the thudding sea. The house sways. I want Doug. Badly. I need to get a message to him that I have Finn, and he's safe. But there is no way to do this. He will be out of his mind with worry.

Muffled sounds—odd, growling noises—come through the ceiling. I just have to leave her up there. Maybe she will calm down without me to shout at.

Feeling the warmth of the stove ease through my legs, I look across at the rest of the photos on the wall behind the sofa. There is a pale rectangle where Jonas's picture had been. In one of the other photos, an orca launches itself out of the waves, droplets flying off its belly. I move closer. It looks like the same picture that was in Susannah's house—the one Finn broke. Suddenly, out of the blue, I think of Harry Halmstrom's torqued face, his talk of big fish and murder.

I seem to be spending a lot of time with lunatics these days.

I just want to go home to Doug. Finn and I are going on the first flight we can get to and I don't care how much it will cost. I just need to see Doug. I realize that I'm no longer afraid of the truth. Nothing he could ever say or do to me could rival the terror I felt today when I thought I'd lost Finn forever.

Next to the whale photo is a smaller one. I lean forward, squinting through the candlelight. Finn lays his head on my shoulder. The glass is murky, but I know my mother, even though she is so incredibly young.

She is bright-faced and smiling—in a headscarf, bell bottoms, and a small T-shirt, square on to the camera. She is holding a baby. I lean further forward. There is no way to see the baby's face, just a tiny hat and a white blanket. But I know I am looking at myself.

I really was here, once, on this godforsaken piece of land. Then I notice a shadowy man in the background of the picture, blurry— and a toddler at his knees, half-hidden between my mother and the house. I peer at them. The man's face is turned away, but one hand rests on the toddler's head. The little boy is squinting at the camera.

He has pudding bowl hair, and red rain boots. His face is blurry. I'm sure I've seen him before somewhere, but I can't think where.

Perhaps my mother brought me here for a final farewell—to shut the place up before going to England—to say goodbye to her colleagues. But she looks happy. She doesn't look like someone who is leaving. She looks like someone who has just arrived.

Who was holding the camera? My father? Or maybe that's my father in the background. Impossible to tell. But of course—this couldn't be a farewell picture because she couldn't have framed it and put it on the wall if that was her last visit.

Then I remember where I saw the little boy in the red boots—this is the boy in the picture in Susannah's bedroom—the one I thought, just for a second, was Finn. Maybe Susannah had another son long ago—born before me—and something happened to him—up here. Finn is about the age now that the boy was in the photos. He even has similar red rain boots. If something awful happened to Susannah's first child, then maybe Finn's similarity to him has brought it all back to her. Maybe her own memories have unhinged her.

Finn is getting sleepy in my arms. I can't stand here all night so I kick the sofa hard, bracing myself for rats to shoot out. Nothing happens. I perch on the sofa cushion and stroke Finn's head, humming to him. I can feel a thought crouching somewhere in the back of my mind, but I can't quite get to it.

Careful not to wake Finn, I gently slide the parka off my body one arm at a time, then ease it from under me and pull it over the top of us, like a duvet. The outside of the coat is damp, but inside the down is still warm and dry. I just have to get through the night. That's all.

I squint up at the shadowy garlands that hang above us and as I gaze at them I realize what I'm actually looking at. They are not yogic flower garlands. They are spiders' webs and creeping weeds.

My jeans are stiffening in the warmth from the stove. Finn settles into me and sighs. I wonder if he can smell his dad, deep in the wool of the sweater I am wearing. I stroke his hair gently. His head still fits my hand. Outside, the storm batters the rocks and gusts of rain rattle the windows of my mother's house.

I remember how I said to Susannah that it isn't possible miss someone you never had. Well I was wrong: I miss the mother I had, but I also miss the one I didn't have; the mother she should have been. I have always missed her—my whole life. But now I miss the missing itself, and the hope around which it was folded.

I look down at Finn's tousled head and I rein in the despair because I have to, for him, and for the baby that's floating inside me like a tiny boat weathering this massive storm.

There is a wicker chair on the other side of the stove. It is so old that its sticks poke out at odd angles like sharp knitting needles. This is a lunatic place to bring a toddler, with all these candles that he could knock over, a hot metal stove, the damp and stink, the deep sea all around, sharp wicker, broken floorboards. This is a death trap.

Rain lashes the house. This is going to be a long night. I rest my chin on Finn's head. He is safe. I have him. Nothing else matters but keeping him safe and taking him home to Doug.

Chapter Sixteen

I must have dozed off. Finn is still heavy on my chest, but I wake with a thudding heart knowing that something has changed. I snap my eyes open.

She is standing above us, lit from behind by the faint red glow of the stove. Her hair is loose on her shoulders, wild foaming gray.

"Shit!" I struggle upright, trying not to wake Finn, pulling the parka back over him. "Susannah!" I hiss. "What are you doing? What do you want?"

My right arm, where Finn's head is leaning, is completely dead. I have pins and needles in both legs. My bruised coccyx feels as if it has seized up.

It is bitterly cold in the room, and not quite pitch dark, but definitely not light either. The woodstove is almost out. I can still hear the thud of waves but the wind has died down. Susannah takes a step closer. She is holding something but I can't see what it is. I press Finn against my chest and jam my spine against the sofa, shielding him with both arms, my heart pummeling at my ribs. She squats, very slowly. Her eyes never leave my face. But she doesn't seem to be seeing me.

It is as if she's sleeping with her eyes open. I can't see what she's doing with her hands. I wait for them to grab my legs—or worse, my neck. But then she gets up. I hear the cartilage in her knees click. She turns and walks away across the room, straight-backed as a water carrier, and through the doorway, placing her bare feet on the stairs, deliberately, one after the other. Then nothing. No pacing. No mutterings. Silence.

My heart is still bouncing off my rib cage. Finn lies, oblivious, on top of me. The room is saturated in dark gray. It's almost dawn. I can feel daylight coming. I can almost hear it. The storm must have passed and there is just the rhythmic bash and suck of waves on the rocks and smaller gusts, rattling the windows. It's okay. Nothing happened. It's okay.

I feel around by the sofa with my foot until it knocks against something. I slide my hand down and my fingers close over a cardboard folder. I pull it up and tip the contents onto the cushion closest to the fading glow from the fire.

I am looking at a sea of old newspaper clippings, envelopes, and photos. I pull out a photo of my mother and hold it up toward the stove. She is young and windswept and freckled with a strand of hair across her mouth. There is another photo of her, out at sea in a yellow oilskin suit, hair flying out behind her, binoculars around her neck. An orca is coming out of the water so close to the boat that she could almost reach out and touch its giant fluke. My mother is looking directly at the whale, and you can see the whale's eye, looking right back at her.

There's a white envelope close to my hand. I tip it over and a single dark curl, tied with white thread, drops into my hand. There is something creepily Victorian about this little love token. I put it back into the envelope and pick up another one, bigger, manila. It feels empty but I tip it over anyway, braced for what I might find, half expecting fingernails, or flakes of skin.

A fragment of white blanket slides out into my palm. It is exactly like the fragment that my mother had in her jewelry box, only without the embroidered *K*. I feel the blood pulse against my temples. Finn shifts against me. I make soothing sounds and slip the fragment of blanket into the pocket of my parka.

Next to my hand is a leaflet for *The Killer Whale Research Institute*. There is information about orca pods, types, sightings, and research studies. One section, called "*Threats*," talks about noise pollution, whales mangled by boat engines or trapped in fishing nets, chemical spills, toxins, harassment. The threats, plainly, are all human. Fifty years ago, a whale would have heard its kin all the way across the ocean. Now it's lucky if it can hear calls from fifty miles away. On the back is a small section "*about us.*"

The Killer Whale Research Institute was launched in the late seventies by a group of scientists from Canada and the USA, in order to establish the size and nature of the threatened orca population of British Columbia. This work grew into a population study that, over the years, has provided unprecedented access to the habits, lifestyle, demography, and population of orcas in this region.

So, this is what she started. Did this make it all worthwhile? I wonder if my mother even knew about this institute. I toss the leaflet back into the file and pick up a manila envelope. The contents seem to relate to the purchase of land in my mother's name, Elena Halmstrom. This land, this house, really was hers. But it is clear that this place belongs to nobody, now, but the sea and the forest and the winds, the wolves and black bears and coyotes and rats and spiders that are slowly reclaiming it.

There is another, yellowing document, folded in three. I unfold it. I am looking at a damp birth certificate. Not daring even to move my fingers in case it disintegrates, I begin to read:

Certificate of Live Birth.
State of Washington, Department of Health.
Child's First Name: Elena Katherine Kalypso

Sex: F
Birth Date: June 28 1953.
Hour: 10:53pm
Name of Hospital or Institution: Capitol Hill Health, Seattle,
Washington.
Name of Father: Theodore Nikolai Kalypso. Usual occupation:
businessman
Name of Mother: Katharine Anne Kalypso.
Mother's maiden name: Katharine Anne Davies

I read the name, Kalypso, again and again. The first two syllables are mine. It makes no sense. I look at the dates again. My mother's dates. This is nonsensical—a false certificate? A forgery? I slip it back into the envelope. The feeling that there's something on the periphery of my vision that I can't quite see is stronger than ever.

I notice an old, light blue airmail envelope addressed to my mother—at our house in Sussex. Across the front, in my father's neat printing: **Return to sender.**

But it has been opened. I fumble and pull out the letter, holding the thin blue paper toward the stove to read the tight handwriting.

Dear Elena,

I have given up any hope that I will hear from you, though I know that one day, when we are old women, I will see your face again. Do you get my postcards? I have sent one every year on the anniversary. Even if you—or Graham—throw them away, it's important to me to send something.

I often think about those early days on the float house and how unfair it all was on you. I felt for you up there alone, wresting with generators and diapers. It wasn't how you dreamed it, was it? Remember how we read Germaine Greer? How does that happen to women? Somehow it always does, again and again, even to women like you, even in places like that.

But I won't go there, not again. I am writing to tell you that Jonas has been coming to the float house.

The first time, a month ago now, I was out at dawn on the rocks staring out to sea, and he rose out of the water—so close to the shore that I could see the droplets on his shining hide. I never noticed before, but orca skin looks like velvet.

He was alone—no other whales. He really is magnificent. His fin is as tall as he was as a man—six foot or more. It's a little twisted at the top. I knew right away, of course, that it was him.

Remember that First People's legend that orcas are the spirits of our drowned men—our fathers, husbands, brothers, sons—and that when we see them close to the coast like this, it's because they are coming to find us? Well, he was coming for me. He is angry, Elena.

I fell to my knees and I felt this strange mixture of awe and fear, but also a kind of peace deep in my heart. This is karma. I shut my eyes and waited for him to sweep me off the rock.

But when I opened them, he'd gone. He didn't come back up for a long time—and I saw him blow, way, way out to sea.

I left the float house that day, and came back to Spring Tide and slept for two days straight. I think now that he didn't come to take me, he came to warn me that I will pay—for the rest of my life. I will never be able to forget.

I've seen him a few more times now further out. Every time I go up there, he comes. But then, last week, he came to Spring Tide, to my new beach, right up close again. I guess he wants me to know that he knows where I am. I can't hide from him. He knows how to find me.

Maybe even if you return this letter you may keep the address, in case you ever want to find me too.

It's a very small community here on Spring Tide. There are artists and potters and writers, but none of the ambition and competitiveness of the Vancouver scene.

This will be a healing place. I have to believe that. I have been through hell. I know you have too—a far worse hell than mine. But the strange thing is that since Jonas came back I've been able to work—for the first time in years.

The work is pouring out of me, sometimes I work twenty hours a day, sometimes I don't even sleep at all. I am mixing clay with copper and silver and burying the pots in the mud by the estuary to oxidize. It makes amazing patterns of light in the clay.

The Granville studio sold for a decent profit—Granville is becoming quite the place to be. I used that money, plus some money from my mother's estate to build a house (she finally died from heart failure in her prison cell last June). I have this crazy idea that one day I will set up a gallery here on the island and that you will come visit. You'll just turn up one day and everything will be just as it was between us. Maybe Jonas will come to see you too: I'm sure he would—if you came.

In the summer, more people arrive on the island and it would actually make a good place for a gallery. But maybe you don't want to hear about my plans. I just wanted you to have this address and to know that I think of you—constantly—still. You are in my heart always and forever. I have a debt to you that is bigger than anything I can ever hope to pay in my lifetime. I don't expect forgiveness. I don't expect you to reply.
Your devoted friend, always,

Susannah.

Ps. I read the other day that they're setting up an institute and establishing listening stations all over the region.

Pps. I travel a lot. I am only at peace on the road—on buses and trains and in airports. Sometimes I imagine that we are traveling together, you and I, and when I see things, I imagine that you're seeing them too, standing right next to me. We have whole conversations, you and I.

I drop the letter.

Through the window I can see that the sky is still dark gray, still too dark to go out. Another fifteen, twenty minutes and dawn will be breaking and we can get out of here.

There is another envelope, the same—airmail, with **Return to Sender** on it in my father's writing. I tip it up and a blurry Polaroid of a newborn falls out. The letter is just a single sheet, written in an even tighter scrawl.

Dear Elena,
I know Gray will send this back—or is it you that sends my letters back?—but I have to write anyway. I try to understand why you haven't ever

replied but I know you believe we are connected—that's why you sent those poems, and so, I am sending you this picture. Yes, Elle, I'm a mother.

My baby boy was born at dawn, on February 8. The birth was amazing. Why do women make such a song and dance about labor? I felt something in the early hours and took myself away to my studio in the woods. I meditated, and sang and moved and danced and eventually, as the first sunlight came through the pines he burst out of me. It was primitive, Elle. I cut the cord with my potter's knife—can you believe it? I didn't expect so much blood, but I was on a high. I felt no pain whatsoever.

Maybe this is a kind of redemption. And isn't he something? He looks a lot like his father, who moved to the island to be near us, though we are not a couple. It's complicated. He's pretty shocked about the way I gave birth, but he can't say anything against it, since he has a healthy son.

Maybe I'll tell you about Marc one day. Or maybe you have no interest in hearing about my life. I have to believe you do because you are still with me, all the time, every day, in my heart, in my breath, wherever and however I travel. I know I will always have a debt to pay but you were with me when I gave birth. You held my hand the whole way through. You gave me strength.

Hey, I never thought I'd become a mother at 42, how about that? I never wanted to have a baby, until recently. I probably didn't feel I deserved to be a mother.

But anyhow, I wanted you to have this picture because I know you will be pleased to know his name. It's Kit.
Namaste,

Susannah.

Ps. Jonas still comes. Though farther out. Not close like the first few times.

I try to swallow. So, the boy in the red rain boots is not Susannah's dead son because she didn't lie to me about that—she did become a mother for the first time in her forties. Who is this boy then? And why did my mother send these letters back? It is still not clear what Susannah could have done to my mother that was so unforgivable.

Among the papers scattered in front of me I see the little face again. A square color-saturated picture; this child is haunting me now. I reach out and pick it up. The familiar face peers up at me. He even has a dimple on his chin, like Finn.

Most of the other papers spread on the cushion are old newspaper clippings. I scrape them up. I'll take them back to England and go through them properly, when I'm calm and can get my head around all this. It's definitely getting lighter. Surely we can go very soon. But as I scoop them one yellowed headline catches my eye: *Chasing Whales.*

I pick it up.

> Dr. Jonas Halmstrom, 36, photographer, conservationist, and renowned orca specialist, was out with his family on a small craft in remote waters near his island home when the accident occurred on May 6. The family was monitoring a newly discovered resident orca pod—when a storm blew in unexpectedly. Tragically, both Halmstrom and his 16-month-old son, Kit, were washed overboard. Rescue crews have been unable to find the bodies. Halmstrom is survived by his wife, Elena, and their newborn baby daughter, Kali.

For a second, my mind goes blank. I close my eyes. The float house sways beneath me.

Then the names begin to roll through my brain—Halmstrom. Jonas. Elena. Kit. Kali. I force my eyes open. I try to read the cutting again, but the words skip and bounce. I put it down. I am shaking all over. There is a metallic taste at the back of my throat. I pick up the next clipping but I can only read bits and pieces.

> "Orca expert Jonas Halmstrom and son drowned in British Columbia."

I scrabble through the papers, pulling them out one by one— there must be ten clippings. I skim them all.

. . . Jonas Halmstrom . . . Kit . . . whale research . . . tragic death . . . storm . . .

Survived by . . . Elena . . . Kali.

Jonas Halmstrom and son . . . drowned . . . tragic accident . . . survived by . . . survived by.

Survived By.

British Columbia, Spring, 1978

They woke to the sound of the sky crashing in. It seemed as if the stars were falling, blowing holes in the ground.

"You hear that?" He was out of his sleeping bag already, pulling on his boots. His tawny hair stuck up all over the place and his voice was gruff.

Elena sat up, too, and fumbled to unzip the sleeping bag. The embers were still smoldering and everything smelled of damp wood smoke and misted cedars. Kali whimpered, just once, next to her.

"Can you get them up?" He zipped his fleece, shoved a hat on his head, rubbed his beard, then the rest of his face with one hand. "I'll take the packs down—I have everything right here."

She shifted across and prodded Susannah's back. "Susannah, wake up." Then she went and knelt by Kit. Two more exhalations echoed across the bay behind the camp. Her little boy lay curled on his side in his sleeping bag, his hair sprouting from the top.

"Sweetheart—wake up."

He opened his eyes and sat up, instantly wide-awake. His hair was static and she smoothed it down. "Some whales are here—you want to come see them on the boat?"

She helped him out of his sleeping bag, stood him up, and tugged a fleece over his head; he wobbled, but didn't complain. Then she put his waterproof suit over the fleece, zipping it up to his chin. He was used to the routine, trying to help her by lifting a leg, balancing, putting each hand up for a mitten. Kali whimpered from her nest over by the fire. She kissed his head "Good boy." There was no time to feed the baby. She just had to hope that she'd stay asleep in the sling for as long as possible.

"Susannah—you awake? Wake up, Susannah." Susannah didn't move.

Jonas was striding off already into the murky dawn, carrying all the gear. She watched the mist swallow him. Another respiration echoed through the camp, bouncing off the wall of pines: they have come right into the bay. Elena scrambled around finding boots, her fleece, a hat. "Susannah? You coming?"

Susannah hauled herself up. "Shit." Her eyes were puffy and small. "What time is it?"

"Almost dawn—we can hear them just out in the bay. Jonas's getting the boat ready. You want to come out with us?"

She hoped Susannah would grunt and turn over, but no—she unzipped her sleeping bag and stood up. She was fully dressed in jeans and a thick, Scandinavian sweater. She turned to Kit and said something that made him giggle, then shoved her boots on. Elena bent to get the papoose.

Susannah really was quite stoic and helpful. But never—ever—again would they do this, all three of them together with the babies on the boat. The past few days had been hell. Susannah had occasionally tried to engage with Jonas, but there was a lack of sincerity in her voice and a quiet hostility behind everything she said. In return, he treated her like an outsider. If he was forced to address her, he did so in monosyllables. He'd been moody the entire trip— growling instructions, and taking off on his own to find firewood or spear a fish for dinner, or just stand on a rock and scan the waters with his binoculars. This trip had been a big mistake. Never again.

She picked up Kali as smoothly as she could and put her into the papoose. The whimper didn't turn into a cry—she stayed curled and solid and warm. Elena shoved her own feet, unsteadily, into her boots, then stretched her fleece and zipped it right around the papoose, sealing Kali deeper into her body warmth.

"Come on!" His voice echoed over the rocks.

Elena picked up the bag of blankets and held out her other hand to Kit. "Come on, honey, let's go!" He folded his small hand in hers and then ran ahead, tugging her forward.

Susannah was bending down to get a scarf.

"Hey, Susannah," she called over her shoulder. "The life jackets are right there by your sleeping bag—can you grab them?"

Their feet crunched over needles and dust. A freezing mist hung above the water. They couldn't see the whales; they must be heading back out to sea already. Susannah caught up with big strides. Littleneck clams crackled underfoot as they scrambled over the rocks to the Zodiac, "You okay?" "I've got you." "Don't slip, okay?"

She could see that the waves were tall beyond the line of rocks. They climbed aboard: Susannah first, Elena holding Kit's hand forward and passing him to Susannah, who lifted him into the boat. Jonas switched on the engine and its roar echoed off the forested mountain slopes behind them. He had his back to her so she couldn't see his expression but she knew it would be fixed and impatient, as if Susannah was single-handedly slowing them all down, which was not true.

Her knees felt shaky as the boat began to move, so she sat down, hoping the bump of the Zodiac would be enough to keep Kali asleep. There was quite a wind. As the boat began to bump over the waves, Susannah stood up to grab a bag that wasn't secured. Jonas sensed her movement. "Sit down," he growled, without even turning his head.

Elena looked up at Susannah. She was staring at the fiberglass floor. Her face was very pale. Her green hat was pulled low and her eyes were down. Slowly, she folded her hands on her lap.

Thank God this was the last day. Tonight they'd be back at the float house and Susannah would be heading south again. She could not wait to be curled around Jonas, back in their warm bed on the float house, body to body with the sounds of the sea filtering up through the hydrophone, their babies sleeping safely next to them, the woodstove roaring below—and no Susannah.

She wondered if the cedar planks had arrived—if so, they could make a start this week on building the woodshed. She knew Jonas's mood would improve dramatically the moment Susannah left.

It wasn't until they were halfway across the bay that she realized Susannah hadn't brought the life jackets.

"No," he stared straight ahead. "If I turn us around they'll be gone." She knew from his voice that he'd never turn the boat around, not even if she got on her knees and begged.

She looked down at Kit's upturned face, lit up by the excitement of waking, and being on the boat already with whales so close up ahead. She made herself smile at him and he beamed back. His hat had slipped, almost covering his brown eyes, and she reached out to adjust it so he could see better. Then she put her arm around his shoulders.

"Can you see them? Right over there?" She made herself sound excited rather than anxious. She pointed at the fins cutting through the water just ahead of the boat. She forced herself not to be annoyed with Susannah. It really wasn't Susannah's fault. Maybe she didn't hear. The boat bumped over rising waves, stern pointed toward the whales. They weren't far off now. She counted nine or ten dorsals— one far smaller than the others. She didn't recognize them, but the visibility wasn't great, and she didn't have her binoculars—Jonas had his though.

"Who is it?" she called. "Can you see?"

"I think it's A5." He turned and their eyes met. She saw the tension in his face. He knew, as well as she did, that they should not be out here without the life jackets.

Her breasts ached as the baby pressed on them. She would need feeding, and soon. But looking at the waves, feeding on the boat just wasn't going to be feasible. Certainly not without life vests. She should force him take them all back. He could come back out and do this alone—but, of course, he'd almost certainly miss them if she made him turn back now. She couldn't face a fight, not this early. And Kit would be so disappointed. It was fine. Zodiacs were unsinkable— that was the point in them. And, anyway, they could get out and back before the storm hit.

Susannah had lifted her gaze and was staring at the horizon, now, with a stiff back. Her face was puffy and her eyes were slits

Her nose was red. She was obviously angry. For a moment, it struck her how strange it was to have this furious woman on their boat. In some ways, they hardly knew each other. There were those six months in California but all that felt like a lifetime ago. There had been intermittent visits in the two years since—all powered by Susannah. Letters, packages. Knitted baby blankets. And of course those anxious few days searching for the float house. But the truth was they didn't have much in common—and never had. Not this, certainly: wilderness, whales, babies, float houses. Susannah didn't belong here. They all knew it. This was the last time.

Jonas steered the Zodiac beyond the coast, following the whales into the open sea. The wind picked up dramatically outside the shelter of the bay. It thumped the sides of their heads and made the inflatable boat bump and teeter. But the mist was lifting and she could see the fins ahead, oiled by the sea, and the blows shooting up in plumes. She glanced at Jonas again. This was the moment when they'd exchange a glance— share the thrill. But he didn't turn his head. She knew why.

Suddenly a big male surfaced just twenty or so feet off—Jonas cut the engine and reached for the camera. He started taking pictures.

Something wasn't right about the wind. The sky, visible now through the clearing mist, was too dark. It wasn't a question of if, but when the storm would close around them.

The other orcas milled in the water ahead of the boat. She couldn't get to her camera in the pack by Jonas's feet, because she couldn't let go of Kit. And anyway, if she started to fiddle around with equipment Kali would wake up and start yelling. She longed for the hydrophone, but with two babies and a storm coming, that would never have been feasible. Anyway, judging from the color of the sky, they couldn't be out here for long.

The big male surfaced again—she'd know that enormous dorsal, with its propeller nick, anywhere, even without binoculars. It was definitely A5.

Jonas had that look of concentrated adrenaline as he shot another roll of film. Nothing else mattered to him right now: he focused and clicked, again and again. This obsession was what she'd always loved about him; it was untouchable, unchangeable—a certainty. As she watched him squint through the lens, she felt suddenly jealous. She'd been like that too, before the babies. But motherhood had changed her in a way that fatherhood hadn't changed him. She wasn't fearless anymore.

Her stomach clenched as a bigger wave lifted the boat up— suspended it for a second before the stern thumped back down. She tightened her arm around Kit's back as he was craning his neck to see behind him, watching over the side of the boat for the next whale to surface. His chubby little legs weren't even long enough to reach the edge of the seat but she recognized the look on his face—the absolute intensity.

"Look at that sky." Susannah's voice was hoarse and dry. "Are you sure this is a good idea?"

"I know. We won't stay out long."

She counted them all—she knew each whale by name—the matriarch with her daughter, and her two big grandsons—the biggest male with his propeller wound and his sister—and then, yes, it really was: Elena half stood up—a new calf! Tucked right next its mother.

"Tlinglit had a baby!"

Jonas had the camera up to his face, pointed at the baby. She turned to Susannah. "Hey—see the calf, right there? It's new. It's a brand new baby!"

But Susannah was still squinting at the sky.

Then Elena turned, too, and she saw the low and heavy clouds and the waves rising to meet them. The wind wailed across the water at them, throwing surf in their faces and another big wave hit, and the Zodiac tilted again. She tightened her arm round Kit's sturdy little body; the other around Kali in the sling. The pit of her stomach felt empty and cold.

"Jonas," she shouted over the wind, "we have to go back."

He glanced back at her. "You have to be kidding me—you know what this is."

"I don't care. We have no life vests and this storm is coming too fast."

But he didn't look at the sky behind her—he fixed his camera on the new calf again. Tlinglit surfaced so close to the boat that every mark on her glossy skin was visible and her little baby followed, as if glued to her side. Elena wondered if she was warning them away from the baby. Kit had both hands on the edge of the boat, craning to see over. Behind him, the dark sky closed in. She held Kit tight, and shouted at Jonas's back. "We have to turn around. Now!"

He didn't even lower his camera.

"Jonas," she shouted over the wind, "look what's coming at us for Chrissake!" He glanced up and she pointed at the horizon. It was closing in, much too fast.

But he went back to his viewfinder. "One minute."

"We have no life vests!"

He focused on the pod.

"Jonas. Turn the damned boat around!"

He didn't. So she stood up. "Go sit with Susannah." She lifted Kit off the seat with her one arm and held him out at Susannah. "Hold onto him—hold him tight," she said, as Susannah took him. "Don't let go of him—don't let go."

She shoved past Jonas, who wobbled, almost dropping his camera. Purple clouds swarmed.

"For fuck's sake Elena."

She grabbed the wheel. If he wouldn't bring their children back to safety, then she damned well would.

"Elena," he boomed at the back of her head. "Jesus fucking Christ."

She turned on the engine. "I'm taking us back."

"The fuck you are!"

She felt his hand on her arm.

CHAPTER SEVENTEEN

I need to get away. I ease Finn onto the sofa and scrape everything into my bag. I can't be here. We have to get out of here. I need to get us home.

I can't think about what I just read.

Survived by . . .

I just need to go home.

I look at Finn. If I wake him, he might cry—and then he'll wake her. I can't have her back down here when I'm trying to get away. But I have to be prepared. We might have to walk for a while out there. I don't know how far away the nearest house is. And what if we get lost? I need supplies from the kitchen—food and drink and diapers.

I tuck the parka over my sleeping boy. Then I tiptoe to the bottom of the stairs, and I listen. Nothing. Just the creak of the float house and the slap of waves. I wait for a moment or two more. I'm reluctant to leave Finn alone on the sofa, in case the creatures that are living in the walls of this house come out and crawl on him. Crawl on my bag. Crawl on the red file. Shred everything with their needle teeth. But I need to know that she's sleeping if I'm going to leave him on the sofa and go into the kitchen.

I take a few steps farther up the twisting staircase. Each step creaks. It is dark. I pause. There is no sound in the bedroom. I get to the top of the stairs, half expecting her to be there, looming out of the darkness. But the doorway is empty. The room is shadowy and paneled. It smells of rotten wood and sea and birds' nests. There is a peaked ceiling and a big bed beneath it. It is bitterly cold up here. As my eyes adjust, I can make out a hunched shape in the bed. There is no movement. I watch the shape, and listen with every fiber in my body. Another gust of wind hits the house and the window-panes rattle. The sea sucks at the rocks and the house sways. She does not move or twitch. She has to be asleep.

I creep as silently as possible back down the stairs.

Finn is face down, as I left him, wrapped snugly in the parka. He's fine. I go back over to the bottom of the stairs again, and listen once more. I'll hear her, anyway, if she comes down those creaking stairs while I'm in the kitchen.

A beige light is seeping in through the kitchen windows and I don't need the flashlight to see the decay; weeds worm through the window frames. There are flecks of peeled paint on the floor. The gingham curtains have been shredded by some animal.

I dig around in the bags of food, finding the bottle of water and taking great gulps of it, wiping my mouth with the back of my hand. I realize I am famished. I grab some bread rolls and a couple of cereal bars and, using the bottled water, I rinse Finn's duck cup, then fill it with milk. Somewhere in the forest, not too far off, something howls. I tear open a cereal bar and bite into it, swallowing the sweetness, gulping water between bites.

Then, I hurry back into the living room.

And I stop.

Susannah is standing with her back to the stove. She is holding Finn. I drop the food with a thud. "What are you doing?" I swallow. I march toward her. "Give him to me."

Finn's face is bleary—she has woken him by picking him up—but he isn't crying. He holds out his arms to me but before I can take him, she swoops him around and away from me. She has my bag, too, strapped across her body, it flaps as she turns and I glimpse the red file inside.

"What are you doing?" I say again. "Stop!"

Finn opens his mouth "Mama!" He struggles against her, squirming to get to me. "Mama!"

"Give him to me, Susannah." Trying not to scare Finn, I keep my voice as even as possible. "Give him to me right now." If I try to grab him there might be a struggle and I can't do that to him. I can't try to wrench him out of her arms. He could get hurt. And it will terrify him. "I'll take him okay, Susannah? Then we'll talk about it. Okay?"

She looks at me oddly, her head cocked. "His father needs to see him now."

"Yes. That's right. That's exactly where he's going, that's where I'm taking him now. His father is in England. His father is Doug."

She scowls.

"Susannah. Please give him to me and we'll talk. I promise. Just give Finn to me now."

"Talk?" she says, lifting her chin high, her strong arms pinning Finn to her body so he can't reach me. He starts to cry. His eyes are frightened and wide. "What do you want to talk about?"

"Nothing." I step toward her. "He's crying, Susannah. You're hurting him."

"Don't move," she growls. "Stay."

"You're confused." I step toward them again. "Just give him to me then we can talk. You can tell me what happened. You can tell me everything that happened. Okay? You can tell me everything."

She steps backward. "Do we really have go over all this again, Elle? Do we? We do? Okay. Fine! Your face was turning blue. I mean, what would you have done? Tell me that? What would you have done? You told him to turn the boat around. The storm was coming so fast. It was madness to be out there, the two of you yelling, and with the babies on board—Kali strapped to your chest for Chrissake—and those whales milling around, too close to the boat—the wind was picking up. It was fucking madness, Elena! Total fucking madness!"

I take another step closer but she raises herself up, pulling Finn to one side, away from me. "He was going to kill you, Elle. He had his hands on you . . . I had to do something."

"Yes." I try to sound soothing. "I know. Of course you did." I step closer. "Now, give him to me, and we can talk about it properly."

"No." Her eyes don't leave my face. "I have to show Jonas that he's back. You told me to."

"I really didn't."

"Mamaaa?" Finn struggles to hold out his arms, but she pins them back down. "Mamaaaa?"

"It's okay, love," I say. "It's okay. I'm here."

"No," Susannah snaps, pulling him further away from me. My bag slaps against her thigh, a flash of red. Finn wails, "Mamaaaa!"

"We were all going to drown out there!" she shouts. "He was attacking you, and the baby too. He was going to crush her against you. He was going to kill you both. I've seen that before, don't forget! I know what it's like."

"That baby was me, Susannah. It was me: Kali. I'm Kali. I'm not Elena. You're confused. You're mixing things up. Now just let me hold Finn, okay?"

"The oar was right there, what would you have done?" She looks at me, head on one side, as if posing a metaphysical question. "Just tell me that, Elena, what would *you* have done?"

"You did the right thing." I edge closer, nodding. "The only thing you could have done. Absolutely, definitely the right thing."

"Maaamaaaa," fat tears roll down Finn's cheeks. I reach for him again, but she whips him away. His hands jerk up and down and he looks startled, then wails with fear.

"I just didn't see Kit, I didn't know he'd gotten behind Jonas—I didn't—he was just too small. You have to believe me, Elena. I had to do something. You would have done the same thing for me. Wouldn't you?"

I step forward again. "Yes of course I would," I say. "Of course. It's okay, Susannah. I completely forgive you. You did the right thing. You really did. Just give me the baby now, okay?"

Finn reaches his hands out to me, sobbing. His tears leave pale streaks on his cheeks.

I lurch forward for him, but she swoops him away again and across to the sofa. "That wave came right up over us, do you remember? For a moment I thought it was that big bull, flipping the boat." One of the hands that is holding Finn flies to her head again and she slaps her temple. "I can't live with these images in my head," she shakes her head. "I think about ending all this—you must too. Don't you?" her face brightens for a moment, as if this is a brilliant plan. "Don't you think we should just end this?"

"No." I edge toward her again. "No, not really, Susannah, I don't think that's a good idea at all. I think you need to give me Finn, give me the baby, and we'll sit down and we'll talk about all this and it will all be okay. I promise. Susannah, you need help. It's okay. I want to help you. Just give me my baby."

"What I need," she smiles, "is to keep this child safe. I know what you're trying to do. I am not going to let anything happen to him this time. I am *not*. And I need to show Jonas that Kit is back and I am forgiven—he needs to see Kit." She shoves my bag back, swishing Finn, too roughly. He wails again.

"This isn't Kit," I wail. "It's not Kit! This baby is Finn—mine, my son. Not Elena's. And Jonas is dead. Susannah, try to think, okay? Think hard. I know you'll know this, if you'll just think. Please. Give him to me."

She looks confused, and for a second I think I've gotten through to her. "You're not Elena . . ." she falters. "But wait. If you're not . . . then . . . she's . . . Oh! I know now. She's here too . . . She'll be coming . . . she'll be out there! They're both out there. They're waiting for him!"

"Susannah. You have to stop this right now. None of this is real. Elena isn't out there. She's *dead*. The whales aren't dead people. That's all got twisted up in your head. This little boy is my baby—he's Finn—and you need to give him back to me right now. He'll be safe with me," I slide closer. I can almost reach him now. "I love him. He'll be totally safe with me, okay?" I hold out my arms, as unthreateningly as I can, and seeing them, Finn launches himself at me again.

But her face twists, and she wheels him away, out of my reach—he lets out a high-pitched shriek. He kicks and writhes and I see her big, hard, dirty fingers, digging into his leg. I throw myself at him. She thrusts out one arm and whacks me square in the chest so that I stagger backward. My spine crashes against the stove. Finn's howls bounce off the wooden walls.

"Stop!" I stagger to my feet, hurling myself back across the room. But she bats me off again with one muscular arm.

My body crashes into a side table this time. It collapses under me into soft slivers. As I scramble to my feet the floorboard gives and one leg plunges downward. I throw my weight in the other direction, yank my foot back and then haul myself away from the hole in the float house floor. Finn's cries are traveling away from me.

I see her disappear through the kitchen doorway—I glimpse his terrified, tear-stained face over her shoulder, mouth open, unable even to scream, his star-shaped hands bumping with each step. Her wasp clasp is loose and her wild hair streams behind her, my bag flaps on her thigh—then she vanishes.

I hurtle across the rotten floor but she's out the door already. I wrench it open and burst after her, into the gray dawn. Freezing mist hits the back of my throat and I gasp—but there she is, running, up ahead. I can just see her through the mist with Finn jolting against her shoulder and his screams echoing through the ghostly pines.

I leap from the float house onto dry land and sprint across the stony ground after them. She is scrambling over rocks up ahead, using one arm to steady herself. Her legs are strong and fast; she is a blurry shape, but I will catch her. My body powers me along faster than I've ever moved in my life, and then I'm in the air as if I've taken off and I am going to fly to Finn—as if I have unfurled vast maternal wings—but I'm falling, coming down, and stones slam into my torso, jolting my teeth inside my skull.

For a second, everything rings and I open my mouth but nothing comes out, no breath will go in or out of my lungs. Then I give a terrific gasp. I am on my front, with stones in my face, spitting gravel and twigs. Finn's cries are further ahead, muffled by the crash of the waves and by the mist. I get up, stagger a few steps—my right leg doesn't seem to work properly—but it has to—it has to—and despite it, I start to run again.

I claw my way to the top of the rock. I am above a white beach, a tiny beach and I can hear Finn, somewhere close by—down there, beneath the ledge of rock below me—but I can't see him. I bend my knees to leap down onto the beach and something hits the back of my head. Everything goes black.

I am swimming. It is so cold, this water, and I am so tired. I can't keep swimming under this freezing water. I have to open my eyes and come up to the surface. I have to breathe.

Stone-shapes—an eyeball, a teardrop, a heart. Something flexes in the background through a shroud of white. Out of the corner of one eye I can see the fur of the parka hood, flickering. I must lift my head. I must get up. My cheekbone hits down hard, and I'm swimming again beneath the surface.

Then I hear her voice, sharp and clear, next to my ear. Open your eyes Kali. Get up. Get up now. Run.

The shingle grinds into my knee bones, stones icy and smooth under my palms. My head is ringing, singing, like the high wind. I sway, hands in stones. But her voice is very clear and firm in my ear. Get up she says. Run.

And I'm up. Something is pressing on the back of my head. I touch it with my fingertips. Then I remember what's happening and where I am.

I open my mouth and I bellow, not a word but a continuous, prehistoric sound that rattles around my skull.

Then I see them. They aren't far away—gray shapes on the rocks—there is a boat and she climbing onto it and I can see him on her shoulder; I can hear his cries.

I scrabble back up the rock, slithering and scratching to the top, and I hurtle toward them through salty mist. My head sings—something in my leg is very wrong but I move it anyway—the bad sensation is far off, irrelevant, a hypothesis of pain—I gasp for air and power toward them.

Pain jolts through me but it doesn't matter. Seagulls wheel overhead, ghostly shapes in the mist. I see her look around, gripping Finn with one arm as she unhooks a rope from a tow post. Her face is grim and her hair flies like snakes.

"Get off of him!" I roar. "Stop!"

My feet hardly touch the ground but the boat engine snarls and it is moving away now—she is in, and driving Finn away from me. It is a small boat, with ropes around the side, and a little cabin and the engine is loud. She is pointing the boat out across the bay, pinning my screaming baby to her side with one arm and steering with the other.

I think about plunging into the freezing sea but I know I won't catch them, not like this. The boat is moving too fast. Somewhere above the engine I can still hear him desperately howling for me.

And I turn. I run again—back over the rocks, aware that my leg is wrong, but that it means nothing. Over the stony path where I fell—I am running through the undergrowth now, jumping over roots and boulders, ducking around the back of the float house in darkness, plants slashing my face and torso. I don't know how I know where to go—I just do. It's instinct that propels me and I am among the trees, dense trunks, the stink of pine needles, and the sea, and the distant rumble of the engine out there in the bay—and I'm pushing past trunks, dodging sharp rocks; my muscles burn but I keep going. I see a crouching animal, fur, yellow eyes—I leap past it—and I am out—on rocks again, above the water. Icy rocks. Mist hangs low. I scrabble to the flat top of the rock—my hands and feet move deftly.

I crouch there, sucking in the freezing mist. My lungs are on fire. There's a drop of about fifteen feet to the water—I see rocks beneath the surface. And I can see the boat approaching, shrouded in mist. It is almost level with me already, passing though the neck of the bay out to the open sea. Susannah is looking straight ahead. She doesn't see me, maybe the mist hides me, or maybe she thinks

I'm back on the beach still. Finn is struggling and howling—she has him wedged against her flank with one arm. As the boat gets closer, I know that there is only one thing left to do.

I kick off my boots and tear off the parka and Doug's too-heavy sweater, hurling them one on top of the other on the rock.

And I leap.

Suspended in midair, I know that if I have misjudged this I will impale myself on the rocks. The shock bites into my flesh, the cold burns; the salt stings, filling my eyes and mouth and nose, pouring down my throat, into my ears. For a moment I am far below the surface, kicking inside a block of ice; I feel the vast frozen body of water over my head, pressing into my eardrums, biting at my skin, clamping at my muscles like teeth, but my feet hit rock and I thrust off it, pushing myself up to the surface with the one leg that seems to work best, and I am out—gasping for air, tossed on a huge wave, then under again, blinded, another lungful of brine. Back up again—back up—choking—a great gasp of air—the boat is right here—just an arm's length away. It is moving too fast. I can't. My limbs are frozen. I can't get it. But I have to.

With every cell in my body I power myself toward the hull and, miraculously I feel the side of the boat—slippery under my palms. If I can't hold on then the next bit of the boat to hit me will be its propeller; my fingers close over the rough rope that runs around the flank. For a moment, I am towed along, swallowing water, gagging, gasping, my legs trailing behind me, gripping the rope with both hands—my arms are wrenched from their sockets, every muscle and sinew is stretched tight. But I hear Finn's cries above the motor and it's like his voice pulls me out of the water—somehow I haul myself up and dive, headfirst, over the side.

I stagger to my feet, bracing myself against the bump of the boat, water pouring off me. My skin is on fire, my head feels tight as if my skull is about to crack open and spew its contents onto the deck.

She is standing at the wheel in a covered area just a few feet away from me. The engine is so loud, but Finn spots me over her shoulder and his tear-stained face collapses. He holds out his arms to me, his little fingers splayed. It takes all my willpower not to move or speak. I can't fight her for him. She'll kill us both.

"It's okay," I mouth at Finn. "It's okay."

"Mama!" he opens his mouth. "Maaaaamaaaa!"

The wind and waves and the sound of the engine roar below his screams, and she still doesn't know I'm here. It is as if she is in a trance. I stare at her broad back in the brown fleece. I have to think fast. I have to act. I look around for something—anything. And then time seems to slow. The colors of the world turn up, all noise quiets, my vision becomes sharper, clearer; nothing hurts now, I don't even feel cold: there is a small cabin to her left. I can see down into it—a few steps to a bed and a sort of sofa. My bag on the floor, the red file spilling out. I could try to shove her in there, lock her in. But I can't risk trying to wrench Finn out of her arms. She's stronger than me. At any moment she will sense me and turn around.

I spot a metal pole, lying along the side of the boat. It has a hook on the end. I swoop to it. It is not heavy and it is hard to make my fingers tighten on the freezing metal but I see her begin to turn and with all my remaining strength I sweep the pole at her ankles and jerk it, sideways.

She topples. I drop the pole—it clangs down—and I throw myself at Finn, wrenching him from her one arm and shoving at her with the other. He comes to me easily—her hands instinctively fly out as her body crashes sideways, and he hurls himself toward me. I see her head bounce, just once, on the fiberglass hull.

Finn's arms whip around my neck. I pin him to me with both arms. "I've got you. I've got you."

Nobody is steering the boat now and it veers to the right over a big wave. I'm above Susannah, with Finn clinging to me so tight that I hardly need to touch him to keep him there, but I do, I hang onto him.

He is silent, perhaps in shock, locked onto my soaked torso. I suck in air, everything inside me is pulsing, throbbing, ready to protect him. Her head is on the floor, resting on one arm. She lifts it, halfway up.

I put a foot on her neck, then, and firmly, but not violently, I press down.

"Don't." The sound of my own voice surprises me. It is deep and loud and threatening. "If you get up I will kill you. I will kill you, Susannah. This is over. You hear me? This is OVER."

The boat is still motoring through the waves, wildly off course now, careening toward the rocky coastline.

I take my foot off her neck and seize the steering wheel with one arm, wrenching it around so that we are pointing out to sea again. Then, not knowing what else to do, I see the keys and turn the ignition off.

The engine cuts. Suddenly there is eerie silence. Just the bump of waves. Sea mist creeps around us. I am shaking so hard that my teeth clatter against each other. I hold onto Finn but I can't keep my arms from jerking. Water drips from my body. I stare down at Susannah. I have no idea what to do. She doesn't move. She lies with her head on her arm. Then I realize that I am no longer scared of her.

"Susannah," I say, "are you okay?"

Her legs crunch up suddenly, into a fetal position. Her massed gray hair covers her cheek.

And then I hear a new rumbling noise. For a moment, I think it's the boat engine, and I've failed to switch it off, but then I see it, over to the left, through the mist: Sven's fishing boat.

I wave one arm. "Here!" I shout. "Help!"

Dawn is breaking through the bruised and misty sky, Susannah is curled at my feet, and Sven is coming. And my baby is safe.

*

As his boat draws alongside ours, I see that there is someone else in the cabin, a crouched figure in a blue woolen hat. He cuts his engine and Ana stands up.

"You a'right?" Ana climbs aboard. I nod, but my body is shaking so violently. "Baby okay?" I can't speak because my jaws are clattering together. I realize that my leg hurts, quite badly.

Finn points "Boat!" he says as if Sven's boat is the first one he's noticed today.

"Yes, love." I squeeze his solid little body and for a moment I feel as if he is holding me up, not the other way around.

"Big boat!" he says.

The pain in my leg is extraordinary, as if there is something burrowing inside the bone. I stand on the good leg, which quakes. The back of my head throbs.

"Susannah." Ana kneels at her side. She calls to Sven, "Blankets!" She points at me.

Susannah still doesn't move but she is breathing.

Ana and I both look at Finn.

She does not seem to require an explanation.

"Down," Finn wriggles. I make myself put him down but I hang on tight to his hand. He looks up at me. "Carry 'oo?" he suggests. I pick him up again.

Sven clambers over into Susannah's boat. He drops a blanket over my shoulders. "Get dry, fast," he mutters. "Hypothermia." My teeth are comedy chattering. I wrap the blanket tightly around us. "Go on into the cabin," he nods at his boat. "There's clothes in there. Get out of those wet things. Fast."

Then he kneels next to Ana. They exchange some mumbled words.

"Susannah," I hear Ana say briskly, "you have to get up now."

Susannah heaves herself off her side and I tell myself it's okay because Sven is here, and Ana. But I still don't trust her. I don't take my eyes off her. My teeth are still chattering insanely. Beneath the blanket my freezing clothes are plastered to my body.

Now Susannah is face down with her legs tucked under her, and arms splayed in front, in a child's yoga pose, but her head is at an odd angle, with her face turned away.

Her hair tangles on her shoulders and across her cheek. I notice her wasp hair clasp is next to my foot. I kick it, hard, and it skids across the deck, through the railings, and into the sea. Her spine is curved like a turtle's shell.

Ana is saying something to her, but I can't hear what. She is bent over and her hands are on Susannah's shoulders. The boat rises and falls with the waves. Sven must have anchored, and I can see that our two boats are lashed together, now, with big ropes.

"Susannah," Ana says quite sharply, "get yourself up."

But she doesn't move. Ana reaches down to her wrist and feels for a pulse. There is something about the movement that makes me think Ana might once have been a nurse. My body feels weak and the pain in my leg is intensifying. So is the solid ache on the back of my head. I need to change into dry clothes and get Finn into the warm boat.

"Silly girl," Ana murmurs. "Silly girl."

"Ana?" I say, quietly. "Is she injured?"

"She'll be a'right," Ana says without turning around. She scrapes Susannah's hair off her face. "There, now."

Susannah suddenly kneels up. Her mouth is slack and she looks like an old woman who has taken her teeth out. A hissing sound comes out of her dry lips.

"Let's get you up then," says Ana. "Good girl."

Sven hauls Susannah off the floor by her armpits and she stands at last, her head and shoulders sunk like a rag doll. Her breathing is labored.

Behind her, down the stairs in the cabin, I see my bag lying half open on the floor—it contains my wallet, our passports, the photos, the red file. Susannah must have taken it out of some confused urge to remove evidence, even though the clippings are not proof of anything, really, except an unspeakable loss.

*

We huddle in the cabin of Sven's boat, opposite Susannah, who sits with her head almost between her knees. She doesn't raise it to look at me. Ana is next to her and Sven is at the wheel, steering us toward Raven Bay. Every now and then, Ana reaches out a dry hand and pulls the blanket up on Susannah's hunched shoulders.

I have peeled off my wet things and I am wearing a pair of Sven's overalls, which are about ten times too big and smell faintly of fish, a huge T-shirt and fleece under them and the blanket over the top of it all. Finn is curled inside the blanket with me, sucking his thumb and pointing, every now and then, at objects, as if he will control the world by naming things. He has never said so many words. It is fascinating, and disturbing at the same time.

"Cup," he says.

And I say "That's right, cup."

Then after a few moments. "Boot."

"Yes, boot."

Finally, he points to Susannah. But he can't think of the word.

I hug him to me. "It's okay, love. It's okay now. I've got you."

The boat bumps onward toward Raven Bay. I wonder if he will be permanently damaged by this experience. He seems calm, but he has been through so much in the last twenty-four hours.

Then I wonder if plunging into sub-zero water can damage an unborn child.

Sven's boat bumps on. I can't move my leg, which is planted inside Sven's enormous Wellington boot. I looked down at it when I changed out of my wet things, and there was blood, and the flesh was pink and raw and open. I will deal with it when we get to Raven Bay. But it hurts badly now and whenever the rubber shaft of the boot presses against it, the pain is searing. I ease my leg gingerly out of Sven's boot and rest it on top of my bag.

I cannot think about what Susannah would have done out there on the ocean with my baby. I cannot allow myself to think about what could have happened if adrenaline hadn't propelled me up the coastline and then off that rock.

I can't think about the contents of the red file. Not yet. But I do know that this is the story that has been crouching in the shadows as I poked and pried and questioned my way through the past few days. In fact, this is the story that's been lurking inside me for my whole life.

That little boy with his dense bangs and red rain boots looks like Finn because he is Finn's uncle. My brother. I had a brother.

I imagine a little boy bravely grabbing his daddy's leg as Susannah's oar smashes down. Jonas topples, Kit clings and the boat tilts, tipping everyone, the wave rising behind the two of them. There would have been a horrific moment when my mother knew what was going to happen—saw the wave and couldn't stop it—then it came over, and took them both, swallowed them.

His father is mine. My father is not my father. I had a brother, not much more than a year older than me—a brother who died.

Other things leap out at me. Harry Halmstrom. He really is my grandfather—and suddenly I understand what his words meant—Jonas was his son. Even through the fog of dementia, Harry Halmstrom knew that something was rotten about his son's death. "*He could swim like a fish.*" He just didn't know about Susannah. If I'm right about this, then Harry Halmstrom is my paternal grandfather.

And I had a brother. I had a brother who drowned because of something Susannah did almost forty years ago and she's been carrying the guilt and terror of that moment ever since. No wonder, when I arrived on her doorstep, she looked as if she'd seen a ghost. She had.

She is unwell. Dangerously so.

My poor mother.

But then again—she lied to me. My mother lied to me my whole life. How could she? So did my father. Both of them have lied to me about everything.

More and more thoughts roar through my head. I imagine my mother up here—out there—with Jonas on these unpredictable seas while my father—while Graham—sat heartbroken in California, cerebrally sketching out blueprints, studying in silent libraries. I remember Susannah saying he was a "fucking saint." She is right about that. He not only forgave my mother, he took her back and remained devoted to her for nearly forty years. He raised me as his own.

The foundations of my identity are crumbling. I am not the first-born. I'm my mother's middle child. I am not my father's biological child at all. I am something—someone—else entirely. My parents are liars. I have different blood in my veins, a different heritage. I am related to an old Swedish man with dementia. I had a brother, a brother who died.

I need to talk to Alice. Alice must know all this too. This will release her from something too. I need to talk to my sister. And to my father—oh my god, do I need to talk to him.

Sven's boat bumps on across the waves. Finn points and names. "Water." "Boat." I hold onto him and I don't want to think these thoughts, but I can't stop.

What on earth was my mother thinking taking a toddler and a baby—me—out on a boat on these dangerous seas to chase after killer whales with a storm coming in? She would never have forgiven herself. It must have eaten her away. It did eat her away.

The guilt has certainly been too much for Susannah. I look across at the matted crown of her head. This is a dreadful burden for anyone to carry. I am not surprised that Finn, with his red boots and his dimpled chin, triggered mayhem in her mind.

Through the mist I can see the flickering lights of Raven Bay. The boat bumps on. Sven mutters into his radio, and it crackles and someone barks back. Susannah doesn't move. She stares at the floor, catatonic, as if sleeping with her eyes open.

I squeeze Finn's warm body closer to mine and I wonder what nightmares my little boy will have of sea and boats and screaming—long after he has forgotten he was ever here.

But he is safe now. And we are going home.

CHAPTER EIGHTEEN

We must make an odd sight, the five of us coming up the quay, our breath mingling above our heads.

There is Ana, striding ahead with a slight stoop under an over-sized man's coat, her hat rammed tightly on her head. There is Sven, supporting Susannah, who is no longer upright, but slumped onto him like a drunkard with tangled hair and legs not quite moving straight. Then there is Finn, toddling along in his pajamas and fleece, holding my hand but bending to look at a rock, a lost pen, a fragment of paper, a stick; trying to pick things up, or poke them or bash them; pointing at buildings, the sky, a person, naming everything he can. And finally there is me, hopping beside him in absurdly large fisherman's clothing, and damp size fourteen Wellingtons. I am hopping, because every time my right foot touches the ground, pain ricochets up my body, bringing a wave of heat, then a chill, then nausea.

But I don't care. This pain doesn't matter. It's just an injury. It will heal.

Sven hauls Susannah down to the Guest House corridor and into Ana's kitchen. The house is so warm and smells of laundry and wood polish. He eases Susannah into a kitchen chair and she slumps, then leans slowly forward until her head rests on the pine tabletop. Her arms hang down like a puppet. Ana comes around and kneels next to her, saying something. Sven stands above them. His beard shines under the bright kitchen lights. He looks ridiculously calm.

I call to Ana that I need to use the phone and then, lifting Finn onto my hip, I go to the hall and dial Doug's cell. It clicks straight to voice mail. I leave a brief message, trying to keep my voice very even, saying everything is fine, and not to worry about a thing, I have Finn and we're going to try and get a flight home tonight. Then I call his office: the answering machine. He never even listens to that but I leave the same message. Then I call home and do the same. I hang up and dial Alice's cell.

"Oh my God—I'm about to go into a meeting, but do you have Finn?"

"Yes."

"Oh thank God. Where were they? The vacation house?" I can tell by the relief in her voice that she was far more worried than she'd let on in our phone call the day before.

"They were at the float house."

"The what?"

"The vacation house. Alice—"

"Christ, Kal. I actually didn't get much sleep last night after you called."

"Nor did I."

"Is Finn really okay? Are you okay? So what happened?"

"I've . . . it's been . . ." my voice wavers for a second. "Holy crap, Alice, I've found out all this stuff—this insane, mad stuff about who I am, and who Mom was. I can't . . . it's . . . I think Dad isn't my real father. He lied—they both did, all our lives, they've lied to us. It explains so much. I think I've just found out that my real father was a whale expert called Jonas Halmstrom. Also, my God, I think we had a brother. I think we had a brother who died up here when he was just a toddler—Mom lost a child—and him—Jonas he died too: they both drowned. Alice, I think Mom and Dad have lied to us our whole lives. She lived up here, and married this man, and had a little boy called Kit, and then me—and . . . Susannah . . . She . . ."

"Kal!" Alice shouts me down. "What the hell are you talking about?"

I take a long, deep breath. I don't blame her: if it were the other way around, I'd assume she was having a breakdown too. She's so used to being the rational one, but for once, I'm the one who has the overview. "Look. Don't worry. Okay? We can talk about everything when I get home. I've got so much to tell you, but I can't do it like this. All that matters is Finn is safe. We're fine."

"Did you just tell me that Dad isn't your biological father?"

"No. No—I don't think he is. Mom was married before, to a man called Jonas. And they had a child before me—they had a boy called Kit. I . . . Christ, Alice. I actually can't really get my head around this myself . . ."

"Right." I imagine her standing up, smoothing down her work skirt. "Okay. I'm getting on a plane. This is all . . . where are you now?"

"No! Don't you dare come out here. I'm back on Raven Island—where I called you from yesterday. I'm perfectly safe. Finn's safe. I haven't gone mad. And we're coming home—I'm going to go and get on the next plane I can. You have to call Doug, though—I've been trying but I can't get through to him. You have to get through to him and tell him Finn's safe, and we're coming home because he'll be panicking. Tell him I'm going straight to the airport the moment I can get off this island and I'm going to get the first flight home."

"You have to promise me you're okay. Promise?" I hear her phone muffle, and the faint "wait." I imagine her, in her suit, her blonde hair pulled back, holding a finger up to a minion—*one minute.*

"I really am. But Alice—my God this is mind-blowing stuff."

"You found out that Mom was married before?"

"Yes. The Halmstrom—it came from him—this man—Jonas. My . . ." but I can't say it.

"Okay. Look. You have to phone me when you know what plane you're on so I can tell Doug, okay? And phone me anyway, the minute you get to civilization. Just . . . how do you know this stuff, Kal? Where did you get this information from?"

"Susannah. Sort of. But it's all true—I know it's true because I've seen newspaper clippings with my name, and Mom's, and his, Jonas Halmstrom, and the little boy—my brother. It's real. I have all the evidence, Alice. I've got it all with me."

"Shit. Can you bring everything home?"

"Of course, I'm bringing it home."

"Shit Kal, I mean—*shit*."

"It's okay, Alice. It's all okay. I promise. I have to go. I'm really sorry I did this to you. I'm sorry I've worried you like this."

"I've worried about you my whole life," she says, shakily.

"Yes, well, you can stop now." I straighten up. "Okay?"

Finn tries to grab the cord of the phone, wriggling his weight forward, "Dat!" he reaches for it, and my foot hits the floor: white hot pain shoots up my leg. "Okay," I half shout. "I have to go."

"Kiss Finn for me. And call me the moment you get off that island."

"I might not have a signal . . ."

But she has already hung up.

Finn is struggling to be put down so I let him—but I keep a tight hold on his hand. He toddles busily toward the kitchen, then spots a big tabby cat sitting on a chair near the doorway.

"Cat!" he gasps. He rushes toward it. "Cat!"

"Be gentle," I say as he plunges both hands into the cat's fur. It leaps up and stalks away.

"Ca-at!" he calls, "Catty!"

Nobody has yet asked what happened up there. Perhaps they'd rather not know.

Sven is putting a steel kettle on the stove while Ana sits quietly next to Susannah.

The pain in my leg is overwhelming and I have to sit. I look down at Finn who is staring after the cat, as it walks, huffily, toward the back door. His legs are planted apart, and he sways, slightly.

"Are you hungry, love?" I ask him. "You must be so hungry. You need your breakfast don't you?" It seems completely lunatic to be here, in the kitchen with the woman who kidnapped and almost killed my child—and possibly me—talking about breakfast. I should be calling the police. I really should call the police.

Ana asks, quite politely, if Finn and I would like oatmeal.

"Yes. Thank you." I get up, taking Finn by the hand, and limping the long way around the table, toward Sven. There is a big black pan on the stove, and when he lifts the lid the warm, milky smell of porridge rises up.

"Maple syrup?" Sven looks down at Finn.

"Sven." I rest my free hand on his thick arm. He looks at me and his blue eyes are steady. I realize how much I owe him. If he hadn't risked his boat and taken me out there, Finn would have been alone with her all night. And the consequences of that are unthinkable. I owe this man everything.

"Thank you for coming back for us today. And for taking me out there last night. I know it was risky. But . . . thank you . . ." I realize that if I carry on talking, I'm going to cry—and neither of us would like that. Sven nods, then ladles the porridge into bowls.

It is a long table. I hobble back to the end furthest from Susannah, with Finn following. But I can see that she is not a threat anymore: she is broken, from the inside. She hasn't even lifted her head. I wonder if someone should call Maggie, or somebody else. What are they going to do with her now?

Finn climbs onto my lap, folds his fist around the spoon, and then begins to wolf down the porridge. I eat too, feeling the warmth spread through my belly, even though the pleasure is drowned somewhat by the pain that radiates through my lower leg. I lean over and gingerly roll up the leg of the jeans. There is a really big scrape—nasty red flesh, rather mangled, some white globules, some muck and darkness. It's probably better not to look. I sit back up.

I hear Ana ask Susannah whether she has any of her pills. Susannah's forehead rests on the scrubbed pine tabletop, her hands hang down and I see the silver thumb ring, the lines of dirt under the nails, the breadth and strength of her palms.

I put down my spoon. "Ana," I don't look at Susannah, "she's been in a very bad state. She's unwell. We really do need to call someone." I don't want to say the word "police."

Ana nods. "Doctor's coming."

I have no idea how they summoned the doctor, since I was using the phone. Then I remember that as we started up the quay, Ana exchanged a word or two with a man who was passing with a dog.

Finn points at Susannah's curved back. "Bedtime?"

"Yes, love, Susannah's very tired."

Suddenly I realize that I don't want to be involved in this anymore. They have it under control. I don't want to talk to police officers or doctors or anyone else. Susannah was certainly a danger to Finn and to me, but when we are gone she will presumably go back to her yoga and her gallery. Without the two of us, she will get her demons under control again. She will round up all the guilt and memories and control them again, with medication—or meditation—or whatever works—and she'll get on with her life.

There is a rip in her jeans, probably from climbing the rocks to the boat. With my fingertips, I gently press the back of my head. It is tender and there is a lump the size of a golf ball, but no blood. I wonder what she hit me with. And then I wonder what Finn saw: did he see me, spread-eagled on the white beach with my eyes closed? I feel anger rising. I should call the police.

I look at the clock above the stove. It's not even seven in the morning.

Calling the police would only make this worse. Nothing is going to change what happened at the float house. The best thing I can do is leave. I will get on the next ferry to Spring Tide Island, then the next one from Spring Tide to Tsawassen. We will go home to Doug. The doctor can decide what's best for Susannah—and these people who clearly know her all too well. Finn and I don't belong here.

Sven puts a mug of coffee down in front of me, and a cup of warm milk for Finn. His hand is massive. I thank him again.

"When's the first ferry to Spring Tide?"

"Midday."

"Shit. Not 'til midday?"

He nods.

But I'll get down there early—I've learned my lesson about ferry times here. First I have to work out what to do about the pain in my leg and the fact that I am in Sven's clothes, and need diapers and a coat for Finn. I sip the hot coffee and feel it sink down toward my stomach, warming me.

"More?" Finn looks up at me.

"Wowee, you're hungry," I smooth his hair away from his brown eyes. He looks just like his dad. And he seems remarkably completely unconcerned about Susannah at the other end of the table. I should take this as a good sign. Children are resilient. Far more resilient than adults.

Then the doctor comes through the front door without knocking. He is grizzled and must be at least seventy, with wire-framed glasses and wild white hair and a long waterproof coat, which he throws on the chair next to me. I see him exchange a glance with Ana before he bends down, stiffly, to Susannah. He asks her whether she's been taking her medication but she doesn't lift her head. I think of the bottles in her cabinets.

None of these people have asked me what happened. Perhaps they know what she did, all those years ago. This is a tiny community, after all. All three of them are watching her closely.

The doctor goes to the phone and I hear him talking in a low voice, but I can't hear what he is saying.

As he comes back in from the phone he notices my leg. He bends, and peers at it without saying anything. Then he holds my foot. He asks me to flex it—I grit my teeth as a sickening pain rolls upward.

"You want to get this X-rayed," he says, gruffly. "You don't want to put any weight on it. There's a clinic over in Spring Tide," he writes down a name. There are wiry white hairs on the back of his hand. As he passes the paper to me our eyes meet. His are wise and sharp, set in folds of flesh, like an elephant's eyes. "I'll clean it up now. Hurts like hell, huh?"

I take the paper from him and I think of how I sprinted over rocks, through the forest of pines, and how I jumped and swam and hauled myself onto that boat, then steered it and pressed my foot into Susannah's neck to keep her down. It can't be fractured. You couldn't do that with a fractured shinbone.

But I know I could have—I could have done just about anything to protect Finn. Something bigger than me took over as I ran through the undergrowth to that headland, as I kicked off my things and as I jumped.

I think about my foot pressing on her neck. I remember reading in the paper about a teenage single mother at home with her one-year-old baby. She took a rifle and shot dead the two men who broke into her house in the middle of the night. I remember the police officer's words: "There is nothing more dangerous," he said, "than a mother protecting her child."

I can hardly touch my toes to the floor now without feeling faint from the pain. The doctor has his bag open. He cleans my wound with a burning antiseptic that makes my eyes water, then he bandages it from ankle to knee. He offers me a couple of Advil. Finn watches with interest. I consider asking the doctor if tranquilizers or a plunge into freezing water would kill an unborn child, but the kitchen is so silent. Then he stands up, and puts his things away. He pats Finn on the head. I realize he never asked how it happened.

I need to change Finn's diaper—it hasn't been changed for hours, and it stinks now. And I am still wearing Sven's clothes.

"Ana," I say, "I don't suppose you have any diapers?"

She glances at Sven, as if handing over Susannah to him, then she gets up. I hop after her, leading Finn by the hand. She pauses at the foot of the steep staircase.

"You stay there," she nods at my leg. "You can't get up here with that leg. I'll get things down. Get you some clothes too. What size feet are you?"

After a few minutes, she comes creaking back down with a bag of Huggies in one hand, some wipes and some folded clothes in the other.

"You change in there," she points to a dining room just off the corridor. I take the clothes and thank her. Our eyes meet.

"Ana," I say, "Susannah's delusional and dangerous, you do know that, don't you? She convinced herself that Finn was . . . a little boy who died nearly forty years ago."

"Yes," Ana nods. "She thought he was Kit."

"Yes!" I stare at her. "Of course—you knew them. Of course you did. My mother . . . my . . ." I can't bring myself to say the word brother. Or father.

"Everyone up here knew your family," she says. "Awful tragedy. I'm sorry for you, Kali. And I'm so sorry for your mother."

I can't let her words sink in. It's too much. "Well," I say, brusquely, "Susannah seems to think that Jonas has come back to find her. She apparently believes that his spirit is alive in an orca—and I think she was taking Finn out to meet him—it. She may also now think that my mother's spirit is alive inside a whale too—because my mother . . . my mother died recently. But anyway, what I mean is . . . she's basically psychotic, Ana. She could have killed Finn. She could have killed us both. And herself probably. Someone needs to know this."

"I know it," she nods. "I know it now."

"So why did you leave me up there alone all night with her?" I snap.

"We don't have any money. Sven's boat's his livelihood," she says, quietly. "And we didn't know how bad she'd gotten. None of us knew that."

Part of their silence today, I realize, is guilt.

"I'm sorry to hear about your mother. I liked her very much. We were friends."

"I don't know what I should do," I feel my throat tighten.

"She's not well, but they'll get it under control," Ana says. "I guess it was seeing you—looking so much like Elena—with your little boy, too, same age and so similar to Kit . . . well. It brought things up for her. But I guess she'll quiet herself again, when you're gone."

Finn tugs my hand. He's trying to get at the cat, which is coming down the stairs. Ana and I look at each other for a moment longer. I want to ask her how much she knows about the accident, and Susannah's part in it. I want to ask her about my mother. But then I realize that it doesn't matter. I just need to get out of here. Finn yanks again. "Cat!" he calls to it. "Mama? Cat!"

"We should at least call Susannah's son," I say. "And tell him what happened."

She shakes her head. "Won't want to know." Ana looks down at Finn, and then at the cat on the stairs. Then Finn breaks loose from my hand.

"Now this one here's called Jessie," she says to him in a grand-maternal voice. She glances over her shoulder at me and our eyes meet again. Hers are self-contained, but warm. She doesn't need anything from me—certainly not forgiveness for leaving me over-night. She just wants to know, I think, that I am all right. No harm has been done. I manage to smile, and she nods. She turns back to Finn. "You can pet ol'Jess, but you be gentle, look, like this."

As Ana and Finn bend to the cat, I look down the corridor at Susannah. Her head is up, now, but her eyes are shut. Both hands are resting on her knees. Her silver thumb ring shines in the kitchen light. The doctor is talking quietly to Sven, over by the stove.

She sits, motionless. Her hair hangs in tendrils on her shoulders and her big hands droop on her knees. But then, as if she's sensed me looking at her, she turns her head, very deliberately and slowly opens her eyes. She looks right at me. Her irises are bleached, like ancient bone.

I look right back at her—the woman who changed the course of my life. The woman who robbed me not just of a father and a brother, but of a mother. And then she tried to take my baby. I wait for the anger and bitterness to kick in, the fury. But they don't. We stare at each other along the corridor, Susannah and I, while Sven and the doctor murmur on, and Ana helps Finn to stroke the ginger cat. Finally, I look away. I am not going to fight her, or call the police. Because all I feel, for this woman, is pity.

Chapter Nineteen

The sun bounces off the sea as the ferry pulls into harbor. Everything seems brighter, sharper and more three-dimensional. Masts
clatter and seagulls circle above. Finn and I are sitting on the
deserted lower deck. I am warm in Ana's white T-shirt, only slightly
too small zippered fleece, a pair of baggy stonewashed jeans with
an elasticized waist, clean socks, and old sneakers, only one size too
big. She even gave me a woolen beanie and a gloves and hat set for
Finn, as well as a spare fleece jacket for him that she said belonged
to her grandson who is now thirteen and won't be needing it.

Finn is still pointing and naming. "Bird," he points over the port.
"Yes, seagull."
"Nuther bird."
"You're right. Lots of seagulls."
"Nuther bird!"
I kiss him. "I love you very much," I say.
"Nuther bird!" he shrugs me off, pointing.
"Yes! Another seagull."

The storefronts are more colorful than I remember, perhaps
because of the sunlight. The main street reminds me of a Cornish
fishing village. I notice a day spa and a yoga studio just across

from the ferry port. This place seemed so threatening that first night in the fog, but on a bright day like today it is just a perfectly pleasant little off-season fishing port.

"Truck!" Finn cries. There is a big crane, lowering a crate off a boat to the right of the dock.

A couple of men are waiting on the quay. One turns and walks purposefully up toward the main street with his dog while the other stands still, watching the ferry arrive. There is something about his posture makes my heart turn over—the slight stoop, the big black jacket, the woolen hat pulled low. I really am missing Doug. I'm missing him so much that I'm inventing him now. I need him. He is part of me. None of this works without him. I have to get home and sort this out.

I stand up on one leg and I press my face against the window. Next to me, Finn does the same standing on the seat, his feet planted wide apart. Then he points.

"Daddy!" he shouts. "Daddy!"

"I know. He does look like Daddy," I pat Finn's head. "We'll see Daddy soon."

"No," he looks up at me, then points again, "Daddy!"

I look again.

The man standing watching the ferry isn't a stranger, colored by my longing, it is Doug. Doug is here.

"Daddy!" Finn shouts, wildly. "Dat! Daddy!"

Doug folds his arms around us and for a long time, we stand in a tight knot on the quay. Then he pulls back and twirls Finn around and kisses him, and Finn squeals and laughs. "Again! Again!"

Over Finn's head, Doug looks at me. Then he lifts the hat off my head with one hand. "Jesus Kal! You cut all your hair off!"

His face is pallid and unshaven, and I can see in his eyes how shaken he is by the past few days, how deeply worried he's been and how shocked he is, of all things, that my hair is gone.

"I know." I run my hand over it, grinning stupidly. Are we really going to talk about my hair?

He puts Finn down. "What the hell is happening Kal?" he says. "What are you *doing*?" He looks me up and down, and despite himself, he smiles. "And what in God's name are you *wearing*?"

I feel as if he might vanish if I take my eyes off him. "How did you *get* here?" I say. "How the hell are you here?"

"Well I literally just got off the ferry from that port, whatsitcalled." He looks at me. "And I was trying to work out how to get the next boat. Christ your hair is short." He pulls me to him again. "Jesus, Kal. Jesus."

"Tsawwassen? But how? I can't believe you got here so fast. I mean how . . ."

"After you called, and then your phone was dead I went to Heathrow and got on the first flight to Vancouver," he says. "Then I got a taxi to the port, and the first island ferry. And I was about to get on that ferry to whatever it is—Raven Island. What the fuck has happened Kal?"

Finn tugs Doug's hand. "Carry 'oo?"

He bends and sweeps Finn up and around and they laugh. "God, I missed you, matey." Doug buries his face in Finn's neck. "My God I missed you."

Finn pulls at Doug's chin. "Truck!" he calls, pointing across the dock. "Dat!"

"Wow," Doug looks at it with him. "Now, that's a big one. It's got a crane, see. For lifting cargo. And look, there's another one, down there, look."

For a moment, they discuss transportation, and I just look at them, and my heart feels as if it will burst out of my chest and soar skyward like a helium balloon.

I don't know what Doug is going to tell me, when we get a chance to talk. But I know that I can face anything he has to say. I can handle just about anything now, though the pain in my lower leg is definitely a challenge.

Behind them both, I can see the main street. There are a few more people out today, carrying shopping bags, crossing the road, stopping to chat. I can see the big pink Cupcake sign for the Rock

Salt Bakery. A woman about my age with an Afro sticking out from under a woolly hat comes out carrying a coffee, with a loaf of bread tucked under one arm and a long woolly scarf the color of cornflowers.

Then Maggie comes out of the door next to the bakery. Her hair is a blood red halo, splintering in the sunlight. She smiles at someone and she has the dogs with her, on leads, one on each side of her. They look like two perfectly well-behaved pets, trotting to heel, their golden coats rippling. She turns down a street and disappears.

I will never know how much Maggie understood about what Susannah was up to. I will never know if she is as naïve as she seemed about her unbalanced friend.

Doug comes back toward me, hugging Finn, who looks even smaller in his Dad's arms. "We can't talk now, but we have to," he gives me a look. "Soon."

"I know." I reach up and pull Finn's hat down over his ears. "I've made some horrible mistakes. But I needed to do this—I can't explain now but I will. Okay?"

"You *needed to do this*?"

I hop closer. "Yes," I look at him. "I really did."

He peers down my leg. "Why are you hopping? Why can't you walk properly? What happened to your leg? Jesus—what has *happened* to you?"

"All I know is I really need to go home. Is that okay? I know you just got all the way here, but . . ."

He looks at me and I can see that he has been—and possibly still is—distraught.

"I came," he says, "to take you home."

*

We get standby seats on the overnight flight to London but it is delayed because of lightning storms.

Finn and Doug are sleeping on an uncomfortable airport chair, Finn against Doug's chest, Doug with legs splayed, his head lolling but two protective arms around Finn's back.

But I can't sleep. My leg is agony and everything is churning through my mind and it's all too much. I get out my phone. I have to e-mail my father. He orchestrated a systematic, monumental campaign of dishonesty for thirty-eight years. They both did. Either of them could have told me at any time, and they chose not to. My parents were in this one together.

To: G.K.MacKenzie
From: Kali
Subject: I know

Dear Dad, I am at the airport, on my way home, and I know everything.

I know about Kit and Jonas, I know about the accident, I know who I am and I know I've been lied to by you and Mom for thirty-eight years. Presumably this is what you were trying to stop me finding out when you told me not to go and see Susannah? Or were you planning to finally tell me, because you had to, when I got home?

You were right about one thing: Susannah is dangerous. Finn almost died at the float house—that's where I've been—and I could have died too. The truth—from you—would surely have been a lot simpler, not to mention safer. I don't know what I think about any of this, it's way too soon to process it all. I think I'm probably very angry with you. But everything is overwhelming right now. Doug came. We are on our way home. Finn is safe. I am safe. But my God Dad. How could you both lie to me like this?

love Kali.

I put my phone away and, to distract myself from thinking, I hobble over to the airport bookstore. On a low table, at the front, among the souvenirs of Vancouver, is the same coffee table book I saw at Susannah's—*The Magnificent Orca*. I pay for it and take it back to sit next to Doug. And I read it, cover to cover, as Doug and Finn sleep on; as the travelers come and go around us, my leg throbs beneath layers of ibuprofen, and our plane delays are relayed across the speaker system.

The killer whale, I learn, is not a whale at all, but a type of dolphin. I learn about orca social organization, the matriarchal culture, powerful mother-child bonds, orca ceremony and traditions. I read about how orcas forage, sending out pulses of sound through the ocean to locate food. I learn how these echolocation clicks allow the whale to effectively see through miles and miles of ocean—to see with sound.

Then I get to the chapter called "*The Language of the Orca*" and the first sentence catches me: "*The complicated vocal, social and behavioral cultures of the Orcinus orca have no parallel in the animal world—other than among human beings.*"

Like humans, killer whales, I discover, have a natural language. Researchers—my mother's academic descendants—have now identified their complex linguistic structures. They have mapped dialects to different pods and clans. They understand that there are three main orca communities—residents, transients, and off-shores, and that these communities essentially don't speak the same language. Though nobody can "speak" these orca languages, researchers have documented a whole lexicon of burst-pulse sounds that signal different states and, probably, emotions.

I realize how precious my mother's notebook and those transcribed vowel sounds is. It is a historical document. My mother was a pioneer of this research, at a time when even the notion that whales were intelligent seemed fanciful. I wonder whether she sat at her desk in Sussex and followed these developments with a pain in her heart. But no. I don't think she did. I think the only way she could have possibly survived that degree of loss—of my brother, and Jonas, and also her beloved whales—was to cut off completely forever.

She became a different person in order to survive. She became a Sussex housewife, with me and Alice and the dog and her easel, in our solid red brick Victorian house, with the apple tree outside and my father's unwavering routines. And this reinvention might have worked—if it weren't for me. I was the bridge between her two worlds.

Day after day she would have seen my brother's face growing up, in mine. She would have seen Jonas in me too, presumably: in my dark blue eyes, or maybe my gestures or my voice or my moods. I could have any number of Halmstrom traits—but I will never know, now, which ones. She loved me but it must have so been hard to look at my face every day. I think I understand why, when she found the lump, she sat with it, watching it grow.

I wonder if she ever let herself imagine what would have happened if she and I had stayed on in the float house after the accident. Maybe she would be one of these researchers—maybe she would have written a book just like this one.

Perhaps it's the late hour, or the exhaustion of the past few days but as I sit there, I feel as if she is living that life after all, and I have just paid her a visit. She is in her little float house in the archipelago. She is silver-haired and fit and strong, without a cancer gnawing through her insides. Her float house is dry and secure, with red geraniums at the windows, water and electricity—maybe even wireless communication by now. She still cuts wood for the log pile with a chainsaw, and collects fungi and herbs and wild fruits from the forest behind the house. And every day she goes out in her boat with headphones and a camera, photographing the whales, listening to them, watching them surface, breathe and then submerge, gathering data. The grief is in her, it always will be, but like the whales, it comes up with smooth, unhurried breaths and submerges again, without a fuss.

At home she keeps her hydrophone dropped through the floor so that she falls asleep at night to their creaks and whistles and squeaks and clicks and wakes in the morning to the sound of orca mothers calling their babies, siblings squabbling and playing: the soundtrack to a world that few of us ever think about. Like the whales my mother lives in two worlds: breathing in one, then diving beneath.

My phone pings. I know whose e-mail has just come in.

From: G.K.MacKenzie
To: Kali
Subject: re: I know

Dear Kali, I am profoundly sorry that you found out this way, and from that woman. Your mother and I were only trying to protect you. All I can say is that we wanted you to feel normal. Your mother was deeply damaged by her loss, but in truth, so was I. This has been a difficult burden for both of us to carry. Our decision not to tell you might not have been the right one—in retrospect it was wrong, since it has endangered you and Finn—but we decided we did not want you growing up with a tragedy hanging over you. We didn't want you to feel different from Alice. You have always been—will always be—my daughter. I am sorry that you found out in this way and from the very person your mother and I both wanted you never to meet. To hear that you and Finn were in danger from that woman distresses me more than you can know. I am very tired now. I have found the past week extremely trying. I am sorry this has come out in this way. We will, indeed, talk when you touch down. Your father,
—G.

I reply right away, wiping the tears off my face with the back of one hand.

Dear Dad, it's okay. Finn and I are both fine and you're right, we can't do this on e-mail or on some long-distance phone call. We'll work this out. It's too soon for me to get my head around it all or to know what I feel, really. Please just get some rest. The flight is delayed but should go soon and we will be home tomorrow and I will call you then. Love Kali.

I am surprised to find that, beneath the anger, I feel protective of my father. It must be agony for him that all this has come out now, when he must feel so alone in the world. He is getting old and he has lost the love of his life. He must be afraid that he will lose me too. And Finn. And maybe even Alice.

I realize that from now on my job is to forgive. At some point I'm going to have to go to Sussex, or meet him at a London restaurant, and we'll talk about all this. And whatever he says, I will have to believe that all they wanted was to protect me.

I suddenly remember Susannah's account of the disastrous Sea Park whale birth. The captive orca was trying so hard to stop her baby from hurting itself on the sides of the tank that she forgot to feed it. The instinct to protect trumped the instinct to nurture.

And the truth is that I played a part in all this, too. Perhaps they would have told me when I was older, if we had been closer, if I had been more reasonable. But I wouldn't let my mother anywhere near me, and I never made the effort to connect with my father.

I shift and a white hot rod of pain shoots up my leg so that I have to grit my teeth and concentrate hard on breathing. I can't fathom how I ran to that rock—how did I do that? Motherhood really is a triumphant, extraordinary force, not to be messed with.

I sit upright. Something has been staring me in the face all this time. I scrabble through the stuff in my bag until I find the crumpled wedding photo. I hold it up to the jaundiced airport lights.

His head isn't visible; the photo is creased down his face, which is in a triangle of shadow cast by the building. But hers is turned up to him, and there is a look of absolute joy on it. My mother is in love. Of course, this body is not my father's—it is broader in the shoulders, more muscular, not nearly as tall. And it isn't raining: there is bright sunlight above the roof behind them. The man in this wedding picture isn't my father at all. This man is Jonas Halmstrom.

There is a sense of possession and loss, both at once, and I have to bend over and rest my hands on my knees just to get my breath back.

I have traveled halfway across the world looking for my mother, putting Finn in terrible danger, and myself, and this unborn baby, but the truth has been staring at me all the time from the crease in this wedding photo. I just couldn't see it because I was too busy running away, spinning stories and pressing them into the blanks.

Elena Kalypso married Jonas Halmstrom. They had a little boy, and then a girl.

I have to show the red file to Alice. This is not something to talk about on a cell phone from an airport. Everything I have discovered is going to release Alice, too. These are the secrets that both of us need to know. It is easy to forget, when you're running away from something that you are always running toward something else.

The orca carving is sitting in my bag still—I never took it to the museum in Vancouver. I will take it into the Pitt Rivers, and, if it is valuable, then I will have it sent back to Canada where it belongs. The grinning demon is still unsettling, with its square rows of teeth, and popping little eyes—but it doesn't spook me so much now. I put it back in the box next to the piece of blanket, with the blue *K*. Kit's or mine—I will probably never know. Then I pull out the folded notebook that started all this. And I remember my mother's diary—tucked in the inside pocket of my parka, on the headland at Black Bear Island, along with my boots, and Doug's warm wool sweater.

For a moment, a sort of panic seizes me—I can't just leave them there. My mother's precious diary is on a rock in British Columbia and I didn't even get to read it properly. The parka that protected me and the sweater that connected me to Doug, the boots that took me to Finn. I can't just leave them all, piled like a totem on a rock.

Then I remember the article I read on the plane on the way out, about Pacific Northwest totems—how they can symbolize quarrels, murders, debts, bereavements—things the people could not talk about but needed to express and remember. Those totems were built to disintegrate, slowly, over time. I lean my back against the uncomfortable plastic airport seat. Maybe it is okay that my mother's diary should stay on that rock, to be reabsorbed by the landscape.

They are sending out the call for the delayed British Airways flight to Heathrow. I shove everything back into my bag—all this evidence, this proof—and then I turn to wake Doug.

Chapter Twenty

I take a sip of the hot chocolate he's made, blow on it, take another sip. Then I lift my painful leg very slowly and inch it onto Doug's lap, flinching as I lower it down. I need more, better painkillers. Tomorrow I will have it X-rayed at the John Radcliffe Hospital.

I can see that Doug has been eating himself up. He is exhausted. He rests his head on the back of the sofa and shuts his eyes. The anxiety of me taking off like that with Finn—and presumably the anger—must have been unbearable. He's still angry, too, rightly so—he is alarmed at how far and fast I went from him. To get that phone call, and think something had happened to Finn—then silence. I have put Doug through hell. It's amazing that he's still here. His hair is all over the place, like a field in a gale. He looks just as handsome, but wrecked.

I look around the room—just the same—why wouldn't it be?—the scruffy white sofas that needs a wash, the Union Jack cushion, the oil painting of the church where we got married, the butterfly picture that Doug gave me for my birthday last year, Finn's fingerprints, the sail white walls above them. Our room is lined with books we've collected separately in the years before we married, and together, in the eight years since. And there are Finn's toys, his ride-on tractor, his blocks and Legos, his teddy bears, his big box of cars.

He turned away from all this, just briefly, he considered the alternative—but I can't blame him for that, because I'd been pushing him away for months. What is extraordinary is how far I jumped in fear, how swiftly I fell—and how deep. I almost lost everything. The tiredness seeps outward from my core and it's all I can do to hold the blue and white striped mug and drink the hot chocolate. There's no way we can talk about all this now.

Finn yelled, climbed, poked, and toddled the entire nine-hour flight—and Doug had to cope with him for most of it, because I couldn't walk around, or even stand for long, with my leg. So we didn't get to talk on the plane. So far all Doug knows is that there was a mix-up, and Susannah took Finn to her float house, I followed her, she turned out to be unstable, there was a fight, I fell. It doesn't quite cover things, I know. Tomorrow I will tell him the whole story from beginning to end, leaving nothing out, but right now I am way too tired—and Doug is unconscious.

I rest my hands on my belly. And then, from deep inside me, I feel a familiar flicker—tiny butterfly wings. I close my eyes tight. There—again—the little wings unfold and shiver. "So you are still there" I say to the baby inside me. "You made it home, too."

"Seriously, though, how could you think I'd have an affair?" Doug opens his eyes, as if we're mid-discussion. "How could you actually believe I'd do that to you?"

Doug's eyes are the exact same brown as Finn's. I am flooded, suddenly, with the enormity of what I have, right here in this ordinary little terraced house. "I was in shock," I say. "I somehow created a whole, convincing story from those two texts and I believed it—utterly—probably because I was so afraid that it might be true. I shouldn't have run away, I know that. But I was in a state."

He cups my chin. "Kal," he says, "I didn't stop her from texting me, and I'm ashamed of that. I was an ass, but I would never, ever . . ."

"I know. I know you wouldn't. You might have been an ass, but I was far, far worse. It's all over now. The good thing is, I'll never be that scared again."

This, above all, is what the whole nightmare has done for me. I have found the part of myself that lies beneath the babble of stories and fears and hopes and insecurities; beneath the threatening chaos of everyday life. I have found the powerful part of myself that remains when everything else has been stripped away. And now I have located it, I will never forget that it's there.

Sometimes you need to run away in order to get somewhere. If I had let Doug come to Sussex with me the day my mother died, then we'd have had talked about the texts at some point and I never would have gotten on the plane. I would have come home to Oxford and we would have gone back to our routines, the resentments and the growing distance. The truth would have sat forever in my mother's jewelry box.

And then where would we all be? I realize that I don't regret what has happened, despite everything—I can't. I am sensible enough not to say this to Doug. Not yet, anyway.

"Doug," I'm so tired that my voice is slurred. "I know we need to talk about all this, it's huge—there is so much to talk about and I've got so much to tell you but I need to sleep so badly . . ."

He steers my face toward his again. "What the hell happened to you up there?" he leans closer. "You're different. It's not just your hair, though that's amazing, but you are . . . changed." He touches my cheek.

The exhaustion rolls over me like a fog. I still have so much to say to Doug. If we really are having another baby then things have to be different this time. I know now that I don't need to sacrifice absolutely everything—my identity, my career, my sanity—to prove to my babies that I love them, constantly, and always will. But I also know that very soon I'm going to fall asleep. I put the cup down, and rest my head back on the cushions.

Doug gives my good knee a tiny shake to bring me back. "Kal?"

I blink slowly at him. "We can talk about everything. We will. But first we really do need to get some sleep."

"You're right."

*   *   *

We climb the stairs to our bedroom, me hopping, leaning on Doug. We stop at Finn's room and stand, side by side at his crib, watching him sleep. He is on his back with both arms by his head. His eyelashes are thick and beautiful. He is just perfect. And safe. Then we go up to our room.

Our bed is soft and white and smells of Doug. His boxers are on the floor. His books are strewn around the place as if he's been up, pacing through the nights. We lie down and I put my head on his chest and for the first time in weeks, months, even years, I know that I am exactly where I belong. Every little bit of me is now in the right place.

My body hums, as if it is still suspended above the Atlantic. My leg aches like hell. But I am here. Home. I lay one hand against my belly and feel the firm rise of it under my fingers, pressing into Doug's flank.

Half of me is Swedish—but not the half I thought. I am not English. And I am completely American. I have met my ancient senile grandfather. I had a brother, a brother who died.

Doug strokes my hair. "Don't go to sleep yet," his voice rumbles under my ear. "I've got to tell you this realization I've had—I just don't care if we have another baby. We are enough, just the three of us. We are more than enough. I can't believe how lost we got. Nothing else matters but this."

I try to answer but I can't make my mouth move in the right shapes.

"Are we going to be okay?" he says. "Kal?"

I make a superhuman effort to speak. "Yes," I say. "We really are."

Rain taps quietly on the roof of our small home. And they flicker across the back of my brain, all of my family, alive and dead: Finn, Doug, my mother, Jonas, Kit, Harry Halmstrom, my father, Alice—then they begin to recede, growing murkier until only one thing is left, sending its little echolocation pulses out through an ocean of sleep.

"Doug," my voice sounds alert. I open my eyes and look at him. "About that baby . . ."

Elena, 1976—

Whenever life got too much—and it often did—she would take herself back to that first day on the boat, the summer of '76, when she woke up certain that someone was on the deck—and she went up there alone, and leaned over the railings, and the whales came.

Sometimes this was the only clear point in a head jumbled with unbearable memories. She never had managed to shut it all out, though she had certainly tried. But that one morning—her first as Jonas's wife—always stayed simple and pure, like a white stone in a beach of complicated pebbles. Right to the end that memory was her place of refuge.

The cedar planks were cold underfoot as she pulled his fisherman's sweater over her pajamas, found wool socks and tugged them on. She stood and listened at the bottom of the stairs, but she could only hear Jonas's deep breaths from their bed, and faint snores, coming from Dean's cabin.

She looked at him in the half-light for a moment. He had rolled onto his stomach when she got up, and was lying face down now in the warm space that she'd left. His face was half buried in the pillow and his beard was in shadows, but she could see the rise and fall of his shoulders and the constellation of freckles across his broad shoulder blades; his skin always tasted of the sea.

When he had sat down opposite her outside the campus café that day, and pushed up the sleeves of his blue shirt, she'd known, right away, that he was her future. When he stood on the stage and talked after the film she hadn't noticed much about him, but two days later, in the sunlight at ten o'clock in the morning, when he started talking about the orca-mapping project, she knew she had to be with him.

It wasn't just the handsome face—his strong nose, the solid chin under his rough beard or the dark blue eyes that never seemed to look away, or the way he leaned forward to make a point and the muscles of his forearms tensed and the tendons shifted. It wasn't just what he said about the whales—though she listened hungrily to it all. It was his voice—his voice vibrated all the way inside her, making every cell in her body sing and come alive. Hearing his voice, she was home.

She tiptoed over to the galley stove, found the matches and lit the gas to brew a pot of coffee. She never believed that she would marry anyone, let alone a man she'd known for just a few weeks in an impulse wedding ceremony witnessed by strangers. She wore her one dress and they bought wild flowers from Pike Place Market. They asked a passing tourist to take their picture, and they celebrated with the wind battering the sides of the campervan and the sound of the sea outside the fogged-up windows. And now—on this first day as his wife—on Dean's boat, heading north: none of it made rational sense. But it felt completely right.

She looked down at her hands on the countertop—the sea grass he'd twisted around her finger on Cannon Beach, turned into gold. She poured out a coffee. She knew someone was up there on deck, waiting for her. She felt them up there. She listened again, but all she could hear was the creak of timbers, the slap of waves on the hull, the distant cries of gulls and Dean's soft snores.

She climbed the stairs with the tin cup in one hand and as she pushed open the heavy door she waited for a body to block the light— but she stepped outside and she was blind.

It was as if cold muslin had been draped across her eyeballs. Somewhere out to sea a foghorn sounded; she rubbed a hand over her eyes as if she could pull the fog away. Invisible gulls let out ghostly cries.

She stepped farther out, sipping the coffee and peering into the grayness. There was still that sense of a presence, very close by, waiting for her.

They'd anchored off the tip of the island. It occurred to her that in this fog they must be invisible. She thought about the gigantic cruise ship they'd seen the day before, steaming toward Alaska. Maybe there was a lighthouse nearby. Or maybe nobody moved boats around in this weather. Presumably, Jonas knew which places were safe and which weren't. He'd sailed the Salish Sea his whole life—he wouldn't anchor somewhere dangerous. She realized that she trusted him. It was a novelty, but she did.

She'd been standing on deck for a moment or two sipping her coffee and staring into the mist, when she heard a giant, exasperated huff. It was so close and so immense, that she jumped with both feet off the floor. Coffee sloshed onto her socks, scalding her toes. She listened, gripping the rail with her free hand: another prehistoric exhalation bounced out of the mist.

She should go down and wake them both—but she didn't want Jonas to come up and explain things, or get out a camera. She needed to experience this for herself. She felt as if they'd come for her, nobody else. She put down the tin cup and held onto the rail with both hands, squinting through the grayness, willing the whales to surface again.

Another vast exhalation—so close she caught the stink of fish and sulfur on the blow and its droplets covered her face. Then it loomed out of the mist, right below her—no more than ten feet away from the boat. She watched its huge curving back, topped with a dorsal fin at least the size of a man. It was surprisingly noiseless, moving in slow motion, slick and smooth.

There was another exhalation—this one slightly farther away—as if someone out there was making a tremendous effort to lift a heavy object—and then a second orca surfaced. All she could make out was the dark shape of its fin as it cut through the waves—a slight pause—before it submerged again. Then a third—just to the right—an explosion of breath and another colossal fin rolling through the water. She leaned over the edge, dangling forward so that she could feel the spray on her face and taste the salt, and—as she hung there—she had the powerful urge to jump.

She forced herself to hold on tight, to stay on deck where she belonged. A whale surfaced so close that if she'd reached out she could have run her hand along its glistening flank and as it passed, it rolled onto its side and looked up at her. She looked back into the steady brown eye and in that instant she felt an unmistakable jolt of connection between them, of recognition and understanding. She felt as if someone had held her very close, just for a moment. Then the whale submerged, again, and passed right under the boat.

The thud of footsteps from below—Jonas burst on deck.

"Hey! You see them?"

"Yes," she laughed. "They're here! Three, maybe four of them."

He came over and put his arms on either side of her and pressed his body against her back so that her stomach lodged on the railings. When the next one came up, he pointed out a scar on the dorsal and explained that these were the things they'd be looking for—any distinguishing marks, and the saddle patches.

"One went right under the boat," she said. "She looked right at me."

"Up in Blackfish Sound the fishermen say there were once so many orca in the water that you could walk across their backs to get to the shore." He sighed. "Shame we can't get photos in this soup."

They stayed like that for a long time, but the whales had moved on.

That first summer, each morning, the three of them hauled themselves out of bed, made flasks of coffee, gnawed on stale crackers and peanut butter, and loaded their day packs and the camera equipment onto the Zodiac. Then they motored out to sea, talking to other researchers or fishermen or tugboat operators via the crackling two-way radio.

On clear days you could see them several miles off—a blow coming up in the distance, or the sunlight catching a dorsal fin. But sometimes she'd hear their voices through the headphones long before they were visible—she'd catch a long, ghostly cry, bouncing through the ocean and she'd raise her binoculars to scan the surface for a blow or a fin.

There would always be that first moment of awe when they appeared. Just for a second, she would remember that she was only separated from them by a thin fiberglass hull. And then she'd get to work, scanning for marks and scars, following their voices as they played, or foraged, or communicated to each other about things she did not yet understand.

For years after the accident she had nightmares and waking flashbacks when she would find herself standing on the Zodiac again with Kali in the papoose, and Susannah pinning her arms behind her. The images came at her like a horror film: trying to get the papoose off, trying to give Kali to Susannah, but Susannah gripping her arms and bellowing in her face, "You can't jump! You can't leave Kali! Kali needs you!" And of course, Susannah was right.

So she clung to the side screaming into the wind until her voice was gone, searching the waves for their faces, for a flash of clothing, skin, anything at all—as the boat tipped and lurched and the storm closed in on them, and Susannah called for help on the VHF, and the waves scooped skyward, the color of tin.

She often wondered whether the orcas dived down with her little boy as he sank; whether they swam all the way to the seabed with him. That would have comforted Kit because he always loved the whales, and was never scared of them.

In those early, unstable years in England, she was sometimes filled with fury—she hated the orcas for what they didn't do. She'd heard firsthand stories of pods saving stranded boats, kayakers—even drowning dogs. They could have nosed Jonas and Kit to the surface. They could have rescued them but they chose not to. Later, she wondered if this was justice—or perhaps even revenge. After all, humans had been destroying orca families for years, taking their babies from them. It made her think of Bella and her mother. Some people might call it karma.

She knew that Jonas would not have been afraid of drowning if it weren't for Kit. She tried to believe that the two of them were together at the end—that Kit was in his Daddy's arms, nursed by gentle, curious whales. She read somewhere that drowning could be a peaceful death.

Gradually over the years, she taught herself to replace these unthinkable thoughts when they came, with that first simple memory. She'd feel it all closing in and she'd take herself back to the time when she woke on a borrowed boat with a ring on her finger, and felt their presence out there—and walked upstairs into the mist and leaned overboard.

She would go back to that throughout her life, right to the very end. But the last time, when the world had shrunk to the contours of her skin and she leaned over the railings, it wasn't the whales that she saw in the water. And so she jumped.